All but one of the warriors who'd managed to
hold on to the raft got back aboard before lizards
could take them down. But, of the fourteen who
went into the sea, only five managed to swim
back and climb aboard to safety.

Such as it was—briefly.

Zilikazi had managed to keep from being
thrown off the raft by holding desperately onto
the pole he'd had fixed near the front of the
raft to hold up his banner. So, he had time—he
certainly had the rage and fear—to bring down
a wave of sheer mental force and fury onto the
creature he knew was responsible. That hateful tekkutu—oh, yes, he recognized his psychic
stench! he was the one who'd inflicted so much
grief on the army in the mountains—who was
the cause of this horror.

Zilikazi could slay anyone outright when he
applied that much power, so long as he could
find and latch onto his mind. Which, he finally
could. He could now see his tormentor, for the
first time. The tekkutu standing at the very edge
of his own raft.

The wave came down, like a mallet striking
an insect.

—from "Sanctuary" by Eric Flint

IN THIS SERIES

To purchase these and other Baen books in
e-book format, please go to www.baen.com

BY TOOTH AND CLAW

CLAN OF THE CLAW
BOOK TWO

Mercedes Lackey & Cody Martin

S.M. Stirling

Eric Flint

Jody Lynn Nye

By Tooth and Claw: Clan of the Claw, book two

Copyright © 2015 by Bill Fawcett & Associates

"Bury My Heart" copyright © 2015 by Mercedes Lackey and Cody Martin, "A Clan's Foundation" copyright © 2015 by S.M. Stirling, "Sanctuary" copyright © 2015 by Eric Flint, "Feeding a Fever" copyright © 2015 by Jody Lynn Nye

A Baen Books Original

Baen Publishing Enterprises
P.O. Box 1403
Riverdale, NY 10471
www.baen.com

ISBN: 978-1-4767-8137-2

Cover art by Stephen Hickman

First Baen mass market paperback printing, March 2016

Library of Congress Control Number: 2015002505

Distributed by Simon & Schuster
1230 Avenue of the Americas
New York, NY 10020

Pages by Joy Freeman (www.pagesbyjoy.com)
Printed in the United States of America

CONTENTS

Song of Petru
XVII

Sword

They fled the sea
Torn by the storm
The way was lost
But He spoke and
Sartas begat Mreiss
And the Lawgiver
Danced the Way

Bury My Heart

MERCEDES LACKEY
& CODY MARTIN

The encampment of the Clan of the Long Fang was not in disarray, but the practiced eye would have seen that there were many things wrong with it. Where were the tents of the Dancers? And there did not seem to be nearly enough tents for all of the Mrem in the camp; Mrem liked their space, except in the deep cold when it was good to pile together and share warmth, but from the look of things here, the Mrem in this clan were crowding as many bodies into each tent as could physically fit there. They were also missing many of the amenities of even the poorest war band; no mills or ovens, only a few baskets or pots arrayed outside the tent-flaps or hanging from the posts, almost no carts or wagons, and barely any herd beasts for a clan of this size.

The Clan of the Long Fang was destitute. Destitute, but alive. This was how the coming of the New Water had left them. They had been the clan nearest the break-through point—or at least, they had been the clan nearest the point where the water had come rushing in that had actually had any members survive. The waters had taken all of the Dancers that

3

had been with the clan, and it was little short of a miracle that many of the elderly, the females and the young had been on a gathering expedition and had managed to climb trees to escape the first of the flood. Many had not been so fortunate, swept away by rushing water mere feet away from their loved ones. It had been another miracle that the hunting males had been able to get to them and get them out as conditions worsened. But the Dancers had all been in camp, on the flat dancing-space where they practiced, and had perished. What hope could there be for a clan without Dancers to pray for Assirra's entreaty to her husband?

Sartas Rewl was not going to lie down and wail in the face of such misfortune. As the talonmaster for his clan, he was now all that stood between them and annihilation. If there were no Dancers, well, then Aedonniss would have to notice their bravery by Himself. He and Reshia, his mate, had herded the bedraggled survivors together with claw and soft words as needed. Reshia had scolded them into scavenging what was left of their tents and supplies from the waters... or, let it be said, scavenging what was left of... someone's tents and supplies. There were hides with markings no one recognized, and eventually, bodies no one recognized among the debris. Soon it was obvious that their plight could have been worse. He had cuffed and cajoled the males into a massive hunt at a moment when all they wanted to do was sit down and howl their grief into the sky. Reshia had done the same with any of the females, the children, and the elderly who could still manage any sort of task—patching tents, hastily smoking the meat that the males brought in, putting together an encampment that would allow them all to survive in the critical days after the initial disaster. Oh, and bullying them into pulling up and moving the camp every day, as the waters rose, and rose, and rose. It seemed like there was no end to all of the water, as it washed away everything the Clan of the Long Fang had fought and worked for for over a generation. "Sing the Mourning Songs," Reshia said sternly. "But sing them while your hands are working. Those who have gone will not be better honored if all of the clan dies."

Reshia was not a priestess; fortunately not a Dancer, as fate would have it, though she had aspired to be one when she was younger. Despite that, she had a granite will to her that commanded almost as much respect as her mate's leadership.

It was not only the hunting males that brought in meat. Some of the elders, whose nerves and stomachs were strongest, scavenged among the wreckage and, at least in the first few days before the bodies began to rot, hauled in the carcasses of those animals that had perished and were good to eat. Kits helped, too, catching the many smerps that had fled the rising waters. What little food they had would not keep indefinitely, and with the devastation from the valley flooding, it was uncertain how much more the clan would be able to procure. The meat they gathered needed to be cured as soon as possible; a complication, but not one they could shirk if they wanted a steady food supply. Hunting was not always to be depended on . . . and with the New Water continuing to rise, could become uncertain. The smoke from the curing fires rose thick; for lack of carry-baskets, the females packed the slabs of blackened meat in layers of leaves and bound them together in bundles, wrapping those in turn in more leaves. More luck, such as it was: the riding and burden-beasts had survived, snapping their tethers and fleeing before the flood. So eventually they came back, or were found, and could be loaded with these provisions as they were created. There was little else that could be done for sustenance; the waters had seen to that.

It was cold comfort to see the Liskash bodies were far more numerous than those of the Mrem in some places. There were always more Liskash, no matter how many drowned or were cut down. Most were the simpler cousins of the Liskash sorcerers; a few, however, bore signs of the cold intellect of the most hated sort of Liskash. It was too much to hope that they had all died in the flood. Even if the ones that had held territory in the hot valley, now underwater, were all gone, those in the lands outside would see this as a chance to expand that should not be allowed to slip away. The Liskash hated each other almost as much as they hated the Mrem, and were constantly fighting one another; one small thing to thank the gods for.

And . . . as Sartas had known would happen, the Liskash came for them. There was no shelter or safety from the Liskash, now. They were on the lizards' territory, and the Liskash would not abide free or living Mrem on their lands. Slavery or death were what the Liskash brought with them for any that stood against them.

By the time one of the roving groups of Liskash had found them, the clan had managed to survive two full moons, always in retreat from the waters, never quite sure what they were fleeing *to*. But a few stragglers from other clans had come through, with a rumor. The Clan of the Claw, always a strong clan, had survived the flooding intact. And they were gathering together any that would come to their banner. They were far to the south, however, across uncertain lands; it would be a perilous journey for the Clan of the Long Fang, even if they were still fully equipped.

So now Sartas's ragged band of survivors had a destination: rally to the Clan of the Claw. And a goal. Survive the journey.

The Clan of the Long Fang had been trekking slowly for the last few weeks. They were slowed by sickness, by lack of food, by the weak and injured, and the elders. More wagons would have helped— but the few wagons they had were needed to carry the tents. With so few arx, all but those that could not move on their own had to walk. They were also slowed by the kits—not that the kits couldn't keep up, but because no opportunity to forage along the way could be wasted. A handful of berries, a few roots, even an armful of edible shoots could mean the difference between "enough to go on" and having another person too weak to keep up.

No matter what Sartas seemed to do, however, his people kept dying. He was walking beside his mount when the news came; the few warriors that still had mounts (no chariots were left) saved them for scouting or for fighting. Everything that was left was precious to the clan, now. The heavily wooded lands that they had favored had suited them well when they had only needed to move to keep hunting grounds fresh... now they had to fight their way through those same woods, and progress was achingly slow. "We need to move faster. We're covered by the trees, but it is only a matter of time before we are found at this rate." Sartas scratched behind his ear in annoyance, the only nervous habit he ever exhibited. Tall and lean, Sartas was very much like the rest of his clan while being so very different at the same time. Unlike some other clans, who boasted members of wildly different coat colors and length, Long Fangers were fairly uniform in color and appearance; dense, sandy-gray fur, shading to cream on the face and underbelly. And they had two very distinct characteristics; tuft-tipped ears, and naturally bobbed tails, both very useful in woodlands. Long Fangers, if tall, also tended to be heavy; it was the short cats that were lean. Sartas was tall *and* lean, and very, very quick. It was a combination that had made him more than usually deadly against the Liskash. Sartas heard the outriders approach; those at the back of the clan's line stirred at their sighting. The formost guards were led by Arschus Mroa and Miarrius

Srell, two seasoned warriors. Sartas hoped that there had been no trouble, but he also knew it was probably a vain hope. Both warriors were riding behind by the clan's lead scout, Ssenna Errol, a rare female warrior. Sartas sometimes wondered if she was part lizard; she was almost as cold and as calculating as a Liskash. That trait was what made her perfect for her role, however. Her face betrayed no emotion as she and the other two warriors pulled their mounts up to him, jumping from their saddles to lead the krelpreps beside their talonmaster.

Ssenna was the first to speak. "We encountered another patrol of roving Liskash. Survivors from the flooding, no doubt. These ones were a mixed bunch, with one of the bigger lizards leading them. We dispatched them before any could escape." Sartas could see some of the blood matted into each of their pelts; none of them looked injured, so it followed that it could only be Liskash blood.

Arschus Mroa was the next to speak. He was by far the largest Mrem that any in the clan had ever seen in recent memory, fully two heads taller than most, and a head taller than Sartas himself, with a slightly darker shade of fur than the rest of his clansmates. "We lost two while fighting them. Sirroc Prell and Nischan Royara. The first fell to a flight of arrows at the start, and we sent the second off at his request after he was laid low with a stinking gut wound." Arschus Mroa hung his head; it was easy to forget how sensitive the warrior could be sometimes, given his immense size and strength.

Miarrius Srell was not nearly as gentle with his words. "Better than bleeding out or having dung-eating Liskash at you while you're down. He went out well, and we'd all best choose that way if it comes to it." Miarrius was the oldest warrior left in the band, and had been even before the flood. His disposition never seemed to change; he was consistently dour and had a scowl that never seemed to leave his face. His fur had long ago started to go gray. He was further distinguished by his missing left ear and the mass of scars that ran down that side of his face, trophies for living through a hard battle long ago. "The Liskash that got those two didn't have such a good end." A smirk curled his lips ever so slightly, as he remembered exactly the end the Liskash they encountered had come to.

Sartas nodded. "Any other injuries? Signs of more Liskash?" Two more warriors gone...it was two too many. The clan's scouts were already stretched thin, trying to find safe passage in the now seemingly crowded woods; the floods had driven out everything into the forest, with much of the traffic concentrated near the new—and ever-encroaching—shore. They would miss Sirroc Prell and Nischan Royara in the coming days, and miss their spears.

"Nothing significant. Those that are hurt are being tended to, Sartas Rewl." Ssenna nodded once. "I'll take another group of riders out to see if there's more to find, however."

"Rotate your complement to the front; send those already at the front to the rear," he ordered. "If you head out again, borrow a fresh mount from someone."

"No need," said Miarrius, "when we have Sirroc Prell and Nischan Royara's. We dismounted to fight; the beasts didn't get much of a workout." Arschus winced ever slightly at the harshness of his friend's words, but said nothing.

"Make it so. We need to find an appropriate place to make camp, somewhere that we'll at least have some cover from prying eyes. Get some drink and then get to it."

The two led their mounts up into the van of the group. Reshia must have seen them and spoken to them, for it was not that long after they left that she made her way back to him.

"I have a little good news to add to your bad," she said, and cheek-rubbed him for comfort. "The kits have been lucky, and we have added much more to eat, enough so that some of our weak have regained the strength to take to their own feet again." She made a face. "At least we do not lack for water. Even if the New Water is salt, there is plenty of fresh water streaming towards it."

"I've never wished for a desert so fervently as I do now. Rather that we had lived in one." He shook his head. "We'll need to keep close watch on the kits, maybe even let them forage once camp has been made; but never on their own. We're not alone in these woods. We lost two more. Sirroc Prell and Nischan Royara. Another group of stranded Liskash."

"We have been lucky. So far we have only encountered those Liskash whose homes were also destroyed. Eventually—"

"I do not think we will continue to be so lucky. At this rate, losing so many so fast..." Sartas laughed bitterly to himself. "At this rate, I'm going to turn into another Miarrius."

"Do, and I shall beat you into good nature again myself," she half-threatened. "Not that such a thing is likely. You are far too handsome to become another Miarrius." This time Sartas laughed honestly.

"We still have far to go, love. We'll see what the forest brings; hopefully, Aedonniss isn't in too bad of a mood."

"You have done what few talonmasters could have, beloved." This time she briefly caressed his ear. "You took a shattered clan with no Dancers, herded it into unity again, and got it moving. If you had asked me before the flood if such a thing was even possible, I would have told you that not even the heroes of an epic could have done it."

Her eyes darkened with too-recent memory; Sartas fell briefly into the same dark place himself.

Sartas thought back. Had it only been a few hands of days? It had all begun with something that only the gods could have caused. Strangely, it had been a fine day. Cool, by the standards of this tropical forest, and the Dancers had elected to take advantage of the weather to make an entire day of practice and prayer. That was fine; Clan of the Long Fang had more than enough hunters that they could afford to do so. Sartas himself had led one of the two hunting parties upland, driving the dangerous root-diggers before them, away from the camp and into a funneling trap. Reshia had taken the kits out to learn foraging techniques, from her wealth of experience in what was edible, what was medicinal, and what was dangerous.

She had been a little concerned that the weather was *too* good, and had been keeping half an ear cocked for the sound of distant thunder. Nothing was harder to deal with than a mob of wet, miserable kits. She saw two playing with each other in the distance, throwing handfuls of grass at each other. A boy and a girl, running and pouncing without a care in the world. It brought joy to her heart, and reminded her of her own upbringing.

It had been during a season when the clan was changing grounds, and had been a great trek. She and Sartas were of an age together, with him only being slightly older. They were like brother and sister as they grew up, inseparable most of the time, twins in mischief. He hadn't been nearly as tall then, of course, but was certainly was on the smaller side compared to the other kits. It colored his demeanor; he always had to prove to others that he was just as good, just as strong and fast. In those days, *she* was the one that defended him. As time passed, he grew from a boy into manhood; no longer was he teased for his size, since he was taller than almost any other male in the clan, with the speed and reflexes of a seasoned warrior instead of the awkwardness of adolescence. He also had a clarity of vision and purpose that few seemed to possess; when Sartas set his will to a task, nothing could sway him.

When Sartas Rewl decided to take her hand as a mate, nothing and no one could sway him then, either. Not that she wanted him swayed. The clan had newly settled—in the same spot where they rested to this day—and Sartas came to her in the light of the new moon. Up until then, she had been the perfect maiden, and had turned down plenty of suitors; some were young, some old, some wealthy, others strong or brave. She would always rationalize that each one had some flaw, but secretly she knew; she was waiting for Sartas Rewl. No one else was her match.

Her pleasant reminiscence had been interrupted by a distant rumble. It wasn't the thunder that she had been half expecting, however. This was deeper and somehow . . . more sinister. Then the ground had begun to tremble, only a little bit at first and then growing in intensity, and she knew that something was horribly wrong.

It had been instinct that had saved them; her instinct, that said *This is not rain, it is not earthquake, it is something else, get off of the ground* and sent her racing around the group, scolding and swatting and sometimes throwing the kits up into the trees. "Climb!" she had yowled at them. *"Climb! Higher! As high as you can!"* The Clan of the Long Fang was blessed with many things by Aedonniss; one of them was deep forests with towering trees. Not just high, but huge in girth, some so big that it took several Mrem with their arms outstretched to ring them. More blessings came in the form of the long water-vines, tough enough for adults to climb and swing from, not just kits, vines that wreathed the trunks of the larger trees and made them trivial to climb.

It was painfully slow progress; first, to get everyone to realize the danger, and second, to get everyone climbing. Many scrambled up the trees, but there were some that could not; the youngest kits that had to cling to their mothers, the elders needed help from the older kits. Meanwhile the distant mutter grew to a growl, the growl to a rumble, and the rumble to a roar. The earth trembled and the trees swayed, and there was a wind rushing through the forest carrying the scents of wet earth and salt. By this point everyone's instincts had kicked in, and *danger!* thrilled along every nerve. Reshia herself swarmed up a huge tree at last, moving as fast as hands and claws could take her, her eyes on the distant top of the tree, her mind fixed on that goal.

Somehow and somewhere along the way she had picked up two mewling kits, both of them clinging to her back, their tiny claws pricking her through the leather of the working-tunic she always wore to forage to protect her from thorns and stings. The kits were terrified at this point, silent rather than crying in terror, digging in like little burrs. More instinct; it would have taken a strong Mrem to pry them off her now, and a good thing as well.

She saw the trees swaying and toppling before she saw the wall of water itself. By that time the roaring was so loud it would have drowned out any other sound. It certainly drowned out the noise of the trees being broken off and crashing down just ahead of the flood.

Reshia didn't recognize it at first for what it was. It looked—it looked like a wall of churning earth, dark brown, roiling with splintered trunks, tossing with broken branches. She had just a moment between sighting it, and when it hit her tree, and the huge tree shook like a sapling in a windstorm. She clung to it as the kits were clinging to her, claws locked into the bark. Some were not so lucky. The impact shook some of her clansmates from their trees, sending them to fall into the water below. Others hadn't climbed up high enough, or were even still on the trunks near the ground. And others still hadn't found a strong enough tree; the force from the oncoming water was enough to topple thinner trees as if they were saplings in the path of an arx. It was all that Reshia could do to hold on to her tree with all of her might as it swayed with the power of the flood.

The power of the water, the horror of what was happening, had bludgeoned her into a state of numb mindlessness. She had only been able to close her eyes and hold with claws that cramped into position, whimpering, until long after the worst was over.

The flood had caught the hunters in a relatively "good" place; somewhat higher ground, and a grove of the largest trees in their part of the forest. It made a good channeling trap.

The rooters they had driven into the trap had given them their first warning; before any of them even heard the first noise, the creatures suddenly went absolutely insane with terror. Insane enough to forget their fear of the Mrem and literally try to run over them...insane enough for some of them to try to climb the trees themselves.

Later, Sartas learned that his instinctive reaction had been the same as Reshia's: to climb the trees. He screeched the order; his battle-trained hunters followed it. The grove stood, although on the side that took the first impact, there was a virtual island of debris piled up against the trunks.

Sartas's first thought, when the initial wave was past and they were stranded in the treetops in a slow-rising flood, was for the rest of the clan. Reshia and the foragers were nearest them—if they survived—

They survived! Reshia is smart! He had to tell himself that, or he would have gone insane, right there and then. He knew where they were going to be, and aside from the water everywhere, he thought he could still find the place. And almost all Long Fang Mrem knew how to travel tree-to-tree. Learned first as kits as a part of playing games, and later honed for survival. There were plenty of Liskash-relatives that were more than big enough to take out a small hunting party, much less a single hunter, and often the only way to escape one was to take to the trees.

"Report!" he snarled, pitching his voice to carry. One by one, the names of his hunters came back to him through the branches. Some, impressively enough, came from *higher* in the trees than he was. "Gather on me!" His tree was enormous, and a little higher than he had managed to get there was a huge limb that was more than enough to take the weight of the entire party without even bending a little. Once everyone had joined him on the massive tree, he called out to them, steeling his voice; any sign of weakness, and panic might overtake them all. "We travel together! We need to find the rest of the clan, get to the kits and elders!" He extended a claw in the direction that Reshia had told him she would take the others to forage. "We will go this way! Use the vines, and only go to a tree that looks sturdy!"

The vines provided a network that strung trees together. While it wasn't precisely *easy*, his hunters knew how to hook their legs over a vine and pull themselves along to get to another tree. If trees were close enough together, it was also possible to leap from limb to limb, extending the claws in midair so that the Mrem could sink them deep into the bark on landing. Twice, his hunters weren't as nimble or sure of themselves as they could have been; two different hunters fell, crashing into the water. Both were able to be saved, but one had a broken arm.

"We can leave you here and come back for you, take you with us and go slower, or leave you to catch up with us however you can," Sartas told the injured warrior, as one of the others bound his arm to a couple of sticks after it had been pulled straight. The Mrem's nose and lips were almost white with pain, but he nodded his understanding. "You might be able to pole yourself along one-handed on a log."

"Go. Save as many as you can. I will manage." Sartas nodded curtly to him as the others finished binding him. The clan—family—always came first, always before oneself. Every warrior understood this, and Sartas was proud to see one of his being so self-less without even a second thought.

"We'll be back for you, along this path. If you aren't here, mark the direction you went; we'll find you." Without another word, Sartas was off again, leading the other hunters swarming back up the trunk and into the treetops.

And he would never forget the moment that he knew that Reshia and the kits were still alive—when he heard them, singing valiantly, their voices cutting through the leaves, her voice rising above all the others. And then, her chiding. "Sing! Sing louder! The hunters will hear us and come for us! Sing!"

Clever. She's always been sharp. The hunters all gave a cry as soon as they heard the singing. After the confusion and biting worry, some wept with relief as they swung to their loved ones. Others were not so fortunate, finding that their mates or kits were not among those in the trees. Sartas, for the moment, had no thoughts for either. His heart was near to bursting as he enveloped Reshia in his embrace. It didn't matter what happened to this world; whether it drowned or burned or was rent to pieces; so long as he had her, there was hope.

There was more heartbreak to come, when they found nothing but a rippling sheet of brown water where the camp had been, and no sign of the Dancers. By this point it was obvious that whatever danger there was, it wouldn't be from the great predators, so taking their cue from Reshia, they had all begun to sing, hoping for some response, any response, from those who had been left in the camp. They did pick up a few stragglers; a couple of agile kits, a handful of adolescents, and one shockingly spry elder, and finally, the injured warrior that had been left behind. When it was painfully obvious that there were no more to be found, they made their first camp of the flood-times in the tree, using vines to tie themselves in place so no one would fall in his sleep.

It was hard living, and it took the clan several days to find good ground at the edge of the flood waters. Sartas Rewl was surprised to find others as they descended from the trees; stragglers and survivors from other clans. Too few, in his estimation; how far had these waters gone? What was left of their world after such destruction? That was when they started scavenging. Some was taken from what had washed up on the edges of the water; very little of it was usable, and much of it had to be repaired. The rest had to be remade from scratch, which was no easy task with almost all of the tools and materials that the clan owned having been swallowed up in the floods. There were trickles of good news as, one by one, some of their mounts and even a few of the pack-beasts came back to them. The snapped reins and broken halters told the tale; like the forest animals, the mounts had sensed the danger, fought their tethers until they broke, and made a run for higher ground. But the water rose with every day, and Sartas began to fear that it would not stop until the entire valley was under the churning, brackish waves.

He wondered where the water had come from. Then, unexpectedly, the kits found the answer one morning. A small group that had been out foraging had strayed a little farther than they were supposed to. In doing so, they had found a small pool of water that had been left behind after the initial rush of the flood. What was left in the pool, however, was not small. They ran back into the temporary camp, breathless and half-terrified. "It's a monster, a real monster!" Sartas's first instinct told him that it was what he feared most: Liskash. His clan was in no state to fight off even a loosely organized attack at this point. Grabbing a spear and gathering the warriors, he set off with one of the kits leading him.

It didn't take the group very long to reach where the kits had found their prize. The waters had come over this part of the woods, and receded. Because of a rather large ditch at the base of a small hill, some of the water had been retained. In that pool of water, half-submerged, was what the kits had discovered. The "monster" was—thankfully—dead. Very dead. And a good thing, too, since it was the biggest animal Sartas had ever seen in his entire life. It was easily fifty times as long as an adult warrior Mrem was tall, probably longer, since it had twisted up in its death-throes. One thing was certain: it could have swallowed an adult warrior whole without thinking twice about it. The creature had two rows of small fins that flanked its sides, with a long barbed crest on top. The thing's head seemed blunted, with the mouth and jaws elongated for several strides before it ended in a sharp beak. Its maw was filled with rows of teeth, interlocked like a saw; Sartas didn't want to imagine what a bite from them would feel like. Assuming it actually bit you before it gulped you down... He'd seen a fisher-flier toss a minnow in the air, catch it, and swallow it whole once, and he could easily imagine this thing acting the same with a Liskash or a Mrem. *What could such a thing prey upon that would keep it fed?*

"What... is it?" One of the junior warriors warily prodded at the beast's carcass, as if to make sure that it was still dead.

Another warrior piped up. "A new horror created by the Liskash? Something we haven't encountered before?"

Sartas shook his head. "Something vomited forth from the sea. There are tales of giants and monstrosities in the deeper waters of the sea. That is why even the Liskash do not venture far out on the salt waters." The Liskash made boats; the Mrem would *use* a boat if they could capture one, but he had never heard of a Mrem *making* anything more complicated than a raft. No matter how delicious water-creatures were, venturing out far from a shore... did not appeal.

"Can we eat it?" It was the kit that had led the warriors to this spot. His belly rumbled, looking at all of the meat sitting there.

"We don't know what it is, or whether it might be poisonous to us or not. Besides, it is already half-rotted. We leave it behind." Sartas knew that there were a lot of hungry eyes that were on his back at that moment, and none of them happy with the decision, but they still obeyed. Things had been very lean for his clan, even with everyone doing whatever they could to forage for food. If it had been before the flood, things might not have been so hard. As it was, everything and everyone had been pushed together along the waters; almost everything easy to reach had already been picked over. It would not be very long until the clan was reduced to nettle teas and bark soups, if they weren't diligent.

Sartas Rewl was silent for the rest of the walk back to camp, consumed by his thoughts. It occurred to him that finding the sea beast on land was a very appropriate sign for what his clan had become; a fish out of water. Hopefully, they'd fare better than the "monster" in this strange new world they had suddenly been thrust into. The question that troubled him the most was how exactly they would do so.

A distant rumble jarred Sartas back to the present day. Virtually every head came up, ears pricked and twitching nervously at the sound. When it died away, proving that it was the sound of thunder and *not* another flood, the tension eased. Mrem were quick to adapt; it was what had saved so many of his clan when the waters came crashing down around them.

But if there was thunder, there would soon be rain, and this was as good a place as any to stop and hunker down. "We camp here!" he called, and saw relief in the adults at his decision. No one wanted to have to make a wet camp. Better to stop now, and get some level of protection and comfort before it was miserable work to try to do so.

And now there was a mad scramble for fallen branches, and a frenzy of cutting down vines. Because, thanks to the still-rising water, there was no promise that the camp you made on dry land was going to still *be* dry when you woke up, so tents were always pitched on top of platforms, so the worst that happened in the morning was that you got wet feet. Ideally, the platforms were knee-high or higher, with shallow trenches dug around them. That was the work of every kit old enough and anyone else who could be spared.

Sartas had too few warriors; with the waters on the rise and only Aedonniss knows what out in the woods, he wanted to keep guards on watch at all times. After a hard day's march and setting up camp, in addition to hunting duties...it became difficult to find anyone that could still stand, much less be alert for threats. Often, he took it upon himself to walk the camp, inspecting preparations and checking the perimeter. He had to keep himself abreast of what was happening among his people. *What starts as a small problem today can become a catastrophe tomorrow, if left unchecked.* The clan was hardy, but even the best of them could only take so much hardship before the edges start to fray and unravel.

But today they were cutting the march short. With luck that meant someone else could help him. Thunder rumbled in the distance again. He twitched an ear. It didn't sound appreciably nearer. He hoped it was a slow-moving storm. Small favors from the gods were to be taken where they could be had, these days.

Sartas was just starting his rounds when he spotted one of his scouts among some of the older kits; Mreiss Lrew, the youngest warrior left to the clan. He was scratching designs in the dirt with a stick, looking positively miserable.

"Shouldn't you be helping the others finish making camp?" Sartas Rewl stood with his arms crossed, looking down to where Mreiss was kneeling. The young warrior looked up with a start, quickly throwing the stick away and sweeping away the dirt when he saw who was talking to him.

"Sir, the kits are all set up, sir," he replied. "And everyone else..." His ears flattened. "Uh...kindly refused my help."

"Chased you off, did they?" He snorted. "Their loss. Come help Reshia. Tell her I sent you." Mreiss nodded once before dropping his eyes to the ground and running in the direction of Sartas and Reshia's tent. *He's troubled. It's best to keep him busy, keep him working. I'll have to keep a close eye on Mreiss Lrew in the days to come.*

The next few hours passed quickly for Mreiss Lrew. As commanded, he assisted Reshia in setting up the tent she shared with Sartas Rewl. Theirs was one of the few that only housed the two of them... but it was tiny, and had been made from pieces that had been scavenged out of the flood. Sartas Rewl made certain that no one in the clan was wanting for anything before he took supplies or provisions for himself and Reshia; he made sure that everyone was fed and had a place to sleep before he looked to himself. He had been a good talonmaster; he was a very good clan leader. At least in Mreiss's opinion. He never talked down to Mreiss, not like some of the others did. When he didn't want Mreiss to do something, he always explained why.

Once Mreiss was finished with that he was set to gathering wood for the small cooking fires, sorting the kindling, and arranging the firepits. After that, Arschus Mroa called upon him to help sharpen spear tips and their own blades. He always liked the time spent with Arschus; the senior warrior was always patient with him, no matter his mistakes. Arschus was quiet by nature, and didn't say much, but when he talked, it was worth listening to. He'd taught Mreiss a lot over the years, just with a few well-chosen words.

By the end of all of the chores, it was well into the night; the camp was made and all within it were ready to bed down. Mreiss shared the meager dinner with the rest of the clan around the main cookfire. There never was very much chatter during supper lately. Before the flood, there would always be laughter and stories; Mreiss liked the ones about battles and ancient heroes from distant lands the best. He always imagined himself as being one of those heroes someday, traveling away from the Clan of the Long Fang and leaving his mark upon the plains. But there were no stories to fuel his daydreams anymore. Everyone sat and ate quietly, the hushed conversations always short and private, as if the speakers were afraid that being too loud would bring some new calamity down upon them. There were no Dancers to lend their wisdom and to calm the fears of the clan. There was only Sartas Rewl, stony-faced and stoic no matter what came. Mreiss hoped it would be enough.

It wasn't until he had bedded down for the night that Mreiss had time to think again; even dinner was a chore, dealing with the unpalatable food and the long silences. He was stuck in a tent with nine kits, all of them younger than he was by a score of years. There was one good thing, though. There was no such thing as a restless, sleepless kit now. After a day's worth of exertions, they all fell asleep soundly and easily. Mreiss was not so lucky. He didn't mind the indignity of being set up with the kits; he had no family left in the clan, as his parents were both killed when he was still too young to remember them except vaguely, as dreamlike blurs and the feeling of comfort. He had been raised by the entire clan from that point on, but always felt different. Some of the kits in the tent were also orphans; parents taken in the flood or dead along the trail.

What kept Mreiss awake long into the night were his memories of that horrible, disastrous day; the day when the flood waters came.

He had wanted to go out with the hunters. The leaders of both hunting parties had rebuffed him. Sartas had at least been kind about it. "We hunt root-diggers, youngling," he had said. "Only the strongest dare that." And he had known Sartas was right; there was no way he could hold a charging spear against a root-digger. "There will always be next time. In a season, you'll be stronger. We'll see you ready by then."

Knowing that Sartas was right didn't do very much to heal Mreiss's wounded pride, however. Having been a loner for as long as he could remember, Mreiss had plenty of practice in going off alone in the woods outside of their village; the years of experience he had doing that were what made him a good scout. He could lose himself in the forest, leave his worries and frustrations behind and just listen to the world. He certainly hadn't wanted to go off with the foragers. They were all kits and the elderly and the women. And though he would very much have liked to stay and watch the Dancers, *they* had chased him off, some with unkind comments about skinny adolescents with stronger desires than his body could meet.

That had been why he had decided that he was going to watch them anyway, whether they liked it or not.

Not just any tree would do, however. It had to be big, very tall, and heavy with leaves, the better to screen him. Best of all would be one so big he could lie down all along a branch, and blend in with the bark. From high vantages like the very tallest trees, he felt like he wasn't a part of the world, but above and outside of it. He didn't dare liken himself to Aedonniss; such would be blasphemy. Mreiss simply wanted to escape from the mundane life that surrounded him, the indignity of being treated like a kit when there was adult work he wanted to do, or warrior's work he wanted to try, but like an adult when there were onerous chores to be done. It seemed the height of unfairness to be told "You are not strong enough" when he wanted to hunt or train against Liskash, but then be told "You are not a kit anymore" when there was water to be hauled or wood to be brought, or heavy objects to be moved. He was caught between two different sets of claws; both hurt, albeit differently.

Mreiss didn't know how long he had been in the tree he had found when it started; he had indeed found one with massive branches that allowed him to lie down fully, and had fallen asleep between his brooding and reverie. He was awakened by a noise, low at first. Mreiss initially thought it was someone growling at him to quit being such a layabout. It took him a few moments for the grogginess to clear from his head and realize he was still up in the tree. When the tree began to shake and the noise grew louder, he looked down at the base of it. *What kind of animal could shake a tree like this and make that sound?* Only then did he notice that it wasn't just his tree that was shaking; the entire forest was moving as the rumble grew louder. Steadying himself on the branch, Mreiss stood up and hugged the tree trunk with one arm while he used his free hand to shield his eyes as he scanned the horizon.

"An arx stampede? An army?" he wondered aloud as he took in everything below. A short distance away he could see the village; the Dancers were in the prominent clearing where they always practiced. Some were under the low shade trees on the far end, resting. They stood out against the ground; years of the action of hands-on-ground had removed the grass in the center to leave a roughly circular patch of compacted sand. Even from this distance, he could plainly see that the Dancers were alarmed as well; some of the ones that had been lounging under in the shade had stood up, looking around.

The noise was getting louder. It didn't sound like a stampede—it took him a moment, but he remembered being with a hunting-party in the spring just after a big rain, when they encountered what had been a trickle of a waterfall and had seen it had become a torrent. The thunder of the waters had sounded just like this . . . only this was much, much louder. *Where's it coming from . . . there! Oh, gods, there!* In the east, he could see large trees shaking with the impact as something struck them, and smaller trees snapping and falling over as if they were just blades of grass being knocked over by a rolling kit. It seemed to Mreiss that whatever was causing it took up most of the horizon, and that it was getting larger as it came closer.

He let go of the trunk and cupped his hands around his mouth, shouting at the Dancers in their clearing. "Run! *Run! Climb a tree, a big one! RUN!*" He pitched his voice high to make it carry over the noise, jumping up and down on his branch, waving. *"RUN!"*

He saw the—thing—his mind didn't even take it in as water at the time, just in time to drop back down to the branch and cling on for dear life. It looked like an avalanche, or a mudslide, a churning, grinding force of rocks and tree-parts and something that was dirt-colored but moving faster than any mudslide he had ever seen before.

One moment, he was staring in wide-eyed horror at the Dancers. Some of them had started to run, but none of them knew where the danger was coming from, or what it was; the trees blocked their view. The next moment, the edge of the flood reached the clearing, and just as quickly it all disappeared under the tumbling water. Mreiss didn't even have a chance to cry out in grief before the oncoming mass slammed into his tree. Several times the tree canted dangerously back before swinging forward a little bit; Mreiss had to cling for dear life, his claws straining at their roots to keep him attached to the tree. He shut his eyes, willing that it was all just another dream, as the sounds of splintering wood and churning water filled his ears.

But it hadn't been a dream....

Eventually, so numb with shock, horror, and grief that he had felt as if he had turned to stone, he began clambering from tree to tree, heading in the direction that the foraging party had taken. The hunters under Sartas had found him a little before he reached them, but well after he had heard their faint singing in the distance, and had known that at least he was not utterly alone.

He had been the one to tell Sartas that he was the sole survivor of the camp. He had been the one to tell the talonmaster that all the Dancers were dead, and that he was certain that none had gotten to safety. He had looked past Sartas to see the faces of those who had heard that their mates, their daughters, their sisters were forever gone, and if he could have managed it, he would have sunk into the ground to hide. He had known what they were all thinking, after the first shock of grief. *So why are* you *still alive?* No one ever said it, of course. It wasn't as if he hadn't been asking himself that same question with every breath he had taken since the waters came.

Just as he was asking it now, lying in the darkness, unable to sleep.

Then, finally, the storm came. Thunder rumbled overhead, rain pounded the tent, and under cover of the storm, now that no one could hear him, he could curl on his side, and cry.

Thunder rolled and the night sky whitened with flashes of lightning up above the trees. It was a good thing the clan had stopped early; it had been possible to make shelters for all of the campfires before the rain came. For once, no one was going to have to go to bed wet.

"I'm not saying that he's wrong. I'm just not saying that he's right, either." Miarrius Srell finished picking his teeth with a bone splinter before tossing it into the fire. He was seated across from Arschus Mroa and Ssenna Errol; the three of them always ended up on their own after the clan ate, to discuss the day and plan for tomorrow. It usually devolved the same way it had tonight; with Ssenna and Miarrius opposed to each other, with Arschus sitting silently and weighing everything.

"Be plain, and say what you want to really say. What would you rather Sartas have us do?" Ssenna, as icy cold as stone most of the time, only seemed to become heated when she talked to Miarrius. The two of them never could agree, and it always vexed Ssenna; Miarrius seemed not to have cared less about how he frustrated her, to the point where others wondered if he did it for his own enjoyment.

"All right, I'll tell you what I'd have our talonmaster do. Stay. Rebuild. We have lived in this valley for over a generation. The mountains and the forests protected us. We can find another home here, where there's still forest that hasn't been drowned in water." Miarrius shifted his weight a little farther back on the stump he was using for a seat. "Joining the Clan of the Claw means the end of the Clan of the Long Fang. I may be old, but I still have pride in my name."

"And just how do you propose to get the water to stop rising, hmm?" Ssenna asked. "You've seen it for yourself. When we backtrack, the water is right at our heels and our side. It would be foolish to stay here; before we could even begin building a permanent camp, the water would be up to our ankles. I don't know where it's coming from, but I do know this; it isn't stopping."

"The water can't keep coming forever. I've seen floods before. This one was costly, and bigger than the others. But that's how things are; the next worst thing is always the end of the world, until the thing after it comes along." Miarrius glowered. "It's just a flood."

"The water, you moron, is salt. Have you ever *been* to the Great Salt?" Ssenna smirked. She had. She knew very well that Miarrius hadn't. "The Long

Valley always was lower than the Great Salt. What if the land that held it back broke? The water will pour in forever until the valley is full."

"And what if Aedonniss thought that it would be a fine time to take a long piss on us? You can guess and wonder what did it until your fur is as gray as mine." Miarrius pointed one finger at her face. "It still doesn't change the fact that our clan dies if we join with the Clan of the Claw."

"And you can flaunt your ignorance as well as your stupidity, but that won't change the fact that we'll drown if we try to stay here. Unless you plan on growing fins and gills."

Arschus Mroa had been stirring the fire with a long stick, gazing into the flames while he listened to his two friends argue. Finally, he straightened up and took a breath to speak. The others stopped talking to listen; whenever Arschus chose to talk, which was rarely, it was usually for a good reason. "You know—"

"Are they at each others' throats yet? It's been a rather dull day, and I could use some entertainment." Rrerren Rras chose that moment to make his entrance. He shook himself mostly free of the rain on his hide just out of range of the fire, which was only polite, then ducked under the leaf-canopy to get as close as possible to dry off. He was carrying a large folded leaf in one hand. "Found something on my way over." He unfolded the parcel, revealing a chunk of meat. "Mind, if you're fighting, please continue. If I can't have a brawl with the Liskash, I'd like to watch one between you."

Ssenna leaned forward, licking her lips. "You bloody fool, How in the world did you get that?" Everyone's eyes were on the unexpected treat; with so little meat for so many in their clan, every morsel was added to a stew or dried out and rationed out. Freshly cooked meat was as rare as mercy, these days.

"With my good looks and charm. How else?" Rrerren picked up a dry stick from the pile of firewood, brushing it off before he used it to skewer the meat. "Oh, don't give me that look. The major share went to the common pot." Rrerren was lithe for a warrior, but not in a lanky way. He didn't need bulk; whenever he moved it was with a casual grace that belied his bravado. In the Clan of the Long Fang, there were no males so handsome as he was, and he knew it. Wherever he went and whatever he did, he always seemed to be wearing the same perpetual smirk, as if there was some joke that only he was privy to. It infuriated some—and made all of the available females of the clan swoon—but that expression never seemed to leave his face. "So, what are we arguing about tonight? The color of the sky?" He cocked an eyebrow at Ssenna. "You know that the only way to get him to admit that it is blue is to declare it is the color of sand."

Miarrius crossed his arms in front of his chest. "The fate of the clan, and our talonmaster's vision of what that ought to be."

"Oh, so nothing too troubling, then." Rrerren's smirk was back. He waited for the old warrior to take his bait while he made a show of carefully skewering and roasting the meat over the cookfire.

It was Ssenna's turn to speak. "No, it isn't troubling. Sartas Rewl has always put the Clan of the Long Fang first, in all things. He's never led us astray, never taken us down an evil path in the years that he's been talonmaster." She unsheathed a claw and poked at the meat on the skewer, checking to see how it was cooking.

Miarrius nearly exploded. "How can you say that? How can you say he puts the clan first, if he takes us to join another and there *is* no clan? Have we endured all of this to be swallowed up and vanish?"

"You don't know that will happen," Rrerren countered. "Unless you've turned Dancer on us. Turn around, let me look under your tail and see if you still have your old equipment. After all, they say miracles can happen." His little smirk turned to a grin as Miarrius flicked a small piece of wood at him. "You'd make a lovely lady. A bit beefy and ancient for my taste, but lovely."

"And you call me a moron," Miarrius growled to Ssenna.

"I think..." Arschus said slowly, and they all turned towards him. "I think, for I have been there, that the New Water comes from the sea, and I do not know how to swim." He reached for the meat, gently taking the stick from Rrerren's hand. He picked off a small piece, popped it into his mouth, and chewed thoughtfully. "And I also think, that if everyone dies here, the clan dies too, and you can bury my heart with it." Arschus gazed into the fire once more, then nodded solemnly before standing up and walking to his tent.

The three warriors sat around the fire in silence, gazing after Arschus. Rrerren was the first one to speak. "You know...he has a good point." He sat for a few moments longer, deep in thought. Suddenly, his eyes widened, and he sat up straight. "And he just stole my dinner!"

It was still raining when the camp roused, which made for a miserable start to the day. But Sartas reminded himself that the fires had been kept burning, so at least their scant breakfast was going to be warm, and they'd been mostly dry while they slept.

It was just around sun-high—not that you could see the sun, given the rainclouds and the trees—when Ssenna came looking for him. The clan was still packing up to resume the trek. She didn't have the sense of urgency about her that would have indicated her scouts had found something dangerous—but her hackles were a little raised, and her scent told him she was profoundly disturbed about something.

"We've found a Mrem camp," she said shortly. "I don't know exactly how to explain it, but I know that you need to see it."

"Are there other survivors?" Usually Ssenna wasn't this guarded about a scouting report; something was wrong, and she didn't want to say it in front of the others.

"You'll just have to come and see, Talonmaster. And I suggest we bring a lot of help, along with a couple of the arx." Sartas called out, gathering some of his warriors. He instructed four of them to stay with the

camp and guard the perimeter, while the rest were
tasked with rounding up the able-bodied to follow
him. Ssenna walked with him when the gathered
Mrem were ready to leave.

"I was checking on the progress of the New Water
before we moved out," Ssenna explained. "Miarrius
and I were having a...discussion...about the water
rising last night, and I wanted to verify something."

"You mean you were fighting about how fast it
was rising, and wanted to use the patrol as an excuse
to prove him wrong. Again." Sartas had no illusions
about that, nor why they were fighting. Miarrius wasn't
precisely *rebellious,* but he was very conservative, and
very protective of the clan, and consequently of the
clan's heritage. He was afraid that for all intents and
purposes, once they joined with Clan of the Claw,
Long Fang would vanish.

*He could be right. But if we stay in the valley, or
what's left of it, we'll die anyway. And if we strike
out on our own, we'll die off. We don't have enough
females. And we don't have enough warriors to fend off
the Liskash on our own forever. Hard to have a clan
identity if you're all dead, after all.* And, of course,
they didn't have any Dancers. Without the Dancers,
a clan had very little it could call a soul.

It took the group about the same amount of time
it would take to boil water four times to get to where
Ssenna had left Rreren and Arschus. When they
reached the village, Sartas almost immediately saw why
Ssenna didn't want to say anything at first. The village
was in perfect condition, aside from being a couple of

hand-lengths underwater. Truly *perfect* condition; the entirety of it looked untouched. Sartas motioned for his warriors to spread out and be vigilant; nearly silent save for the light splashing of their hands through the water, they moved through the village.

"I observed this place until the sun was halfway to midday, Talonmaster. Nothing was moving here, except the water. There's no one here, at all." Ssenna was back to her usual stony demeanor, her eyes still scanning the settlement. Sartas decided it was time to see for himself. He walked through the water into the village proper, and several things immediately stood out to him. A kettle sitting over an extinguished fire outside of a hut, still full of food; by the look and smell of it, it couldn't have been left out for more than a day. There was a sitting mat next to another tent, and in the water next to it, scattered, as if the project had just been dropped in a hurry, were arrows, half-fletched. More such projects were around the village; hides stretched on frames, half-scraped. Toys dropped carelessly, or tossed aside. Grain half-pounded in a mortar, or only partially husked from stalks. Even swords, spears, and shields were left behind; something no warrior would ever abide. The oddest—and the one that put *his* hackles up—a skewer of cooked meat just under the surface of the water, half of it gone, and a bite torn from one of the pieces still on it.

It seemed that everything was left here but the Mrem that once owned and lived in this place.

Sartas's ears perked up when he heard a cry from the far side of the village. Snatching up his spear, he started to run towards the sound. As he got closer, it became apparent that it wasn't a scream or a yell; it was whooping and excited shouting. He turned the corner of one building when he saw two of his warriors, standing in front of an open hut with their teeth bared in grins.

"What is it? What have you found?" They were both so busy jumping up and down and clapping each other on the back that they didn't realize it was their talonmaster talking to them at first. When they finally recognized Sartas Rewl, they sobered up somewhat, but kept smiling.

"You won't believe it...*food!*" The one that spoke went inside and came back out with a large pot. He opened the covering on top, and then pulled out a handful of grain. "There's so much food! Some of it is wet, but most of it was in pots or hung on the rafters. Fresh food!" By this time the rest of the party had arrived to see what the commotion was about. It didn't take long for the rest to join in the celebrating; after so many weeks of being hungry every day, food had become the only thing that some thought about.

After allowing some time for his people to enjoy the discovery, he held up a hand for quiet, and eventually got it. Ssenna was again at his side.

"What do we do, Talonmaster?" Ssenna asked quietly.

He thought about it. In a few more days, all this was going to be underwater—wasted. "Did you look for the clan this belongs to?" he asked. Miarrius, Arschus, and Mreiss all walked to the front of the group to face him.

"We did," said Rrerren, as Arschus nodded. "We did a fast running-scout, covering as much territory as we could. We went a *long* way, Talonmaster, and there was nothing. Not so much as a tuft of fur." He reached into a bag of jerky—presumably from the storage hut—and began chewing on a piece. "Not even any tracks. Though, with all of this rain and the flood, that isn't so surprising."

Sartas nodded. "All right then. In a day, no more than two, this will be ruined. If we run across the clan it belongs to, we can share it back, but for now, we take everything that is still useable. It will do no Mrem any good underwater."

While the rest of the group were merrily grabbing baskets, pots, and hanging meats, Sartas held Ssenna back. "This troubles you the same as it troubles me. Tell me why."

"The things left here . . . no clan can survive very long without them. We had no choice; much of what our clan owned was washed away while many of us were out, either hunting or foraging. These ones . . . this place *wasn't* swept away by the flood. It's only now starting to get a taste of the water; it couldn't have started any earlier than last night for this part of the land." She bit her lip and furrowed her brow. "I don't know what happened here. I'm not sure I want to know, Sartas."

He looked into her eyes for several very long moments before turning back to the group. "I don't know what happened here, either. I just hope we don't find out what happened to these Mrem the hard way."

His hackles wouldn't go down. He had, perhaps, too good of an imagination to feel easy about this situation. Had one of those monsters from the Deep Salt survived and attacked the village? Was it some new Liskash deviltry? Did the clan become hysterical when the floods came, run off in every direction and been lost that way? Kits wouldn't survive alone for long... but why wouldn't their mothers have taken them? Look how Reshia's group had done! Could it have been something else? Some new madness or plague?

Had the gods themselves simply come and taken everyone?

And his conscience still bothered him about his order. This all had belonged to someone, and they were taking it. But necessity dictated he looked to his people first. And as he had said, in a day, it would be so far under water that it would all be useless. Wasn't it better for Long Fang to have it, than have it go to waste?

There was only so much ground left, anymore, that the Mrem who lived here could be on. If they were found, they would be returned their goods, with the hope and understanding that they share with his clan. If they weren't—somehow, Sartas knew instinctively that they would never find the Mrem that lived here. That thought frightened him more than the New Water ever had.

There was too much to take in one trip. Sartas was forced to tell the clan to make camp again as soon as they found a secure spot, and prepare to divide up the . . . well, he could only call it "loot" . . . and dry out what needed to be dried. He didn't want to stop, but he didn't have a choice. What was the point of rescuing all this stuff if half of it spoiled or rotted or went otherwise bad because it hadn't been properly dealt with? "Fires for drying, fires for more smoking," he decreed, because if they re-smoked the wet tent hides, they had a very, very good chance of saving them even if they *couldn't* completely dry them out.

Miarrius was happy, or at least as happy as he ever was; Sartas knew why. He thought, once the clan had settled for a day or two, it would be easier to get Sartas to agree to stay and give up on the march to find the Clan of the Claw. But the land here was different than where they had their village, and things were still shifting. They hadn't seen a Liskash in a number of days, but that could change at any time. And there were still the flood waters to worry about; each day, the water rose, and the clan would be forced to go higher. The camp they had made for now was nowhere near as "permanent" as Miarrius fondly hoped. Soon, they wouldn't have the cover of the forest to help keep them hidden.

Sartas saw signs that some of his people shared Miarrius's desire to end the march. It had been a long and hard path, and it had cost them dearly. Compounded with the fact that they still had so very far to go to reach their goal, it was almost too much for most of them to bear thinking about. They wanted a place to stay. They wanted a home. A home where they needn't worry about drowning, starving, or being killed by the Liskash at any given moment. While only a few were vocal in their desire to end the march, many behaved in a way that showed how ready they were to accept that decision. An older smith that had joined them from another clan was starting to plot out a new forge for himself. Sartas almost didn't have the heart to point out that his fires would be underwater in seven or eight suns.

But weavers were setting up their weighted looms again, and some were sending kits out to forage, not for wood for the fires he had ordered, but for reeds and whip-tree branches for basket-making. And the potters were considering a kiln. Not good. Not good at all.

But at the same time . . . the kits were playing again. They hadn't even gotten more than their first meal out of the bounty, and already one good meal had revived them so much that he was shocked. He hadn't noticed how worn down they all were. That was especially worrisome; *he* hadn't recognized how badly deteriorated his people were becoming. Sartas tried to rationalize it away, thinking that he had to keep focused on getting as many to their destination alive and quickly. His doubts weren't quieted, however.

Or was it only that he'd been forced to think about other things? True, he hadn't been with the main part of the march since it began.

But he should have noticed. Shouldn't he?

Sartas sensed Reshia walking up behind him before she even spoke. No matter how quietly she moved, he always knew it was her, always knew she was there;

partly it was that he had honed already keen senses to be some of the sharpest in the clan, partly it was the closeness they had.

"You are unhappy," she stated. "I, too, am concerned. It is good that we rest for a little, and better that we have had this gift of food and goods. I am no Dancer, but I have tried to thank the gods for it, and if the clan that left these things behind is truly lost, I have tried to thank their spirits. It means life for us. But . . . I am concerned."

He turned to face her, studying her features. Reshia was a few fingers shorter than Sartas, and with a figure that would have made her a fine Dancer if she had chosen that path. Leaner than the norm for Long Fang females, her fur was fine and not as dense, more gray than sand. The tufts at the ends of her ears were longer than the usual, which would have given her features a kittenish cast, had they not been so severe. This was not to say she was not beautiful, certainly she was the most lovely Mrem *he* had ever seen, but she had none of the softness, the roundness, that most males seemed to prefer. And she had a trait he had only ever seen in Ssenna's face; the tips of her fangs showed, ever so slightly, all the time, instead of being hidden by her lips. It made her look just a little dangerous, just a little feral. The thing that Sartas loved the most about her, however, was that they shared the same heart; in her own way, she was every bit as much the warrior that he was.

"Is it that plain?" Sartas sighed heavily, shaking his head and peering behind her to look at the camp.

"We cannot become too comfortable here. If we do, we may never get moving again."

Reshia turned her head to the side, watching him as she talked. "But you have doubts."

He nodded. "Sometimes I feel as if you know me better than I know myself." A group of kits ran past them, chasing one another, laughing and shouting. "I set us out on this journey, and when I decided to do so, I knew it would be hard and unforgiving. I fear I may have blinded myself to our people, though. We've all suffered since the New Water came, and I forgot that not all of us are warriors; we may need time to heal." He pointed a claw at the group of kits that had passed by moments ago. "I see sights like that, with the kits laughing and looking healthy, and I wonder if perhaps Miarrius is right; we end the march, settle somewhere on the ridge, or even find high ground that will be an island, where the waters can't find us. I wonder how much more of this trekking what is left of the clan can take." Sartas looked to the ground, shaking his head again. For that moment, his guard fell, and Reshia could see how much this was paining him. She waited the space of many breaths before she spoke.

"We can do as you say and as Miarrius and those that will listen to him want; we can stay here, end the trek. But we will not." She placed a hand upon his arm. "You know the danger we're in, how real it is. We have no Dancers; the messenger that brought us news of the Clan of the Claw was weeks ago, looking for other clans to inform. None of the stragglers is a Dancer, and not one of the females that are left to us has had the gods speak to her and tell her she should take up the heritage. And if that was to happen? Who would teach her?"

He hesitated. "That is true."

But she was by no means finished. "Even if the Liskash were to leave us in peace—if, say, we managed to settle on land that became an island and successfully hid ourselves..." She shook her head. "I cannot see that happening. We are not adept with water. Only a few of us swim, and we do not know how to make boats, only rafts. We have never fished; well, except by accident. Do you see us being able to hunt, to forage, under such a circumstance? We have no trade, no contact with any other clans. We are cut off, and we are the only ones that can change that; sitting around and waiting will not do it." She patted his forearm. "Let us rest another day, and finish drying and preparing what we found. Then call a council. Let everyone speak. I...will have a few words with some of the others."

"Words? Try not to beat Miarrius too badly; we'll need his spear arm in the future."

She purr-chuckled. "No, no, I mean to speak with... shall we say, those who worry a great deal. It does no harm to plant doubts. You know of whom I speak... Ssenna for one. She is the sort to look at a cloudless day and assume in the night there will be a storm."

"Yes, but then she prepares for it, and if there is a storm, is near-unbearably smug, and if there is not, says 'Well, the thing you take care against never comes.

Perhaps I prevented it.'" He laughed, then embraced Reshia. "You are my rock in this storm, love. Thank you for helping me remember that." Turning back to face the camp, he left his arm around her shoulders, pulling her close. "The hard part is still to come. Convincing the rest."

It was at the campfire the next night when everything unraveled. Sartas had heeded Reshia's words, and waited for another day for preparations to finish; he was clear to everyone that they were to begin tearing down what they could in preparation for the next day, when the march would begin again. In retrospect it was a mistake, and one that would cost him; he was simply doing what felt right, however, and was at the time ignorant of the consequences. Shortly before the campfire, he sent word through the camp that there was to be a council held at that night's fire, and all were to be there and be heard.

Everyone had already been fed when it was time for the council; Sartas thought that was good. Being fed before the discussion might've quieted some who would otherwise have been loud in their opposition. He only hoped that Reshia's words had quieted the others, or helped them to see reason. Once it looked to him that everyone was assembled, he raised a hand for silence.

"We will be leaving again, soon. On the morrow or the next day." Sartas waited while the expected murmuring quieted. Finally, he began to speak again. "Perhaps none of you have gone to the New Water to see how far it has risen since we camped here," he said. "I can understand that. But I tell you we cannot stay. In three suns, the water will be here. In four, this camp will be ankle-deep. Before the water is here, other things will be; serpents, poisonous insects, perhaps disease. They, too, flee the water. It is time to move on. We have all rested, recovered our strength, and now it is time to seek the Clan of the Claw again, where we can unite with them and find safety."

One of the elders stepped forward feebly. "What of the oldest of us? This journey has been hard on everyone, but we cannot recuperate so quickly in so few days. Many of us have died, and more will die if we continue on much further." There were some nodding their heads in agreement at this. "It places strain on the rest of the clan in helping us, as well, along with the injured and sickly. How is it fair for us, at the end of our lives, to steal the energy needed for the kits, who are at the beginning? We cannot go on like this. Our wisdom has value, but is it more valuable than the future of the clan? Better to stop for a while so we can have both."

One of the females spoke up now. "I had five kits before the New Water. Now I only have one." It pained everyone the most when one of the young ones was lost; Sartas could scarcely imagine what she must have been going through. "It was not your fault, Sartas Rewl, but that doesn't bring my kits back to me. I cannot lose my last; my husband was gone in the floods, and all I owned; my child is all I have left."

More stepped forward. "Those of us with kits still need to care for them. They forage on the march and grow weaker with every day out there. They need rest. Those poisonous creatures you say are coming, well, we can at least *see* them coming when we are in a camp—but my kit was bitten by a serpent on the march. How can we defend against things we cannot see, that we blunder into? We are not, and our kits are not, trained hunters. We do not know these things are there until we step on them and they turn on us. You drive us before you, and we are defenseless against these dangers. It is time to stop, Talonmaster."

One of the smiths called to speak. "We cannot make a living at our trade on the march; we're no better off than the women, and unable to help the clan, unless we have a place to do our work. A forge doesn't work so well on a wagon bed. We need weapons, we need hunting implements. We need to be able to repair and refurbish the ones we have. We can't do any of that on the march." A potter joined him in his complaint. "How can we replace all the storage jars that are broken without a kiln? We have tried firing pots overnight in the ashes, as our ancestors were said to do, but it just doesn't work! Are we to turn basket-weavers now?"

"We'll turn into corpses if we continue this." This was a voice that Sartas was not familiar with. It belonged to a young male, one of the ones who had joined them shortly after the flood. He wasn't as tall as Sartas, but he was very fit; stocky, functional strength. He was not of the same body type as the

Long Fangers. Unlike them, he had no ear-tufts, and he had a long and very mobile tail. He was tan with subtle reddish and cream markings rather than tan with a heavy frosting of gray. He had heavier jaws and a longer face, too, which had the effect of making his eyes look smaller. Scars on his face and shoulders said that he was used to fighting. But he had not become one of Sartas's warriors. He didn't seem to do much of anything around camp, either; just enough to keep anyone from bothering him. "Continuing is foolish. If it weren't for your obsession with tucking tail and bowing down before the Clan of the Claw, we would have found a new home already."

Sartas sized the young male up instantly. *A bully, and used to getting his way.* "Who is this that is speaking? I don't know you." Sartas had to tread carefully here, but already had an idea of what this would ultimately come to. There was only one thing that this young Mrem had on his mind right now: a challenge. For him, it was a no-lose proposition. Long Fang did not have so many young warriors that they could afford to cast him out even if he lost the challenge. And if he won? He would be the new clan leader—though probably not for very long—a jump in status that under ordinary circumstances he could not have dreamed of achieving.

"I am Shar Enthiss." The young hothead puffed his chest out and stood tall, putting his fists on his hips.

"Strange, I've never heard of the exploits of Shar Enthiss. I haven't heard how many war bands he has led, or how many Liskash he's killed." Sartas Rewl paced around the fire as he talked, keeping a wary eye on the bully. "I haven't heard of his skill with javelin or sword, either. Yet here he is, it would seem." He stopped, turning to face the male. "My only concern is the survival of the people of this clan. If that is what I'm obsessed with, as you put it, Shar Enthiss, then it's not something I'm ashamed of."

"Your words are strong, but your actions show the opposite," the youngster huffed. "Here you have mothers with kits, the elders, and the injured and ill begging with you to leave off this pursuit of yours, and still, in the face of harm to your own clan, you insist on trying to find another clan. And you don't even know where it is! How long do you propose to drive us? Until everyone is dead?" There were more voices joining his in agreement, now. "You started us on this path, and now you need to end it. If you won't, then—"

Miarrius Srell stepped through the crowd and snarled for quiet. Shar Enthiss, confused, went quiet. Miarrius looked around at the gathered Mrem, taking his time before speaking. Sartas held his breath. This was the last thing he needed... when Marius supported this youngster, there would be an avalanche of support piling up behind him.

"If we continue on, more will die. I assure you all of this." *The old bastard has sunk me.* Sartas Rewl felt as if there were a block of slick ice in his belly, dragging him down. Miarrius fixed him with a stare, his face revealing nothing. "I can also tell you that if we stay here, *all* of us will die. In the lowlands, we were protected. Now, we are not; there are no more lowlands, only the New Water and the Liskash holdings that surround most of it. If we stay, we will either drown or eventually be found. Either way, we die." Miarrius turned back to the bully, pointing at him and glaring now. "We are too committed, but more than that, the New Water will drive us no matter what our wishes are; we continue on if we want to save anyone." He let out a heavy sigh. "I do not want to join Long Fang to Claw. But I also do not want to watch as our elders and kits starve or are slaughtered by Liskash. As the saying is, 'when the avalanche has begun, the pebbles must go, whether they like it or not.'"

Sartas took his eyes off the youngster for just a moment to see what the rest of the clan was doing. Their body language would tell him everything he needed to know. Most of the ones closest to Shar Enthiss had shied away from him, and very few at all seemed as friendly towards him as they were moments ago.

"Sartas is our talonmaster, and has been for many seasons," said Ssenna, from out of the crowd. Then her voice turned contemptuous. "What do we know of you, Shar? Only that *somehow*, you survived out of all of your clan." She left unspoken anything else that might be implied; Ssenna was very good about saying only enough, and no more.

Someone else in the crowd—Sartas could not tell who it was—snickered and added "Dung always floats."

"We know why we of Long Fang lived," put in

another of the hunters. "Because Sartas with the hunters, and Reshia with the foragers, both recognized something terrible was happening in time to get us to safety. I do not think we should abandon a path Sartas thinks is wise, given that."

Shar Enthiss was not pleased to see the conversation turning against him. Abruptly, he kicked a log in the fire, sending sparks skittering out. "Enough of this pointless yammering! If you're all too addled by your love of this fool, then I'll handle this myself." He unsheathed his claws and lowered his head, growling low. "I'll lead this clan to safety. Not you, Sartas Rewl."

Sartas nodded once, walking through the edge of the crowd into an open area. "If this is the way it must be, then know this; after it is done, there will be no more trouble from you, and you will do your share for this clan." The younger male roared once and charged, barreling over some of the crowd to reach Sartas. At the last moment Sartas unsheathed his claws and squared his shoulders to meet the charge. Just as Shar reached him, Sartas grasped the bully's shoulders while rolling back with his momentum. Arching his back as they rocked to the ground he simultaneously planted a hand in his opponent's chest, kicking him off and behind him. Shar impacted the ground with an audible thud, landing awkwardly on his back. Sartas had already spun around and readied himself in a low crouch; the youth was dazed for only a moment before he regained his senses and lifted himself from the ground.

Shar Enthiss still had plenty of fight left in him. He

was more careful this time, however. They circled each other for several long moments before he lashed out again; two quick swipes and then a bull rush. Sartas dodged both blows, and sidestepped the rush; as Shar went under his arm, Sartas chopped the back of his neck to send him off-balance. His opponent recovered quicker than he had anticipated, and retaliated by raking his claws across Sartas's ribs. A slick of red colored the tips of Shar's claws; he grinned ferally, emboldened by drawing first blood.

Shar made what looked like another rush...but then, just before he would have hit Sartas, he suddenly dropped to the ground and rolled. He hit Sartas's legs, knocking them out from under him before Sartas could avoid him, and turned the roll into a pounce. Sartas threw his arms in front of his face, blocking his opponent's hammer blows. Shar raised up both arms to bring them both down in a powerful strike; Sartas countered by striking him in the chin with a palm, then flipping him off to the side. As a parting gesture, he took a backhanded swipe, digging into the flesh of Shar's shoulder.

Time to end this. Shar could wear Sartas down, if he had endurance enough; he was certainly large enough to overpower the leaner Mrem. And Sartas had to show the clan something decisive. He stood up from the ground, allowing his arms to drop to his sides casually. Shar was confused by this; Sartas was dropping his guard, leaving himself wide open for attack. Not wanting to waste the opportunity, Shar moved in and stabbed his claws at Sartas's face, looking to blind him. At the last second before the claws reached him, Sartas locked an arm around Shar's outstretched one at the elbow. The talonmaster used his free hand to push against the bully's shoulder, forcing him down to the ground; he then wrenched the arm, twisting it back and taking the strength out of it. Shar screamed in agony; his screaming grew higher in pitch when Sartas planted a hand against that same shoulder, standing on it as he bent down to place a claw at the rival's throat.

"Do you yield?" Shar ended his screaming to huff and grunt in pain instead. Sartas applied more pressure to the joint he was standing on. Eyes going wide in agony, Shar managed to yelp, "I yield! Stop, stop!"

Sartas let go of his arm but took his time in removing his hand from Shar's shoulder. "Tend to your wounds. But do it somewhere else." He waited while Shar slinked off into the darkness beyond the light of the fire before turning to face the crowd. "As soon as preparations are made, we will ready ourselves and continue on the march. Does anyone else wish to contend this? If so, speak, and it will be heard." The entire clan remained silent, but it was an approving silence, with thoughtful nods. There was no more grumbling or chords of discontent within the crowd, now. Finally Miarrius spoke up.

"I would request a full day of tomorrow to properly pack, rather than the hasty thrown-together packing we have been forced to do until now, Talonmaster," he said, with great dignity. "Proper packing will enable us to move efficiently, and if any of the food has not dried completely, we can arrange for it to be eaten first, rather than spoil slowly in the bottom of a basket."

"That is wise. We'll make sure it is done." The gathered Mrem began to disperse, then, to talk about what had just happened, and to discuss how to get ready for tomorrow. Reshia waited until after the last of them were gone from the fire before she approached Sartas.

Her ears were flattened. "That did not go as well as I had hoped," she said, in a voice loaded with chagrin. "Let me tend your wounds."

"Better you than Shar." He winced as she began to inspect and poke at the claw marks. "I don't think we will have any trouble from that one anymore, however. Thugs are easily broken when they find someone truly willing to stand up to them." He watched her as she worked, speaking softly. "What are you thinking, my heart?"

"I am thinking that the clan is behind you, but even with this rest, they are weary and will only get more weary. Is there any way to make the march easier?" She sighed, and cleaned the blood from the slashes on his shoulder.

"Ask the gods to dry out the valley, to burn the Liskash from the lands, and grant us jars and baskets of clean water and food that never need to be refilled." She ticked his nose at the jest. "Honestly ... there is nothing more to be done, other than to continue forward. We have limited means. If it weren't for the village that Ssenna had found ... I don't think we would be able to continue. Perhaps that was a mercy from Aedonniss; I hope we will gain more, but I do not count upon hopes to see me through."

"I did not expect so much opposition," she said slowly. "I hope it has been settled, but it surprised me, and I am not sure what to think."

"Talking helps to lessen pain, especially when there are so many to listen. There may have been those that you did not know about, that needed to talk." Sartas shook his head. "I agree, though. I did not expect to see so many that were ready to lie down and give up the march. They are tired, and they have every right to be. But this world is not fair; it is cruel and harsh. We must be strong and tough enough to face it, or we do not deserve it."

She made a face. "Well, that is true, but no one ever wants to believe it. There. I think you will heal." She smoothed down his head-fur. "I am glad Miarrius stood up for you. That he did, after openly grumbling, I think is what convinced many. They saw as he did in the beginning, and then as he did in the end."

Sartas looked at her with puzzlement. "I thought you had spoken with him, like the others that expressed a wish to end the march. I was certain he was going to go against us until the very end."

"I did speak with him. And he was still grumbling and saying that you were completely in the wrong when I left him." She tilted her head to the side. "I do not know why he changed his mind; it was certainly none of my doing."

Sartas looked up at the stars overhead, and spoke in faux wonderment. "The gods do still smile on us."

Reshia punched him in the shoulder, which caused him to look at her, smiling. "Maybe we have a chance after all, love."

Miarrius had been right about one thing; taking the time to properly and efficiently pack everything and distribute the loads more evenly was already making a difference. Even the kits could manage small packs—their own bedding, for instance—and every bit that was distributed to someone else made things easier on the pack-beasts and the adults. For the kits, having their own little packs seemed to be a source of pride; each competed with the other to have the smallest and best organized.

The food had been divided up into meal-sized portions, which meant, in addition, that everyone could carry his own midday meal. That meant the midday stop for the group wasn't lengthened by trying to sort out food and squabbling over portion sizes. Everyone knew what they were getting, and it was done impartially with considerations made to the sick, young, and elderly. That in itself was a relief. It translated into less time and energy wasted on arguments and more on the task of surviving.

The edges of this valley were . . . a challenge to negotiate. Gnarled roots and vines everywhere, with boulders at the edge of a heavy slope to make walking difficult even if they hadn't needed to fight their way through. No obvious paths, or even game trails.

Also, no sign of that missing clan, either. The empty camp still haunted Sartas. With the New Water in their way, and the edge of the valley on the other side, there were only so many places that a clan could have gone. Long Fang was on one of the only ways out, following a "path" of least-resistance and least-growth in the direction they needed to take; neither he, nor any of his scouts, had seen any sign of that missing clan.

Could Shar have been from that lost clan? There had never been any time to press him on how he'd survived the flood and where, exactly, he had come from. It didn't seem likely, but this world had recently had a spate of the unlikely afflict it. *Well at least he's acting like a productive member of the group now.* Sartas didn't trust him as a scout, but he was doing fine as a guard on the rest, and carrying a full pack, too. In time, he would be a worthy addition to the clan. *If we live that long.* The thought stayed in the back of Sartas's mind, constantly toying with him. There was still such a long way to go, across unknown land with undoubtedly many dangers ahead. Not to mention needing to actually *find* the Clan of the Claw.

It seemed that Sartas's fears all came true two days later. The sun was out, but it looked as if there were another storm coming from the direction of the Great Salt Water. Everyone still kept an eye for a renewed flood; if one part of the valley walls could come down, why not another? The New Water still kept rising, or so the scouts behind said. Slowly, but inexorably. It was the new constant for their world, it seemed.

The trail had been clear for the last few days, with the clan hardly seeing anything moving aside from the odd game animal. Sartas was at the head of the march again, talking with one of the wagon riders when Ssenna came from the rear of the line, riding her krelprep at breakneck pace. She leapt from her krelprep at the last moment, landing at a run before stopping next to the talonmaster. "Sartas Rewl! There is news!" Miarrius was a breath behind her. He looked even more grim than usual; never a good sign.

"What is it? What has happened?"

"Liskash, Talonmaster." Ssenna bit her lip, baring her fangs more than usual. "Hundreds of them. You know we have made no effort to hide our backtrail, and they are on it; even without a trail, there isn't any other way for them to go other than to follow us. From what we saw, they are a motley group at best. They have no nobles that we've seen, and don't look to be as organized as other Liskash forces. Still, their numbers alone are enough to overwhelm us. There is one large scaled-fiend that seems to be in charge of them, however."

"They've got archers, sling-throwers, and plenty of footmen with pikes. They're a force, to be sure." Miarrius shook his head. "They'll be caught up with us in three days' time, maybe four if we're lucky. They aren't burdened with wagons or elders like we are; they're a pillaging force, taking what they find and destroying the rest."

"Not even slavers?" Sartas growled under his breath. Slavers were less likely to charge in with wanton violence; capturing Mrem was their goal, not slaughtering them. This spelled doom for the entire clan. A pillaging party would leave no one alive. Even an enslaved Mrem could scheme to escape, as long as he wasn't mind-wiped by one of the Liskash magicians. It was better to die than to lose one's name to one of those foul bastards.

"They had no slaves with them, nor the means to keep any. They're out for blood and meat, and nothing more." Miarrius took a deep breath. "We could try to hide our backtrail, but that would delay us a great deal, and I do not know how effective that would be. I am a warrior, not a hunter."

"There's no time for that, at this point. Even if we could hide our trail, there's only so many places that we or the Liskash can go. They're also more numerous than we are, and will find us eventually." Sartas looked to Ssenna.

"We need to draw in the other patrols immediately, gather our strength to the center. We have very little time left to prepare."

"Go, all of you. Bring all of our scouts back. We need to meet tonight, and decide—"

Mreiss Lrew chose that moment to ride in on his krelprep, pulling up short of the talonmaster and the rest where they had stopped. "I've got news, Sartas Rewl!" Mreiss paused for a few moments to catch his breath. "There's a series of cliffs well ahead of us. A day and a half's ride, by my ranging. They're near impassible, with the wagons and whatnot. I tell you truthfully, I could hardly climb them, even with only my harness and sword—" He paused, canting his head to the side. "Why are all of you looking at me like that? Did I say something wrong?"

"How far do these cliffs go?" Sartas asked carefully. "Half a day? A full day? More?"

Mreiss shrugged. "As far as I could see in either direction. More than we could travel in seven sunrises, to be sure."

Sartas looked to the others. "Be quick about your tasks. We have even less time than before." He explained the situation to Mreiss; all of the color drained from the young warrior's face as he came to know the full extent of the clan's troubles. Almost stumbling over himself, he left to make preparations. Only Miarrius was left once the others had gone.

He stopped, laying a hand upon Sartas's shoulder, looking to the ground before meeting the talonmaster's eyes. "I was wrong, Talonmaster. You were right, and I was wrong, when I urged us to stay, and said that you were driving the clan too far. If you had listened to me, we would already be dead." Without another word, Miarrius strode off to fulfill his talonmaster's command. *Wonders upon wonders*, Sartas thought, as he contemplated what new evils they would face. It wasn't enough that the clan was battling starvation and disease at every turn, that they now be plagued with a storm of Liskash, with no way to escape? How much more would they need to endure before there was respite?

And had he saved them this long, only to destroy them in the end?

Sartas Rewl knew he would not be sleeping this night.

❖   ❖   ❖

"I tell you, if we do this thing that you say, then we'll all die."

The meeting that night was even more heated than the last one. Everyone had a different idea about what to do concerning the oncoming Liskash horde and the cliffs that were blocking them in ahead. It didn't help that each Mrem seemed to be utterly convinced that their plan was the best to lead the Clan of the Long Fang to salvation and glory. The only ones that weren't talking were Sartas Rewl and Arschus Mroa; both took in the debate in silence.

The one that had everyone's attention at the moment was Rrerren Rras. "We should split up into several different groups, all heading in different directions. We'd cover our tracks, and agree to meet up at a predetermined point after we've lost the Liskash bandits. They can't follow everyone, and either all of them will pursue a small, fast band of us that can evade them, or they'll split up and get lost from each other. You know what happens when they lose their leaders; they fall apart."

"And where would you propose we meet up, warrior? Not a one of us knows this land; the farthest that we've scouted are those cliffs, which the Liskash will smash us on if we're wandering aimlessly looking for each other!" That was one of the smiths; he'd lost one of his legs on the trek, and had been forced to hobble behind everyone else on a crutch when he wasn't riding a wagon.

"Both of you are wrong." Another Mrem that Sartas didn't immediately recognize stepped forward. "The clan needs to head to the water. We can make rafts, and float along out of range of their javelins and arrows. The Liskash wouldn't dare follow us out onto the water—"

"For good reason, you mindless smerp! The New Water is death! Were you asleep in a wagon when the kits found that carcass? There are beasts from the sea in it, not to mention rotting things from all that died in the floods. And snakes and poison insects and who knows what else hiding in the trees, starving and just waiting to drop on you because they can't reach land!" The female pointed at the maimed smithy. "How many of our wounded or elderly would drown, besides? We're not fish."

"Hey, that's not a bad idea! We go into the trees! It'll be like we just vanished into thin air. We've traveled in the trees before, and those dirty Liskash don't know how to climb all that well. The ones that fly can't see us through the tops of the trees, as well."

"...except that the trees end in less than half a day's ride from here." Ssenna was crouched by the fire, poking the embers with a long stick. "Between the end of the forest and the cliffs, it's just open ground, with a small valley with some hills on either side."

"We can fight them." Miarrius was a few paces behind Ssenna; the way that the shadow and the light from the fire were playing across his face made him look like a demon incarnate. "We stay in the forest, keep moving, double back on our tracks. Keep the women and kits ahead of us, while we strike at them and then fade away, wear them out." The old warrior was caressing the pommel of the sword on his side.

"Once they've bled enough, they'll lose the taste for chasing after us."

Mreiss Lrew shook his head. "There's not enough room, not with the New water on one side and Liskash holdings on the other. With only half a day's ride of forest left, we'd be pushed out onto the fields soon enough." He looked around, suddenly seeming unsure of himself. "Besides . . . what if they got around the attackers? Who would be there to defend the rest of the clan?"

"Well, why not lay traps? Pit traps, deadfall traps, all kinds of traps!"

"Not enough time to lay enough traps to slow the Liskash; they number in the hundreds." Ssenna interjected. "By the time we'd have enough traps in enough places to make them start to be careful, they'd be upon whoever was making the traps."

"Mreiss, what is the territory ahead like?" Sartas asked slowly. "Exactly."

The youngster gathered up a pile of leaves, sticks and stones and squatted down, clearing off a space of ground. He scattered leaves over half of it. "This is the forest we're in." He laid a line of twigs along one side. "These are the cliffs, they go on . . . well, for a long time. Longer than I was able to go, since I needed to come back and report. Far enough to reach both horizons." He laid in two groups of stones with a space between them. "These are the hills, and the pass between."

Sartas dropped down on his heels, and studied the construction, pondering it. Then he stood up. "I have a plan. I believe it will save the clan, the kits, the females, the elders. But it will mean that those who stay with me will die." The entire gathering was silent, now, with all eyes on the talonmaster. He took a handful of seeds and put them at the pass through the hills. "A single small force, using traps first, then themselves, can hold the Liskash here. And meanwhile, the rest of the clan can get up the cliffs. The longer that force can hold, the likelier it will be that everyone gets to safety. By the time any Liskash that are left break through—and they will, with the numbers Ssenna describes—there will be no trace of those who scaled the heights. The trail will be cold, and in any event, even the Liskash are not going to pursue a few Mrem up a cliff and into the territory of some other god-king." He looked about, and shrugged. "That is all I have. If anyone has a better plan, please speak up now."

Arschus Mroa held a finger up. "There are no other plans; *this* is the only plan that will guarantee the survival of the Clan of the Long Fang." He looked to Sartas. "Might I make a suggestion, though, Talonmaster?"

"Of course."

"I suggest that we kill every bloody one of those Liskash fiends. Even if we die trying."

The entirety of the clan gave a roar in approval, the warriors thrusting their javelins into the air and whirling swords above their heads. Sartas was filled with pride to see his people looking strong and courageous again. He only hoped that their strength and courage would see them through the battle ahead.

❖   ❖   ❖

Sartas Rewl was at the edge of the camp again, well beyond the light of the fires. He was staring back towards the direction that the Clan of the Long Fang had come from. It was now the direction that the Scaly Ones were coming from; if he was wrong about this plan, then it would mean the end of his entire clan. This wasn't the first time that they had been faced with dire circumstances; the entire trek, starting from the flood of the New Water, had been fraught with danger and death. But this was worse, if such a thing existed. A Liskash horde. No nobles, thank Assirra; without any Dancers, the clan would have been defenseless against Liskash spells. The numbers that the Liskash had more than made up for it, however; even with all of his warriors, Sartas knew that they could not hold for long against even an undisciplined mob of a few hundred Liskash.

Perhaps we will hold long enough. Long enough to save the clan, at least, to have our name carry on.

Reshia came out from the camp, her eyes fixed on him, her posture a little stiff, her face full of suppressed grief. "Is it that certain?" she asked, when she was close enough to speak. "Is there no other way?"

Sartas turned to face her. "None that I have been able to see. We must do this thing, or the rest of the clan dies as well. I do not know if I am right about this plan; it might not help at all. But it's the only thing I can see to do." He cursed, spitting onto the ground. "If we had more warriors, or more time, working chariots, then maybe I could come up with something else. But Aedonniss hasn't granted us any of those things, and we have no Dancers to plead to Assirra for us." He looked back to her, suddenly weary. "I do not want to leave you, love."

She sighed, bitterly, and her blinking betrayed that she was fighting tears. "If I were a warrior, I would fight at your side, and then we would never be parted. But I would be of more hazard than help." Her fists clenched, betraying how much she was fighting saying anything else, words that would also do more harm than good.

The talonmaster took her chin and forced it up so that her eyes were meeting his. "Speak. If I cannot share my mind with you, and have you do the same with me, then we're all already lost."

"This is not *fair*!" she wailed. "To have come through so much, for this! I do not want to be alone!" And she flung herself on him, clinging to him.

Sartas held her as close as he dared until he could scarcely breathe. "For a moment, I thought of taking you and our fastest krelprep and riding away. Just leaving everything and trying to make it on our own." He pulled her back by the shoulders, resting his forehead on hers as he closed his eyes. "I couldn't do that, though. Just as much as we're the strength of our clan, they're the strength of us, as well. If we left them, they'd fall, and then we would, too."

She had no answer for that, only tears, tears that they both knew were their farewell.

"I need you to do something for me, love."

She lifted her face from his shoulder. "You have only to ask. Only do not ask me to give you my blessing for this. I cannot bless what takes you from me forever."

He smiled at that, trying to help lessen the burden on her heart. "I would never dream of asking your blessing on this, love. I only ask that you remain as strong as I know that you are. The clan is going to need someone with a strong spine to see it through the rest of the journey, and find the Clan of the Claw. You're the only one that can do that."

"Then I promise I will harry, hound, scold, scream, and drive them before me until they are safe," she replied fiercely.

Sartas's smile grew and became more heartfelt. "I haven't a single doubt that you will." He took her face into his hands again; it was part of the closeness they shared. "You need to remember that even as I go off to kill these Scaly Ones, that I will never leave you. Sure as Aedonniss makes the sun rise. So long as you and the clan live, no one will ever bury my heart."

It was a hard push to the hills, with everyone moving as quickly as they could. They spared no pity for the beasts; after all, they were either going to be abandoned at the bottom of the cliffs, or left with the warriors at the hills. In either case, there was no point in sparing them. Everything but the krelprep were slaughtered; what meat that couldn't be smoked and taken with was gorged upon. For some, it would be their final meal.

Farewells had all been said the night before. At the pass in the hills, the clan moved on at the same pace, while the warriors remained behind. So far as Sartas could tell, no one, not even Reshia, looked back. *Good. It will be easier on them, and on the warriors.* This was the way life was in their world; the warriors fought to protect the clan, and often died doing so. Still, after having lost so much already to the New Water and the horrors that had followed, it was a testament to his clan's strength of spirit that they were able to press forward.

They had laid traps at the edge of the forest, counting on the Liskash to become careless and bloodthirsty at that point. They'd made no effort to conceal their trail; they hadn't before knowing of the Liskash, and with a group their size to try was pointless. Sartas also instructed his people to make no effort to trap it until the end of the forest, either; better to draw the Scaly Ones in, thinking that their prey was running scared. Sartas had reckoned that a little time spent at the end of the trees would be worth it in Liskash casualties.

They had managed to use the gifts of the forest to hastily construct some unpleasant surprises for the oncoming raiding party. Spiked pits concealed from view on and off of the main trail, snares, and deadfalls comprised the majority of them. He was particularly pleased with the swinging logs. *Someone* was going to get his long, scaly neck broken. Several someones, if there were any justice in the world. Sartas wasn't fool enough to think that these traps would be anything but a minor inconvenience for the Liskash following them, however; if anything, it would only incense them. But, an angry Liskash wasn't a thinking Liskash, as much as they ever did think. It was something that he could use against them. His warriors being able to keep their heads would double the effectiveness of his force.

His warriors waited at the pass, most mounted on their krelprep with shields and javelins ready. Rrerren was on one end of the line, telling jokes and boisterous tales of his own exploits to lighten the moods of those around him. Miarrius and Ssenna were on the other, arguing about some new trifling. Arschus Mroa and Mreiss Lrew flanked him on either side; the latter was fidgeting with his harness and his weapons, while the former was seemingly as still and impassive as a carved rock. Sartas had inspected the line; in all, he had thirty fighters. Most were warriors, but some were untrained and simply chose to join the battle. He had done his best to make them as ready as possible in the little time that they were all left. One of the males that joined them had surprised him; Shar Enthiss.

The young male walked in front of Sartas's krelprep, keeping his head bowed and only raising it slightly so that his eyes met with the talonmaster's briefly. "Sartas Rewl."

"Speak, if you wish." Sartas was curious as to what was going on here; he didn't quite know what to expect of the young upstart.

"Before this fight, I just wanted to say... I was wrong in what I did, and did it for the wrong reasons. You are the greatest talonmaster I've seen. I'm honored to fight by your side; it's what little honor I have left." Shar pounded the haft of his javelin to his chest once before casting his eyes to the ground again.

Sartas nodded. "If you fight against the Liskash half as well as you fought against me, Shar Enthiss, you'll surely have no shortage of honor and glory. I'm glad we have your spear to aid us; I'm even happier that it isn't against us." Shar looked up then, and a mean grin spread across his face. He stood up straighter, raised his spear in salute, and walked off to rejoin the line.

Arschus Mroa leaned forward in his saddle. "That was a kindness that you did him now. Especially for one that, not so long ago, wouldn't have minded having your throat in his teeth."

"Kindness is as rare as nectar, these days. With what is to come, it is of no cost to spare even one such as Shar some kindness." He turned and beckoned to Mreiss. The young male wheeled his krelprep to face the talonmaster, eager to hear what Sartas wanted of him.

"Yes, Sartas Rewl?" Mreiss did his best to puff his chest out and hold himself high in his saddle.

"To you goes the most important task of all, young warrior," he said gravely. Mreiss bounced in the stirrups of his saddle, waiting, no doubt, to hear that he was to lead a charge, or something similar. "I want you—up there." He pointed a talon to the top of the tallest hill behind where the battle lines would be. "I want you to watch everything. Above all I want you to *survive*. You are *not* to engage the enemy. And when we are done, I want you to race back to the clan, and tell them everything that you saw." He leveled a stern gaze on the youngster. "Listen to me: it will take more courage, and more will, to do this, than it will to fight. There is no harder task. And none more vital."

"But—I can't *leave* all of you! I *won't*!" It was plain for any to see how conflicted Mreiss was; he wanted to do his duty, to do as he was ordered to. Yet he did not want to abandon his fellow warriors when they were in their darkest moment.

"You *will*. You are not a heedless kit anymore, Mreiss Lrew. Will you leave the clan without a senior warrior to fight for them?" He didn't roar, he growled. "Your duty is to the *clan*. Not to a band of its warriors. The *whole* clan. They *must* know what happened. They must know everything. Then they must have a strong, young, seasoned warrior to lead what is left of the fighters. You are not 'the one that can be spared.' You are my *best* choice. You are fast. Your mount is fleet. You are clever. You've been trained by Ssenna to be a scout. By Miarrius to be crafty. By Arschus to be strong. By Rrerren to be gallant. You can evade any Liskash that are left. You are my best choice for this; no one else has as much likelihood of making it back to the rest."

"I—"

"You'll follow your orders, Mreiss Lrew, as a true warrior must." Every word pained Sartas to say, but he did not allow any of it to show on his face. This must be done, for the good of the clan.

"I'll . . . I'll do as you command, Sartas Rewl. For the Clan of the Long Fang." Without another word Mreiss turned his mount to face the hill where he was to observe the coming battle. He paused for a moment next to Arschus Mroa.

"In the next life. Warrior." Arschus laid a massive hand on Mreiss's shoulder for a moment. Then Mreiss spurred his mount to gallop towards the top of the hill where Sartas had pointed.

Sartas and Arschus watched until Mreiss was so high up on the hill that he and his mount were barely visible against the earth. Then they made sure that he had concealed himself so well not even their sharp eyes could spot him. Sartas nodded. "He has learned his lessons well. Now it is time for our task. The Scaly Ones will be here soon."

Arschus appraised the entrance to the pass, below them. "I imagine they will wish they hadn't survived the coming of the New Water after they see what is waiting for them."

No sooner did the large warrior finish speaking than did the first Liskash rounded the bottom of the hills at the beginning of the pass. First one, then four, then forty Scaly Ones. And more kept coming. Soon the entirety of the entrance to the pass swarmed with Liskash.

Arschus hissed. "They look like carrion-bugs." Even at this distance, the Liskash were clearly a motley and sorry group; very few had any armor, and whatever they were wearing was mostly in tatters or ruined with filth. Despite that, they still had the numbers to be more than a credible threat. And they were *hungry*. It was to raid and pillage or to die, for them.

"Soon they will be feeding carrion-bugs," Miarrius said. "Something will, at least. Bugs will be getting a full meal today, one way or another."

Rrerren galloped to the center of the line to join Sartas and the others. "You worry too much, gray-hair. In fact, take a nap; I'll take care of these interlopers."

Ssenna, quiet as death, moved her mount within the vision of the others. "I don't think your jokes will be any more lethal than they already are, Rrerren."

"Maybe he'll just bugger them to death." Miarrius slipped his sword and dagger from their sheaths, eyeing the approaching Liskash. "He's buggered damn near everything else in the clan."

"That will do." Sartas did not turn to stare at his warriors, he let his tone of voice tell them that the time for joking was over. "Every arrow, every javelin, every thrust is precious and cannot be wasted. Make each one count. If you can't kill, maim, cripple. I don't want a single Liskash in that horde to be unmarked. Remember that we are buying time. *Hurt* these forsaken lizards. Make them know that the Clan of the Long Fang lives for their blood!"

All of the warriors roared as one at that. The oncoming Liskash seemed to pause at the sound of the battle cry. It was only for a moment, though. They began to advance again; Sartas saw that their archers and those with slings had crowded to the front. Their lines weren't nearly as well organized as if they should have been; the orderly formations had been replaced with a crush of Scaly Ones, gathered together in smaller groups behind the front rank. *Ssenna was right; they don't have a noble leading them. This is not a coherent force, this is a mob.* For a moment he had a glimmering of hope. Was it possible they might survive this? Soon they were in range to start firing arrows and slinging stones, cutting off his thoughts. "Shields!"

As one, all of his fighters brought their large shields up over their heads; the shields covered most of their bodies and the front of the krelpreps. Arrows, stones, and then javelins came down in uneven volleys; the Liskash weren't coordinating their archers at all, it seemed. The rain of projectiles slackened and finally became a drizzle. No one seemed to be hurt, beyond one unlucky krelprep that caught an arrow through the neck. *They must be running out; with no way to resupply, perhaps they're down to their last.* "The stupid beasts are out of ammunition!" he roared. "Send some back!" Again as one, all of Sartas's fighters threw a volley of javelins; only one, since they had so few to begin with. Some of those that were left without any picked up the javelins that had just moments ago been thrown at their hides. Their javelins found good purchase in the Liskash ranks; most found their marks, with the Liskash being too focused on their victims to worry about their own safety.

Sartas dropped the large shield while swinging a lighter one from his back; the first was covered in dents and protruding arrows along with one Liskash javelin. He noticed that there was dried blood on the javelin; the sight of what was probably Mrem blood caused his anger to burn in cold waves throughout his body. He raised his javelin into the air, then pointed it towards the Liskash. "Forward!" Tucking the butt of the javelin under his arm, he spurred his mount, sending it surging forward with a whinny in protest. His fighters roared in response, following him down the path. The Liskash were at the base of the rise where his warriors had gathered; any ground they hoped to gain would have to be taken while fighting uphill. This gave Sartas's riders and the fighters on foot the advantage of momentum for their charge. Only a few of the Liskash raiders were able to position their shields or ready javelins for the oncoming charge; most of them were still pushing forward, too eager to be the first to kill one of the Mrem.

No time to think, now. This was the work for training, reactions, and the will to survive. Sartas was the first to meet the Liskash line; on instinct, he worked his javelin at the final moment, leveling it at the enemy. His spear found the first Liskash with a shock of contact, lodging in its mouth; he instantly withdrew it and thrust it out again before the first had even fallen; another was taken in the throat, and the one after that through its eye. The rest of his fighters were right behind him; they had formed into a wedge, the better to pierce through the massed Liskash. Those without mounts crashed through Scaly Ones that had been off-balanced by the charge; javelins and swords and axes flashed, and the ground was quickly stained with blood. The Liskash were reeling; they couldn't have expected their foes to attack so ferociously against their superior numbers. Here they thought they had been pursuing refugees like themselves, fleeing before the New Water. They had never expected the pursued to turn and bare their fangs in defiance.

Hunters often grew in fervor when a prey-beast ran in fear; so it was with these Liskash. They had not taken into account the terrain that had become the battleground. Scores of the Liskash were paying for this miscalculation with their lives and limbs.

Even with the flow of battle on their side, there were just too many Liskash; after Sartas lopped the head off an archer, his mount took a javelin to its side, followed by two more javelins once it reared up with a scream of pain. He was able to leap from the krelprep and land on his feet without it toppling over on him. The beast was still kicking in its death throes when he came up, shield and javelin in hand. Several of his warriors dismounted near him; the killing resumed immediately. Arschus Mroa had eschewed a shield in favor of using both hands to wield his axe; it was suitably large to fit his gigantic frame. Swinging it back and forth, he cleared Liskash two or three at a time from around him, as if he was knocking the heads off flowers.

Rrerren Rras had both of his long swords out, and was whirling them while laughing raucously in between dispatching Liskash; he was graceful with each dodge and feint, every parry and slash. Two Liskash sought to attack him from front and back at the same time; deflecting the tips of their spears at the last moment, he redirected the points into the Liskash on opposite sides as they charged forward so that they impaled each other. "Careful! You slimy lizards might hurt someone with those things!"

Ssenna was on the edge of the fighting, standing on her fallen mount; she would spot opportunities in the fighting, and loose an arrow at a Liskash; sometimes a breath before it would have delivered a killing blow, other times to take pressure off of a harried comrade. She never missed with a single arrow, always calm and methodical in her aiming and firing. For a moment, Sartas wondered if he should have allowed Mreiss to stay; with his lightning reflexes, slim build and shorter stature, he could have dashed among the fighters retrieving spent arrows for her. Well, too late now. Miarrius was doing his best to cause as much havoc as quickly as possible in Mreiss's place. For such an old warrior, he was surprisingly spry. He rolled between the legs of one Liskash, slashing its ankles as he moved. Springing from a crouch, he skewered another through its throat, and then turned to parry a javelin-thrust with his dagger. Slashing the offending Liskash across its snout, he dashed inside of its guard, hacking off its arm first and then its head. The final Liskash that Sartas saw Miarrius kill was taken down after the warrior had tripped it and used his legs to immobilize it before disemboweling the Scaly One.

As well as his fighters were doing, Sartas had his own hands full. For every Liskash that he cut down, there were three more to take its place. He gave the head of his javelin to one of them; dying, it reached for the haft and held onto it as it fell backwards, taking the javelin out of the talonmaster's grip. Snarling, he ducked under a sword just in time as he pulled his own blade from its sheath; he felt the tip of one of his ears trickling blood. *Too close.* He chopped at the Liskash that had swung at him, forcing it back.

Feinting to the left, he ducked low and stabbed quickly with the short sword, catching his opponent in the chest with the tip of the blade. The Scaly One didn't have time to hiss as it fell off the blade, dead.

There were already others to take its place, however. A slung stone grazed the side of Sartas's shoulder; he whirled and dropped to a knee as two more went sailing over his head to impact with a foe behind him. He charged forward again, shouldering a Liskash in the back; it stumbled forward, impaling itself on one of his warrior's javelins. He knew that he couldn't stop moving; more would be crowding at his back. Sartas slashed one lizard across its legs, spinning with the cut and opening its throat with another blow as it fell to the ground.

Finally, the inevitable happened; they started dying. One warrior fell, followed by another; javelins and swords and claws from the mob came in unending waves. Even with all of their ferocity and bravery, Sartas's warriors could not fight in such a melee forever. Sartas had just cut a Liskash from stem to stern when he noticed that Rrerren had suddenly stopped laughing; whirling around to where he last saw the warrior, his heart dropped. Rrerren was standing with a sword through his back and out his chest, a confused look on his face. Then he spun on a heel, decapitating the Liskash that had run him through. Sartas sprinted through the fighting, dodging Liskash and Mrem alike to reach Rrerren's side just as he fell to his knees.

"Already?" He sputtered, trying to grin as he was

coughing up too much blood. "I've only killed twenty more Scaly Ones than Arschus has. I can't let—" The light left Rrerren Rras's eyes in that moment, and he went slack in Sartas's grip, still smiling. Sartas came up from the ground roaring, baring his fangs and looking at the surrounding Liskash with unadulterated murder in his eyes. He surged forward, blocking a javelin with his sword; he collapsed the throat of the javelin-wielder with the edge of his shield. The Scaly One doubled over, unable to breathe; Sartas swung his sword with all of his might, cleaving off the enemy's head and shoulder with a single blow. The other foes all backed away from him, none of them wanting to be the next to face his wrath.

Sartas took a step towards them, intending to find a new victim for his fury. He stopped suddenly, feeling as confused as Rrerren had looked. He couldn't move his left leg. Looking down, he saw that there was a javelin going through the meat of his thigh, still quivering. The Liskash around him saw the opening, and came for him; he was put on the defensive, swatting away swords and javelins while not being able to maneuver at all. Soon, they would swarm him, and that would be the end. He could see that more of his warriors were failing and dying; in twos or threes or alone, they killed and were cut down in turn.

Just when it looked like the onslaught was going to overwhelm him, Sartas saw that some of the others were coming for him: Ssenna and Miarrius, fighting as a pair, with Arschus carving a path through the Liskash from a different direction. The throng of Liskash separating them from the talonmaster was too strong; every time they pushed forward, they were driven back just as quickly. He tried to call out to them, to tell them to leave him and fight for themselves. It was no use, however; the din of battle drowned out every word he said more thoroughly than the New Water had drowned the valley.

Arschus disappeared behind a wall of Liskash. He had several arrows and javelins sticking out from his hide, but he did not stop; whenever the Liskash came at him, he cut them down with swings of his axe. He eventually slowed, however, until he progressed no further; the last Sartas saw of him, before the Liskash got between them, he was splitting one of the Scaly Ones in half while throttling another to death with his left hand.

Miarrius and Ssenna had been stopped by the mob of Liskash between them and Sartas as well. They were fighting back to back; Ssenna was cradling her left arm while stabbing Liskash with one of their own javelins. Miarrius was bleeding from a dozen wounds, but that didn't seem to have slowed his assault. A slung stone struck his hand, causing him to drop his dagger; with that hole in his defense, three Liskash swords bit into the flesh of his chest. Miarrius killed two of them, rending the throat of the second one with only his claws before he finally fell to the ground. Ssenna finished off the third Liskash, standing over Miarrius's body. The Liskash pressed in with spears; from the sound of things, Sartas knew that she did not die alone.

The wounded talonmaster hissed at the Liskash around him. *We all go together here.* He was committed to make his friends' sacrifice worth it, and to match it. He gathered his strength, willing himself past the pain from his wounds. Sartas snapped the haft of the javelin that had pierced his thigh to free himself, then leapt into the air off of his good leg. Driving the splintered wood down, he lodged it into the eye socket of a Liskash, sending the scaly horror down gurgling.

Another opponent came swept in from Sartas's left, narrowly missing the talonmaster with a poorly aimed bash from his shield. Sartas struck the Liskash on the temple with the pommel of his sword, spinning it in his hands to turn the point downwards before stabbing the Liskash in its back from above. Just as the spray of its blood washed over his face, he felt his body shake. An arrow had slipped past his arms and through his armor, lodging in the side of his gut. Sartas stumbled backwards, barely managing to wrench his sword loose before he lost his balance completely.

"I'm done for." Sartas said it for no one other than himself. He had seen enough arrow wounds to the belly to know that he didn't have long. With no Dancers to heal him, never mind the fact that he'd never get off of this battlefield, the outcome was certain. He'd bleed out. So he had better take as many of the bastards with him as he could before he no longer had the strength to move. Propping himself up on one arm, he held out his sword with the other, keeping the blade as steady as he could. "The next one of you dies. The one after him won't be as lucky, you sons of snakes."

Sartas couldn't hear any of the sounds of battle; no more swords on shields or other swords, the whack of javelin hafts meeting, the screams of the dying. Was he really the only one left?

"*SARTAS REWL!*" The Liskash around him opened their ranks just enough so that he could see who had called out his name. It was Shar Enthiss. Sartas had not seen him during the fight, save for the very beginning. After that, it had been hard enough for any of them to keep track of anything besides the enemy immediately in front of them. Shar had lost all of his weapons, and his shield. His armor looked like it had been clawed and ripped away from his body, with his harness left in tatters. His fur was utterly drenched in blood, his ears were tattered, and clumps of fur around his face were torn out. Sartas could not tell how much of the blood was Shar's and how much of it was Liskash. His doubts were dispelled in the next moment, when Shar dug both of his clawed hands into the belly of a Liskash and nearly *pulled* it apart. Gore splattered everywhere, but Shar did not stop for a moment. His eyes were wild, and any Liskash that came across his path met its end. With claws and fangs, anything he was able to touch he would rend to pieces.

Shar had breached the circle of Liskash that surrounded Sartas. They all backed away from him, some trembling visibly; Shar looked like something from a terrible afterlife full of blood and rage. Upon spying the talonmaster, Shar smiled, baring yellowed teeth between red-covered lips. His smile left him just as suddenly as it had come when a javelin pierced him just below his breastbone. He looked down at the offending javelin as if it was rude to interrupt him. The Liskash that was holding the javelin tried to pull it back out, but Shar *grabbed* the shaft of it. The Liskash began to pull on the javelin more frantically. That's when the young warrior *pulled* himself along the javelin towards the Scaly One, impaling himself further. Shar stabbed his talons into the Liskash fighter's arms when he was close enough, screaming, *"CLAN OF THE LONG FANG!"* He then sunk his teeth into the lizard's neck, ripping out its throat. A look of deep satisfaction was the last thing to cross Shar Enthiss's face before he fell to a dozen swords and javelins.

The Liskash were gathering in closer around Sartas now. They were hissing and spitting, with swords raised. He was losing strength, fast; too much of his blood was gone. A wordless roar pierced the air; all of the Liskash around him went quiet. An opening formed in the circle; beyond it was the largest Liskash Sartas Rewl had ever seen. It was armored in patchwork bronze scales and pieces of discarded hide. Sartas's eyes went wide at what it was holding, however; the mangled body of Arschus Mroa. The Liskash fiend dropped the corpse, licking its lips as it stalked over to Sartas. It stalked closer until it was next to him.

The Liskash, clearly the leader of the others from the deference they showed him, pointed a single scaly claw at Sartas. "You die," it said in broken Mrem. "We take all." Its expression remained unchanged, but Sartas could tell it was relishing this moment. Sartas took several deep breaths, then propped himself up on an elbow. With a monumental effort, he brought himself to his feet.

"No. We both die." Sartas pulled the javelin from his thigh, a gout of blood spurting sluggishly from the wound; he would bleed out that much quicker because of it, but he could also move better now. The Scaly One must have understood Sartas; tilting its head back to roar, it sprinted towards him. Sartas dashed at it; he would have to have perfect timing for this to work. The Liskash swung his sword down just as Sartas knew he would. The talonmaster raised his sword to meet the blow, but held it in a loose grip. At the last moment, he pulled the sword closer so that it was the tip that made contact with the Liskash blade. The swords meet with a clang, and Sartas's spun out of his hand into the air. As quick as a blast of lightning, he snatched the sword with his off hand, and swung it laterally; it caught the Liskash leader in the ribs, snaking under the edge of its armor. Sartas tugged on the blade to carry it through, then pulled it out. The ground trembled as the leader fell to its knees, clutching its ruined belly. With a final scream, Sartas raised his sword above his head, then brought it down with both hands through the Liskash's spine.

There was absolute silence for a long time, as Sartas stood, swaying in place. Then the air filled with hisses, in tones of panic, and the Liskash backed away—slowly, at first, then scattering like the leaderless lizards they now were. In a few more moments, he was alone on the field of battle, surrounded by the dead.

His vision went black around the edges, and he found he was unable to stand any longer. He fell to the ground, but no longer felt any pain in his leg or his belly. The last thing he saw was the sun, partially hidden behind some clouds. *That seeing the sun like that...always reminds me...of Reshia....*

On the hill above, Mreiss Lrew dashed the water from his eyes with the back of his hand, and watched the panicked mob of Liskash scatter to the winds. It would take them a long time to organize themselves, get over their fear, and come back. But it would happen, he had no doubt of that. Maybe not that particular group, but these were Liskash lands; it would happen under one of the nobles, or another strong warrior.

By that time, he needed to be long gone.

More treacherous water blurred his vision, but he gathered up the reins of his mount, and scrambled onto its back. Lashing its rump with anger, he startled it into a gallop. He wasn't going to worry about saving it now. He would be leaving it at the base of the cliff anyway.

In the meanwhile, he would get all the speed out of it that he could. And maybe the wind would dry his eyes so that he did not disgrace himself in front of the clan.

When he reached the cliff, his mount was stumbling; he snatched what was left of his belongings off its back and turned it loose with a final slap to its rump. There was no sign of the clan, not even the eldest or the most feeble. Good. Sartas and the rest had bought them enough time.

Damn his eyes! They would not stop watering!

But he didn't need to see to climb.

With the aid of a lifetime of practice, he swarmed up the face of the cliff, claws finding sure purchase every time he planted them. In what seemed like almost no time his hands met empty air; he was at the top. He hauled himself over the edge, and peered to the horizon.

There they were, made small as fleas by the distance. He began to run.

Mreiss reached the clan, panting hard and sweating heavily. The others all crowded around him when he came. Every new person had a question for him.

"Did the others make it?"

"Where is everyone?"

"How many Liskash did we kill?"

"Did we win?"

He ignored all of *them*. But he didn't ignore *her*. When Reshia came forward, all of the others went silent.

He saw by her lack of expression that she already knew the sum of what he would tell her. But she didn't know all of it, not the details, not the whole truth. Closing his eyes to concentrate, he began to recite, calling up even the smallest action in his mind, for none of this should be forgotten. There were three of the elders that were singers and tale-tellers; vaguely, he heard them murmuring to themselves as they committed his words to memory.

Finally, he was almost done. Silence fell heavily on the Clan of the Long Fang. He opened his eyes, to look into Reshia's face.

"Reshia..." He took a deep breath, fighting back the cursed water from his eyes; he must not break now, not in front of her and the rest. "Sartas...he was the bravest...he—"

"He did what he must for the Clan of the Long Fang." She placed a hand upon his shoulder. Just for that moment, Mreiss saw a flicker of what she was really feeling; the loss, the pain, and also the resolve to survive. "As you must now do."

He remembered what Sartas had told him; how the clan would need a seasoned, fit warrior to lead it. There were elders who were seasoned, but not fit. There were fit males that could become warriors who were not seasoned. And there would be fit and seasoned warriors who could not lead if their lives depended on it. Now it was clear why Sartas had given him the orders that he had. Now, in this moment, when the others were listening to him, when they were looking at him with eyes that begged for *someone* to tell them what to do, he could be that person, that leader. Letting Sartas down...was not an option. There was only one thing that he could do to honor the memories of his comrades, his mentors... to honor his friends, who had all died so valiantly.

Mreiss Lrew was certain of what must be done; he

hadn't ever wanted it, and still didn't, but honor and the survival of the Clan of the Long Fang demanded it.

He drew himself up and planted the end of his spear in the ground at his feet. "The Liskash that pursued us are scattered, but we are still in Liskash lands, and we have a long way to go." He looked about him to see who was left. "Hwrarall, take three of your choice and scout the path ahead. Reshia, please lead the van and keep them in order; stop when you see a good place to camp for the night. I will take Llrariss, Shorwa and Mrawwa and cover the rear." He pointed towards the horizon.

"We travel to the Clan of the Claw, as Sartas Rewl, talonmaster of the Clan of the Long Fang, wished."

Song of Petru
XXIX

By the Claw

The Land was dry
Their hearts drier
Many were lost
All enslaved
But by the claw
And by the rock
Freedom was found
The Trek joined

A Clan's Foundation

S.M. STIRLING

HALT!" KRAR CALLED.

His tongue came out and licked his nose, but it was sandpaper-dry. He wrinkled his nostrils again, straining to scent something besides dry earth and rock and dry-season grass and the rank smell of males and females and kits pushed beyond endurance.

Water! He thought. *Water is worth halting for. Thirst can kill us as dead as Ashala's troops would if they catch us.*

True, Mrem could keep going on willpower. But herdbeasts would just lie down and die if you pushed them too far.

If the stock die, we die too.... But the Liskash need less water than we do. They are of the scale-kind, not beings-of-fur. They will not let their slaves go easily.

He looked around. Yellow grass almost the color of Mrem fur stretched in all directions in a hissing, swaying tide reaching to his waist. Now and then there would be a flat-topped thorny tree with dark leathery leaves, and weaver-nests hanging from the branches in untidy bundles. More occasionally a rocky hillock clothed in olive scrub. Wings hung overhead, from tiny creatures to great gruesome scavengers.

He smelled the wet earth nearby and yearned towards it, thirsty as he was.

"Follow," he rasped.

Spears bristled behind him as he loped; he was a big tawny Mrem, with a longer tail than most and scars from Mrem claws as well as Liskash whips. The spring was at the foot of one of the rocky hills, trickling down the reddish sandstone of a cliff. Below, it collected and spread to a fair-sized pool. With an effort of will that made him snarl he kept watch while others drank, then plunged towards the cool water.

"Ahhh," he sighed, wiping his face and whiskers with the back of a hand. "Bring the others! Fill the pots!"

They were two days and a night away from Ashala's holding, barely stopping long enough to water the stock at any scum-filled hollow and let them graze for short periods. Every animal and Mrem needed to rest.

Krar trotted back to the main body and raised a brawny arm; with much confusion the caravan eventually halted in response. He shook his head.

We're in trouble. A herd of wild bundor has more order.

If Ashala's troops caught up with them the living would envy those killed outright. The Liskash were cruel by nature, and coldly murderous when crossed or defied. He wanted to thrash his tail in frustration and worry, but was too cursed tired. The need to push on warred with the need to rest.

That and the fact that the krelprep pulling the

wagons were practically dragging their noses in the dirt, their gaunt flanks heaving. They couldn't afford to lose even one more of them. The wagons carried their food and water. Those jars and bales let them endure between springs and not delay by spreading out to forage.

We move so much more slowly than soldiers would, or a party of hunters! The sick and the kits will die if I push too hard... but we will all die if the Liskash catch us.

The dried food was holding well enough and they could butcher a beast when they had to, but water... water was always a problem.

There was good grass here and even some high ground to give them a look down their back trail. He stared at the rocky face of the low cliff across the water hole. Yes, that would do very well for a lookout post. Krar wished he knew what was going on behind him, but he didn't think anyone was going to volunteer to hang back to find out. And his leadership was tenuous, so it was unlikely he could order someone to do it. If he tried he had no doubt he'd be invited to do it himself. Too many of them thought being free of the Liskash meant doing just what they wanted at any given moment.

Mrem were making their way towards him, anxiety in their eyes, though their faces were blank in the way that habit and necessity made common among slaves.

"Is something wrong?" Mrownes asked. He was a few summers older than Krar with a whip scar across his face. A friend and hopefully a supporter.

"Nothing; something's right for a change." Krar gestured at the water. That was when he noticed the herds of bundor and hamsticorns surging forward. The heads of the krelprep were up, their nostrils quivering. The drivers were barely holding them in place.

"Curse it," he swore. "Mange upon them!"

He and the other Mrem moved together as the animals pushed around them, their attention all on the water. Occasionally someone would snarl when the herdbeasts jostled them, and the sound of predator anger would make them shy away a little even in their thirst.

"It'll be hours before the mud settles and we can fill our jars."

He looked at one of the herders. "Next time we come to a water hole keep them back so that we can get our water first," he snapped.

"You hold back hundreds of thirsty animals," the Mrem suggested. "I can't. Maybe you have some magic that will control them, eh?" He spat. "You might as well ask me to bring you a star in my hand while you're at it."

Krar frowned but had to admit to himself that the herder was right. Maybe bringing the herds was a mistake, even if it saved so much time from hunting. It seemed that every decision led to another problem. Sometimes it was overwhelming, not the glory and pleasure he'd thought being first would bring. A slave simply had to obey....

"Can you at least keep them from drinking till they're sick?" he asked.

"Don't tell me my business, Krar. You take care of yourself, we'll see to our herds."

Without another word, Krar stepped up behind the herder and grabbed him by the scruff of his neck, giving him a sharp shake, then shoved him down.

"The herds belong to all of us now," he said. "Don't get the idea that they belong only to the herders."

The herder glared up at him, then leapt to his feet, teeth bared and fur bristling around his head and shoulders.

"Who says they don't belong to us? We guide them, we take care of them, they wouldn't be here if it wasn't for us! The Liskash masters took the growth of our work, but—"

"*I* say. And for now my word is law. When we have time we'll decide who will lead us, but until we have that luxury, *I* am in charge here. Unless you would like to fight me for that honor?"

Krar narrowed his eyes and locked them with the other Mrem's; his hand drifted towards his knife and the tip of his tail twitched ever so slightly. The herder scowled, then lowered his head and shook it until his ears rattled, glancing aside and down and blinking as if the confrontation suddenly bored him. Krar suppressed a savage impulse to make the other male roll on his back and expose his belly.

"Now ... can you keep them from drinking until they founder?" he demanded, danger in his voice.

"Yes, great god, we can do that." The herder spat to the side. "We just can't stop them from getting to the water in the first place."

"Thank you," Krar said, "that's all I wanted to know."

As he pushed his way through the jostling animals he glanced at Mrownes who raised his brows at him. Krar frowned but shrugged.

"I don't want the herders getting the idea that the herds belong only to them. It's important that they and everybody else knows we're in this together."

"I can't argue with that," Mrownes said. "Just don't come down too heavy or you'll have a rebellion on your hands. As you said, we're all in this together."

They'd come to the first wagon and Krar ordered the driver to put the wagons in a wide circle, then take the krelprep to the water hole.

"Having the wagons in a circle may keep the herds from wandering through our camp," he explained to the driver.

As they walked on to give orders to the other wagon drivers Mrownes grinned at him.

"What?" Krar snapped.

"Now you're getting it," his friend said slapping his shoulder. "I'll go tell the others. Here comes Tral looking like he wants to talk to you."

Krar gave Mrownes a brief smile of thanks, then turned to the healer.

"How's your patient?"

"I have many, but I assume you mean the stranger."

The free Mrem prisoner had sparked the slave revolt. Just the *knowledge* that there were Mrem who were free of Liskash domination had set his people wild.

"He's unconscious, but given the shaking the wagon's been giving him that's a mercy."

Tral looked at the rocky cliff face beyond the water hole. "If it's possible I'd like to take him up there, away from the smoke of our campfires and the noise. It's not far and a litter would be easier on him than the wagon. And the flies... I couldn't tell you why, but I think they're bad for the sick."

Krar looked at the cliff thoughtfully; he respected the healer's judgment.

"I'll send someone to see if it's possible," he said. "I wanted to post someone up there as a lookout anyway."

He looked at the healer. "How is he? Do you think he'll live?"

He held his breath as Tral thought it over. If the stranger died it might mean the end for all of them.

"I don't know, because I don't know him," the healer replied. "He's been badly used and he has a fever. A lot depends on his will to live. I'm guessing he has that from the way I saw him fight the Liskash. That and whether the fever breaks soon. Wesha—"

Krar frowned; that was a female name, and the Liskash had kept the sexes apart among their Mrem slaves except at breeding time.

"The female's healer, she is helping me and she's highly skilled, so he's getting the best care we can give him. That's all I can tell you."

The younger Mrem put a grateful hand on the healer's shoulder in an amicable grooming gesture.

"That's all we can ask for." Turning he called out: "Fetys!"

A young Mrem came running, lithe and quick. Krar pointed at the height.

"See if you can get to the top of that and check along our back trail. While you're there see if there's an easy way up. The healer wants to bring a patient up there."

Fetys nodded and moved off, threading carefully through the herd of massive stocky hamsticorns, then wary and alert among the horns of the bundors.

Then Krar noticed the others watching him. "Make camp!" he called. "We'll stay here a day and night! Dry wood only for fires, we don't want smoke."

Being leader mostly seemed to mean work and worry. The problem was...

If anyone else was doing it, I'd worry even more.

The thought that he was the most cunning and fierce and able had made him proud. Now it...

Makes me worry.

They'd killed a bundor and parceled the meat out to various groups. The herders and the females and the laboring males all kept to themselves as they had on Ashala's holding. Clinging to habit in a hostile wilderness made them feel a little less lost. They'd hated their life at the Liskash fortress, but it was all they'd known.

A group of the younger males had found something they'd known but never tasted, a jar of forbidden wine in one of the wagons. Krar heard their high-pitched *chirrs* of excitement, and the hissing and spitting as it was handed around, or grabbed. He yawned and stretched and headed their way.

I should have smashed it, he thought. *But the healers wanted it!*

"What've you got there?" a burly young Mrem demanded of a group of females when the last drop was licked out of the tall jug. "Give me some, I'm hungry!"

He staggered over to the pot warming on some rocks by the fire and grabbed it, swiping up the contents with his hand and stuffing it in his mouth.

"Here now!" one of the females said. "What do you think you're doing?" She stepped towards him and he pushed her down.

"I'm free now," he snarled. "That means I can eat as much as I want."

He leered at the female staring at him wide eyed from the ground. "And I can have any female I want, when I want, not when some master says I can." He tossed the pot aside and lunged for her.

Krar halted his own dash. The pot the young male had just tossed aside crashed into his head and he dropped to the ground, his head covered in sticky lumps of meat and thick gravy.

"Rav, I know you," Mahssa, the leader of the females said coldly, flexing her fingers as she stood watching him. She was a gaunt grizzled female, with part of her left ear missing.

She dropped the fragment of pottery in her hand, her ears flat with anger. He looked up at her with his mouth open, then struggled to his feet staring and weaving where he stood. Krar smothered a snicker at the way he tried to straighten up, looking like a sulky kit that had just had its nose whapped.

"You were a good kit when you were with us. It

saddens me to see that you've become a bully," Mahssa continued implacably. "Your mother would be ashamed to see you like this."

"Where is she?" Rav demanded his eyes filling with tears; he'd completely forgotten that he could see his mother now.

Mahssa compressed her lips and looked down, blinking slowly in compassion.

"She died of a fever last winter," she told him. "I'm sorry you had to find out this way. I remember her tears as they took you away, Rav. She never got over missing you."

"She's dead?" Rav asked, sounding lost.

"Yes. I'm sorry."

"It was the cursed Liskash," the young Mrem snarled, suddenly bristling.

Now he's really dangerous, Krar thought. *His tail's puffed out like a soapweed plant after the rains.*

"They kept her half starved, no wonder she died of a lil thing like a fever. *I'm* not gonna starve, I'm gonna *take* what I need and nobody's gonna stop me!"

Krar grabbed him by the shoulder, spun him around and slapped. He kept the tips of his fingers rolled back, but the open palm into the angle of the jaw was enough to lift the young Mrem off his feet. He fell in a heap, blinking and panting, then turned himself to rest on his elbows and shake his head, making a *mrew-mrew-mrew* weeping sound.

"You will not take from the females and the kits while I'm alive to stop you," Krar snarled, baring his fangs. "The food was shared equally and it was more than you would have had from Ashala's hand. But you, like a sneaking coward, had to have more! The wine was being saved for the sick who couldn't eat, and now it's gone. Thief! We ought to cast you out to find your own way, to eat all you can of what you can catch. You make me sick, you worthless coughed-up clump of hair!"

Mahssa put her hand on the leader's arm. "Have mercy," she said. "He's just found out his mother is dead. I remember him as a youngster, he was good then. I think the problem here is the wine and now that's gone the problem won't come again. His punishment will be tomorrow when he's very sick from what he's drunk."

Krar was silent a moment as he thought. "I hear you Mahssa," he said at last. "But I will think of something to add to nature's punishment for this fool."

He glanced at the old female. "You are too kind to him." He pointed. "He's broken your good pot with his useless head."

She blinked. "Yes, well, it's his fault anyway and it can't be replaced." Her lips thinned. "We could use help in carrying the younger kits. They crawl around and drop off if they're put on the wagons. May we make him our beast of burden?"

With a smile, Krar nodded. "An excellent idea. Rav! Until I say otherwise you are at the service of the females. Whatever they ask of you, you will do. Do you understand?"

Rav struggled to his feet, shaking his head and pawing at it as if wondering where the stew had come from.

"No, no, no." When he was standing as upright as he could manage, he carefully said, "You can't do that. Nobody made you leader."

Krar strode up to him and Rav moved back quickly. But Krar crowded close and spoke into his face, eyes locked and head half-turned to give the full view of his fangs in a lunge-to-the-throat posture:

"*I* lead us, and you are in no condition to dispute that. When you are, if you want to challenge me to be first among Mrem, come find me. In the meantime, you'll do as I say!"

The last was a shout, high and shrill and tearing with a hiss in it. He let his claws out, holding them up to show that his slap could have ripped out the other male's jugular; his whiskers were back and his ears were flat.

Rav's mouth worked and he pointed aggressively at Krar's chest but didn't quite touch him.

"I won't forget this," he said breathing hard with anger and wine making his breath musky. "You wait, you'll see. You can't treat me like this."

Krar was satisfied to note that as angry as Rav was, as drunk as he was, his claws were still retracted. Disgusted, he gave him a slight shove and the younger Mrem stumbled back, barely keeping himself from falling.

"Go back to your friends tonight. Then tomorrow bring yourself and your gear and do whatever Mahssa tells you to do." He took a step forward. "Don't make me come looking for you," he warned.

They glared at one another for a moment, then

Rav glanced at Mahssa and with a grimace, stumbled away, tail down.

"You always were bossy," Mahssa said after he had gone.

Krar looked at her and smiled. He shook his head briskly and his ears rose.

"I daresay you were, too, when you were a kit."

She laughed. "I was. I am. But now it's what I'm supposed to do." She sighed. "Your status will have to be confirmed and soon, you know, and not just by who's quickest and has the sharpest claws. You can't just keep giving orders. Not until at least the elders say you can."

"I know," he agreed. "But I'd like to see us a bit farther from the great go—from Ashala's holding before we take the time."

"We need at least a day here to rest," Mahssa said, squinting up at the dust-hazed sun sinking in a great red ball behind the hill. "Maybe we elders can snatch some time to find an agreement on this." She nodded. "I'll see what I can do."

"And do you want me to be our leader?" he asked.

She looked at him with her eyes narrowed. "I think I do," she said slowly. "Besides, I can't think of anyone more suitable. And if there *are* wild Mrem out there we're going to need someone to speak for all of us. Unless you can suggest someone other than yourself?"

He snorted. "Honestly, Mahssa, I wish I could. It's one thing to make another back down over a trifle and then stalk around with the fur on your back up, looking everyone in the eye. But taking care of all these people, seeing that things are shared and sentries posted and . . . it's all more like *work*. Still, someone has to do it or we're lost."

She patted his shoulder. "That's what I was hoping to hear."

Thak flicked his tongue out to taste the air, only the tip of his muzzle above the grass that almost matched the patterns of his scales. There was the smell of water, much stirred, and bundor and hamsticorns, as well as the stink of far too many Mrem in one place in the middle of nowhere for his liking.

Mrem belonged in the slave pens, not wandering around loose. He knew this waterhole; it was the best for many miles, but well downhill of here—the land wasn't as flat as it looked. From here, he was above even the level of the hill over the pool. And it would be dark fairly soon. . . .

The translucent membranes flickered across and back over his eyes, and his narrow whiplike tail curled and uncurled. It looked like, wisely, they'd kept the bundor and hamsticorns separated; that gave him the beginnings of a plan.

"Gisshah, Asoth, Vess, Poth come here."

When the other Liskash scouts joined him he gave them their orders.

"Asoth, take over the lead herd beast of the hamsticorns and head it toward Lord Oglut's steading. Gisshah and Poth, take over the herders, get them to guide the herd. Vess take over the lead bundor and some of the others and have them stampede the

Mrem camp. When they're really on the move they should keep going without your guidance, then you follow us."

The scouts nodded, hissing their pleasure at the joke they were about to play.

"It's good," Poth said. "A few hundred juicy hamsticorns to sweeten the bitter news we bear. The great god will be pleased."

Thak looked at him. This was exactly his thought and it unnerved him to have it plucked from his head like that. He had dreaded bringing his god word that a great herd of Mrem and their animals were about to march over the Lord Oglut's land. Perhaps the prize they brought with them would win them their lives.

He flicked his hand at them. "Then go," he said.

Without further discussion they went to follow their orders.

Tral had decided to move all of his patients up to the top of the cliff. There was an easy path and it did seem the air was clearer up here; it would be pleasantly cool in the night, good for the ones with fevers, and they could drop a bucket on the end of a rope down the cliff to get water. He looked around the rocky expanse, noting with approval how the shelters broke the wind and the quiet peace of it.

Now he was checking on his most important patient, the mysterious wild Mrem.

"Are you awake?" he asked quietly. The Mrem was all bandages and burnt hair. His eyes were closed, but Tral sensed that he was conscious. "I have brought you some meat stew," he said, waving the bowl teasingly under his nose.

The stranger opened his eyes and looked at him. "I'm awake," he growled.

Tral filled a spoon and offered it. The wounded Mrem opened his mouth and took the food.

"Where are we?" he asked, after his tongue had cleaned his whiskers.

"I've no idea really," Tral told him. "We're heading east, but we've never been so far from where we were born. We're on top of a cliff beside a water hole if that helps."

The stranger nodded silently. Then: "More, please." And took another spoonful of the stew.

"What's your name?" Tral asked. "We can't keep calling you *the stranger*."

"I'm Canar Trowr," he said. "And I can feed myself."

"Not with your hands in the condition they're in. Be patient and you'll be feeding yourself in no time."

He offered another spoonful, which was accepted. "Do you know where we are?"

"I think so. You should head north and east, it increases the chance of your joining with my people. Who are you?"

"Tral, I'm a healer. My next question is, how do you feel?"

"How do I look?" Canar Trowr asked.

"Bad."

"And that's how I feel. But I also feel like I'll live. They wanted me to talk, not die right away."

Tral smiled. "That's good hearing. We're resting

here for the night, maybe for tomorrow. I'm hoping for that, the rest would do you good. Would do all of us good."

He paused in his spooning as the camp below them erupted in shouts and screams, the squealing of animals and the thunder of hooves.

"What's going on?" Canar Trowr asked, his ears struggling to rise; they were rather long and tufted by nature, but looked ragged now.

"I don't know," Tral said. "I shall find out." He put the bowl down and rushed to the edge of the cliff. The slits of his eyes went wide in shock, painting the dim scene below with a flat silvery radiance.

Below the bundor were on the move, charging in a panic directly toward the camp. Some Mrem were already running for the heights beyond the water hole, some just stood in shock. A few went racing to the krelprep who'd been staked out well away from the water hole because they wouldn't stop drinking.

The hamsticorns were moving north in a slow, eerily calm manner given the blind terror of the bundor.

Tral's breath stopped in his chest as he watched in horror. Many Mrem climbed into the heavy wagons or took shelter beneath them, many more might make it up the height he stood on. First among these were the ones who led the krelprep.

As he watched the herd stampeded into the camp and some fell beneath the bundor's heavy feet. Other bundor slammed into the wagons, threatening to topple them as those inside them screamed in terror.

It seemed to take forever, but at last the bundor

were through and running back down the beaten path toward Ashala's holding.

Tral turned and ran to get his bag of medicines and bandages.

"Stampede!" he paused to shout, then raced down the cliff path to see what help he could offer.

They were still gathering the wounded, over fifty so far and Krar was grateful it wasn't worse. There were twenty-three crushed and broken bodies lined up on the ground, and the air stank of blood and wastes. But they would have no time to bury them. Some of the kits couldn't seem to stop crying no matter what the females did, and all of them were badly shaken. The thin mewling sound grated at their ears, adding to the rage and fear.

The krelprep had been saved, which was a miracle and the heroes who had done it deserved much praise. Krar resolved that they should have it. When there was time. The wagons had survived as well, though several of the water jars had been cracked. Some of the bundor had stopped running and their herders had rounded them up.

"What happened?" Krar demanded of their leader.

"Nothing!" the Mrem said, his tail swishing in his distress. "There was no reason for it. All at once the herd leader and several others went off like they'd gone mad and the others followed. I've never seen the like before. I swear to you there was no reason for it. None!"

"It's possible," another of the herders said, "that

we can round up more of them if you'll give us a few days."

"A few days?" Krar demanded. "We can't just sit here for a few days! The Liskash are sure to be after us. We took their food, their wagons, their herds, not to mention ourselves, and ran away on them. They're going to come looking for us, they're surely looking for us right now. We have to find shelter with the wild Mrem or we'll be slaves again; if we're lucky enough to survive!"

"For pities sake, Krar! Let us rest! Give us time to mourn," a female said.

"I would like to, I promise you I would," he answered. "But we have no choice."

A male spoke up then. "I say we should wait for Ranowr to catch up to us. He'll know what to do."

A chorus of ayes greeted this statement and Krar lost all patience.

"If he were alive he'd be here now!" he shouted.

There was a collective gasp at that followed by a stunned silence. Then a female spoke.

"It's true," she said slowly. "Ranowr is dead, of poison he took willingly. He killed the young goddess and died himself to give us a chance to get away. His last words to her were: *I die for my people. You just die.*"

Startled, Krar turned to see that it was the beautiful golden-furred Prenna who had spoken, her green eyes so wide the whites shone all around and the pupils dilated to circles even in the firelight. He reached out a hand toward her, wanting to offer her comfort. Mahssa stepped forward and put an arm around the young female's shoulders.

"When she's like this she's never wrong," the old female said.

Krar frowned. "What do you mean?"

With a shrug Mahssa said, "She just knows things sometimes. Others among the females can do it to a lesser extent. But Prenna always knows."

He felt a chill touch the back of his neck and took a step back. The uncanny caused fear that even the bravest would not be ashamed to admit. Then he shook it off.

"Ranowr was a good Mrem," he said quietly.

He hadn't liked him, but he'd respected him and now he owed him. And what he owed was the lives and safety of all those Ranowr had sacrificed himself to save. His voice grew louder.

"And we will mourn him and honor his memory when we are safe. Until then we must move."

"Krar!" a voice called.

He turned to see a hamsticorn herder pushing his was through the gathered Mrem towards him.

"The hamsticorn herd is heading north, all of them! With six of our brothers! We're going to follow them and bring them back."

"If they stampeded there's nothing you can do to bring them back. Who can say how far away they are by now? That's why we're not chasing the bundor. We don't have the time or the Mrem to spare."

How many times am I going to have to explain this?

"You don't understand! Their tracks say they just walked away, there's no sign of panic."

"It's true," Prenna said. "They were forced to leave and the herders with them."

Krar thought he could get tired of her doing that.

"Who forced them to leave?" Krar asked, genuinely puzzled.

"Liskash," Mahssa said. She bit her lips. "Ashala forbade her people to use their power over our minds. She liked to rule by fear alone, by her power to burn with her mind."

All of the younger Mrem stared at her, while the elders shifted uneasily.

"Exactly what do you mean?" the young leader demanded, certain he wasn't going to like her answer.

"The Liskash can take over our minds and force us to serve them," Tral said. "There is no defense against it."

"When were you planning to tell us this?" Krar snarled.

"So our brothers are helpless prisoners?" the herder asked at the same time.

"Yes," Mahssa said. Her ears twitched nervously. "To be honest there hasn't really been a chance to tell you. Besides, it would only have frightened you; it is not a good memory that we elders have. As Tral says, there is no defense against it."

"We have to go after them," the herder said. "We can't let the Liskash beasts get away with this."

Krar felt like his head was spinning, or he'd found a huge patch of blissweed and was feeling the effects of rolling in it all day long. Was there no end to this?

"I can't stop you," he said at last. Then frowned. "Are all of you going?"

By this time the other twelve hamsticorn herders had lined up behind their speaker and all of them nodded.

"Then each of you take a sword and a spear with you. But know this, we can not wait for you." Krar turned to Mahssa and Tral. "Have you any advice for them?"

"Do not get too close to them, do not let them know you are there," Tral said.

"If they can see you they can control you. Never forget that," Mahssa added.

"And to find us again head north and east, for that is the way we'll be going," Tral added.

Krar raised an eyebrow at that; it was the first he'd heard of it.

The lead herder nodded his thanks. "I am Whar," he said and turned to Krar. "Thank you, leader. We will return and we will have our herd and our brothers with us. Possibly some Liskash tails."

"I wish you luck, Whar. Our thoughts will be with you."

Each of the herders said his name and then followed their leader to the wagons to get their supplies. Then without another word they jogged off in pursuit of their friends.

As Krar watched them leave the head bundor herder stepped boldly up to him. It was the Mrem he had confronted at the water hole and his tail thrashed once before he could stop it.

"If they can go and get their herd then I think we should be allowed to do the same with ours," the herder said belligerently.

The young leader turned to him with a sigh. "If all of you go, then who will care for the bundor we have left? Because I don't know how to move them and neither do the rest of us."

"Of course we'll leave some to watch the remaining herd. We want our bundor back and you can't stop us from going. Especially not if you're going to allow *them* to go."

Krar studied him with his arms folded. Apparently there was a rivalry between the herders. But more importantly... "I hope when you say 'our bundor' you mean the bundor belonging to *all* of us."

"Well," the herder spluttered, "if we go and gather them up at risk of our lives it's only fair that they should belong to the herders."

"I don't see it that way. The herds belong to all of us. Or are you and herds planning on living on your own?"

The herder huffed and thrashed his tail, his ruff rising in agitation. "What do you mean by that?"

"I mean that you are either with us or against us. If you deny that the herd will be held in common, but will be all your own wealth and the rest of us can die hungry and poor then you're not welcome here."

Krar looked each of the bundor herders in the eye, just long enough to signal seriousness.

"I mean this. What's more, if you go after them we will not wait for you, any more than we will wait for the hamsticorn herd."

The herder stared at him with his mouth open, then clenched his jaw and took a stance. "And will you also supply us with swords and spears as you did them?" he demanded.

Krar looked thoughtfully after the departing ham-sticorn herders. "All right," he said. "If you agree that the herds belong to all of us." He gave the Mrem a questioning look.

Reluctantly, and with every appearance of resentment, the lead herder nodded, his tail lashing.

"Then, even though I think we're throwing them away, since you insist on running into the arms of the Liskash, you may arm yourselves. Do not become so obsessed with recapturing every one that you forget we're moving away from you as fast as we can."

"Remember," Tral said, "north and east."

"Thank you, Tral," the herder said, ostentatiously turning his back on Krar.

He gestured to his followers. Fourteen Mrem followed him; the rest, mostly older, looked uncomfortable at staying but glad they weren't going, either. Whether it was because they were missing out on the adventure or because their leader had just disappointed them by releasing their claim to the herds only they knew.

Or maybe they think their glorious leader is leading the rest to certain death or slavery. Because I certainly do.

Whar and the other hamsticorn herders moved fast through the dimness of the savanna. The stars were many and bright, and the moon two-thirds full, plenty for Mrem eyes—Liskash were much less at home in the night.

The trail was easy to follow, a broad trampled swath through the tall grass, and the herd hadn't pounded it to dust as they would have if they were moving at speed. They jogged on relentlessly until Whar called a halt. They were tough Mrem, used to a hard life, but they were also very tired. And tired Mrem make mistakes.

While they rested squatting on their hams they gnawed on jerky, alternating leathery bites torn loose with strong teeth and sips of water of stale leather-tasting water from the bags.

"I'm hungry," Shum said, "I'm starving. But I'm so tired I'm ready to give up on this dried krelprep shit."

"You'll save energy if you just shut up and eat," Vrar suggested.

The others rumbled a tired laugh.

As they'd traveled the ground had risen around them and the herd was moving through the narrow space between hills. So far they hadn't encountered one stray. Though they had found the body of a calf that had apparently died of exhaustion. No sign of its mother though, which struck them as strange. Usually when a calf died the cow wouldn't leave it for at least a day.

"That calf—" Vrar suggested.

"The meat wouldn't have been any good by this time," Whar said.

"No. The mother ... maybe that's the mind control that the elders were talking about."

"Thank you for this thought, Vrar," Whar said sardonically, looking at the moon in over-elaborate politeness. "Perhaps you think this jerky was poisoned, too?"

Vrar frowned and twitched his ears. "No, I don't—"

"Shut *up*! We've rested long enough. Let's go get our herd."

"Bedding down for the rest of the night," he whispered two hours later.

Mrem had better hearing than Liskash, too.

"Confident monsters aren't they?" Shum said, lying not far away, running a thoughtful thumb along the edge of his spearhead.

"They have no reason to think they'll be followed," Whar said. "They're not heading for Ashala's holding, so they weren't after us. They're not the Liskash whose slaves we were. I think they just happened on us and took the chance to steal our herd."

"Enemies of Ashala?" Shum asked.

Whar shrugged. "Even Liskash don't like Liskash. I'm sure she has many enemies."

A whisker-twitching grin: "I know I'm one of them."

They approached the herd carefully, staying well away and downwind. Below they could see a campfire start up and in its light they saw Liskash soldiers, their spears slanting into the night. One of the Liskash sent two of its fellows off toward the herd.

"Guards," Shum murmured.

Whar nodded. "Arrogant to think they'd only need two," he said.

One of the Liskash went around the herd to the far side, while the other climbed partway up they hill from which they watched.

Suddenly, Hath, who was farther down the hill closer to the herd, stood up. He swayed where he stood and then took a stop forward. Whar rose and whirling his lariat over his head dropped the braided-leather rope over Hath's shoulders. Then he and Shum pulled him in as the herder struggled to go forward. Then, just as suddenly he turned and ran toward them, dropping to the grass beside them, panting as though he'd run a race.

"It took me!" Hath said in a panicked whisper. "The elders didn't lie, if you get too close they can just make you do their will!"

The herd leader put a hand on his shoulder to calm him. "What did it want you to do?"

"Guard the herd. I didn't hear words or like that, I just knew that was what I was supposed to do." He shuddered. "I didn't even want to get away."

The Liskash below them had turned to look up the hill toward them, flicking its tongue out. After a few moments it turned back to the herd and sat down, taking off its boiled leather helmet.

"If we can't go near them we might as well not have these," Shum said lifting his spear off the ground. "The swords are useless, too."

Whar picked up a good sized stone. "But not these," he said, detaching his sling from his belt.

He whipped the sling around his head with a flexing motion of arm and body and released the stone at just the right moment. There was a subdued *crack* as the stone struck the narrow scaled head, lost in the buzzing and clicking and animal-calls of the night.

"Is it dead?" one of the others asked.

"It's dead all right," Whar said. "I've killed wild

bundor at that range and Liskash skulls aren't as thick." He snarled slightly. "How long I've wanted to do that!"

"Now to get the others," he said. "Find some rocks and follow me."

They all had a supply of small stones, used to move a recalcitrant hamsticorn, but what they wanted now where those of a size that might kill.

For now the Liskash on the far side of the herd was safe. There was too much risk they'd be seen if they tried to approach it. The campfire, on the other hand . . .

Some four were asleep, or at least lying down, two were eating. Those would be dealt with first.

"Don't miss," Whar told his fellows. He stood, whirling the sling and released the stone. It struck one of them right in the forehead and the Liskash went down, its body twitching. Two others were struck as successfully, but the other three sprang to their feet and took up their bows.

The Mrem had the advantage of being in complete darkness as far as the Liskash were concerned and their arrows fell far short. Meanwhile the herder sent stone after stone out, invisible in the night and a brief flash of speed when they came in range of the campfire. Another fell, his head bloody, and the remaining two ran to the herd. The hamsticorns parted almost miraculously from before them and the Mrem knew this must be more of the Liskash mind tricks.

The herders held back, fearful that they, too, would be taken over. Then the herd began to move, the exhausted animals calling out in protest, but following their leader none the less. They moved up the hill toward the Mrem; massive creatures, usually placid . . . but right now they represented a serious, unstoppable danger. The herders sought to move out of their way.

"You head that way," Whar told them. "I'm going down to cut some throats."

"I'll watch your back while you do," Shum said and followed him, while the others led the hamsticorns.

Whar found that two of the Liskash were dead and he made short work of the third. Then he felt the strangest sensation, as though a band had gone around his head. Without hesitation he took off running in the opposite direction from the herd. He'd gone about a hundred paces when he noticed that the sensation had stopped and he turned. That was when he realized that Shum wasn't with him.

He dropped to the ground and crept back toward the campfire carefully. Stopping just within sight of the small campfire.

Shum was just standing there, his head and shoulders bowed, while a Liskash with a bloodied head came toward him.

Whar crept forward until he felt that strange sensation and then pulled back. While he watched the Liskash went up to Shum and viciously slashed his throat.

They will pay! Whar thought, keeping the snarl that lifted his lips silent. *How they will pay!*

He crawled in a wide circle, careful not to approach too closely.

Then, one by one, the captive herders came into view. They stopped by the Liskash, their arms dangling awkwardly, heads bowed. But Whar knew each Mrem and his heart stuttered in his chest in dread.

"Come out!" the Liskash bellowed. "Come now or I'll cut their throats one by one!"

Whar put a large rock in his sling and stood. After a moment he began to whirl it around his head until it had reached a good speed, then he ran forward as fast as he could roaring at the top of his lungs. He felt the band fall over his head and kept running, when he felt his will slip he let the rock fly. For a moment his mind completely stopped.

Then the stone struck the Liskash full in the face, shattering the delicate bones and driving them into the lizard's brain. It fell thrashing to the ground and after a moment was still.

One by one the captive Mrem raised their heads and looked around, several dropped to the ground in exhaustion.

"Shum!" one of them said, reaching out for his friend's body.

Whar came up to them then and kneeling put his hand on Shum's forehead.

"Shum was a good Mrem," he said, his voice choked. Then he turned to his friends. "We cannot rest," he told them. "There are three Liskash left and they're driving the herd after our brothers." He handed his water flask around. "Take their weapons and follow me."

They loped off toward the herd, following carefully lest they come under Liskash influence. Whar vowed that if they survived this he was going to sleep a day and a night.

Vrar and the other herders ran from the hamsticorns for a while. Then at his signal when they were briefly out of sight of the herd they moved to the side, hiding in the tall grass to let it flow past them. The exhausted beasts went by bawling and complaining all the way.

They lay still, watching for the Liskash. At last they came, the three of them spread out behind the herd, following them at a distance.

For some reason the Mrem felt no compulsion from the Liskash and each of them knew cautious relief. They watched them go by, noticing that the missing Mrem were not with them.

"Stupid Liskash can't see in the dark," Vrar said softly.

"What shall we do?" Hoff asked.

"We shall kill them," Vrar said with more confidence than he felt. He and the others spread out, stalking their prey with a natural silence.

The Liskash stopped and gathered together while the herd went slowly on. The Mrem froze and watched carefully. The three lizards seemed to argue, one pointing back the way they'd come while another waved in a general way around them, the third pointed to the herd which had begun to slow.

"What do you think they're saying?" Hoff asked softly.

"Who cares?" Vrar said. "Let's get them while they're distracted."

He held up a stone the size of his palm and the others hefted rocks of their own. Then the Mrem began to creep forward, slowly, carefully, the grass barely whispering with their passage. When they were about fifty paces from the Liskash they rose almost as one and let fly.

One of the lizards had time to point at them before the stones found their marks knocking them to the ground.

Vrar was the first one to reach them and his sword was out and flashing down before he came to a full stop. Within moments the Liskash were so much dead meat and the Mrem were hooting with victory.

"Stop it!" Vrar said, coming to his senses. "We'll scare the herd. You, Hoff, take six Mrem and guard the hamsticorns. The rest of you come with me." He turned toward the Liskash encampment and, he hoped, Whar and Shum.

They hadn't gone far when they met with Whar and the six missing herders. There were embraces and backslaps all round.

Then Mazer asked: "Where's Shum?"

Putting a hand on his shoulder, Whar said, "Shum was a good Mrem."

Mazer gasped and went to his knees. "Shum is no more?"

Whar shook his head and the other Mrem caterwauled grief. He and Shum had been lovers. The others stood around him, silently offering support.

After a few minutes, Whar knelt beside him and gently said, "We must go. We will have to mourn later, there is no time for it now. The others are moving away from us as we weep."

Mazer nodded, took a few deep breaths and got to his feet. "Yes, we must go." And with that he started back the way they had come, the others following.

It had been Ashala's Holding, before the Mrem rebelled. Then her daughter Hisshah's Holding, briefly. For about twenty minutes.

Captain Thress lay in his own filth in the dark cell and cursed his life; cursed Hisshah who he had always despised; and cursed the guards who ignored him. He heard the door open and wondered if they'd finally come to kill him.

Sheth, Thress's former second in the military hierarchy of the Holding, came into the cell. A soldier behind him put down a stool and at a gesture from Sheth left the cell. He didn't bother to lock the door.

"You still can't move," Sheth observed.

"Can't I? I hadn't noticed," Thress sneered. "Give me some water."

"I no longer have to obey your orders, Captain." Sheth sat on the stool, flicking his tongue once disdainfully. "You stink."

"If it displeases you then it pleases me," Thress said. "What do you want?"

"Maybe just to admire how the mighty Thress has fallen."

The captain turned his head away and there was silence for a while.

"I thought you might like to know what's going on," Sheth said. "Hisshah's pet slave Ranowr poisoned her, and all the nobles are wrangling about who is now the god among us."

Thress barked a laugh; Hisshah had used that Mrem to humiliate him over and over again. He strongly suspected that the fuzzy beast had enjoyed it, despite the beatings.

"And I thought I would never smile again!" he said, and looked at his second in command. "And do you aspire to take Ashala's place?"

Sheth snorted. "Not I. I am but a humble soldier. My parents are still alive as far as I know, and I have no particular desire to kill them. So I lack the basic qualification for leadership."

"You do," Thress agreed drily. "Why haven't I heard screams and cries from the Mrem?" he asked. "The torturers seem strangely idle. Hearing him suffer would complete the joy of this day."

"Ranowr? He convinced Hisshah to drink by drinking *first*. Really quite well done for a beast."

"Then why not torture a few of the others? Screaming is one of the few things they do well."

The other Liskash studied the ceiling. "It seems the Mrem have all escaped. Every last one of them. Along with our bundor and hamsticorns and seven wagons and fourteen draft krelprep. Not to mention seven wagonloads of supplies. Oh, and weapons. It was probably a mistake of the great god to have them trained in the use of weapons."

The captain stared at him in disbelief, then laughed until he started to cough. His numb, inert but awkwardly still living body jerked.

"Oh, thank you for visiting me. You've made my day quite jolly." He looked at his former subordinate. "Has anyone gone after them?"

"I've had no orders to do so. If we do I think it will be a token gesture. It's only a matter of time before our more aggressive Liskash neighbors make a move on us." He shrugged. "Why should we exert ourselves to enrich them?"

Thress chuckled. "Why indeed?"

Sheth leaned forward and put his arms on his legs. "Who do you think will come after us first?" he asked.

"Oglut," the captain said at once. "He has two grown sons to worry about. He *needs* a new holding to keep at least one of them busy. How will you feel about serving a foreign god?"

Sheth tipped his head to one side, considering. "About the same as I'd feel about serving one of locally grown would-be gods." He shrugged and leaned forward confidentially. "I live to serve."

"It's good that you know your place," Thress ground out.

The other Liskash stood up and adjusted his sword belt. "I think the stink has grown to be too much for me now. I shall take my leave."

As he turned to go Thress said, "Kill me or give me water."

Sheth turned and shook a finger at him, tsking. "Once again you forget that I no longer have to take your orders, Thress."

He cocked his head and tapped his teeth with a claw. "But you have amused me. I think I'll keep you alive for a while. You'll be a talking head for me. Very well," he said, turning to the door. "I'll give orders that you're to be watered and fed . . . and cleaned up. At least for now."

And with that he was gone, leaving the door wide open. Hisshah had had only a *small* power, the ability to move light objects. Her pet Ranowr had been the one who pointed out the potential of a *small* power, when applied to the interior of other beings' bodies. The spine, for example, was quite vulnerable.

Thress cursed him, thrashing his head from side to side. He extended his will, trying to take over his second's mind, ordering Sheth to kill him. Far down the corridor he heard the other Liskash laugh and knew he'd failed. He lay there torn between rage and black despair.

Perhaps if he was insulting enough he could get one of the guards to kill him.

Hormr, the lead bundor herder, shook out his long whip and faced the massive bundor bull before him. The creature stood in front of his harem of seven cows and shook his horns aggressively at the Mrem.

Hormr wasn't impressed.

"I don't want your females, you walking feast-day dinner," he snarled. "I want you to *move*."

The bundor didn't see any reason to move; it was free of the annoying presence of the rest of the herd, the grass in this slight declivity was fresher than in most places because water collected beneath the soil, and there were no predators. Except the Mrem with the whip.

Hormr drew back his arm and flashed the whip forward, flicking the bundor on its tender nose with practiced skill—the whip could cut like a knife if you mishandled it, and he didn't want that. The bull bawled and drew back, its big eyes rolling, then turned and moved in the direction Hormr urged it with a whip flick on its flank. The cows moved to follow it.

The round-up was going well. They'd come across some large groups and several small ones like this one, in little dry valleys and the lee of rocky hills. By now they had about a hundred and fifty. Hormr's heart was very happy.

It makes me feel rich, just looking at all that meat and leather. Herding it all these years for others, and now it's mine.

He was wishing he hadn't brought the spear. It was a cursed nuisance to carry and he'd only used it once. He'd poked a bundor with it and made a wound. Bad herdcraft, that; there was always the risk of infection or maggots if you broke a beast's skin. And so he carried the stupid thing because he didn't want to hear Krar's complaints if he came back without it.

Then he thought of how that cursed Krar had tricked him out of the herd and he swore. They'd just see about that. It wasn't fair, wasn't right that he and the other herders did all the work, but the other do-nothing Mrem shared in the herds. Well, nothing was set just yet. He was certain he could get the elders to see reason and they were the real power among the Mrem.

His temper got the better of him and when he

used the whip on a slowing cow it was hard enough to make her bellow. The bull turned toward him, but Hormr snapped the whip loudly and the bundor turned away, heading toward the gathering herd.

The others were already talking about taking what they had and following the other Mrem. "We're too close to Ashala's holding," they insisted.

"Fools," Hormr muttered to himself. *A risk, but think of the reward!*

Then he heard to sound of a large group of bundor. The bull turned its head toward the sound and started to move in that direction.

All right, the lead herder thought. *The more, the better.*

As they came over the crest of the hill the first thing he saw was a small herd of about thirty bundor and his heart leapt. Then he saw the Liskash sitting on the side of the hill below him.

He grabbed the bull bundor by a horn and started to pull its head around. The animal protested with a loud bellow and the Liskash looked up.

Hormr's hand fell from the bundor's horn and the bull trotted down the hill to join the herd. He stood there as the Liskash came toward him; he was not afraid, not angry, not anything.

By this time other Liskash had noticed his presence and they were coming to get a look at him.

"Well, well," one of them said. "What have we here?"

"One of our runaways, sir."

"I believe you're right," the Liskash said. "Where are the others?" he asked the Mrem.

"Far away, and getting farther," the Mrem answered in a monotone.

The Liskash slapped him. "Call me great lord," he said.

"Great lord," Hormr said.

All the Liskash laughed.

"And where are they going?" the Liskash asked.

"Great lord they are going east and north."

"Why?"

"To join the wild Mrem."

Their leader clicked his tongue thoughtfully. "I think we will take these bundor and this slave back to the holding with us," he said. "The nobles should know these things. They'll tell us what to do."

He gestured to the small herd and told Hormr, "Round them up and take them to their pastures. If you see any others take them, too."

Hormr uncoiled his whip and went to work, somewhat to the Liskash leader's surprise and pleasure. He hadn't mind controlled a Mrem slave since he'd been young and he'd forgotten the pleasure it brought. It was a bit of a strain, but would probably take less effort the more he did it. This would certainly make it easier on them, the leader thought. The slave was used to these beasts. The nobles would be pleased.

Canar Trowr had gone from lying on the folded tents in the wagon back to sitting beside the driver. Grass bowed ahead of them; dust smoked in their wake, making the air scent slightly spicy. The lowering sun turned a scrim of cloud in the west to gold.

Being wounded is irritating. Everything itches, and I am bored, but there is nothing to do but endure and heal.

The shaking of the wagon as it passed over rough ground had been making him queasy when he was lying down. He was still miserable but at least he didn't think he was going to lose his meager breakfast. He wished he could walk, but knew he was too weak. Besides, the Liskash had torn out all of his toe claws and it would hurt too cursed much.

Can you skin a Liskash without killing it? he wondered, not for the first time. *That scaled skin is tough. It should make excellent leather.*

He'd been holding himself aloof from the driver because he was afraid if he opened his mouth only whimpering would come out. Then he noticed that the driver was holding aloof from him. Now he wanted to talk, just to be annoying.

But these Mrem didn't talk much, he'd noticed. They spoke softly and in short bursts as if afraid they'd be overheard. Because they'd been slaves, he supposed. Part of him looked down on them for that. Part of him respected their courage in escaping with what must have been a fair portion of their Liskash master's wealth.

It still amazed him that they'd actually believed that the lizards were gods. He smiled at the thought, then grew serious. It made it all the more amazing that they'd walked away.

Canar Trowr had to admit to himself that he was coming to like these strange Mrem. Tral and Wesha were fine healers and Krar was solid. But they knew nothing of civilized ways. They weren't even a proper clan. And apparently they only possessed one name each. He'd never heard of such a thing.

He looked down to see a pure white female, obviously young, trudging along beside the wagon. The shape of her ears was exquisite, with just the hint of little tufts right at the tips. When she licked her nose the skin of her lips was the most delicate pink, and her canines were so sharp that the tips seemed to fade out into air.

Very sexy, he thought. *Rrrrowr!*

"What's your name?" he said to her.

She looked up at him and he found himself staring at one of the loveliest faces he'd ever seen; she had huge green eyes. He caught his breath and wondered who her lucky mate was; such a beauty would never go unclaimed.

After a moment's thought she said: "Prenna." Then she looked down again, silent.

The rather mushy accent of these slave-Mrem sounded charming on her lips, soft and alluring.

"Just Prenna?" he asked, smiling.

She nodded, then looked up at him again. "Why would I have more?" she asked. "I am the only Prenna here."

"All of my people in the Clan of the Claw have two names," he told her. "It is the Mrem way."

She stared at him with her brow furrowed. "We are Mrem, but it is not our way."

He thought she felt insulted and he made a gesture of apology. "It is the way of the clans," he explained.

Prenna looked back at the following Mrem. "Aren't we a clan?"

Canar Trowr shrugged. "Are you? Have you all agreed to be? Do you have a clan name?"

They would need these things to be accepted by the other clans he knew. Right now they were just a mob of refugees. Especially now that their herds were gone. He frowned. He would have to encourage them to unite as a clan or his people and the other clans might refuse to accept them.

"You look like a priestess," he told her.

She looked up at him, puzzled. "The . . . Ashala," she said carefully as if the name hurt to say, "called her handmaidens priestesses. But they were Liskash. Can a Mrem be a priestess? And a priestess of what?"

He was shocked. Somehow it hadn't occurred to him that they wouldn't know of Aedonniss and Assirra. That was like not knowing which direction the sun rose.

"Surely you know about the great god Aedonniss?" he said. "He created the world!" And he told her all about that.

Prenna nodded politely when he'd finished.

"What do you think?" Canar Trowr asked when she remained silent.

"I think it's a very pretty story," she said. "But we were fooled once into worshiping a false god. I don't think we'll give our faith so easily to another. Besides," she said thoughtfully, "if he created everything and he is a Mrem in shape, then why did he make the Liskash so powerful? Or at all for that matter?"

He stared down into those big, green eyes and had

no answer. "I'm only a soldier," he said. "Not a philoso-
pher. There are such among the Clan of the Claw. If
you care to seek them out perhaps they could tell you."

"Look," Prenna said pointing ahead.

There in the distance was a dust cloud, a fairly
substantial one. And here, running towards them as
fast as he could was a spear-carrying scout.

"Hamsticorns!" they heard him shout. "Our hamsticorns!"

The word spread rapidly and the Mrem all cheered
and clapped their hands in joy. Krar came jogging up
to the head of the caravan and consulted with the
panting scout. Then he gave a shout and ran the way
the scout had come.

As soon as the caravan joined the herd they made
camp. The first thing they did after circling the wagons
was cut out a beast to kill and roast. Everyone was
cheerful at the thought of fresh meat.

Mrem, Canar Trowr reflected, *were made to eat meat.*

As the feast finished, thunder rolled and they hastily
erected the huge tents they'd been hauling. As much
as they liked meat they disliked being rained on. It
was unnerving, too, to have rain so far out of season.
The wise in the Clan of the Claw had told Canar
Trowr that it was because of the new sea. Apparently
all that water was changing the weather.

"We'll be here for a day or so with this," Tral said,
handing him a skewer of meat chunks. "The trails,
such as they are, will be too muddy for the wagons
to travel."

"It's good you'll have a chance to rest your stock," Canar Trowr said. "Besides, it's past time you all had a meeting to decide what you want to do."

Tral looked at him. "I suppose it is. Our idea when we escaped was to join up with the wild Mrem," he said thoughtfully. "But that's not much of a plan."

"The preferred term is 'free Mrem.'" Canar Trowr told him. "My people don't think of themselves as *wild*."

The healer laughed. "No, I suppose not. Thank you for pointing that out. Perhaps you could tell me the best way to approach your people. All our hopes are tied to traveling with you to someplace far from the Liskash."

Canar Trowr nodded. "I thought you'd never ask," he said.

The next day the remains of the bundor herd caught up to them, and again there was much rejoicing. Not least from the bundor herders who had feared being left hopelessly behind.

That night they gathered together for a long delayed meeting. The Mrem stood in a circle around a central fire; even the kits were among them for this was an historic event. In a cleared space before the fire stood the acknowledged elders.

Mahssa and Tral as the eldest among them took charge. They'd long since felt out the other elders about confirming Krar as their leader. The others had hemmed and hawed and said they'd like to ponder, but when pressed acknowledged that he was the best candidate by far. Still, they insisted on putting it up for a vote and so that business led off the meeting.

"Does anyone have another they'd like to propose?" Tral asked the crowd.

"I object to Krar as leader," Rav said. "He's a bully who pushes people around."

"You mean he pushed you around when you were acting like a rampaging bundor." Mahssa sneered and her tail thrashed. "And the question was who else could be our leader? Are you suggesting yourself, Rav?"

The young Mrem held up both hands in negation and took a step back.

"We don't have time to waste," Tral said. "If there are no others then I move we vote now." He looked around at the serious faces. "All those in favor of Krar for leader say aye."

The entire crowd roared "Aye!" with one voice.

Krar stood a moment longer among them, then strode into the center of the circle.

"I swear to lead you to the best of my ability," he promised. "I also swear to place your good above my own and to strive to be an honest and responsible leader. I will always listen to you."

He lowered his head and snorted softly. "I can't and won't promise to always do what you want. I can only promise to try to be fair and just to all of you."

When he was finished the crowd roared approval and Krar smiled, fit to burst with pride.

Then Canar Trowr shuffled painfully into the open circle.

"You may not know me," he said to them. "I am Canar Trowr, soldier and scout of the Clan of the Claw. It is good that you have finally selected a leader.

But now you must do more. You must become a clan. All of you will be bound by this. It means that you are like one family, loyal to one another and to your leader. It means that if you go off on your own you might not be able to come back. Because each member of a clan relies on every other Mrem in the clan. You must become a unit. And your clan must have a name that you will all acknowledge."

This threw them all into an uproar. They actually were all related. Sisters and brothers, mothers and cousins, fathers as well, though because of the way the Liskash had arranged things, fathers never knew their kits. But the groups had been segregated and thought of themselves as members of those groups and not, as Canar Trowr proposed, as a single unit.

After a time Krar stood forward again and asked, "Can we do this? Can we be as one?"

There was a pause and then a rather lukewarm, "Yes," came from the crowd.

"We will do this with a whole heart or not at all," Krar commanded. "We need to be a clan for our own sake, and because it will cause the free Mrem to accept us. Now . . . are we a clan?"

"Yes!" came back to him in a mighty shout.

"What will you call yourselves?" Canar Trowr asked.

Prenna came forward into the speakers circle.

"I think we should be the clan Ranowr," she said. "To honor the hero who brought us to freedom. Without him we'd be laboring on Ashala's holding—slaves still."

Krar held back the disbelieving laugh that threatened to escape him.

Did I hate being under Ranowr's shadow? he asked himself. *Now I shall labor all my life under his shadow!* He shook his head.

Then thought: *On the other hand, Prenna is right, he is ... was ... a hero, well deserving of the honor. What's more he's dead, but I'm alive and the clan's leader. And,* he glanced at Prenna, *if I work it right, I might end up mated to the most beautiful female in the clan.*

There was a more solemn pause and then, one by one each Mrem said, "Aye."

Krar managed to say his "Aye," late, but not last.

They resumed their march two days later, well rested and feeling certain that Ashala's people did not pursue them. Now that they had become a clan the groups mingled more and they relaxed with one another.

After another four days scouts came back to report that the free Mrem had been spotted. The Clan of Ranowr greeted this news with joy and trepidation mixed.

Krar, Tral, Mahssa and Canar Trowr went forward to meet them in one of the wagons.

At first all they saw was the dust cloud, even a heavy rain didn't keep the ground damp in this heat. In what seemed like a very short time they were in sight of the great caravan of Mrem and their stock. From out of the cloud strange vehicles came towards them, pulled by strange creatures.

Krar pulled the wagon to a stop and stared anxiously, not certain they wouldn't be met with weapons instead of welcomes.

"What are those things?" he asked Canar Trowr.

"Chariots!" the wounded scout answered. "And unless my eyes deceive me that is Rantan Taggah himself coming to greet us!"

"He is your leader?" Krar asked.

"Talonmaster of the Clan of the Claw," Canar Trowr answered. "Just as you are talonmaster of the Clan of Ranowr, and so you must identify yourself." He put his hand on Krar's shoulder. "My people will welcome you, I think. Be happy! Be proud!"

"Yes," Krar said quietly. "I am."

Song of Petru
XXXIV

Heart

Lost and alone
Amid Liskash hordes
They sought the path
The way to home
Instead they found
A Sacred Path
A Blessed Home
Song of Petru

Sanctuary

ERIC FLINT

CHAPTER 1

Sebetwe

Knest died toward the beginning of the *durre kot,* the witching time before sunrise.

It was a dangerous period. Not as dangerous as midnight, but still perilous—especially this early into *durre kot.* Knest's soul would have to withstand the assault of pejeq and milleteq and whatever other demons might be lurking on the great mountainside until the sun finally rose above the horizon and Huwute's brilliance drove the demons back into their lairs.

Even the strongest disciple would be hard-pressed to survive that long. As the sky brightened, the demons would be driven to greater and greater fury in their assault on Knest's soul. That was especially true of the pejeq, who were undoubtedly in great numbers at this altitude. Milleteq were often sluggish, but not their hungrier and more ethereal kin—and the greater danger the pejeq faced when Huwute's rays began piercing the heavens would make them frantic toward the end.

Only the firmest disciple's soul could hope to pass through that ordeal intact. And Knest...

"He was a weakling," Herere said harshly. "He won't last even halfway through the *durre kot.*"

Aqavo stared down at Knest's corpse, hissing softly as her eyes traced the long wound left by the grek wadda. The venom had left the flesh pale, putrid-looking, altogether horrid. Fortunately, the plant's venom rendered its victim unconscious before it began its deadly and hideous work. Knest had at least not died in great pain.

The fourth member of the party, Nabliz, gazed at the horizon where—much too late—Huwute would finally rise. "Herere is right," he said softly. "You know she is, Sebetwe."

Sebetwe did know it, but he hesitated to give the order. Aqavo, probably the kindest of the group, put his reluctance into words. "That would be the true death for Knest. His soul gone forever."

Herere shifted her weight on her haunches. "When his soul is taken by a demon he will also suffer the true death—and we will be at great risk ourselves."

She was right. A pejeq riding a captured soul or a milleteq enlarged by devouring one would be able to attack them throughout the night. At dawn and dusk also—any time except when Huwute's glory filled the sky.

"We must do it, Sebetwe," said Nabliz.

Aqavo said nothing, but her slumped shoulders indicated her agreement. Herere glared at Sebetwe, then down at the corpse of Knest. After a moment, she drew her knife.

Sebetwe raised a hand. "I will do it," he said. "Aqavo, start the fire."

He drew out his ax. It was typical of Herere that

she would think to use a knife to cut open a skull. The huge female was always prone to displaying her great strength. Sebetwe, average size for a male Liskash, would use a more reliable tool for the purpose.

Delay was dangerous. So, with none of the ritual formality he would have preferred, Sebetwe smashed open Knest's skull. Two more blows of the axe were enough to expose the narrow brain case. Then, using a taloned hand, he scooped out the brain. He laid it on a bare rock, since Aqavo's fire was only starting to build.

While he was busy at that task, Herere sliced open Knest's chest and abdomen. With Nabliz's help, the dead disciple's heart, lungs and liver were soon removed from the body.

The heart and lungs, they would eat, to keep what might be left of Knest's valor and spirit in their midst. Could they have done the same with the brain, they might have been able to save Knest's soul as well. But that would be perilous. Devilkins usually infested the brains of dead people; not powerful ones like pejeq or milleteq but sly and malicious ones who sought to infest those who ate such brains.

So the brain would have to be burned. Had Knest died at home, or at least in safer surroundings, they could have performed the rites and embalming rituals that would have preserved his soul long enough for it to pass into a newborn.

The liver would also be burned, lest whatever sins and evils had lurked within Knest should escape into the world with his death.

❖   ❖   ❖

By the time they were done, Huwute had fully risen. The goddess's splendor was still dim enough that one could gaze upon her without danger, but that would not last long. Huwute was vain and thus dangerous, as deities so often were.

Sebetwe knew that most Liskash tribes actually worshipped Huwute. Primitives, not much more than savages, who could not distinguish the manifestations of the Godhead from itself. In truth, it was sloppy thinking to visualize the sun as a "goddess," though most disciples did it anyway.

Sebetwe knew that Huwute was not really a deity, simply the manifestation—not the only; but certainly the greatest—of the Godhead's self-consideration. Dangerous, not in the way that a conscious beast is dangerous but in the way a fire or a rockslide is dangerous.

It was not always easy to remember the teachings, though. Sebetwe found it hard not to resent Huwute's stately and self-satisfied progression. Could the goddess not have hastened her steps a bit, to keep Knest's soul in the world?

The work was done, all their belongings back in their packs. Sebetwe straightened and gazed up the mountain. They still had a long way to go before they reached their destination. The trek up the slope would be arduous. The thin and cold air of the mountainside would sap their energy, making them more sluggish as the day passed.

That was how Knest had died, in late afternoon

of the previous day. His brain had become dulled; so dulled that he had not noticed the filaments of the grek wadda lying in wait against the rocks until the monster struck.

They would have to be careful—and ever more so as they neared their goal. The gantrak of the mountains guarded their nests fiercely.

Achia Pazik

Lavi Tur slid down the slope to come to rest beside Achia Pazik. Despite the peril of the moment, the Dancer was amused by the young male's graceful flamboyance. Because of his age, Lavi Tur was not formally a warrior yet—a fact that aggravated him no end because he felt, probably rightly, that he was as strong and agile as almost any warrior in the clan.

"Probably" rightly? Achia Pazik asked herself silently. The question was a bitter one. After the disastrous outcome of the battle three days ago with Zilikazi's army, Lavi Tur was almost certainly as strong and agile as any warrior in the tribe. She didn't think there were many left who weren't dead or captured or so badly wounded that they were unavailable for any more fighting. For a time, anyway. And the casualties among the Dancers had been worse than those suffered by the warriors.

Zilikazi had targeted the Dancers from the very beginning of the battle, sending massed units of mounted warriors at them. The mind power of the Liskash noble who lorded it over the lands bordering on the great southern mountains had been incredible.

No scaled noble they'd encountered before had been nearly as domineering.

The Dancers had been stunned, the warriors even more so. The battle had been over within two hours. Only small groups of the tribespeople had escaped; the rest, killed or enslaved. Most of those who had escaped, Achia Pazik thought, had fled back in the direction from which they'd come, to the northeast. But she and the handful with her wound up, in the chaos and confusion, being separated from all others and making their escape to the south. They'd apparently moved completely around the huge Liskash army, although they'd had no conscious intention of doing so.

But it was too late now to do anything more than continue south. Trying to retrace their steps would surely be disastrous. Achia Pazik wanted no further contact with Zilikazi until and unless she could figure out some way to counteract his incredible mental force. And how was she supposed to do that, with no more aid than could be provided by one other Dancer, five warriors, one not-quite-a-warrior, four other females—one of them elderly, albeit hale and vigorous—and three kits?

Their only chance was to make it into the mountains. Hopefully, the dropping temperatures would deter Zilikazi's soldiers from pursuing them. Liskash didn't like cold; it made them sluggish.

"Chefer Kolkin says the way is clear as far ahead as he can see." Lavi Tur spoke in a hissing whisper, which Achia Pazik thought was a bit dramatic given the very content of what he had to say. If the way was clear, why worry about being overheard?

But she didn't chide or tease him. Like most young-lings, Lavi Tur was sensitive to criticism.

"All right," she said. "Pass the word to the others. We've rested long enough. We have to get higher before nightfall."

After Lavi Tur left, Achia Pazik looked up the slope. She was in a slight depression and couldn't see the peak of the mountains whose side they'd been climb-ing. But she knew they still had a long way to go.

A screech somewhere in the distance caused her to tense. That had been made by some sort of animal, not a Liskash scout. A big animal, from the sound.

What animal? She had no idea. To the best of her knowledge, no Mrem had ever gone into the great southern mountains. There had been no reason to. Mrem were more resistant to cold than the reptiles, but they still didn't like it—and with the plains avail-able, why go into the mountains?

But the plains weren't available now. There might never be again. Not those plains dominated by Zilikazi, at least, and they were the only ones within reach.

So, up they would go, no matter what dangerous animals might live up there. Achia Pazik didn't see where they had any choice.

Zilikazi

"Kill the injured," Zilikazi said. "Any who can't move without assistance."

He gave one final glance at the huddled mass of Mrem captives, and then decided he'd better qualify that. His underlings were prone to interpreting his orders excessively. He could hardly complain about that tendency, given that he'd fostered and encouraged it himself. But he saw no reason to waste captives unnecessarily.

"By 'assistance' I mean any who need to be carried on a litter. If they can walk with the support of one or two other Mrem, we'll keep them alive. For now, at any rate."

He didn't bother to wait for his lieutenants' gestures of assent before turning away and moving back toward his pavilion. That abruptness was another trait he'd fostered over the years. For him to wait to accept an underling's sign of obedience would suggest there was a possibility the underling might *not* obey Zilikazi, which was unthinkable.

Zilikazi's dominance resulted mostly from his immense power. But he'd buttressed that innate ability with shrewd methods of rule as well.

As he moved toward the great pavilion in the distance, his palanquin followed in his wake. The four Liskash who bore that palanquin were lucky that Zilikazi was still young enough to be energetic and chose to demonstrate that vigor publicly on most occasions. The palanquin was already heavy due to its construction and ornamentation, even without someone riding in it.

As he walked, the Liskash ruler contemplated his next move in the great conflict that had erupted since the sea broke through the eastern mountains and began flooding the lowlands. The migrations of the Mrem clans had unleashed war all across the lands to the north. Wars between Liskash nobles, often, not simply clashes with the furred barbarians. In the nature of things—Zilikazi was no exception—Liskash nobles were always alert to opportunities to enlarge their domains. A noble weakened by Mrem was like a bloody fish in the water, drawing predators from all around.

Now that he'd crushed the Mrem who had dared to invade his own territory, Zilikazi was tempted to send his army north, to seize what lands he could from other nobles. Keletu was badly weakened, he was sure; so, most likely, were Giswayo and Sakki.

But, in his cold and calculating manner, he suppressed the urge. Unlike most Liskash nobles, Zilikazi had trained himself to patience. His mental power was greater than that of any noble he knew—or had ever heard of, for that matter. So what was the hurry? He was still young; still had plenty of time to forge the greatest Liskash realm ever known. It was better to continue the path he'd always followed; the patient path, that consolidated gains before adding new ones.

That meant he had to anchor his position against the southern mountains before he sent his army to the north. The Kororo Krek probably posed no real danger to him, since the religious order seemed disinclined toward conquest. But who knew what ideas might come into the heads of fanatics?

Their overly complex, phantasmagorical notions belonged in the addled brains of Mrem, not sensible Liskash. If those notions spread more widely, mischief might result. Zilikazi hadn't been able to make much sense of the prattle of the Kororo disciple he'd had tortured. But one thing had emerged clearly out of the muddle: the Krek placed no great value—perhaps none at all—on the established customs of the Liskash.

Not even the most powerful noble—not even Zilikazi himself—could rule without those customs. If one had to maintain control by the constant exertion of sheer mental force over each and every underling...

Impossible! One had to sleep, after all. What made orderly rule possible was accepted and entrenched custom. Once a noble demonstrated his or her power, those who were inferior acquiesced in their subordination. Willingly, if not eagerly. Thereafter, the nobles needed only to demonstrate, from time to time or in clashes with other nobles, that their power had not waned.

So. The Kororo Krek had annoyed him long enough. It was time to crush them and bring those who survived under his rule. The soldiers wouldn't like campaigning in the mountains, of course. They would complain bitterly in private to each other. But what did that matter? Soldiers always complained. As long as they kept their grievances to themselves, Zilikazi could safely ignore them.

As for the conditions in the mountains, they couldn't be *that* bad. The Kororo had been up there for at least three generations now. And they weren't a single sub-species which might have become hardened to the environment, either. They were a mongrel breed, accepting Liskash from everywhere. If such could survive up there, so could Zilikazi's soldiers.

Njekwa

"What news?" Njekwa asked quietly, after Litunga entered the cooking tent and came to her side.

"The warriors I spoke to said we are marching south, starting tomorrow." The old shaman lowered her voice still further. "Zilikazi plans to crush the Kororo, they think."

Njekwa grunted skeptically. Litunga would have spoken only to common warriors, not officers. Such were hardly likely to be in the godling's confidence. Rumors were generated and spread in the ranks of the warriors like weeds.

Still . . .

"What should we do, Priestess?" asked Litunga.

"There's nothing we can 'do,' and you know it as well as I do. What you really mean to ask is 'what is our attitude?' Do we support the godling or stand apart?"

Which was also a rather pointless way of putting it, thought Njekwa, although she didn't say it out loud. Zilikazi was barely aware of the Old Faith's existence. He didn't care one way or the other whether its adherents considered the Kororo to be heretics—and he certainly didn't care if they supported him or stood aside when he marched against the Krek. As far as Zilikazi was concerned, the only proper religious belief was the one that recognized him as a god. All others were beneath his contempt.

Nonetheless, the question mattered to the Old Believers. Ever since the rise of the Kororo Krek, a few generations earlier, they had wrestled with the issue.

On the one hand, as members of the Krek themselves freely acknowledged, the Kororo creed had arisen from the Old Faith. It rejected outright the pretensions of the nobility to divine status. Spurned the notion with scorn and derision, in fact.

On the other hand...

The Kororo rejected much of the Old Faith as well. They considered ancestors worthy of respect, but not veneration. They did not seek their enlightenment, much less their intervention in current Liskash affairs. They placed no special status on the female nature of the Godhead—indeed, they argued that the Godhead had no gender at all.

For them, so far as Njekwa had been able to determine, the Godhead was more in the way of a disembodied universal power than anything she or her shamans would call a deity at all. The Kororo even went so far as to claim that all the goddesses and gods—even mighty Huwute herself!—were illusions. Figments of the imagination; names given to a mystery so vast that no mortal mind could ever grasp more than a shard at a time. And that shard was more likely to be distorted than true.

Quite interesting concepts, actually. In certain moods—usually after one or another misfortune—Njekwa found herself half-agreeing with them.

Some of them. The notion of a genderless Godhead was preposterous, of course.

"So what should we do?" Litunga repeated.

Njekwa gave the usual answer. "For the moment, nothing."

Meshwe

"Couldn't I try first with a huddu?" asked Chello plaintively. "Or maybe a mavalore?" Squatting on her haunches with her hands splayed on the sand, the youngling stared apprehensively at the tritti sprawled a short distance away in the little arena. For its part, the horned lizard stared off to the side. To all outward appearances it seemed oblivious to Chello's presence.

But tritti could move very quickly. And their fangs might be short but they were very sharp. As small as they were, their venom was not fatal to a Liskash, even a youngling. But it would hurt. It would really, really hurt. For a long time. And if it bit her in the wrong place, Chello might lose something like a finger.

Maybe even a foot. One of the older females, Kjat, had lost three toes because of a tritti's bite—and that had happened in an arena just like this one. True, Kjat was pretty dim-witted and should probably never have tried to become a tekkutu in the first place.

Still...

"No, you can't try first on a huddu or a mavalore," said Meshwe. "It wouldn't do any good. No animal whose life is guided by fear can serve your purpose. Only in a ferocious mind can you find the strength you need. You know all this, Chello. It has been explained to you often."

His tone was patient. The mentor had been through this many times over the years. Most younglings trying to become tekkutu were afraid the first time they went into the arena—usually, many times thereafter too. Tritti bites hurt, sure enough, and the little predators were quite willing to attack creatures much larger than themselves if they felt threatened.

Which they did, of course, when they found

themselves trapped in a small arena whose walls were too high for them to leap over and too smooth to scale.

"Now, concentrate," commanded Meshwe. "Find the hunter's mind and merge with it. From the hunter, take its fierce purpose. To the hunter, give your own serenity. Out of this exchange, surround your mind with impervious walls."

Fierce purpose, the tritti surely had. Unfortunately, Chello's serenity was as shaky as that of most six-year-old younglings. She started off rather well, but then got anxious and fumbled the exchange. The hunter reacted as such hunters are prone to do when their little minds are penetrated by strange and unsettling sensations. (You couldn't call them thoughts, really; not even notions—a tritti's brain is quite tiny.)

Strike out—and there was only one visible target.

"*Aaaaah!*" Chello began capering about, shaking her leg frantically. "Get it off me! Get it off!"

Tritti transmitted their venom down grooves in their teeth, not through hollow fangs like serpents. So they had to chew for a bit where a snake would strike and immediately withdraw. But not for all that long. By the time Meshwe could climb over the wall into the arena the horned lizard had already relinquished its hold and fallen back onto the sand.

The mentor lifted Chello over the barricade and passed her into the hands of a healer who'd been standing by. Then he drew the trident from its sheath on his back and turned to face the horned lizard.

The creatures were really very ferocious, given their size. The tritti leapt forward again and bit Meshwe on the ankle.

Or tried to. The mentor, unlike the youngling, was not clad in a light tunic. His upper body was unarmored, but his legs and feet were encased in thick boots that reached almost all the way up to his groin.

The fangs were unable to penetrate. Frustrated, the monster fell back and gathered itself for another leap. But the trident skewered it to the sand.

Meshwe waited for a while, as the tough little creature thrashed out its life. It was too bad, really. This tritti was fearless even by the standards of its kind. Had Chello's attempt been successful, the hunter would have made a splendid familiar until she was ready to graduate to a greater challenge.

But, she'd failed. And now the tritti would be inured to any further such attempts, either by Chello or any other youngling. It would simply attack instantly if it found itself placed in the position again.

Chello was still wailing. She had a very unpleasant few days ahead.

Too bad also, of course. But the Kororo Krek had never found any other way to raise up tekkutu.

They'd been left in relative peace for years, here in their mountain sanctuary. But it wouldn't last. Any attentive youngling could learn the basic precepts of the order. Only a few of them, however, would manage the task of achieving *tekku*. And only tekkutu could hope to withstand the mental domination of the nobility.

CHAPTER 2

Sebetwe

The hatchlings might be too old. That much was already obvious from the volume of sound being emitted from the nest somewhere above and still not in sight.

"At least two, maybe three," Nabliz said softly.

All four of them were huddled together under an overhanding rock on the steep slope. The vegetation was getting very sparse now and there weren't many places to find concealment.

"Too old," grunted Herere. She had the odd quality of being pessimistic as well as aggressive. The combination often irritated Sebetwe—as it did now.

He started to say something but Aqavo spoke first. "Maybe not, Herere," she said. "Sebetwe is very—"

"Powerful," Herere interrupted, impatiently and a bit sourly. "Yes, I know. This is still not magic."

The word Aqavo had actually been about to use was *bradda*, Sebetwe thought. The term was subtle and while it had much in common with *gudru*— "powerful"—it suggested more in the way of influence and persuasion, even charisma. The fact that Herere did not understand the distinction was much of the reason she herself had never risen very far in her ranking as a disciple.

For Herere, all conflict came down to strength against strength. That had served her well enough as a child at establishing her mastery over creatures like tritti and even paqui.

But today they faced great gantrak of the mountains. No Liskash disciple, no matter how great their *gudh*, had any chance of simply dominating such monsters. You might as well try quenching a bonfire by force of will.

There was no point trying to explain any of this to Herere, though. No mentor of the Krek, not even Meshwe, had ever managed to do that. So Sebetwe simply shifted his shoulders in a slight shrug and said: "Maybe I can, maybe I can't. We'll find out soon enough."

Another chorus of screeches came down from above.

"They're hungry," said Nabliz. "We'd better move quickly."

He was right. The mother would be away, hunting for her brood. The father...could be anywhere, but there was no point in worrying about that. Male gantrak were every bit as protective of their brood as females, but they had little of the same territoriality. The brood's father might be a mountain range away.

Or could be asleep in the nest itself. With males, behavior was hard to predict.

"Let's get going," Sebetwe commanded. "I'll continue directly up the slope with Nabliz. Herere, you take that little draw to the left. I think that'll bring you above the nest." A little diplomacy here. "You're the strongest, so you'll have the best chance of handling the mother if she returns."

"And me?" asked Aqavo.

Had he been fully honest, Sebetwe would have replied: "You stay here, because you're only a novice, not yet a full tekkutu, and won't be any use to me in the capture. And you won't be any more use if we have to fight."

But he liked Aqavo as much as he disliked Herere, so he coated the answer. "Stay here and make ready the harnesses. We won't have any time to spare."

"How many?" she asked, sounding a bit relieved.

"Only two. If I can capture any at all, it won't be more than that."

Aqavo started rummaging in the sacks they'd all unloaded when they reached the overhang. Herere was already out, heading for the draw.

"Ghammid be with you," said Nabliz after her.

Aqavo whistled softly. "Don't let Meshwe hear you say that or you'll get a lecture."

Sebetwe grunted his amusement. It was true enough. He could hear it already. *The so-called "God of Good Fortune" is simply another manifestation of the Godhead as we can perceive it. No more a real deity than the sun or the moon—and you have as much chance of improving your luck by invoking her as you do of changing the dawn or the tides by invoking Huwute or Ishtala.*

Sebetwe didn't doubt Meshwe's teaching. Not for a moment. Still . . .

"Ghammid be with us," he murmured, and headed up the slope, shaking his catchpole slightly to make sure the noose was not tangled.

Achia Pazik

"What *is* that thing?" hissed Chefer Kolkin. The warrior's grip on his spear was tight enough for his knuckles to stand out in sharp relief—quite unlike the veteran's usual relaxed manner when handling his weapons.

Part of his tension was due to the unearthly shrieks coming from somewhere above them. Most of it, though, was simply due to the uncertainty of the moment. Should they fight? Flee? Hide? And looming behind all of those questions was a still greater one—who was to decide? Which of them was to give the order, whatever that order might be?

By strict seniority, Chefer Kolkin himself should perhaps be in charge. But as doughty a warrior as he was, Chefer Kolkin had never displayed much in the way of leadership in the past.

Neither had the other surviving Dancer, Gadi Elkin. Besides, although she was older than Achia Pazik, she did not match her in skill—and rank among the Dancers was based mostly on ability, not age.

Of the other four soldiers, the half-brothers Tsede Zeg and Elor Zeg generally kept to themselves, to the point of being almost rude. Zuel Babic was too young—not more than two years past Lavi Tur's age—and Puah Neff was cut from the same hide as Chefer Kolkin. Brave and fierce in battle, capable at other tasks, but not suited to lead more than a handful of warriors.

So . . . it would have to be Achia Pazik herself who took the position of leader. Until now, she'd been able to avoid that task, because they'd simply been fleeing. The only decision to be made was *this way!* or *that way!* and any one of them could do that much. There was no need to make a formal proceeding out of the matter, though, even if they had the time to do so.

"I think it's more than one thing, whatever it is," she said. She pointed to a narrow ledge that moved up the side of the mountain to their right. "I think we can follow that around, and stay away from ... whatever they are."

Chefer Kolkin nodded. "I will take the lead." He moved off, crouched over so as not to show his profile above the terrain. Not until he had taken eight or nine steps did Achia Pazik realize that the warrior had displayed as much adroit skill in tacitly accepting her leadership as he had in moving up the mountain. Apparently, there were subtleties beneath than stolid exterior.

She stayed in place, waiting for the other warriors to reach her. As they did, she passed along the same instructions: *Up the mountain using the ledge. Follow Chefer Kolkin.* No one disputed her authority, either because they accepted it on its own terms or because they supposed Chefer Kolkin had made the decision. Again, there was no point in forcing a formal agreement, even if they had the leisure time. Hopefully, as time passed, the warriors would come to accept the situation without quarrel.

She expected no dispute from the other Dancer—and, indeed, Gadi Elkin did as she was told without hesitating. So did the four females and their kits.

Lavi Tur brought up the rear. And he, of course, raised the issue. Being quick-witted at his age was a very mixed blessing.

"Who put you in charge?" he demanded, in a tone that was both challenging and amused.

"I did," she said curtly. "Do as you're told."

She was half-expecting an argument, but all she got was a smile. An instant later, Lavi Tur was moving up the mountain.

She followed, after taking a long look behind to make sure nothing was pursuing them. Nothing she could see, at least. Because of the folded terrain, she could only see a short distance. There might be an entire army on their trail, for all she knew.

But she thought it was unlikely they were anywhere near. Liskash generally did not move as quickly as Mrem. That was true even in the hot lowlands. Here, in the cold heights, they would be more sluggish than usual.

Sebetwe

Sebetwe was cursing his own sluggishness that very moment. Liskash were not cold-blooded, in the way true reptiles were. But they were still more susceptible to low temperatures than Mrem or other mammals. In high altitudes like these, they needed to absorb sunlight after dawn in order to get moving quickly, and they needed to rest more often than they would in the lowlands. That was so regardless of the difficulty of the terrain—which, if it *was* arduous to travel across, required still more often and longer rest periods.

Not a big problem, perhaps, for someone taking a leisurely hike simply to enjoy the scenery. But when you were hunting gantrak...

He tried to raise his spirits by reminding himself that gantrak, while they lived in the mountains, were not mammals either. They too would be sluggish this early in the morning.

The thought was not very cheerful, though. Sluggish in the morning or not, a fully grown gantrak would weigh half again what Sebetwe did, had talons three times as long as his own, fangs that made his teeth look pitiful—leaving aside the scaly armored hide and the thick bony ridges guarding the creature's skull.

Not far now, judging from the sounds being made by the hatchlings nesting somewhere above them.

Achia Pazik

Elor Zeg almost slipped off the narrow ledge, he came back down in such a hurry.

"Liskash—up ahead!" he hissed. "Chefer Kolkin sent me back to tell you." He hesitated briefly, and then added: "He wants to know what you think we should so."

From the slight frown on his face, it was clear that Elor Zeg had his doubts about the propriety of a noted veteran warrior like Chefer Kolkin seeking instruction from such a young Dancer as Achia Pazik. But, thankfully, he kept whatever reservations he had to himself.

She suspected those same reservations had distracted Elor Zeg from passing along the critical information she needed to make any decision.

"How many are there?" she hissed in return, trying to speak as quietly as possible. "And are they warriors?"

Elor Zeg grunted slightly with embarrassment. If

he'd neglected to include that information in a report he'd given Chefer Kolkin himself, the older warrior would have berated him. Pretty savagely, too.

"Only three, that we can see. And we're not sure if they're warriors. Exactly." He seemed a bit confused. "What I mean is, they're carrying weapons. I guess. Of a sort."

Achia Pazik was getting exasperated. Neither of the Zeg half-brothers was exactly what you'd call a mental giant. "What do you mean, 'you guess'? What sort of weapons?"

"They're more like snares than weapons. Ropes mostly, attached to poles, with odd loops at the end. They also have big knifes, but those are still in their sheaths."

Ropes with odd loops...

Some of the Mrem tribes used devices called lassos, she knew. Her own people didn't, because the animals they herded were too big to be held against their will by mere ropes. But there were tribes whose herd animals were a lot smaller and more manageable.

So far as she knew, though, the lassos were simply ropes designed to be cast in such a way as to loop around the necks of their targets. She'd never heard of any attached to poles.

Then again, she'd never actually seen a lasso. Her knowledge might simply be faulty.

But this was no time to let her thoughts stray. There was a decision to be made.

"They're above us on the mountain?"

"Yes. Climbing still higher, too. They haven't spotted

us. I don't think they're paying much attention to anything below them."

They must be hunting something, then. Whatever was making the hideous shrieks?

Possibly. But it didn't really matter, one way or the other. If the Liskash were preoccupied, the small band of Mrem could pass them by without being noticed.

Hopefully.

"Tell Chefer Kolkin to stay on the trail." *Tiny narrow treacherous ledge* would have been a more apt term to use than *trail*. But everyone's spirits needed to be kept up.

Elor Zeg left without a word.

Or anything else. Warriors taking orders from their superiors were normally in the habit of making a small gesture when they did so. A sort of hand-clenching coupled with a forward thrust of the fist. But Achia Pazik was not about to insist on formalities. It was enough that no one was openly challenging her authority.

Well, almost no one.

By the time Elor Zeg and Achia Pazik had finished their little conference, the rest of the party had crowded up the trail and come close enough to overhear the last exchange.

"I think we ought to attack them," said Lavi Tur brashly.

Before Achia Pazik could reply, Aziz Vardit spoke up. She was the oldest of the females in their party.

"Thankfully, you are not in charge," she said. "Achia Pazik is. So be quiet."

Sebetwe

They were almost there. Close enough to separate the tones of the hatchling screeches. There were two of them.

No adults. By now, they would have made their presence known. Gantrak did not tolerate much in the way of obstreperousness from their offspring. If there had been an adult in the nest above, she or he would probably have silenced the noisy hatchlings.

That was the good part. The bad part was that gantrak hatchlings wouldn't be making that much noise if they weren't hungry—which suggested, at least, that an adult might be returning with food soon.

But there was no way to know, and they couldn't possibly stay on the mountain for another night. Not this high up. At least one of them would die, and quite possibly all four.

Sebetwe glanced around. Nabliz was also in position. He couldn't see Herere because the big female had moved far enough around the slope of the mountainside to be out of sight. But whatever her other failings, Herere could be counted on to be in position also. In the field, as long as the task didn't involve subtlety and indirection, she was extraordinarily capable.

Time, then. Being careful to keep his snare out of sight of the hatchlings above—that involved an awkward extension of the pole, sticking out almost directly behind him—Sebetwe began creeping up the final stretch.

He never once thought to look down the mountain behind him. If the adult gantrak were returning to the nest they'd either be coming from the other side of the mountain or they would have already spotted the Liskash advancing on the nest. In which case there would be no need to scour the mountainside looking for signs of them coming. Their screams of fury would have been heard already. Gantrak were even less given to subtlety than Herere.

CHAPTER 3

Sebetwe

He was at the rim of the nest, now. On the other side of the mound of stones, the noise being made by the hatchlings was almost deafening. Glancing to his left, he saw that Nabliz was ready also.

Sebetwe couldn't see Herere—he could have barely heard her if she were shouting, in the midst of the hatchling racket—but he would just have to assume that she was in position as well.

It would be no great matter if she weren't. He was now sure there were only two hatchlings in the nest, which he and Nabliz could handle. Long enough for Herere to arrive and lend her assistance, anyway.

There was no point in waiting.

No point in issuing a war cry, either. Trying to shout over the screeching of the hatchlings would be an exercise in futility.

So, he just came upright and leaned over the stone rim, bringing his snare into play.

Two hatchlings, as he'd guessed. It was almost comical the way the creatures became instantly silent the moment they spotted Sebetwe. They stared up at him with their jaws agape, their eyes large and as round as such eyes could be.

His cast was perfect. The noose came down over the head of one of the hatchlings, down its sinewy neck and over the slender predator's shoulders. With a powerful wrench to his right, he brought the rope tight, pinning the young gantrak's forelimbs to its body.

Now a wrench to the left brought the creature down. As he clambered into the nest, he saw that Nabliz's cast had been much poorer than his. Nabliz had failed to get the noose over the shoulders of the other one. Now, he could only lift the small gantrak into the air, choking it with the rope around the neck. Unless someone came to his aid—and soon—he would kill the hatchling instead of capturing it.

Nabliz had no choice in the matter, though. Even a hatchling gantrak was dangerous if left to run wild.

But Sebetwe could spare no more than a glance at Nabliz. His own hatchling was still not subdued. He slammed the pole down and stepped on it with his foot, keeping the hatchling pinned. Then, squatting to bring himself close to the little monster—not *too* close; a swipe from one of those thrashing and well-taloned rear limbs could easily tear out an eye—he compressed the thing's mind under his *gudh*. Within two seconds, the hatchling was completely still, paralyzed.

Being *gudru* had its uses, but Sebetwe was already readying his *bradda*. The mental exercises needed for that took some time, though, which was the reason he'd started with a crude but straightforward use of his *gudh*.

The exercises were mostly a matter of rote for him now, so he took a bit of time to see how Nabliz was faring.

Much better. Herere had arrived and immobilized that hatchling's rear limbs with Nabliz's own snare. Between them, she and Nabliz brought the creature down to earth. By now, the hatchling was half-suffocated and dazed. Moving deftly and quickly, Nabliz loosened his noose and slid it over the young gantrak's shoulders.

That one was now completely immobilized also. Herere, showing the good sense she usually exhibited in combat, switched snares with Nabliz. She would now hold the creature still while Nabliz readied his own *bradda*.

Everything was shaping up well.

Until the pile of debris in a far corner of the nest suddenly erupted.

Achia Pazik

The screech that now came from the slope above made the ones issued earlier seem like the peepings of small birds. Achia Pazik froze, her eyes ranging up and scouring the mountainside, looking for the source.

Sebetwe

A gantrak—fully grown, with a red-and-blue male crest—came up from the pile of debris. It must have been sleeping there.

The scream it issued paralyzed Sebetwe for a moment. But not Herere. She flung her snarepole at Nabliz, shouting something that couldn't really be heard above the monster's scream. Sebetwe thought it might be *Here! Hold the hatchling!*

Then she rose, drawing her knife, to face the gantrak.

It was an act of courage bordering on sheer madness. There was no way Herere, armed only with a knife, could overcome an adult gantrak. Even the male ones, although smaller than the females, outweighed any Liskash—and if their fangs and talons were any smaller than a female's, Sebetwe couldn't tell the difference.

And so it proved. The gantrak's charge drove Herere off her feet entirely. But not before she grasped the monster's crest and drove her knife into his chest.

Or tried to. The armor there deflected the blade— she'd have done better to try for the throat or belly— and all her knife did was gash a nasty-looking but shallow cut in the creature's hide.

It was enough to unbalance the gantrak, though. Between that and Herere's tight grip on the crest, the monster stumbled and knocked both of them over the rim of the nest.

The gantrak screamed again. A moment later, he and Herere had fallen out of sight somewhere down the mountain's slope.

Achia Pazik

Two intertwined bodies came rolling down the mountain. One of them was a Liskash, that much was obvious. The other—

What was it? She had no idea.

But whatever it was, it was big and clearly dangerous. And it was coming straight for the section of the ledge which she thought Chefer Kolkin had reached.

Chefer Kolkin

Achia Pazik's assumption was mostly correct—that *was* the portion of the ledge Chefer Kolkin had reached, moving ahead of the other warriors. But it was no longer a ledge. That section of the trail had broadened out into a small terrace. Almost a meadow, except the only things growing on it were lichens and a few scrubby little bushes.

Chefer Kolkin heard the bodies tumbling down the slope before he could see them. And when he did see them, it was at the last moment—in what seemed like a mere instant, he was knocked to the ground by the collision.

A moment later, three bodies separated themselves out from the jumbled pile.

Chefer Kolkin himself, a bit bruised but otherwise unharmed.

An unusually large Liskash, who seemed to be covered with gashes and wounds but was still alive and conscious—barely.

And . . .

Some sort of hideous monster. It reminded Chefer Kolkin vaguely of a flat-bodied crested lizard he'd once seen in the desert, except its limbs weren't splayed out—and it was easily thirty or forty times as big as any lizard he'd ever seen.

So were its fangs and talons.

Chefer Kolkin rose before the Liskash. That was his first mistake. The monster, which had been crouched over the Liskash and ready to tear it into pieces, immediately had its attention drawn to him.

And immediately charged him.

The charge was terrifying. Unlike any lizard Chefer Kolkin had ever encountered, of any size, this one rose on its hind legs and surged forward with its front limbs spread apart and raised, its talons ready to slash.

Or grapple. Chefer Kolkin had no idea what the beast's fighting tactics were—and had no desire to find out. So he lunged forward with his spear, aiming below the armored chest for what he hoped was the softer and thinner hide of the monster's belly.

His aim was true and his guess that the creature's belly was less well protected than its chest was correct. But "less well protected" is a relative term. It was still like striking armor with his spear head. The blade penetrated only a short distance before the monster jerked its torso sideways, causing the spear to leave nothing more than a shallow cut that didn't pierce the body chamber.

That sideways twist also unbalanced the creature, so it didn't slam into Chefer Kolkin with the driving force that it had obviously intended. The veteran Mrem warrior was no stranger to battle and twisted his own body out of the way.

But as it passed him, the creature struck with its taloned paw, slamming into Chefer Kolkin's left shoulder. The warrior's own armor kept the talons from shredding the flesh beneath, but he was knocked off his feet.

On the ground, half-stunned, Chefer Kolkin saw that the monster had also stumbled and fallen. But a moment later it was back on its feet and spinning around to charge again—this time crouched on all fours, it seemed. Which was logical enough, given that Chefer Kolkin himself was sprawled flat on the ground.

The creature surged forward. Desperately, Chefer Kolkin tried to interpose his spear. But he knew he wouldn't have time.

Suddenly, seemingly from nowhere, the Liskash was there. Now standing, blood oozing over much of its body, holding a big rock in its hands. Apparently it had lost whatever weapons it once possessed.

The rock did splendidly as a substitute, though. The big Liskash threw it down with great force, striking the monster's skull. The impact flattened the creature and seemed to daze it somewhat.

Somewhat. A sideways blow of a front limb struck the Liskash's lower leg, tearing another gash and sending the Liskash sprawling.

By then, thankfully, the rest of the Mrem warriors had arrived. The Zeg half-brothers had their spears ready, holding the monster at bay, while Puah Neff and Zuel Babic came to Chefer Kolkin's side and began tending to him.

The monster was coming out of its daze quickly—if it had been in one at all. Thwarted in the direction of the Mrem by the spears of the half-brothers, the creature turned its attention to the Liskash.

Who, for its part, was now all but helpless. The Liskash still seemed to be conscious, more or less, but that last wound—or simply accumulated damage and exhaustion—had left it unable to do more than feebly try to lever itself up on one arm while, with the other, it tried to find a rock with which to defend itself.

The monster crept toward it. But then, suddenly, a second Liskash interposed itself. A considerably smaller Liskash—and one who seemed to possess no weapons at all. What did it think it could do?

Sebetwe

There was no chance Sebetwe could control the gantrak, even as battered and confused as it was due to Herere's incredible fight and the completely unforeseen intervention of the Mrem. But he thought he might be able to keep the gantrak stymied long enough for...

Whatever. Perhaps the Mrem would finish it off. Perhaps Herere could be rescued once the rest of the Liskash arrived and they could flee.

Whatever. He had no great hopes or expectations.

He tried to apply *gudh*. But, as he expected, it served no purpose. The great predator's mind was simply impervious to mental bludgeoning.

And thankfully so, all things considered. If Liskash nobility could control the world's most terrible predators with their minds, they would be even more powerful than they were. But that sort of sheer will simply didn't work well on hunters, unless they were small or young.

So, it would rest entirely on Sebetwe's *bradda*. To

make things worse, he hadn't had time to do more than the first of the needed exercises—and certainly didn't have time now. The gantrak was less than two body lengths away and about to charge.

Sebetwe began with a spike of pure glamor, doing his best to surround himself and the recumbent Herere with an aura that would make the monster wonder— leave the creature puzzled, at the least, hopefully tinged with a bit of awe.

It was the greatest such spike he'd ever created. By far. Why? He had no idea. Perhaps it was the peril of the moment. Perhaps it was the exaltation of trying such a feat against such a creature. For all he knew, it was simply caused by the lightheadedness brought on by the rarified atmosphere.

Whatever the cause, the gantrak's forward creep stopped immediately. The monster's head came up. Its two forwardly-focused predator's eyes scrutinized Sebetwe intensely. Somewhat in the manner that such creatures studied their prey, but more like...

Sebetwe's concentration was almost disastrously broken by a laugh. *But more like a possible mate is studied.*

He did not want that much glamor! Again, he had to force down a laugh.

The humor swelled his self-confidence. Now, through the veil of the glamor's aura, he began to insinuate other emotions. The key one was kinship. Gantrak were not pack hunters. But they did mate for life and spent years raising their young. That was enough, he hoped—and blessed be whatever gods and goddesses did exist and never mind what the teachings said—for the tie of kinship to take hold. Long enough, anyway, for whatever else . . .

Might happen. He still hadn't given that any thought at all. Any more than he'd been able to think about Nabliz's situation. The last he'd seen, Nabliz had been trying to control two hatchlings with a snare in each hand. Good luck with that!

The arrival of another Mrem on the open space barely registered on him at all.

CHAPTER 4

Achia Pazik

When she reached the open space where the ledge widened, Achia Pazik was frozen for a moment by the bizarre scene in front of her. To her left, now pressed against the side of the mountain in a half-supine position, was Chefer Kolkin. The warrior was being tended by Puah Neff and Zuel Babic. He seemed shaken and perhaps dazed, but she could see no blood or open wounds on him.

In front of those Mrem crouched the Zeg brothers, their spears leveled at an incredible monster. But the creature was paying them no attention at all—neither them nor the badly injured Liskash lying unconscious on the ground. Instead, the huge predator's attention was fixed entirely on a smaller Liskash kneeling not more than two arm's-lengths away.

Who, for its past—most bizarre sight of all—was doing nothing more than peering intently at the monster. The Liskash not only had no weapons in its hands, the hands themselves were simply pressed flat to the ground. Its pose was not even one of preparation for sudden flight. More like...

A pose of prayer, almost. Except that was insane. *What was the Liskash doing?*

Suddenly, she sensed something familiar. The kneeling Liskash was emanating—if that was the proper term; the power's nature was unclear to Mrem—the same sort of mental aura that Zilikazi had used to destroy her tribe.

Except... not really. The aura was quite different in some ways. That it was some sort of mental force was certain. But it had very little if any of the sheer *will* that had suffused Zilikazi's power. It seemed more like...

She had to grope for a moment before she found the analogy. And then she couldn't help but choke out a half-laugh, half-cry of surprise.

The Liskash was trying to *coax* the monster! Yes! Just as you might try to inveigle a nervous and wary pet to let itself be stroked.

Achia Pazik would never have imagined such a thing was possible. And...

After a few moments, she realized that the Liskash was not succeeding in its purpose. The monster was growing restive, its narrow but fierce mind chafing at the restraints being placed upon it.

And if it got loose, it was likely to kill or at least injure more than just the two Liskash before it was finally brought down.

But if she ordered the Zeg brothers to attack, the monster was sure to break free of whatever strange binds the Liskash had placed upon it. At which point anything might happen. The creature was certainly more likely to go after its assailants than the Liskash.

As she'd been wrestling with this immediate quandary, a thought that had been congealing elsewhere in her mind suddenly came into clear focus.

Whatever powers the kneeling Liskash was trying to wield, she now realized that they actually had little in common with the forces Zilikazi had controlled. Instead, oddly, they reminded her more of the mental aura that she and other Dancers created in their war dance—which was not a "force" so much as a shield. And not a shield deployed in a way that stops a blow directly, but rather deflects it.

Confuses the blow, befuddles the blow.

Again, she choked down a half-laugh. You could even say, seduces the blow!

Without thinking about it, she'd come to her feet and began the first shuffling steps.

This was madness! Yet . . .

Who could say? All of these powers were mysterious and poorly understood.

Within seconds, she was into the full rhythm of the Dance.

Why not?

Sebetwe

Sebetwe had begun to despair when he felt a sudden surge of strength.

No—not strength, so much as a heightened awareness, a better and more acute grasp of the way the gantrak's mind worked. It was as if he could suddenly understand a language that had formerly been nothing but a half-meaningless argot.

His new understanding was not fluent, but good enough that he could insinuate himself—his mind, his spirit, who knew what it was, exactly?—into the creature's mind and quell its growing fury.

Again, he had to qualify. He was not quelling the fury so much as he was undermining it. He was persuading the animal that he was neither prey nor enemy, and doing so in the ancient manner common to most predators—by triggering its surrender reflex.

Most predatory species fight amongst themselves, but rarely do those fights result in death or even severe injuries. At a certain point, the animal that felt itself losing would submit to its opponent; who, for its part, would accept the submission and leave off any further battle.

So too, here and now. Steadily, inexorably—Sebetwe had never felt this sure of himself, this filled with mental acuity so great it transcended normal notions of power—he was bringing the monster to an acceptance that it had fought—fought well; fought furiously—but was simply overmatched.

Where this new capacity had come from, he did not know. He was far too preoccupied with the needs of the moment to even give the matter much thought, beyond a passing wonder. The gantrak was on the verge of surrendering, but Sebetwe could still lose the contest if he fumbled even the least because he was distracted.

Achia Pazik

The Dancer understood the Liskash better than the Liskash understood itself.

No, himself. By now, and in her own very different way, Achia Pazik had penetrated the thing's mind.

His spirit, rather. She could grasp no precise concepts, no clear ideas, nothing that could be given a name. Except, perhaps oddly, the thing's own name. The Liskash called himself Sebetwe.

She was coming to know the Liskash also, far better than she would have ever thought it possible for a Mrem to understand such a creature.

No creature, now. Such a person.

There was great skill here, subtle skill—even sly skill. In its own fashion, Sebetwe's power was as fearsome as Zilikazi's. But it simply couldn't be applied the same way. Sebetwe's method was based on intuition, understanding—recognition. One being shaping another's purpose not by forcing its will upon it but by persuasion.

The form of that persuasion was crude, of course, working with the mind—such as it was—of a savage predator. Achia Pazik did not think it would or could work the same way if applied to an intelligent mind. Sebetwe was not causing the gantrak—from somewhere, that name had come to her also—to hallucinate. He was not tricking the monster into thinking that Sebetwe himself was an even greater one of the same kind. Rather, he was . . .

She wasn't sure what he was doing, in any way she could have put into words. But as she continued the Dance, she *knew*. She had perhaps never been closer to any person than she was in this moment to Sebetwe the Liskash.

She Danced, and Danced, and *knew* that Dakotsi Danced to her left and Mareko to her right. All the tales placed the goddess of wonder and the god of caprice in tandem at such times.

Chefer Kolkin

Chefer Kolkin had recovered enough to be able to follow what was happening. More or less, from the outside. He had no sense of the complex weaving of minds that was transpiring between the still, kneeling Liskash and the whirling Mrem Dancer. But he could see that—somehow—the Liskash was controlling the fearsome monster that had almost killed him. And he could see that—somehow—Achia Pazik was aiding and supporting the Liskash in its effort.

"What does she think she's doing?" hissed Tsede Zeg. But it was a soft hiss, almost a whisper. "Is she crazy?"

"Be silent," Chefer Kolkin commanded. The younger warrior obeyed. On this level, Chefer Kolkin's authority was paramount.

Nabliz

Farther up the slope, in the nest, Nabliz was as puzzled as the Mrem warrior below. He'd expected the effort to control two gantrak hatchlings to be enormous; quite possibly more than he could manage. Even as small as they were—small compared to their parent; each of them still weighed a third as much as Nabliz—and caught in the snares, they were gantrak. Ferocity incarnate. There were larger land predators, but none who would willingly face a gantrak in direct struggle.

And, indeed, so it had been at the beginning. But then, something...happened.

Nabliz had no idea what it was, except that it coincided with the cessation of the noises of fighting coming from down the mountainside. The adult gantrak's screams of fury had died, of a sudden. Thereafter—silence.

That silence was echoed, as it were, up in the nest. The hatchlings had ceased their own screeching and thrashing. Within a few moments, they'd become almost listless, as if they were half asleep.

Nabliz was pleased by the change, of course. Pleased and relieved. But some part of him worried all the more. Whatever else, the gantrak hatchlings had been a known quantity.

What was happening?

Sebetwe

Finally, it was done. The gantrak rolled onto its back, exposing its belly. Its underside was not exactly unarmored, given the toughness of the monster's hide. But it was covered with none of the spines and plates that made so much of its body almost impenetrable by any hand-held weapon.

By now, Sebetwe knew enough of the creature's instincts to make the appropriate response. He leaned over, placed his palm on the gantrak's belly, and then leaned on it with all his weight.

But only for a moment. This was no pet to be

stroked! That one brief but firm touch was enough to close the surrender reflex cycle. Henceforth, the gantrak would be submissive to him.

Not docile, though. Docility was simply not in the nature of a gantrak. But the predator had accepted Sebetwe as his superior.

Might it be possible to actually tame the creature? No adult gantrak had ever been tamed by Liskash. For that matter, Sebetwe knew of only one instance in which an adult gantrak had even been captured alive—and that had been an instant in more senses than one. Within a short time, the monster's captors had been forced to kill it before it managed to break loose from its bonds.

It was hard enough to tame gantrak hatchlings. More than half of those had to be killed also.

But if it could be done...

The power and force of the great predator's spirit, if it could be tapped by a Liskash adept, would be of tremendous assistance against Zilikazi's mental power. It still wouldn't be enough to beat down the noble—Zilikazi's strength was incredible—but it would be enough to fend him off for a time. Perhaps quite a bit of time.

He decided it was worth trying. Provided...

He rose to his feet and turned to the Mrem whose dancing had given him such acuity, in some way that he still couldn't fathom but knew to be true, as surely as he knew anything.

The only way to tame the gantrak would be with the Mrem's continued assistance. Sebetwe had no idea how to persuade the Mrem to do so—even if he knew how to speak its language.

Which he didn't. He knew none of the Mrem tongues. There were said to be dozens of them. Apparently, their mammalian quarrelsomeness extended to speech also.

But to his surprise—certainly his relief—the Mrem spoke in his own language. Even with the dialect of the Krek!

Achia Pazik

Somehow or other—she understood this no better than anything else—Achia Pazik had learned the Liskash's language during the Dance. Quite well, in fact, even if she didn't think she was fluent.

"I am Achia Pazik. And you are Sebetwe, I believe. Of the Kororo...I'm not sure if a 'Krek' is a tribe. But I know you are enemies of Zilikazi."

The Liskash stared at her. "How did you know my name? And the Krek is a creed, not a tribe. All may join, no matter their origin. And, yes, Zilikazi is our enemy. Our greatest enemy."

No matter their origin...

She was pretty sure that sweeping statement had never been intended to included Mrem. But...

It was worth trying. As bizarre as taking shelter among Liskash might be, they needed to take shelter somewhere. On their own, as few of them as there were, running through the wilderness, half of them would be dead before much longer, even if Zilikazi didn't catch up with them.

She was not so naïve as to believe that the enemy of her enemy was necessarily her friend. But, for the moment, she'd accept a simple lack of enmity. They managed so much right here on a mountainside, fighting together against a monster. Who was to say they couldn't manage as much fighting side by side against a much greater monster?

"I learned your name—as I learned to speak your language—when our minds intertwined against the gantrak. Now, Sebetwe, I have a proposal."

After Sebetwe accepted, she explained the situation to the others.

"You're crazy!" exclaimed the Zeg brothers, speaking as one.

"Be silent," Chefer Kolkin commanded. "Achia Pazik is our leader. She decides."

CHAPTER 5

Zilikazi

The third day of the march began late in the morning. Zilikazi would have preferred to begin sooner, as he had done the first two days, but practical reality dictated otherwise. They had entered the foothills by the middle of the afternoon the day before, and the temperature had dropped noticeably. If he ordered his soldiers to begin marching too soon, before they'd been able to soak up some heat from the rising sun, they would be sluggish. The huge train of camp followers who brought up the rear would be still worse, and not even a noble of Zilikazi's power could override the ties between his army and their camp followers. Mates, children, the elderly—no matter how fiercely Zilikazi lashed his soldiers' minds, they would resist simply leaving their folk behind. Not openly, of course; but resistance could take the more subtle form of lethargic incompetence. The soldiers would be taking two steps sidewise and one step back for every four steps forward.

Besides, he didn't want his soldiers unready in case combat erupted. Zilikazi wasn't expecting to encounter any armed resistance yet, but it was hard to predict the behavior of religious fanatics. If the leaders of the Kororo Krek had any sense of military tactics, they'd wait until Zilikazi's much larger and more powerful force was well into the mountains. The terrain would then favor the defenders. Even such a crude and simple tactic as rolling large stones down the slopes would cause casualties.

But who could be sure what the Kororo would do? From what little Zilikazi had been able to glean from the babble of the one he'd had tortured, the Krek's beliefs bordered on outright insanity.

Like all nobles, Zilikazi had little interest in the elaborate theology of the Old Faith. Whatever power the old gods might have possessed had mostly been superseded by the power of the newly-risen nobility. That those decrepit ancient deities still lurked about somewhere, Zilikazi didn't doubt, but they mattered very little any more.

That said, he didn't have any reason to question their nature. First, they were beings, with personal identities—names, genders, personalities. Zilikazi was dubious of some of the specific claims made by the priestesses. The sun deity Huwute, for instance, was almost certainly not female. Only a male god could shine so brightly.

But the errors and biases of the priestesses of the Old Faith were pallid compared to the ravings of the Kororo.

No deities at all, just abstractions given names? Mere facets of a greater and mysterious so-called "godhead"?

Preposterous.

The Kororo didn't even have proper priestesses and shamans—or even priests. Their religious leaders were called "tekkutu." So far as Zilikazi had been able to determine, the term meant "adepts of tekku." Apparently, this so-called "tekku" referred to some sort of mental power over animals.

That such a power might exist was plausible enough. As children, members of the nobility often played with manipulating the minds of animals. But the intrinsic limits of that activity soon made it pall. Most animals simply didn't have enough brains to make controlling them useful. If you tried to force one to open a gate by lifting the latch with a foreleg—assuming the beast was big enough to manage the task at all—it would fumble it, at best. More often than not, the beast's mind would simply shut down under the pressure.

Unless they were predators, especially large ones. Those would resist fiercely and usually successfully. Some would even attack the noble who tried to force his will upon them.

And this fragile mental activity was the source of a Kororo tekkutu's power?

Preposterous.

The Kororo fortifications might be a bit of a problem. They were reputed to be quite strong, in a primitive sort of way. The terrain would certainly be a nuisance. But the end result was not in doubt. Zilikazi estimated it would take him no more than a month to crush the mystics.

Njekwa

The slaughter of the Mrem too badly injured to move on their own or with minor assistance took place at noon. By then, the able-bodied Mrem had already been sent about their slave chores and duties, so there were few around to put up any resistance, and all of those were also injured.

The task was done quickly, efficiently, and with a minimum of fuss, the way Zilikazi's well-trained soldiers went about such things. There weren't really that many badly injured Mrem left by then, anyway. Days had passed since the battle where they received their wounds, and the majority of the wounded had either started to recover or had already died.

Njekwa and the other priestesses and shamans made it a point not to be present at the killing. They raised no public objection, of course. To have done so would have brought the noble lord's wrath down upon them. But the savagery of the deed fit poorly with the precepts of the Old Faith, and none of its practitioners wanted to be in the vicinity when it happened.

The issue wasn't so much one of mercy. Liskash understood the concept, although it figured less prominently in their moral codes than it did (at some times and in some circumstances) for the Mrem. But the Old Faith did place a great premium on *khaazik*, the general principle that harm should be kept to the minimum necessary. Killing those who had no chance of survival was acceptable; indeed, in some situations, a positive good. On the other hand, killing creatures, especially sentient ones, for no greater purpose than to avoid minor inconvenience went against *khaazik*.

Duzhikaa, it was called, which translated roughly as *trespass-upon-observance*. As misbehavior went, it was not as severe as outright criminality, but it was still frowned upon. Severely so, if the misdeed came to the attention of Morushken, goddess of thrift.

But it was in the very nature of Morushken to appreciate all manner of thrift—such as the thriftiness of a high priestess who sheltered her adherents from avoidable punishment. Njekwa was quite sure the goddess would look away, so long as she and the other priestesses and the shamans stayed out of sight and sound of the killing.

Unfortunately, as it turned out, some of her adherents were unclear on the nature of thrift. Youngsters were particularly prone to that error—and especially the one who came before her with two Mrem kits hidden in her basket. This was not the first time Zuluku had been a problem.

"There is no need to kill them," Zuluku insisted. "It was their dam who was badly hurt, not they."

Njekwa looked down at the tiny creatures in the basket. "They are still suckling age, and will be for some time. I think." She wasn't sure how long, because she didn't know that much about the barbarian mammals.

But it didn't matter. A few days would be too long. Newborns of any advanced species required constant feeding.

"They're mammals, Zuluku. Without their dam and her milk, they'll die soon anyway."

The young female looked away, her expression seeming a bit...

Furtive?

The dam is still alive also—and this young idiot is hiding her!

Njekwa started to say something. She wasn't sure what, except that it would be harshly condemnatory. But then Zuluku looked back at her with a new expression. A very stubborn one.

Njekwa hesitated. She had to be careful here, she realized. Young adherents tended to get impatient with the necessary caution their situation required. Some of them—not many, no, but the number might grow—were becoming contentious.

Two had gone so far as to seek refuge with the Kororo in the mountains. Njekwa was afraid others would follow, now that Zilikazi was marching on the Krek. You'd think any Liskash with half a brain would realize that fleeing to the Kororo right when Zilikazi planned to destroy them was sheer folly.

But youth was prone to folly. She had been herself—just a bit—at Zuluku's age.

Best to deflect the matter, she decided. She could shield herself easily enough, and if a young adherent to the Old Faith fell foul of their noble lord, so be it.

"I saw nothing. I know nothing," she said, turning away. A moment later, she heard Zuluku's departing footsteps.

She began composing herself, reaching out for serenity to Yasinta, goddess of the evening. With time and application, Njekwa could forget everything she'd just seen and heard. Well enough to sink below Zilikazi's notice, at least.

Nurat Merav

She woke to pain. Terrible pain, on her left side below the ribs; aching pain most everywhere else.

But fear rode over the pain. Where were her kits? They were much too young to survive on their own.

Her memory was blurred. Despite the age of her kits, Nurat had left them to join the other Dancers once it became clear that the Liskash threatened to overwhelm the warriors because of their noble's mind power. She remembered bits and pieces of the battle that followed, then...

She'd been injured, obviously, but she didn't remember how or when. Her last memories were of stumbling—often crawling—back to the place in the camp where she'd left Naftal and Abi.

The great relief when she'd found them, still quite unharmed even if they were squalling because she'd abandoned them while nursing.

Then...

Nothing.

She pressed down on the injury and was surprised to encounter bandages. Thick ones, even if they were crusted with blood—but the blood seemed to have dried. And the bandages were well placed and tightened by a cinch around her waist.

Who had put them there? She certainly hadn't. The best she'd managed was a crude poultice that she had to keep in place with one of her own hands.

She looked around. She seemed to be in some kind of tent. But it was of no design she recognized. The frame was a circular lattice over which were stretched hide walls. All of it was covered with a dome made of thinner wood strips that supported some sort of felt. There seemed to be a thick lacquer spread over all the roof's surface.

She tried to picture what the structure would look like from the outside, and almost instantly realized that she was looking at a Liskash yurt. She hadn't recognized it for what it was immediately because the interior had none of the decorations that would adorn the exterior. If "adorn" could be used to describe garish colors that usually clashed with each other.

She was a captive, then. And soon would become a slave, once the noble who lorded it over these Liskash turned his attention to her.

A Liskash female came through an opening in the yurt that she hadn't spotted. The opening wasn't a door, just a place where two hides overlapped. She thought the female was quite young.

The hide flaps moved again, and another female came into the yurt. Then, still another.

Three of them, and all young. They were staring down at her intently. What did they want?

She tried to remember the few words of Liskash she knew. Or rather, the few words of the tongue spoken by the Liskash who'd lived in the lowlands near when her tribe had once lived. She had no idea if these Liskash spoke the same language. Mrem dialects—at least, on this side of the newly formed great sea—were all related, many quite closely. But the Liskash had lived here for ... ages. No one knew how long. She'd heard that their languages could be completely different from each other.

Before she could utter more than a couple of halting syllables, however, the second Liskash to enter the yurt spoke to her. In a Mrem dialect that was not her own but was still mostly comprehensible.

"What you *<garble something>*." Nurat wasn't sure, but she though that last word might be a slurred version of "name." And there had seemed to be an interrogative lilt at the end of the short sentence.

Acting on that assumption, she said: "Nurat Merav. What is your name?"

Liskash expressions were unfamiliar to her, but she suspected the stiff-seeming appearance of the creature's face was the Liskash version of a frown.

"You mean my *<garble something which sounded like the same word>*? That was definitely a question.

"My *<slurred version of 'name'>* is Zuluku," the Liskash continued.

Naftal mewled softly. Abi did the same.

"Quiet must!" the Liskash hissed, softly but urgently, as she passed the kits to her. "Very must!"

The three young Liskash females stared at the yurt entrance. They seemed tense and agitated.

Nurat didn't understand what was bothering them so much, but it was clear they felt the kits had to be kept silent. She saw no reason to argue the matter; and, besides, the kits were hungry. So she began nursing them.

After a while, the Liskash seemed to relax. The one who called herself Zuluku turned away from the entrance and stared down at Nurat.

"Why are you doing this?" Nurat asked.

But no answer came. Perhaps the Liskash had not understood the question.

Zuluku

In fact, Zuluku had not understood the question, although she'd recognized most of the words. But even if she had, she would have found it difficult to answer.

Perhaps even impossible. She did not clearly understand herself why she was hiding the wounded barbarian. Part of her motive was certainly her sense of *khaazik*. But only part of it. *Khaazik* was not something that normally moved people to acts of daring, after all.

Most of all, she was driven by deep frustration. At every turn and in every way, her spiritual urges were stymied and suffocated. As a youngster, she'd once heard a Kororo missionary speak to a secret gathering of Old Faith adherents. She had understood very little of what the Kororo had said—almost nothing, being honest—but she'd never forgotten the missionary's sense of sure purpose.

She'd dreamed of that purpose ever since, and gathered around her other young Old Faith adherents who shared her dissatisfaction. None of them had any clearer idea than she did of what their goals should be. They simply felt, in an inchoate way, that they should have some goals that went beyond the never-ending passivity of their religious superiors.

Njekwa seemed to have no goal beyond survival. They wanted more.

In the end, perhaps, they sheltered the badly wounded Mrem and her kits simply because they'd finally found something they could *do*.

CHAPTER 6

Meshwe

"Tekkutu! Tekkutu!" Little Chello came racing toward Meshwe. Chello was still limping a bit from the lingering effects of the tritti-bite, but was so excited that she ignored the pain.

Excited by what? Meshwe wondered. He could see nothing behind her but the narrow lane winding between the town's yurts. Although, now that he concentrated, he thought he could hear some hubbub in the distance.

He wasn't certain, though. At his age, his hearing was mediocre at best.

"What is it, child?" he asked, as the little one raced up. She tried to stop too abruptly, stumbled, and would have fallen if he hadn't caught her.

"It's Sebetwe and the others!" cried Chello. "They're back. And they brought with them—oh, you won't believe me! Come see for yourself!"

The youngling got back on her feet and began tugging Meshwe by the wrist. "Come see! Come see!"

As they neared the town's central plaza, the hub-bub resolved itself into the excited speech of a large crowd. Judging from the tone, the crowd seemed agitated but not panic stricken.

Once they got still closer, Meshwe could distinguish a single voice rising above the others. That was Sebetwe, he was sure. So the hunting party must have returned, then.

Finally, just two rows of yurts from the plaza, Meshwe could make out the words Sebetwe was shouting.

"Stay back, you idiots! If we lose control of them, some of you will get killed!"

That sounded . . . dangerous. Even if the crowd's hubbub still didn't seem that frightened.

"Come on, tekkutu! Come on!" Chello was so excited she finally let go of his wrist and raced ahead of him. He hurried his steps but didn't break into an outright run. At his age, running was not the least bit enjoyable.

He came into the plaza and stopped. Very abruptly. The sight before him was without a doubt the most bizarre thing he'd ever seen—and Meshwe had lived a long and varied life.

In the center of the plaza were two adult and two juvenile gantrak. Judging by the size and subtleties of coloration of the adults, one was female and one was male. A family group, presumably. The trappers who'd gone out to capture (hopefully—the prospect was always chancy) a juvenile gantrak were positioned on either side of the predators, keeping a wary eye on them. The leader of the little party, Sebetwe, had a look of intense concentration on his face.

Meshwe recognized the expression. It was that of a skilled tekkutu maintaining control over a predator.

But controlling an adult *gantrak*? It was unheard of! Meshwe himself would not dare to do it, not even if he had several other tekkutu to assist him.

Then, further back, Meshwe spotted a still more outlandish sight. There was a party of Mrem in the rear. Two handfuls, perhaps more. And in the fore were two Mrem he thought to be females. Both of them were advancing with a peculiar manner—a bizarre one, actually. They were prancing and capering about as if possessed by demons or under the influence of one of the jatta syrups.

It took him a few moments to realize that the Mrem females were engaged in that weirdly frenzied mammalian version of dancing. And another few moments to remember that according to reports the Krek had gotten from its spies in the lowlands, Mrem dancers were able in some unknown and mysterious way to counter the mental power of the Liskash nobility.

Was it possible that...?

Ignoring the noise and excitement around him, Meshwe squatted and began the process needed to place him in tekku. There were several stages to that process—the exact number varied depending on circumstances—and with his long experience and proficiency he was able to pass through the initial ones quickly. But then, entering the phase known as *efta duur*—merging with the target spirit—Meshwe encountered an obstacle.

Not an obstacle so much as turbulence, he realized. It was as if, wading into what he'd thought was a pool, he'd encountered rapids. The clear, crisp, harsh minds of the great predators he sensed nearby were constantly being undercut—perplexed; disarranged, disoriented—by...

What, exactly? He could detect Sebetwe's presence in that turmoil. The young tekkutu seemed to be guiding the gantrak through their confusion, giving them desperately needed clarity and focus. It was only that controlled orientation that kept the ferocious beasts from running wild.

But how was he doing it? No tekkutu, no matter how strong and adept, could possibly maintain that control while simultaneously undermining the normal instincts of a predator. It would be as hard as trying to run a race while juggling knives. Possible theoretically but not in practice.

It was the Mrem, he realized. Somehow, in some way, their dancing—or rather, the mental concentration—no, it was more like force, vigor, tension—they derived from the dancing, was the main factor keeping the gantrak off balance. The mammals, with their weird prancing about, unsettled all of the predators' normal rhythms of behavior. In desperation, the gantrak then leaned on

Sebetwe's tekku presence to provide them with a focus. Their spirits converged with his, as it were.

He was not controlling them in the normal manner of a tekku handling a predator. With minds this great and fierce, that would be impossible. Instead, he was guiding them through the chaos, reassuring them. He was not their master so much as their mentor—it might be better to say, their spiritual counselor.

No—ha! who could have imagined such a thing?—he was their shaman!

Zilikazi

The first attack from the Kororo came as Zilikazi's army was marching up a narrow and steep col two days after they entered the mountains. He'd been expecting it and had warned his commanding officers to be prepared, but it was still an unpleasant surprise.

The surprise—certainly the unpleasantness—came from the manner of the ambush, not the casualties it caused. Empathy was an emotion that, while not entirely absent from the caste of noble Liskash, was very limited in its range. More so for Zilikazi than most. The sight of his soldiers crushed and mangled by the rocks that had come crashing down the slopes was purely a matter for tactical calculation. Suffering casualties, including fatal and crippling ones, was a necessary feature of soldiers, no more to be rued or regretted than the rough hides of draft animals.

What *did* bother Zilikazi—not quite concern, but close—was the method used by the Krek's warriors. The Kororo had been able to trigger the rockfalls while staying far enough away to nullify Zilikazi's mind power. He could detect them, but their mental auras were somehow obscured as well as dimmed by distance. Trying to impose his will upon them, at this range, was like trying to catch fish swimming in a murky stream with your bare claws. He might be able to move fast enough but he couldn't detect their location well enough.

How were they doing that? And how were they causing the rockfalls? Presumably his soldiers would discover those secrets once they advanced farther into the range. In the meantime, there was nothing to be done but heal those who could be healed and euthanize those who would never recover.

Zilikazi did not maintain a medical corps, as such. He relied on the females who still adhered to the Old Faith to serve him in that capacity, since the witless creatures insisted on maintaining their silly beliefs and rituals. They might as well be good for something. He did, however, keep a cadre of medical inspectors who would ensure that the females did not waste valuable resources tending to those injured soldiers who were doomed anyway.

The Old Faith's notions of *khaazik* and *duzhikaa* were not absurd, in and of themselves. Any sensible and capable ruler understood the principles of thriftiness and obedience to norms. But the relative weight that the Old Faith assigned to those beliefs was impractical at best. Why keep a soldier alive who was so badly injured that he would never again be able to serve his purpose? That was simply a waste of food and healing supplies. Better to put him down quickly and efficiently—and painlessly, so far as possible, there was no need to be cruel—in order to concentrate resources on those who might someday be able to rejoin the ranks and be of use to Zilikazi.

But he spent little time musing on the matter. The medical inspectors would take care of the problem for him.

Zuluku

"What should we do?" asked Raish, peering through the slightly open flap of the yurt. Her anxiety was plain in the timber of her voice. "The inspector will be here soon. If he comes in, he's bound to discover..."

She nodded toward the far side of the yurt, where they'd hidden the Mrem and her kits under a mound of hides and thrushes. That had been enough to fool the soldiers who'd carried in their terribly injured comrade and given him over for treatment. They'd been in a hurry, since Zilikazi's officers didn't tolerate slackness when it came to minor tasks like tending to the wounded. But it wouldn't be enough to fool the inspector. Adherents to the Old Faith had been known to hide severely damaged soldiers and the inspector would be on the alert for that. He'd poke through any piles that were big enough to hide a large body.

Zuluku wasn't worried about the wounded soldier himself. He was barely alive and certainly wasn't conscious.

What to do...?

Raish drew back from the open flap, a look of surprise on her face. A moment later, Njekwa came through into the yurt, pushing Raish aside not by physical force but by her sheer presence. When she chose to be, the priestess could be intimidating.

Njekwa cast a quick, knowing glance at the pile of hides and thrushes, and then looked down at the wounded soldier.

"Idiots," she said, her tone calm and even. "Did you give any thought to what might happen?"

The priestess knelt and gave the soldier a quick and thorough examination.

"He has no chance," she said. "Not once the inspector sees him. Bring over the blade and the bowl."

Zuluku, realizing her intent, hesitated.

"*Now*," Njekwa commanded.

Whatever her qualms and doubts might be, Zuluku had obeyed that voice since she was a youngling. She and Raish moved quickly to bring over the implements.

"Hold up his head," Njekwa said. "Over the bowl. You know—"

She didn't need to say anything further. Zuluku had done this before, on three occasions. She lifted the soldier's head, as gently as possible, and brought it over the wide bowl that Raish held in position.

Neatly, quickly, efficiently, Njekwa severed one of the great veins in the soldier's neck, being careful not to slice the artery. The cut was as small as possible for the purpose, not a great gash that would allow fountains of blood to spill everywhere.

It didn't take long for the soldier's life to drain away. Thanks to Brassu, the goddess of tranquility, he never regained consciousness.

When it was done, Raish removed the bowl and Zuluku lowered the soldier's head back onto the hide he'd been resting on. After cleaning the blade, Njekwa assisted her in rolling the hide around the corpse.

Zuluku was about to finish the process, covering the face and tying the laces, when Njekwa said: "Wait." The priestess's head was turned toward the entrance flap.

Listening, Zuluku could hear footsteps approaching. A moment later, the medical inspector came into the yurt. He took two steps within, gazed down at the corpse and the three females—one of them still holding the bowl full of blood—and grunted with satisfaction. Then, without a word, he turned and left the yurt.

Sighing, and trying not to quiver from tension, Zuluku said softly: "Thank you, Priestess."

Njekwa's responding grunt held more in the way of sarcasm, perhaps, than satisfaction. But she said nothing further and a moment later, she too had left the yurt.

Meshwe

"Now I understand," said Meshwe to Sebetwe. "The Mrem dancing gives us strength—say rather, finer control—at the same time as it confuses—say rather, confounds—the gantrak."

Sebetwe issued the throaty Liskash version of a chuckle. "I'm still groping for the right words. I think we may have to invent some. But, yes, that's about my sense of what happens also."

Both of them studied the gantraks. They had to look up to do so. It had taken the better part of the afternoon, but the family of predators had now settled down, more or less. Working hard under Meshwe's commands, members of the Krek had erected a fair imitation of a gantrak nest atop a small hillock on the edge of the town.

Then, they studied the Mrem. The mammals had been given three yurts not far from the hillock. They were supply yurts, not personal dwellings. But they were clean and had been emptied of their former contents.

Most of the Mrem were inside the yurts, no longer visible. But their leader, the young female called Achia Pazik, was squatting outside one of the yurts and returning their scrutiny.

Calmly. And there was obvious calculation in that gaze.

Good signs, both.

"We will need to find more Mrem dancers," Sebetwe said.

Meshwe made no reply. The conclusion was also obvious.

The scouts had come back with their reports. Zilikazi was coming. The traps would damage his army, but not enough.

CHAPTER 7

Nurat Merav

Nurat had watched the quick and efficient slaughter of the badly wounded Liskash soldier carried out by the females in the yurt. She'd also observed the encounter between the females and the male who'd briefly entered the yurt afterward. He'd seemed to be an official of some kind.

Her view of the incidents had been limited, just what she could see through the small opening—no more than a slit—she'd created in the pile of hides and thrushes the females had hastily piled on top of her and her kits. She'd understood none of their speech, either. She thought she recognized two of the words they'd used, although she wasn't even sure of that.

But, by now, one thing was clear to her. For whatever reason, the female Liskash were protecting Nurat and her kits. They'd not only provided her with healing treatments but they'd gone to considerable length—and considerable personal risk, she suspected—to keep the Mrem hidden.

Hidden from whom? She didn't know, precisely. But whatever Liskash officials they were hiding them from, ultimately they were hiding them from Zilikazi himself.

How could they be doing that? Nurat had felt herself the Liskash noble's incredible might. She wouldn't have thought a small group of female Liskash could counter that mental power.

But, then, she understood very little of the way that mind control worked. Perhaps it could be evaded, if not directly countered.

If you knew how to do it, which she didn't.

And why hadn't Zilikazi detected her, for that matter? He'd seemed to have no trouble finding the minds of the Dancers and the warriors in the battle and crushing them like so many eggs.

Everything was a mystery, everywhere she looked.

She would have to learn the Liskash language, as fast as she could.

This Liskash language, she reminded herself. Unlike the Mrem, the Liskash had a vast array of tongues and speech.

Nurat Merav had always been adept at learning different Mrem dialects. Hopefully, that skill would apply here as well.

Zilikazi

Something was stirring up the females. Zilikazi could sense their unease—and what seemed to be unrest, perhaps even a small amount of resistance. But his mental powers did not enable him to understand the actual thoughts of others, only their emotions—and those, only blurrily.

The ability of a Liskash noble to force others to do his (and very occasionally her) bidding rested, ultimately, on the noble being able to grasp the emotions of those he would subordinate. But the grasp was that of a hand—and a gloved hand at that—upon a crudely-felt object, not that of delicate fingers probing the subtle texture of a surface. A noble could crush an egg, so to speak, but he could not really feel it or even give it a slight crack.

Besides, Zilikazi was preoccupied with the campaign against the Kororo, which was proving to be considerably harder than he'd anticipated. So he gave little thought to whatever might be happening with the females. Why bother? There would be plenty of time after the campaign to deal with any problems that might exist. As long as he controlled his army, what difference did it make what got females agitated? Like eggs, they too could be crushed.

Another rock slide came crashing down the slope of the mountainside. Once again, Zilikazi's mind tried to find and destroy the will of those who opposed him, but he could not find them. It was as if his gloved hand groped at slippery fish wriggling down a fast-moving stream. He could sense them but not their precise locations.

This, he now realized, was what the Krek meant by their concept of "tekku." He had thought it to be nothing much more than twaddle, but he'd been mistaken. Somehow the Kororo were using an attunement to certain animals—predators, he thought, with clear and simple purposes—to provide them with a shield against him.

Tekku was a real mental ability, then, albeit subtle and certainly nothing compared to his own in terms of sheer force. Eventually he would pin them down and force them to submit.

Sebetwe

"They've reached Nesudi Pass," reported the runner from the Krek warriors trying to resist Zilikazi's advancing army. "We can probably fend them off for two more days, but no longer."

Despite the distance he'd traveled as fast as he could, Khuze was not breathing hard. He'd had to rest for the night before reaching the Krek, and had taken the time in the morning to warm up before resuming his run. That last stretch had taken only a short time, as runners measured such things.

Watching Khuze as he spoke, Sebetwe found himself—as he did quite often of late—envying the ability of the Mrem to handle cold temperatures as well as they did. There were major disadvantages to being a mammal, to be sure. The amount of food the creatures needed to consume was astounding! How did they get anything done besides eating? But he still envied them, every time he or the Krek had to wrestle with the drawbacks of living in the mountains.

Khuze's statement had been greeted with silence. A bit belatedly, because he'd gotten distracted by his musings, Sebetwe realized the Krek guiding council was waiting for *him* to respond.

Why? He was the most skilled of the younger tekkutu—more skilled than any of the older ones except Meshwe, for that matter—but he was not a war leader. Like any adult Kororo he was proficient in the use of weapons and knew the basic principles of tactics. That was as far as it went, however. There were three or four people squatting in the command yurt who would have a far better notion than he did of how to handle the current situation.

Once Zilikazi's army forced its way through Nesudi Pass, there would be no obstacle to their further progress until they reached the next range of mountains, where the Krek eyrie was located. They'd be passing across a broad and fairly flat plateau which provided little opportunity for the sort of long-distance ambush that had been the Krek's most successful tactic thus far.

Let Zilikazi get close enough...as was bound to happen if Kororo warriors had to fight the noble's army at close range...

There would be no way to resist him. Not even with the help of the gantrak. Sebetwe could only control one of the creatures, and then only with the assistance of the two Mrem dancers. He could not be certain, of course, without making the attempt. But he didn't think he could withstand Zilikazi's power at close range.

If they had more dancers, the situation might be different. Although even with the help of two gantraks, Zilikazi couldn't be held off indefinitely.

If they had more gantrak...which would require still more dancers...

He came to his reluctant conclusion.

"We must leave the eyrie and retreat through the mountains," he said. "In the ranges, we can slow down Zilikazi. Even without rock falls prepared ahead of time, we can improvise traps and barriers. On the plateau, we can't. It's as simple as that."

He looked around the circle. "And we need to find more Mrem. Without more dancers, we can't control enough gantrak to make a big enough difference."

One of the Krek's two main war leaders grunted. Logula, that was. "If we can find enough gantrak in the first place. The beasts are not plentiful, and not easy to catch."

There was that, too. But Sebetwe still didn't think they had any choice.

"Perhaps Zilikazi will turn back..." That tentative musing came from Nokom, the oldest of the females on the council. "There is really nothing here worth his while."

Meshwe make a sharp gesture of negation. "That's an idle fancy. If Zilikazi were going to turn back he would have done so already. And there *is* something here worth his while to destroy—the Krek itself. So long as we exist, he will consider us a threat to his rule."

He swiveled his head and gazed at the wall on the southeast side of the yurt beyond which, still a considerable distance away, was the Dzundu Sea. There were rumored to be lands on the other side of that sea, but its far shores had never been observed by any of the Kororo scouts who had ventured that far. Their reports only spoke of a large island a fairly short distance from the mainland.

"Fairly short" was an abstract measurement, however. The span of water between the mainland and the island was quite large enough for the huge monsters who swam in the seas. The scouts had seen them coming to the surface.

Needless to say, no scouts had ever made the attempt to cross over to the island. Swimming would be simple suicide, even if anyone were strong enough to get all the way across, and using a boat wouldn't be much safer. It might be possible to build a raft big enough to withstand the assault of a sea monster. But no one knew for sure.

With the exception of a few clans, neither Liskash nor Mrem were skilled at sea travel. Whenever they did venture onto the sea—even very large lakes—they generally used simple skiffs and coracles and stayed very close to shore. Marine and aquatic predators were much bigger and more powerful than even the largest land carnivores.

"We will have to hope that one of two things is true," Meshwe continued. "First, that once we retreat far enough Zilikazi will be satisfied that we no longer constitute a danger to him and will turn back."

Logula issued another grunt. "Not likely. There is no more persistent noble in the world."

Meshwe nodded. "Still, he can't pursue us forever. We can travel faster than he can, with that huge force he has. Which brings me to our second hope, which is that we can continue retreating once we reach the sea."

Nokom looked up with alarm. "We don't *know*?"

"I am afraid not. Our scouts never followed the shore for any distance to the south. We have no idea what might lie in that direction."

"What about following the shore toward the north?" asked Logula.

"Not possible," said Meshwe. "Not for the whole Krek, at any rate. A few particularly hardy individuals might manage to do it. There is a very deep canyon with a swiftly moving river at the bottom. Almost sheer cliffs, according to the scouts who discovered the canyon some years ago."

"Canyons can be crossed, even ones with swift rivers," said Logula.

"Yes, certainly. But not without building bridges and laying guide ropes—and how long would that take? We can't move *that* much faster than Zilikazi. Long before we finished constructing what we'd need to get through the canyon, his army would have arrived—and we'd be completely trapped."

Again, Logula grunted. The sound, this time, conveyed agreement, if not satisfaction.

Meshwe now turned back to Sebetwe. "And that brings us to the next and perhaps most difficult questions. Can we find more Mrem? And would they agree to help us?"

"I don't know."

"Find out."

Achia Pazik

"I don't know the answer to either question," Achia Pazik said to Sebetwe. "But since the answer to the second question depends upon answering the first, we should make plans to that end."

"Yes, that makes sense," said Sebetwe. "Where are more Mrem from your tribe most likely to be found?"

Achia Pazik had to restrain herself from throwing up her hands in a gesture of futility. "I don't know the answer to that question either," she admitted.

Sebetwe got an expression on his face that resembled a yawn. Achia Pazik thought it was the Liskash equivalent of a smile. It was hard to tell. The features of the reptiles were stiffer and less mobile than those of her people.

"So it seems we need to address that one first," he said. "How many of your people can you send out to accompany our scouts? I think without you to talk to anyone we encounter, they will not be willing to listen to us."

Achia Pazik chuckled. There wasn't much humor in the sound. "They'd be much more likely to try to kill you."

CHAPTER 8

Meshwe

The Krek began its march two days later. By then, Zilikazi's army had made its way entirely through Nesudi Pass and had come onto the plateau. Had that army been made up only of warriors, it would have been able to move more quickly. But it was not. For every warrior there were three or four camp followers, most of them females and younglings.

The Krek was not moving much faster. The Kororo also had younglings, elderly and infirm members, some of whom had to be transported if they could not move on their own. In addition, as was true of Zilikazi's army, they had to bring supplies with them. They could not count on foraging—not enough, certainly—while on the march.

If anything, their burdens were even heavier. Beyond supplies, the invaders were bringing nothing with them except simple yurts. The Kororo, on the other hand, were trying to salvage as much as they could of all their belongings. Even if they were able to return to the eyrie someday, Zilikazi's warriors and camp followers would plunder everything left behind and burn whatever they could not carry away.

But the Kororo had a greater incentive to move

quickly, of course. The situation was another illustration of the old saw that, in a chase, the hunter runs for his lunch and the hunted runs for his life. Every member of the Krek knew full well that if they couldn't stay far enough ahead of Zilikazi's army, the noble would shackle their minds. The powers of the tekkutu could shield them to a degree, but that degree depended largely on distance.

Calling tekku a "shield" was misleading, actually. The main effect for a tekkutu of drawing upon the consciousness of a predator was to withdraw, in a sense, from the psychic realm in which the nobles held sway. A predator's fierce and narrow mind ignored the faculties of the nobles altogether. They simply did not exist for them, any more than such a predator would be swayed or influenced by logical reasoning or argumentation or peroration—or poetry, for that matter.

That made the mind of the tekkutu partnered with the predator something slippery, its presence sensed but its location uncertain, undetected—hidden in a fog, mentally speaking.

But even the thickest fog can be penetrated, if the observer gets close enough. So it was here. Most of the Kororo tekkutu trailed behind the main body of the Krek, using their powers to veil them from Zilikazi's mindsight. But they could only do so successfully if enough distance was maintained from the oncoming army.

Initially, Meshwe had hopes that Sebetwe's control of the gantraks might enable them to hold off Zilikazi indefinitely. But that proved not to be true.

For one thing, they could only use one gantrak at a time. They'd found that if they tried to harness both of the adult predators simultaneously and make them leave their younglings behind, the creatures resisted fiercely. The risk of losing control of them entirely became too great.

So, the tekkutu could only use one of them if they left the Krek's current immediate vicinity. And the strength of just one of the great predator's spirits was simply not enough to enable Sebetwe—or any tekkutu including Meshwe himself—to withstand Zilikazi's mind control if the noble got close enough.

That said, by coupling with a gantrak Sebetwe *could* accomplish two things. First, he could get much closer to Zilikazi than would have been heretofore possible. Not close enough to assassinate him, but still close enough to bring back much more precise information than they could have obtained by spying on the noble's army from a great distance.

More useful, though, was the second ability Sebetwe gained. He could shield a number of the Krek's warriors for much longer than he could have without the gantrak. Long enough to enable them to create bigger rockfall traps in Zilikazi's path than they'd expected to be able to, and traps that could be set off with better accuracy and timing because Sebetwe could stay behind for much longer. They wouldn't have to rely on mechanical triggers, which were imprecise and susceptible to being discovered by scouts and disarmed.

None of this allowed the Kororo to do anything other than retreat, true enough. But they could retreat in reasonably good order and at a pace that the entire Krek could manage.

What was perhaps most important was that the additional time Sebetwe could provide them would help their own scouting parties, both those ranging ahead seeking the best routes as well as those which were spreading through the mountains in search of other Mrem bands who had also managed to escape Zilikazi's crushing of their tribe.

Nabliz

The leader of one of those scouting parties was feeling disgruntled, and for a variety of reasons.

First, because the terrain they'd been passing through for the past three days was rough, with little even in the way of animal trails. Second, because at this altitude and at this time of year, he and his fellow Liskash warriors were very sluggish in the morning.

Third, because the Mrem accompanying them, a warrior named Chefer Kolkin, seemed to have no trouble at all getting started at daybreak.

Fourth, because it was obvious the miserable furball managed that annoying feat by eating twice as much as anyone else in the party!

Being fair about it, the Mrem was carrying his own food.

Being petty and ill-humored about it, his food smelled bad.

Being *really* petty and ill-humored about it, the food didn't taste very good either—which Nabliz knew because the miserable furball had offered him some, thereby upsetting his well-constructed view of the inherent selfishness of furballs.

(They ate too much. It followed that they had to squabble over food, didn't it? And didn't it thereby also follow that they were by nature a squabbling and quarrelsome breed?)

(Apparently not—which just gave Nabliz yet another source of vexation. He disliked it when reality did not match his preconceptions. Especially in the morning.)

On a more positive side, Nabliz knew from experience that his foul temper would fade away within two hours after sunrise. A wiser and more charitable soul than himself—Meshwe, and probably Sebetwe as well—would have accepted all along that the disagreeable nature of the Mrem at dawn was really a function of the Liskash's own metabolism, and that the furball was quite innocent in the matter.

The knowledge did him no good at all at the moment, though. It just gave him a sixth reason to be grouchy. Early in the morning, Nabliz disliked wise and charitable souls.

Being fair about it, early in the morning, Nabliz disliked pretty much anything and everyone. At home, back in the comfort of the Krek, he'd still be asleep at this wretched time of day, as would any sensible Liskash.

So, he spent the next hour or so detesting Zilikazi, who was, after all, ultimately responsible for Nabliz's foul state of mind that morning.

And every morning, for that matter.

And every afternoon and evening too, now that he thought about it. The vile noble had a lot to answer for.

Chefer Kolkin

Now that he'd had a bit of experience dealing with the Liskash at close quarters, Chefer Kolkin had learned to keep his distance from them in the morning. The reptiles tended to be surly in the first hour or two, especially if they arose as early as they had been since they began this expedition. Even though he was the grouchiest of the small group at that time of day, the one named Nabliz who was in charge insisted that they all be ready to resume the expedition by dawn.

Chefer Kolkin understood the reason for their peculiar behavior—or thought he did, at any rate. The Liskash were not exactly reptiles, although Chefer Kolkin routinely used the word to refer to them, as did all Mrem. They seemed to be somewhere between mammals and reptiles, in terms of their energy and activity levels. Unlike true reptiles, they had a certain—fairly large, in fact—reserve of energy which they could draw upon even when they were cold. They benefited from basking in the sun, especially at daybreak, before they tried to engage in any activity that was more energetic than eating. But they weren't as dependent on using sunlight to raise their energy levels as true reptiles were.

Perhaps oddly, what Chefer Kolkin found most unsettling about them was how little they ate. More precisely, how little they ate most of the time—and how much they gorged when they did finally sit down for what they considered a real meal.

There hadn't been any of that on this expedition, though. The similarity between Liskash and true reptiles was most evident after they'd gorged themselves. The next day, they were almost as torpid as a snake who'd swallowed whole prey. They weren't very active the following day, either.

In the safety and comfort of the Krek's eyrie, that hadn't been a problem. But it was clear to Chefer Kolkin that Nabliz had ordered his warriors to refrain from any heavy eating on this expedition. They couldn't afford to waste a day or two just digesting a big meal. So, they made do on what the Liskash seemed to consider light rations—which, from Chefer Kolkin's point of view, barely qualified as snacks.

For the first time in his life, the Mrem warrior was contemplating the idea that perhaps there were some advantages to being a Liskash instead of a Mrem. The notion was unsettling, of course. But he was an experienced warrior and a proficient scout, and it was a simple fact that for all their grumpiness in the morning, the Liskash were covering at least as much ground as a party of Mrem were—in part, because they weren't laden down with the heavy packs that a Mrem needed to carry his food in these barren highlands.

As Chefer Kolkin did. And the pack chafed. Especially in the morning.

True be told, he was feeling pretty peevish himself.

Lavi Tur

As it happened, a Mrem still too young to be a warrior was contemplating the same idea. In his case, though, without the irritation of a heavy pack weighting him down since he was walking alongside the litter carrying what few possessions his Mrem band had retained when they joined the Kororo and—never let it be said that diplomacy didn't have its uses—Achia Pazik had persuaded the Kororo to give them two beasts of burden to do the work of hauling those possessions.

True, the beasts had their full share of reptilian sullenness at this high altitude. You had to be careful not to place your feet where they could step on them or the rest of your body where they could nip you. Surly brutes.

But they didn't smell bad—they hardly seemed to defecate, either—and a bit of wariness was far less tiring than hard labor, when you got right down to it.

Lavi Tur also had the benefit of his age. He'd often been irritated by the limits that age placed upon him. But he also lacked the much deeper irritation of a full life spent being limited by experience. His mind could range freely; more than those of most Mrem.

So, he was contemplating the possibility that the very nature of the Liskash could, at least in some circumstances, give them a mental advantage over Mrem. Less able to deal with reality by the use of sheer vigor, perhaps they compensated to a degree with reflection and meditation. A Mrem had to remind himself to look before he leapt; to measure before he cut; to think twice before he acted. To a Liskash, those things came rather naturally.

This much he had concluded so far, in the manner that brash youth sniff disdainfully at the stolid certainties of their elders: even from what little Achia Pazik had translated for him, it was clear to Lavi Tur that the Kororo creed was far more sophisticated than the one he'd been raised within.

When you got right down to it, Mrem tribal beliefs—he thought they barely qualified as religion—were childlike. Downright silly, in many cases.

From what little he knew of them, he thought traditional Liskash creeds were no more sophisticated, and probably even less.

The teachings and beliefs of the Kororo, on the other hand...

The day before, Achia Pazik had explained to him that the old Kororo priest (or was he a shaman? possibly even a sorcerer?) named Meshwe did not believe *any* gods were real. Not, at least, in the way that the Mrem envisioned Aedonniss and Assirra—as real beings, who could not be seen simply because they were so gigantic and powerful that their forms fell beyond mortal vision.

Meshwe didn't believe in any of the Liskash gods, either—even though the Liskash had far more of them than did the Mrem. They had gods or goddesses for everything, it seemed. Achia Pazik had told him of some of them:

Huwute, the sun goddess.

Ishtala, the moon god.

Ghammid, the god of good fortune.

Yasinta, the goddess of the evening.

Morushken, the goddess of thrift. She also seemed to be a deity given to pity and compassion, but those aspects were less prominent. The Liskash had a thrifty sense of mercy, apparently. As an almost-warrior, Lavi Tur didn't really disapprove.

But however many deities the Liskash professed to believe in, the creed of the Kororo was that none of them were truly real. They were simply manifestations of what they called "the Godhead," produced by the inherent limits of mortal minds. In the very nature of things, neither Liskash nor Mrem could grasp divinity in its full and complete splendor. So, mortals essentially invented "gods and goddesses" as a means of comprehending at least some of the aspects of divinity—and those, only poorly and in part.

Meshwe had told Achia Pazik that mortals were like insects trying to grasp the nature of a Liskash. (Or a Mrem, he had added, perhaps out of politeness.) With their poor vision, able to see only a portion of a Liskash at a time, they would come up with the idea that there was "a toe goddess" and a "claw god." And they would imagine those toes and claws in their own insectile manner.

Lavi Tur had no idea if Meshwe and the other Liskash priests were right in their beliefs. What he did know was that those beliefs were far more interesting than the tales of Aedonniss and Assirra.

What a marvelous adventure this was turning out to be!

CHAPTER 9

Nurat Merav

"Are we finished with the mountains?" Nurat Merav asked weakly. The past few days had been very hard on her. Despite the best efforts of the young Liskash females who'd been sheltering her and her kits, the rigors of travel through rough terrain had almost killed her. So it felt, anyway.

Twice, they'd had to dismantle the yurt completely, since the trail was too steep for the big draft animals that normally carried it perched on a great litter. Too narrow, rather—the beasts were immensely strong and surefooted, but they had to be able to march two abreast to carry the litter. During those periods, Zuluku and the other females had concealed Nurat Merav within a great rolled bundle carried by one of the animals.

They'd been warm, at least. But the constant jolting had been stressful, and the lack of food even worse. It seemed that during times like this, Liskash simply went without eating for two days or even more. They'd made up for it when they reached the plateau by preparing a great feast.

While that sort of regimen might have suited the reptiles well enough, it was not good for Mrem, even healthy ones. For someone trying to recover from injuries like Nurat Merav's, it was far worse.

She hadn't complained, though. She knew the reason the female Liskash hadn't fed her during those periods was because they couldn't. At Zilikazi's order, all foodstuffs and cooking equipment and implements had been stored away. They'd most likely have been spotted if they'd tried to feed Nurat Merav and her kits.

Thankfully, her kits were not much given to squalling. It was a good thing, too. While the Liskash beasts of burden made quite a racket themselves, there was precious little resemblance between their basso grunts and bellows and the high-pitched squeals of unhappy Mrem kits.

"Yes," Zuluku replied. "For at least four *<garble something>*." Nurat Merav wasn't sure, but from the context she thought the word she hadn't understood meant *days*.

"And after that?" she asked.

Zuluku looked unhappy. From experience, the Mrem Dancer was coming to recognize the facial expressions used by Liskash. She'd found they substituted subtleties in the way they moved their jaws for the lack of mobility in other parts of their faces. This particular half-open, lower-jaw-skewed-to-the-left grimace indicated a mixture of distress and apprehension, but one which fell short of extreme anxiety. *That* would have been indicated by jaws held wide open.

"Not sure," was the answer. "If the Kororo fight *<garble something>*, travel may become very hard again."

The lower jaw closed further and shifted to the right. That seemed to indicate something along the lines of *dawning-hope*, or maybe *anticipation-of-improvement*. A Mrem would assume an exaggerated upside-down smile and a wag of the head.

"But the warriors I talked to *<garble something>* that was not likely." That word must mean *thought*, or maybe *believed*. "They say the Kororo can no more use *<garble something>* because they won't have time to *<garble something>* the way they did before. If they try, Zilikazi will get close enough to *<garble something>*."

That seemed... fairly clear. If she was interpreting Zuluku correctly, the Kororo would not be able to put up enough resistance in the next range of mountains to require Zilikazi and his army to move off the road into the narrow trails. The yurt would remain intact, which would make it easier for them to keep Nurat Merav and her kits hidden—and fed.

Moved by a sudden impulse, she said: "You have been a good friend. I thank you for it."

The expression that now came to Zuluku's face was not one Nurat Merav had seen before. It seemed to have traces of *uncertainty* and... *chagrin?* No, more like *doubt*.

But all the Liskash said was: "We are <*garble something*> by Morushken to be thrifty in all things."

Zilikazi

After the frustrations of the passage through the mountains, Zilikazi was almost enjoying the march across the plateau.

Exasperating, that had been. The traps, pitfalls and rockslides set off by the Kororo had taken a toll on Zilikazi's equanimity as well as his army's numbers. Many more of his soldiers had been injured than killed, it was true. But Zilikazi wasn't sure if that was a blessing or a curse. While on campaign, one wounded warrior required two or three to tend to him. Injury depleted an army's strength faster than death did.

But the wounded could not be left behind, or dispatched, unless they clearly couldn't survive their wounds. There were limits to any noble's power, even one as mighty as Zilikazi. His control over his warriors depended more on their acquiescence than his sheer force of mind. If nothing else, he had to sleep—and who would protect him from his protectors then?

In the end, as in any society of intelligent and social animals, the power of the masters depended on a great lattice of custom, ritual and accepted practice. Brute force was needed to maintain that lattice, for there were always those who sought to unleash chaos. But force could not substitute for it.

So, the wounded were tended to—and well; better than they would have been in most Liskash armies. And the army's lord and master accepted the need for patience.

But he was glad now that he had made the decision to bring his whole realm on the march. He had left no one behind except those too ill or infirm or old to march, and the few needed to take care of them. Doing so had run the risk of allowing one of his neighbors to overrun his lands, but he had deemed it a risk worth taking. If need be, he could retake the lands when he was done with the Kororo and he thought all his neighbors understood that quite well. He'd already beaten the most powerful of them, had he not?

The greater danger had been rebellion. He could not predict how long the campaign against the Kororo would take, for some of the terrain would be new to him—most of it, if the Kororo chose to flee. (As, indeed, they had chosen to do.)

If Zilikazi's absence from his lands was prolonged, and if he'd left a large force behind, one of his lieutenants was likely to grow ambitious. After the successful wars he'd waged against his neighboring nobles, the strongest enemy he could face would come from within his own ranks, if he let slip his grip.

No, best to bring everyone with him. Under his direct and watchful eye, none of his subordinates would even think of rising against him.

Meshwe

"You're certain?" Meshwe asked.

The scout nodded firmly. His fellow added: "There's just no way, Tekkutu. It's not a deep ravine the same as it is trying to the north. But the river that runs into the sea on the south is very wide, and there are marshlands on both sides. We could certainly cross it, given time—"

"A *lot* of time," the first scout said.

"—but I don't think we'll have much time. Not enough."

Meshwe looked away and pondered the matter. "But you say the area is wooded?"

"It's something of a forest, even down close to the shore," said one. "But it isn't dense enough for us to hide from Zilikazi in it. Not the whole Krek."

Meshwe shook his head. "I understand that. But is there enough wood to build rafts that would allow us to cross over to the island?"

Now, the scouts looked confused.

"Well . . . Yes, certainly. But . . ."

"But . . ." his companion chimed in.

Meshwe grimaced. "I know the strait is full of

monsters. But surely some of the rafts would make it across. And what other option do we have?"

Sebetwe

The trap was almost ready. Sebetwe just had to hold Zilikazi's mind at bay for another five minutes. By then, the lead elements of his army would be too far into the gully to make their escape when the dam was ruptured.

The flood that followed wouldn't be enough to hurt most of that great army. They'd only had two days to let the water pile up behind the dam, and it wasn't a great river to begin with. More in the way of a large creek, really. Still, there'd be enough of a flood to kill dozens of Zilikazi's troops; maybe as many as a hundred, if luck went their way.

Looked at from one angle, that wouldn't be much more than a pinprick. Sebetwe had now gotten close enough to have a good idea of the size of Zilikazi's army. There had to be at least six thousand warriors down there. More, if you added those still too injured to walk but recuperating.

There were other factors involved than simple numbers, however. Sebetwe was pretty sure the morale of Zilikazi's army wasn't too good right now. Better than it had been two or three days ago, yes, due to the greater ease of traveling across the plateau. But if they suffered a sudden and sharp blow just as they entered the next range of mountains...

That army had its own scouts, who'd been ranging ahead off to the sides. By now, at least some of them would have returned and given their reports. The gist of which would be that this next mountain range was wider than the first had been, and if the terrain was no worse—might not be quite as bad, in fact—the roads were ancient memories and the trails were mostly figments of the imagination.

Zilikazi would order the scouts to remain silent, but they were bound to talk to their mates nonetheless. As word spread through the noble's army that they still had many days of slogging ahead of them, their morale would sag again. The flood would damage their spirits far more than it would their bodies.

There came another unseen blow from Zilikazi's mind. The noble was now just trying to batter his way past Sebetwe's shield. He'd apparently given up trying to penetrate the psychic fog that Sebetwe had created.

The force of that blow was well-nigh astonishing. It was almost like being struck by a physical blow delivered by an ogre. But, again, Sebetwe was able to shed the force. The pure focus—you could even call it indifference—that the gantrak's narrow fierce mind gave to Sebetwe was in its own way also well-nigh astonishing.

Whether he was real or not, Sebetwe whispered a murmur of thanks to Ghammid, the god of good fortune. The day the god's blessing—or fate, or destiny, or sheer blind chance, it didn't really matter—brought Achia Pazik to them, had been a most fortunate day indeed. Without her, Sebetwe could never have hoped to keep the gantrak under any control, much less the tight reign he needed to withstand Zilikazi.

Just three minutes, now.

Achia Pazik

Achia Pazik was tiring, but neither she nor Gadi Elkin faltered in their steps. The two Dancers had been trained in a harsh school that prized endurance and they came from a breed of folk who were contemptuous of self-pity. They'd drop unconscious before they began fouling the Dance.

Which...they might, if Sebetwe kept this up much longer. With experience, Achia Pazik and Gadi Elkin had learned how to modify the Dance in ways that suited this purpose better. The initial effect was to make the strain of the Dance less harsh. They were working *with* a Liskash tekkutu and his predator partner, not directly against a noble. Still, the force of Zilikazi's mind, even when it came secondhand and filtered through Sebetwe, was wearying. As he got closer, it felt more and more like they were Dancing in a sea of spiritual mud.

Finally, she saw Sebetwe give the signal. A moment later, grinding noises from above were followed by what sounded like a thunderclap in the distance.

Sebetwe rose and moved toward the gantrak. The beast was perched on a nearby rock, seemingly oblivious to her surroundings.

"Let's go," he said. "You can stop the Dance in two minutes, Achia Pazik. By then, the turmoil in the minds of Zilikazi's troops will require his full concentration."

Two minutes. Not so bad.

She and Gadi Elkin even finished with a flourish.

CHAPTER 10

Zilikazi

In the event, it took Zilikazi quite a while to calm down his troops after the dam burst. The water rushing down the ravine carried not only rocks and logs with it, but specially designed spears as well. The Kororo, exhibiting a fiendish imagination that fit poorly with their philosophical claims, had tied crude blades to both ends of many bundles of reeds. The buoyant reed bundles raced down atop the surging flood, spinning and whirling. The blades added their share of carnage to the damage done by the force of the water and the other debris.

It was a fairly small flood, and brief in duration. But the ravine was steep and because of the difficulty of the terrain the soldiers had been packed too tightly. Their officers had become complacent, certain that the Kororo wouldn't have had time to prepare any more elaborate traps—or, if they had, wouldn't be able to stay close enough to set them off at the right time. By now, the troops had gotten adept at spotting and disarming inert triggers left in place. So the deaths and injuries produced were much worse than they should have been.

Zilikazi was quietly furious with those officers, and made a silent vow to punish those most responsible. But he had more pressing concerns at the moment—and, being honest, was at least as angry at himself. He'd consistently underestimated the powers of the Krek's so-called "tekku." To make things worse, the Kororo shamans were either getting stronger or he had finally started encountering those among them who were most powerful and adept at their peculiar mind skill.

He still didn't really understand the nature of that skill. How could harnessing the pitiful brains of animals be of any real use?

In the distance, he heard the screech of a gantrak, but paid it little attention. The mountain predators were ferocious, certainly, but they would never dare attack such a large group of Liskash. The creature was just angry that its hunting territory was being encroached upon.

Sebetwe

Zilikazi was wrong about that. The gantrak's screech had been one of triumph, not fury. The predator was not an intelligent animal, but she was far smarter than most dumb beasts. She understood, in some way, that the creature she and her mate had mysteriously become partnered with had just scored a great victory—and she shared in that victory herself.

For his part, Sebetwe winced. Whether it derived from anger or elation, the screech of a gantrak up close was hard on the ears and unsettling on the nerves.

He managed not to jump, though.

Achia Pazik

Achia Pazik didn't jump either. But that was only because Gadi Elkin, tired by the Dance, had stumbled over a root and Achia Pazik had barely managed to catch her before she fell. The gantrak's screech jolted her nerves, but her grip on her fellow Dancer kept her steady on her feet.

"I'm starting to hate that thing," hissed Gadi Elkin, once she regained her balance. "Aren't you?"

Achia Pazik let go of her grip and shrugged. "Not as much—not nearly as much—as I hate that Liskash noble down there. The worst the gantrak will do is bite your head off, but at least your mind will still be yours right through to the end."

"That's a low standard!" the other Dancer said, grimacing. "Lose your head or lose your mind."

"Our choices are pretty limited right now." Achia Pazik started up the slope, following Sebetwe along what might be called a "trail" if you were in an expansive frame of mind. "Let's try to keep both."

Nabliz

The first little group of Mrem they found were of no practical use. There were two females in the group, but it turned out neither of them were Dancers. The two warriors also in the group wouldn't be any help, either. One had suffered injuries which, even if he recovered from them—a process that would take months—would still leave him lame. And the other was really too old to still be serving as an active warrior.

The young male in the group might be of use, eventually. But the Krek's current circumstances made concepts like "eventually" lame as well.

Still, Nabliz took it as a good omen. If two groups had survived from the catastrophe the Mrem tribe had suffered at the hands of Zilikazi and his army, surely there had to be others.

Two warriors were detached to escort the Mrem to the Krek. The rest, including Nabliz and Chefer Kolkin, continued their search.

Chefer Kolkin

Chefer Kolkin was pretty sure the Liskash would have simply left the small Mrem party they'd found where they were, once they discovered there were no dancers among them, if Chefer Kolkin hadn't insisted otherwise. The reptiles were sometimes astonishingly callous. Not cruel, no, at least not in the way Mrem understood cruelty. Even at their worst, there was always something a little cold-blooded about Liskash. The sort of hot rage which sometimes led Mrem to commit acts of utter barbarity was just not something that seemed to afflict Liskash. On the other hand, they had much less in the way of simple compassion, either.

It took some getting used to. But so, Chefer Kolkin reminded himself, did many things that turned out in the end to be beneficial. Spices took some getting used to also, when you were a youngling. Yet for an adult, food without them would be horribly bland.

Njekwa

When the priestess came into the yurt, followed closely by the shaman Litunga, she glanced around and then headed unerringly toward the one pile of hides and thrushes which was large enough to conceal a big animal. As she went, she gave Zuluku and her two companions a peremptory summoning gesture.

"Get up," she said. "We haven't much time."

Once she reached the pile, Njekwa crouched and flipped back the two hides on top. Now visible below were a Mrem female and, pressed closely to her side and staring up at the priestess also, two of the mammal younglings. "Kits," she thought they were called.

There was no expression on the adult Mrem's face. None that Njekwa could discern, at any rate, but she was not very familiar with the creatures. One of the kits seemed frightened; the other, either less anxious or less intelligent, simply looked curious.

"Can she move at all?" Njekwa asked, turning her head toward Zuluku but not taking her eyes from the subject of her scrutiny.

To her surprise, the Mrem answered. "I can move a bit. Not far, not quick. But I can move."

"You speak our language?"

"A bit." An odd little twist came to her mouth. "Not far. Not quick. But I can speak a bit."

By then, Zuluku was squatting next to the priestess. "What's wrong?"

Njekwa issued the little whistling noise from her nostrils that served Liskash as the equivalent of a snort of derision. "What do you think is wrong? Everything is wrong. It is wrong that you sheltered this creature. It is wrong that the Old Faith is ignored. It is wrong that nobles such as Zilikazi lord it over all others. For the moment, though, what is most wrong is that Zilikazi led his army into another trap, the soldiers are angry and upset, he is trying to quell them, and naturally he is resorting to ancient ruses which always seem to work even if they require everyone to be stupid."

Zuluku stared at her, uncomprehending.

"Zilikazi says treason must have been the cause," Litunga explained. The old shaman's jaws snapped twice wide with sarcasm. "Would you believe, it seems some of us are harboring Mrem spies in our midst?"

Now wide-eyed, Zuluku stared down at Nurat Merav. The notion that the badly injured Mrem female was a spy—and what would she have spied upon, anyway?—was ludicrous. But...

They were indeed harboring a Mrem in their midst.

"What do we do?" she asked Njekwa. Her voice didn't...quite...squeak with fear.

Say what you would about the priestess, she had steady nerves. In times of crisis like this, whatever doubts about her the young females might have, they instinctively looked to Njekwa for guidance and leadership.

The priestess studied Nurat Merav for a moment. "If she can move at all, you need to take her out of the camp. Her and her younglings, all of them."

"Take them where?" That question came from Raish, who was now squatting by the pile also, along with Selani, the third of the young Liskash females who'd been tending to Nurat Merav.

Litunga jerked her head toward the wall of the yurt facing north. "There is a grove not too far away, and a small gully that leads most of the way to it. Once night falls, you can move them through the gully and hide them in the woods."

Raish glanced at the entrance flap, as if to reassure herself that it was still closed and no one could see inside the yurt. "Can we wait that long?"

"I think so," said Njekwa. "The search for supposed spies is starting at the other end of the camp, among the warriors and their yurts. It will take the inspectors half the night before they come this far. They may not even try to search this side of the camp until tomorrow."

"They might search the grove too, then," said Zuluku.

"They will almost certainly search the grove," said Litunga. "We were told they were searching anywhere in the army's vicinity where spies might be hiding."

Zuluku looked down at the Mrem. "She might— probably can—make it as far as the grove. But then..."

Njekwa gave her a sidelong look. "And so now you finally realize that recklessness has its own reward? Stupid child. The 'but then' is obvious. Once you get to the grove—all of you, not just the mammals—you and Raish and Selani will have to carry her away on a litter."

The three young females looked at each other. "Carry her away, where?" asked Raish.

Again, Njekwa issued a derisive whistle. "How should I know? The camp is too dangerous. I suggest you try to find her own people, wherever they might be, and hand her back into their care."

"But—"

Zuluku looked down at Nurat Merav. The Mrem was obviously trying to follow the discussion but having a hard time of it.

"Where your people are," Zuluku said to her. Then,

remembering the lilt at the end of a phrase that the Mrem used to indicate a question, she rephrased the intonation: "Where your people are?"

Nurat Merav's face got scrunched up the way Zuluku had come to recognize was the Mrem way of indicating puzzlement and uncertainty. "Don't know. Most were captured. Killed. The rest..."

The mammalian face-scrunch got more pronounced. "Don't know your word." She raised her hands and made little fluttering gestures with her fingers. "Like straw in wind."

"Scattered," provided Litunga. "You'll likely never find any of them. Better you try to reach the Kororo. Even carrying a litter through these mountains you'll be able to move faster than the whole army."

For the first time, Selani spoke up. "Why would the Kororo take her in?"

"They probably wouldn't," replied Litunga. "But they'll take *you* in. It'll be up to you to persuade them to take the Mrem also."

She shrugged. "Whether they would or not, I have no idea."

"There's a fair chance, actually," said Njekwa. She gave Zuluku an intent gaze. "But you have to do it right. Talk a lot about Morushken—no, don't do that; you'll just get a tedious philosophical lecture about the unreality of deities. Just talk about your adherence and devotion to the principle of thrift."

Yet again, her jaws snapped sarcastically. "You shouldn't have any trouble with that, since it's true. You idiots."

The priestess rose. "Litunga and I will come up with a story to explain your absence—if the inspectors even ask, which I doubt. And now, you'd better get ready to leave. You only have a few hours until nightfall."

She turned and left the yurt, Litunga following behind.

The three young Liskash females stared at each other, then stared at Nurat Merav. Then, they went back to staring at each other.

Finally, Zuluku said, "We can make a litter easily enough. Can't we?"

Having a practical problem at hand steadied them all. "Oh, yes," said Raish. "We can make the poles out of—"

CHAPTER 11

Meshwe

The situation at the coast was just as bad as Meshwe had feared. If anything, the river was even wider than the scouts had made it seem—and, what was worse, the marshlands bordering it were extensive. He'd half-hoped that they could cross the river on rafts, but now that he saw the terrain for himself he could see how impractical that would be.

The delta was so clogged with debris—logs from upstream mixed in with brush and decaying pieces of who-knew-what—that only small rafts could hope to wend their way through it. More like big coracles, really. And they'd make slow going of it. Too slow, with Zilikazi's army not more than four days behind them.

In any event, the monsters might be just as dangerous in the river as they were in the strait. The very biggest did not seem to enter the delta, neither the huge tentacled shell-creatures nor the things that looked like seagoing versions of gigantic lizards. But other hunters were found there. Just in the short time he'd been studying the area he'd already seen three of them. Strange beasts, that looked like a turtle crossed with a snake.

None of the turtlesnakes he'd seen was big enough to capsize a large raft. But they could probably tip over a coracle, and even if they couldn't they could easily pluck Kororo right out of their vessels. Those sinuous snakeheads looked like they could reach quite a distance.

Warriors could fight off some of them, but how many were out there? And even if they could fight off all the turtlesnakes, the effort would slow them down still further. Zilikazi's army would probably arrive long before most of the Krek could cross over the river.

And even if they arrived later than Meshwe expected, they could cross the river much faster than the Kororo. Zilikazi's army was so large that they could simply build pontoon bridges across the river and cross all at once. Then the pursuit would begin again—and where would the Krek flee? No scout had yet crossed that huge, marshy river. No one knew what lay in the lands to the south. They could very well just find themselves trapped against an obstacle that was still worse than the ones they faced here.

No, better to make the attempt to cross over the

strait to the great island he could see in the distance. They could do that in big rafts, which wouldn't take much longer to build than small ones.

Would they be safe from the monsters, in big rafts? There was no way to know until they tried. The giant lizards could probably capsize any raft—or simply smash them to pieces. And those hideous tentacled things might be able to seize a raft and pull it apart, or even pull it under entirely.

Could, yes—but *would* they? It was possible the huge creatures simply wouldn't see the rafts as prey to begin with, and would leave them alone.

Of course, should that prove to be true, then Zilikazi could cross the strait on rafts also. But that was a problem for a later time.

Besides . . .

The thought taking shape in Meshwe's mind came to the fore. *Insane thought,* he would have said, not so long ago. But who could say? Not so long ago he would have thought the idea of taming a gantrak was insane also. Yet Sebetwe had managed to do it, with the help of two Mrem dancers.

If they could find more dancers . . .

That assumed the dancers would be willing to help, but why would they not? The position of that shattered Mrem tribe was even more desperate than that of the Kororo.

He turned to his small cluster of aides. "Send runners to find Sebetwe and bring him here. I have a better use for him than setting more traps for Zilikazi."

"And the gantrak?"

Meshwe considered the matter. "Yes. I need the dancers here also. Without Sebetwe and those two the gantrak will run wild if we don't bring her back."

Her mate and their two younglings were getting restless anyway. By now, they'd found that even without the dancers, any group of three tekku could keep the gantrak under control, so long as they were fed and left alone each night. But there was no telling how long that might last if they grew still more restless at the prolonged absence of the mother.

Two of his aides left to find runners. To the remaining four, he said:

"Start building rafts."

"Small ones, for the river?"

"No. Big ones. As big as we can make them and still be able to cross the strait with oars and sails."

He pointed to the island on the horizon. "We're going there."

Was it an island at all? he wondered. They didn't know the answer to that question either. They'd been assuming it was because it *looked* like an island, but it might just be a promontory extending from another continent.

He could remember a time—vaguely—when he'd thought uncertainty was rather pleasant.

Zilikazi

The army was now far enough into the second mountain range that the danger of traps and rockfalls had receded considerably. The terrain was not exactly a plateau but it had fewer of the steep slopes and narrow gullies that enabled the Kororo to make best use of their ambush techniques. Better still, none of the remaining streams and creeks were large enough, even when dammed, to produce devastating floods like the one that had struck the army when they first entered the range.

There was something else, too. Zilikazi was almost sure that the extraordinarily skilled tekkutu he'd faced earlier had withdrawn. He still didn't know the Kororo's identity, but over the course of their contest he'd come to recognize his presence—his psychic taste, as it were.

That taste had been missing for more than a day now. Halfway through the morning yesterday it had disappeared.

Where? Zilikazi had no idea. It would be nice to think the tekkutu was dead, but he was almost certain that the two of them were not done yet with their struggle. Of whose final result there was no doubt, of course, but it was still aggravating.

Zilikazi had little experience with long and protracted conflict. This was the first time in his life since attaining his full adult strength that he'd been unable to just overwhelm his opponent in short order.

He could remember—vaguely—a time when he'd thought easy victories had grown a bit boring.

Nabliz

The next encounter with a party of Mrem almost erupted in a fight. This was a large party—twenty-eight of the mammals, in all, including four dancers. Unfortunately, there were also six warriors in the group and their leader was pugnacious. His name was Jora

Ashag, and it seemed that Chefer Kolkin knew him quite well. That was a very mixed blessing, however, since it also turned out that the two warriors detested each other and had almost come to blows on several previous occasions.

As they might have this time, given the added tension of the unusual situation. Luckily one of the dancers, an older female named Yaffa Barak, had more authority than Jora Ashag in whatever manner authority was reckoned by Mrem, something which was still unclear to Nabliz.

Also luckily, given Jora Ashag's belligerent nature, the Mrem female was not timid herself. Not in the least—especially when the male warrior made the mistake of trying to bully her. At that point, Yaffa Barak did a fairly good imitation of a gantrak in full fury, and Jora Ashag withdrew into sullen obeisance.

Good enough, so far as Nabliz was concerned. They had reached the limit of their search, anyway, since Meshwe had ordered him not to travel farther than three days from the Krek's current location. Estimated current location, rather. By now, Nabliz was not exactly sure where the rest of the Kororo were to be found. They'd probably reached the sea, or were within a day's march of it.

So, once the initial antagonism subsided, Nabliz ordered the now-much-enlarged party to start toward the sea also. He was careful, however, to discuss the matter with the older Mrem female first, using Chefer Kolkin as his translator, and then successfully presented the order as coming jointly from the two of them.

Yaffa Barak made no objection. Nabliz hadn't thought she would. With his increasing experience in dealing with Mrem, Nabliz was coming to recognize the mammals' personal characteristics. A bit to his surprise, he'd found these weren't really that much different from those of his own folk.

Yaffa Barak, for instance, was a familiar type. She reminded him of one of his aunts. An older female with considerable status and prestige, of which she was quite cognizant; not stupid, certainly, but not especially bright, either; ultimately rather easy to manipulate so long as you were careful to remain respectful and outwardly deferential at all times.

Njekwa

"They're gone," Litunga reported.

"All of them?" Njekwa asked.

"Yes, all three. And the Mrem and her kits, of course. They even did a good job of clearing away any traces of her presence in the yurt." The shaman whistled amusement. "One of them—probably Zuluku; she's headstrong but she's smart—even thought to let a kessu run loose inside. She must have caught it rummaging in the garbage."

The priestess made a little grimace of distaste. Kessu were scavengers who were annoying but harmless enough, except for their noisome odor. The stench was strong enough to overlay whatever traces might have remained of the mammals' stay in the yurt. The Mrem scent was not especially objectionable, but it was distinctive.

Njekwa thought the precaution was probably unnecessary, since there were a number of Mrem slaves in Zilikazi's army. It would be easy enough to explain the smell of a Mrem in the yurt to one of the inspectors, if they even inquired about the matter.

Still, she was pleased. If Zuluku—and, yes, it had almost certainly been her idea—had been careful enough to use that ploy to cover their tracks, she'd presumably be careful enough to get away from the encampment altogether.

Njekwa hoped so. She was rather fond of Zuluku, even if the youngster often aggravated her. She would not enjoy disavowing her and her companions if they got caught by Zilikazi's inspectors.

She'd do it, nonetheless, and leave them to their punishment, which would certainly be harsh. Whatever else, the Old Faith had to be protected.

Zuluku

Zuluku and her party were already far outside the army encampment. Far enough, she thought, to be safe from the inspectors. They'd passed through two groves where they might have tried to hide. Ahead of them was a low ridge, half-visible in the light of a crescent moon. Once they were beyond it, which they should be before sunrise, they would be completely out of sight of the army. Not even the sentries on the outer towers that Zilikazi's engineers erected every day when the army camped would be able to see them. Thankfully, the towers were not very tall. They were temporary structures—not quite what you could call flimsy, but close—which had to be light enough to be erected and dismantled within a short time. Zuluku had never stood atop one of the things, since they were only for warriors. But they were not much more than twice the height of a tall Liskash, which was certainly not enough to enable a sentry to see over the ridge.

She was glad of it. They were all very tired by now. By the time they made it over the ridge, they'd be completely exhausted and would have no choice but to rest.

Rest wherever they could. Blessedly, from what she could see of the sky, it didn't look as if rain was in the offing. They wouldn't have to build shelters—which was a good thing, since she wasn't at all sure they'd have the strength and energy to do so anyway.

They started climbing the slope of the ridge. It was rather steep, but at least the footing wasn't too treacherous. And it wasn't a very tall ridge. Even moving as slowly as they were, they'd be across it well before dawn.

It was Zuluku's turn to rest from carrying the litter, so she didn't have to devote all her attention to her feet. She looked down at the Mrem. The kits were asleep—they did that a lot; more than Liskash of that age would do—but their mother was awake.

Awake, and looking back up at Zuluku.

"Thank you," the mammal whispered. "You are a good friend."

Zuluku didn't know how to respond to that. She supposed it was true, as Mrem gauged such things. But

Liskash—adherents to the Old Faith, at any rate—did not think the same way.

Duty and obligation, not emotion, were paramount. She finally settled on: "It is the thrifty thing to do."

But she felt good, she suddenly realized. Really good. For the first time in her life, she was *doing* something.

CHAPTER 12

Sebetwe

"So who are they?"

"I have no idea, Sebetwe." The scout, still breathing heavily from her long run, needed a moment before she could continue. "Three Liskash females—all young, from what I could see at a distance—and they're carrying somebody on a litter. A Mrem, I think."

"Why do you think so?"

"I think I saw fur. There's at least one little one riding in the litter also and it's not acting like one of our younglings. It's acting..."

The scout gave Achia Pazik a sidelong glance that was partly apprehensive and partly apologetic. "You know. Weird."

Sebetwe rocked back on his heels and considered the matter. It was true that Mrem kits and Liskash younglings behaved quite differently, especially at a very early age. Much more differently, truth be told, than adults did. Mrem kits were all but inseparable from their dams, whereas Liskash younglings started to roam about as soon as they could engage in any sort of locomotion.

Crawling, tottering, stumbling, it didn't matter. The moment a Liskash could do so, it went exploring.

It was a bit odd, really. As adults, the mammals were generally more inquisitive than sensible Liskash. But not their kits.

He looked at the dancer. "If the person on the litter is a Mrem, who would it be?"

Achia Pazik shrugged. "Could be almost anyone. Although, if there are kits, it will almost certainly be female."

Her face contorted in that overly mobile way the mammals had. Sebetwe interpreted this particular facial contortion as sarcasm. No, more like derision.

"You won't catch a Mrem male anywhere nearby, when kits need tending," she said.

That was another peculiar trait of the mammals. There seemed to be quite a bit of tension between the genders, to go along with what—from a Liskash viewpoint, anyway—was an excessive degree of mutual attachment. Sebetwe supposed it wasn't surprising that creatures with such a surplus of energy would have to expend it in often frivolous and pointless ways.

He rose to his feet. "Only one way to find out. Let's go see."

Zuluku

Zuluku was astonished to see the group who accosted them just as they entered a meadow. It was a mixed party of Liskash and Mrem—but unlike their own, the two species seemed to be completely intermingled.

Seven of them, in all. Five Liskash and two of the

mammals. Both of the mammals were female. By now, from tending to Nurat Merav's injuries, Zuluku could easily spot gender traits, which were more distinctive among Mrem than they were among Liskash.

Of the five Liskash, at least three were clearly warriors. She was not sure of the other two. Both of them carried weapons, but no armor, and there seemed to be something . . . different about the way they carried themselves.

Could these be the famous Kororo "tekkutu"? Zuluku hoped so.

Desperately hoped so, in fact. They were becoming very weak. The work of trekking through the mountains was hard enough in itself, without having to carry the litter as well. Worst of all, though, was the hunger.

Liskash were not often hungry. Not, at least, in the way Nurat Merav said her folk experienced the sensation. Mammals needed to eat often—two, even three times a day!—because their feverish bodies burned energy so rapidly. Liskash could normally go for days without eating much, or anything at all, because their bodies stored fat efficiently whenever they feasted.

(There was this to be said for those feverish mammal bodies, though. It got very cold here in the mountains, and they'd learned quickly that by huddling around Nurat Merav they could get through the nights much better.)

But Zuluku had never experienced the sort of strenuous effort this journey through the mountains had required. And it was so cold! None of the Liskash females had any experience with hunting, and even if they had it wouldn't have done them much good because they hadn't thought to bring any weapons with them.

They had knives, of course. Liskash females always had knives. But they were small ones designed for the sort of work needed around a village or camp. They were not really weapons, and they certainly weren't suited for hunting.

Raish had tried tying her knife to a long stick with a cord and using it as a spear. She might have scared a couple of small animals with it, when the cast spear landed somewhere in their vicinity. Not much, though. Neither one of them had scuttled or hopped more than a short distance before settling back down.

They'd tried eating some succulent-looking berries they'd come across on the second day. Fortunately, Zuluku had insisted none of them eat more than two berries without letting enough time elapse to make sure the things were not poisonous before eating any more.

Fortunately, indeed. Within a short time, all three of them had gotten sick and started vomiting.

At least they hadn't lost any food already eaten. Their stomachs had been empty of anything but digestive bile and what was left of the treacherous berries.

As the party of strangers grew near, Nurat Merav raised her head from the litter and peered at them. Immediately, both Mrem cried out her name and came rushing forward. A moment later they were clustered over the wounded Mrem, jabbering at her in their own tongue too quickly for Zuluku to understand much of what they were saying.

This much was clear, though: the Mrem were very

pleased. One of them even broke off from jabbering at Nurat Merav long enough to give Zuluku a quick embrace.

A "hug," she thought that was called.

Odd creatures, Mrem.

Sebetwe

"You're saying she is the best dancer among you?"

Achia Pazik shook her head. "No, Sebetwe."

"Achia Pazik is our best Dancer," said Gadi Elkin. "Nurat Merav is not really very good at all."

"Then why are you so pleased—"

Achia Pazik interrupted him with a raised hand. "You don't understand. Nurat Merav is our..." She looked aside, her expression frustrated. "What is the word? It means something like designer of the Dance."

Sebetwe gaped his jaws a little. "I doubt if we have any such word. We Liskash don't dance very much."

"And thank the gods for that!" said Gadi Elkin. Her own jaws gaped in that manner whereby Mrem showed amusement.

Sebetwe was not offended. It was a simple truth that Liskash didn't begin to have the fluid and supple grace—not to mention the sheer energy—that Mrem used in their dancing.

"All right, then," said Achia Pazik. "We will use our word for it. Nurat Merav is our *choreographer*."

"Koree—koree...a-gra-fuur?" The word was awkward on his tongue.

"Close enough," said Achia Pazik. "She is the best among us—"

"The best in any tribe!" interjected Gadi Elkin proudly.

"—when it comes to understanding how a Dance must be shaped to accomplish whatever its purpose might be. *Now* do you see how important it is that she has been rescued?"

Dimly, Sebetwe did begin to see. If a real expert, someone with great talent, could analyze a dance and see how it might be modified and adapted to do something as unheard of as merging with a great predator like a gantrak...

He began to feel some of the Mrems' excitement. So much so that he almost ordered an immediate resumption of the march.

But he didn't. They'd taken a rest not simply or even primarily for the sake of those who'd been alternating the duty of carrying the litter. Mostly they'd stopped because the person on the litter was weaker than any of them.

Person. Not for the first time, it struck Sebetwe how easily that word came to him these days. There was still much about the Mrem that was peculiar, even unsettling at times. But at some point—he didn't know when, exactly—they had become people, not just intelligent creatures.

Nurat Merav

It took her a while before she finally grasped the full extent of the ambition. When she did, she hesitated a moment out of sheer disbelief.

"*With* the Liskash?"

Achia Pazik waggled her hand back and forth. "It would be more accurate to say that we use the Dance to provide the Liskash shaman—they're called 'tekkutu,' by the way—and the gantrak with a rhythm that can sustain them both. The tekkutu are really the ones who work directly with the animals."

Nurat Merav pondered the matter, for a time. Partly, because she was very tired; but mostly because the concepts involved were so outlandish.

And yet...

A wedding Dance worked in somewhat the same manner Achia Pazik was describing. What would happen if you modified the chain turns in the middle of a wedding Dance and blended them with the insistent, fierce rhythm of the whipping steps that provided the war Dances with their basic framework? The end result might be...

The Liskash they called Sebetwe who seemed to be their leader came up to the little group.

"How soon will you be strong enough for us to resume the march?" he asked Nurat Merav.

She waved that question aside impatiently. "How soon will we get there once we do?"

Zilikazi

They were almost out of the mountains. Two days' march, no more than that. Then, another day's march—perhaps two—down the foothills to the seashore where the Kororo were finally penned.

"They're building rafts, you say?"

"Yes, lord," answered the scout. "Big ones, at least

seven of them. Too big to go on the river with. They must be planning to cross over to the island."

The scout's jaws gaped with derision. "Crazy plan. You should see the monsters there! Some of them could probably swallow a raft whole."

"I *will* see the monsters there," Zilikazi stated.

Personally, he doubted the scout's assessment that a sea monster, no matter how large, could just swallow a raft in one gulp. It was not impossible, he supposed. He'd seen great snakes swallow prey as large as they were. But by all accounts he'd heard, the really huge predators in the sea did not include snakes.

There seemed to be three types. One was basically a giant lizard that had adapted to marine conditions. Another was a reptile that had a snake's head and neck perched on what resembled a turtle's body. But that was supposed to be the smallest of the big sea predators.

The one that apparently grew to the greatest size was the strangest of them all. It was said to have tentacles, much like the small squids that were sometimes caught near the shore. But the body was quite different. According to the accounts, the creature's entire body was nestled inside an enormous coiled shell.

Experience with the sea was rare among Liskash, but not entirely absent. It was said by those who had that experience that the shelled monsters—ammonites, they called them—were rarely attacked by other predators, and never once they reached a certain size.

Some of them fed exclusively on the tiny shrimplike creatures that swarmed in parts of the sea. But others were hunters of much larger prey. It was said that the very biggest could even devour the giant lizards.

Zilikazi was skeptical of all these tales. Not so much because he disbelieved them but simply because he was skeptical by nature. That tended to be true of all Liskash nobles. Having the power to coerce others by sheer force of mind had the side effect of making the wielder of that power suspicious of all claims made by reason and observation.

Reason was what they said it was, no? And observation was always subject to interpretation—and who but a noble had the final authority to interpret everything?

No matter. He'd find out the truth soon enough. Three days, maybe four. After that, the Kororo Krek would be just a memory—and it would be Zilikazi who dictated the nature of the remembrance.

CHAPTER 13

Meshwe

"Can you do it?" asked Meshwe.

Sebetwe raised a hand in a gesture for silence. His eyes were closed, his mind searching across the water for...

What would you call it, exactly? Meshwe turned his head and looked at the incredible creatures who had been slowly gathering around the narrow spur of rock—a miniature promontory, as it were—that jutted out into the strait.

There were five of them, now. Two huge ones and

three who *would* be called huge if they'd been placed alongside any other creatures. In this company, they just seemed very, very big. Half-amused and half-appalled, Meshwe contemplated for a moment the possible necessity of developing fine distinctions with regard to size. Which words should indicate the larger monster? Huge, gigantic or immense?

What added to the eeriness of the scene was the silence and near-immobility of the creatures. Unlike the giant sea lizards, who seemed to be constantly in motion, these ammonites were just floating on the surface. Their only movement was an occasional slow flutter of tentacles to keep them in position so their eyes could gaze steadily at Sebetwe.

Huge eyes; lidless eyes; unwavering eyes. Meshwe thought he might have nightmares about them when he slept.

Next to him, Sebetwe finally spoke. "Join me, Tekkutu," he said. "I need your wisdom."

The suggestion was . . . unusual. Tekku did not work well—as a rule, not at all—when more than one tekkutu tried to meld minds with a predator. Such beasts invariably had a narrow psychic focus, which did not react well to complexity.

But were these ammonites really predators, in the normal sense of the term? Meshwe wasn't sure.

Yes, they ate meat. But they were not active hunters in the same way that the sea lizards or the turtlesnakes were—or gantrak or any land predator, for that matter. They *grazed* for meat, as it were. Their great nest of tentacles would reach out and engulf anything around them. They seemed quite indifferent to the nature of their meal. Fish, large and small; crustaceans scuttling across the sea floor; incautious sea birds; anything at all—even other ammonites, if they were considerably smaller and foolish enough to come too close.

It was done quite casually, to all appearances. There was none of the intent focus of a hunter chasing after its prey. If a fish managed to wriggle out of the tentacle mass, or a crustacean scuttled quickly enough under a rock—or another ammonite fought them off long enough to escape—they seemed quite indifferent. There would always be more food coming along, soon enough. And meanwhile, as they floated on the surface, their eyes looked elsewhere.

Meshwe took himself into the tekku trance; quickly, with the skill of long practice.

He found Sebetwe's mind almost immediately. The younger tekkutu was by now almost as skilled as Meshwe—more skilled, when it came to this new facet of the art—but he'd been his student for years. Meshwe could have found him in an ocean of mental turbulence.

Almost as quickly, he became aware of Sebetwe's... *audience*, was the only term Meshwe could think of. His guess had been right. The minds of these ammonites were not at all similar to those of predators he had encountered in the past. They were much more akin to the minds of plant-eaters, except—

They were vastly greater. Those must be huge brains, nestled somewhere inside the floating behemoths.

Strange brains, judging from the strange minds. They were like nothing Meshwe had ever encountered.

Not intelligent; not, at least, in any sense that would mean anything to a Liskash or a Mrem. But very far from dull-witted, either. And there was a sense of cool space to their minds—a sort of vastness, you might call it.

They were ultimately quite passive, he realized. So big, so powerful, so well armored that fear was essentially unknown to them. And so also were fear's cousins, aggression and fury. So dominant by their very nature that they had no need, no instinct, to dominate at all.

They were observers, more than actors. Very curious. Indeed, as his own mind probed deeper into theirs, he realized that their strongest emotion was probably curiosity itself.

They didn't need food. Food came to them; food was a given.

He didn't think they needed to mate, either, although he wasn't sure. For all their immense size, these creatures were still akin to those little shelled creatures who simply scattered their seed with careless abandon. For them, reproduction would be simply another given. It would have no roots in passion or lust.

He almost laughed aloud, then. The monsters were *bored.*

Well, not bored, exactly. Boredom needed intent focus also. It might be better to say that the giant ammonites passed their lives in a state of mind so placid that any sort of entertainment would fix their attention.

Fix it *mightily,* he thought.

Mightily enough, perhaps, to allow an entire people to find their sanctuary.

He withdrew from the mindmeld.

"I will be back soon," he said to Sebetwe, placing a reassuring hand on his shoulder. "In the meantime, keep them interested in you."

Sebetwe nodded curtly, but his eyes remained closed. Meshwe strode off the little promontory and headed toward the clot of dancers on the nearby beach.

Nurat Merav

She stared up at the old Liskash, wondering if he were serious.

His jaws opened in the Liskash version of a smile. "Yes, I am quite serious." He motioned toward the dancers, still moving through their steps. "This wedding dance is not right. Close, but not close enough. It is too ceremonial. We need something that conjures simple joy and delight. No solemnity at all."

Achia Pazik had broken off her part in the Dance when she'd seen Meshwe approaching and had come over. She joined them in time to hear the last few sentences.

"What about the Jottuk Festival Dance?" she suggested.

Nurat Merav stared at her. "But... That's just a kit's dance!"

Achia Pazik shrugged. "True. But you have to admit it's joyous and delightful. Not a trace of solemnity to be found anywhere."

"Do you even remember the steps?"

Achia Pazik grimaced ruefully. "I think so. We'll probably miss a few, at first, until we've practiced a bit."

She looked at Meshwe. "Do you think that will be a problem?"

He turned his head to look out at the great shells floating in the distance. "I doubt very much if they would know the difference. What matters is simply capturing the delight, and the joy."

Achia Pazik and Nurat Merav looked at each other. Then, at Meshwe. Then, back at each other.

Nurat Merav tried to lever herself upright in the litter—which was more in the way of a pallet, by now, with added cushions and hides. Hissing with concern, Zuluku and Selani helped her to sit up. Not knowing what else to do, Zuluku and her companions had continued to serve as Nurat Merav's caretakers.

Once her head was high enough, Nurat Merav sheltered her eyes from the sun with a hand and stared at the monsters in the sea.

"Do I understand this correctly? You want me to shape a Dance for—for—these—"

"I think they are much like children, in their own way," said Meshwe. "Please, Nurat Merav. Indulge an old tekkutu."

"If that's what you want." She leaned back, supporting herself partly on spread hands but mostly on the strong grips of her two Liskash tenders. Then, after thinking on the matter for a while, she looked up at Achia Pazik.

"I've forgotten some of the steps myself. It doesn't matter, though, since we'll be modifying it a lot. I think mixing in some of the steps from the Drunkard's Dance would probably help—and it would sure be a lot easier to do on a floating raft."

Achia Pazik frowned. "Why would we do it on a raft?"

Nurat Merav grinned. "Haven't you figured it out yet? The crazy old tekkutu here"—she nodded toward Meshwe—"figures we can keep the shelled monsters happy while we cross the strait to the island."

The Dancer stared at Meshwe. "But . . . What about the sea lizards? Do you think they'll be kept happy also?"

Meshwe whistled his derision. "Not likely! From what I can tell, the only thing that keeps those things happy is devouring something. Maybe mating would excite them too, but I haven't seen them doing that yet. For which I am truly thankful."

More seriously, he added: "But I've been watching them and one thing is obvious: they stay well away from the ammonites. I think they're afraid of them. Wary, at least."

He shrugged. The gesture was quite similar to the one used by the Mrem. So similar, in fact, that Nurat Merav had found herself wondering if one race had learned it from the other.

It was possible. They'd coexisted for a long time now. Not too happily, perhaps, but they'd still managed it for centuries. Maybe longer. No one knew.

"It's a risk, I admit," said Meshwe. "All of it's a risk. But I don't see where we have any choice."

He pointed now to the mountains rising in the west. They were some distance away, since the slope down to the sea was shallow and the foothills between were wide. Still, they were easily visible.

"Zilikazi's army will be starting down the slope soon. By tomorrow morning, our scouts say. And there's no way to stop them. They'll be coming through the same broad saddle pass our people used. You remember it, I'm sure. Gentle slopes on the sides, very few rocks, and no streams beyond little rills. Their warriors outnumber ours at least eight-to-one. Our only chance now is to find sanctuary on the island."

"And what will stop them from crossing after us?" asked Achia Pazik.

For whatever odd reason, that question banished all of Nurat Merav's doubts and hesitations.

"Ha!" she exclaimed. "You think that scaly snake"—realizing she was perhaps bordering on insult, she gave the Liskash around her an semi-apologetic smile—"meaning no offense to anyone here—but if you think that—that—"

"Scaly snake," Meshwe offered.

Nurat Merav grinned. "That *scaly snake* can keep monsters as entertained as we can, you've never see what a really well-designed Dance can do!"

Sebetwe

When Meshwe returned to the rock spur, he brought two other Kororo with him. One of them was Zinzile, the oldest and most experienced tekkutu other than Meshwe himself. The one with her was her son Tofar, who had only a smidgen of her experience but was a very talented tekkutu in his own right.

"Sebetwe, show them what you're doing and how you're doing it," Meshwe commanded. "They can take over keeping the ammonites interested—"

"We should call them the Sure Ones," Sebetwe interrupted. "It's how they see themselves, I think. That, or maybe the Constant Ones."

"As you wish. Once Zinzile and Tofar can take over with the Sure Ones, you and I need to make plans. I have come up with an idea."

The old tekkutu's jaws gaped. Sebetwe felt himself grow wary. He remembered that look of amusement well. Meshwe's jaws had gaped just so the day long past when he'd half-tossed a then-little and very scared Sebetwe into the enclosure to face a tritti.

The little monster had *bitten* him. It *hurt*. But Meshwe's jaws had only gaped wider.

On the other hand, they'd gaped wider still a few days later when another tritti—not the same one; Meshwe had killed that nasty wretch and good riddance—had come to sit placidly on Sebetwe's outstretched forearm.

CHAPTER 14

Zilikazi

After all this! Zilikazi was so furious he had to restrain himself from shattering the scout leader's mind. The effort was almost physical, so great was the urge.

And then, as his thoughts cooled a bit and he realized what his only course of action could be, he *did* strike down the scout leader. Terror now had to be marshaled. Great terror. It was the only thing that would drive his army to do what had to be done.

It would have been simple to crush the scout's mind. Fear, then unconsciousness, then death. All in less than a minute. There were not many nobles who could kill that easily just with the use of their minds.

But while that would produce fear and dread, it would not produce the sort of near-gibbering terror that Zilikazi needed to instill in his troops. So, he spent the time and effort to force the scout leader to shatter his own body. The terror he sent coursing down every channel in that body caused muscles to spasm so ferociously that they snapped bones and ruptured vertebrae.

When it was over—the scout not quite dead, but his body a mass of broken flesh that would not survive more than a short time—Zilikazi fixed his subordinates with a basilisk gaze.

"Henceforth, this will be the punishment for failure." He paused briefly, allowing time for anyone who dared to point out that by no reasonable criterion could the scout leader be said to have "failed." Failed at what? He'd sent warning to Zilikazi that the Kororo were crossing the strait as soon as he realized himself, had he not? What was he then supposed to do? Swim out into the strait with his handful of scouts and somehow capsize the great rafts they were using to make their escape?

No one spoke, of course. He'd have been astonished if they had. He'd simply paused to allow all of them to contemplate the fact that Zilikazi was being completely unreasonable.

As he was, indeed. The time for reason was now past. Against all expectations, the Krek had continued to elude his grasp.

Now was the time for *will*.

He pointed to the woods and groves on the lower slopes. They came almost right up to the beach.

"If they can build rafts, so can we. And we will build many more of them, and we will build them faster."

Again, he paused. Not long.

"Do as I command."

Zuluku

Zuluku was almost gibbering with terror herself. So were Raish and Selani. The only thing keeping them steady enough not to was the close presence of Nurat Merav. Much as they had during the cold nights of the mountain crossing, the three young Liskash females were huddled around the Mrem's pallet.

Zuluku would have been happier if that pallet had been positioned in the very center of the raft, instead of against a railing. She could perhaps then have been able to ignore the horrifying creatures that were themselves clustering nearby. But the center of the raft was empty, so that the Mrem dancing there—Achia Pazik, she was called—had the room she needed for a dance that was insanely acrobatic.

It didn't look like a dance at all, to Zuluku. Dancing was not unknown, among Liskash. But it was a slow and ceremonious affair, usually done as part of solemn rituals, not this mad whirling and capering and leaping about.

And screeching! The Mrem shouted and cried out as they danced. The noise was almost as chaotic as their movements.

It helped—a bit—that Nurat Merav's kits were completely oblivious to the peril of the situation. Both of them were peering about with keen interest. By now, they were quite unafraid of their dam's Liskash companions. Indeed, one of them—the female kit, whom Nurat Merav called by the name of Abi—had climbed onto the low railing that had been placed on the sides of the pallet and was balanced there precariously, steadying herself with both hands on Zuluku's left shoulder.

For some odd reason, Zuluku found the pressure of the tiny hands reassuring. Perhaps the innocence of infants would protect them from madness.

For madness this surely was. The rafts the Kororo were using to make the crossing to the island were big, true, but they were hardly what anyone would call sturdy. There had been no time for anything but crude designs and even cruder workmanship. The rafts were just piles of logs roped together with piles of more slender rods—stripped branches, half the time—roped on top at a perpendicular angle to make what was laughingly call a "deck."

They'd made crude sails, too, but so far those had proved useless. The sails were much too primitive to do anything but run with the wind—and the wind was blowing from the wrong direction. Sails would have just driven them along the shore toward the great rocky cliffs to the north where another river entered the sea through a deep gorge.

So, they were forced to row their way across, with oars that were every bit as crude and clumsy as the sails. Basically, they were just big poles swiveled against upright posts. The paddles at the ends of the oars had been made from the dismantled parts of wagons. They were also attached with nothing better than ropes, and already one of the paddles had disintegrated from the pressure.

Which—this was the one bright feature—was considerable. Since every raft was packed with people, there were plenty of arms and backs able to strain at the oars, with plenty of replacements whenever someone got too tired to continue.

They'd kept rowing with that oar, by just attaching a pile of brambles to the end. It made for a heavy load when the rowers had to lift it out of the water for the return stroke, but it was better than nothing.

Needless to say, their progress was slow. They'd launched at dawn, but they'd be doing well to make landfall on the island by sunset. If need be, she'd been told, the Krek's leaders planned to keep rowing through the night. Luckily, there was enough of a moon to be able to see the island even after sundown.

Assuming it didn't rain, of course. Zuluku had no idea if that was likely or not. The sky looked clear—bright blue and almost cloudless, in fact—but she had no experience with the weather here by the sea. For all she knew, bright blue skies by day meant terrible storms at night.

She heard Raish issue a little hiss of fear. Glancing toward her, she saw that one of the ammonite monsters had come almost to the side of the raft. The hideous thing was looking right at her!

With that huge, unblinking eye. Then, one of its tentacles looped lazily out of the water and curled over the railing.

They were doomed! It was going to capsize the raft and eat them all!

Little Abi squealed with excitement and tried to reach the tentacle tip with her hands completely extended.

The gruesome tentacle—it had suckers! with *teeth* in them! in every single one of them!—rose from the railing and extended itself to meet those hands. For just an instant, before Zuluku could snatch her back, Abi's fingers touched the tip of the tentacle.

The tentacle curled away; and a moment later it fell back into the sea. The great eye just kept staring at Zuluku.

If only it would *blink*.

Meshwe

"It's going quite well, I think," said Meshwe. He and Sebetwe were taking a break. They'd found that mindmelding with the Sure Ones, while it lacked the acute stress of merging with a predator, produced its own form of psychic fatigue. Liskash—Mrem even less—were just not well-suited by nature to maintain a constant equanimity.

Profound equanimity. It was now clear to Meshwe

that the minds of the Sure Ones were completely unlike any minds he'd ever encountered.

Reptiles he knew, mammals he knew. There was even a carnivorous giant frog that he'd melded with on a few occasions. But those minds were all closely akin to his, practically cousins, compared to these. Meshwe knew that some of the shamans who specialized in the study of nature thought that squids and ammonites were actually related to such things as clams and oysters.

He'd been doubtful of that claim in the past, but he was doubtful no longer.

Cold, cold, cold minds. There was no fear in them; nor fury, either. But he knew that should they choose to kill, they would do so with an implacability every bit as sure as everything else about them.

The Sure Ones, indeed. They named themselves well—so well that the name was accepted by Liskash and Mrem, even though the Sure Ones had no language with which to speak that name. Nor any way to even think it. They simply were. The Sure Ones.

So well named, happily, that even the great lizards of the sea understood their nature. It was obvious that the lizards were feeling frustrated. They were now swarming in the strait, surfacing constantly and sometimes even leaping half out of the water. Circling and circling the flotilla of rafts and its ammonite convoy, but never approaching too closely.

The huge, scaly predators didn't know—exactly— the nature of the peculiar beasts that were floating through their waters toward the island. But theirs were simple minds.

There was food. There were mates. There were competitors for food and mates. All creatures large enough to be noticed at all fell into those three categories. So what were these?

They were frustrated; in their own way, curious; and always prone to aggression. But they were not mindless. The strange beasts were surrounded by the shelled ones, and those could be dangerous. For one thing, they were almost impossible to kill. Not even the greatest of the sea lizards could bite through that armor. And while the tentacles could be attacked, the reverse was just as true—the tentacles were the shelled ones' own teeth and claws. Attacking them was akin to matching bites with another sea lizard.

Risky. There wasn't room in the tight and narrow minds of the sea lizards for many concepts, but that one was well understood.

Risky. So, they kept their distance.

The turtlesnakes didn't come anywhere near the rafts. The river delta and its immediate environs seemed to be their natural habitat. They were great and fearsome predators in their own right—as any land animal discovered, even the largest, if they came too close to the water. But their normal diet was the fish and amphibians that dwelt in the delta. They would not last long if they tried to match themselves against the lizards or ammonites of the open sea.

"Yes," Sebetwe said. "It's going well. But..."

He glanced at the island, slowly drawing near, then looked back at the shore. His eyesight was very good and he could easily see the advance elements of Zilikazi's army. Some of them had already reached the beach and he was pretty sure of the activity of those farther back, in the woods.

They'd be building their own rafts.

He glanced now at the tekkutu who were taking his place and Meshwe's for the moment. Chikwe and Kudzai, those were. Neither was especially talented but both were solid and experienced. They would manage for a while.

"We need to talk to Nurat Merav again," he said.

"I agree." Meshwe's jaws opened a bit. "She'll be delighted to discover we want a new dance from her."

Nurat Merav

"Are you *joking?*"

CHAPTER 15

Zilikazi

Zilikazi had eventually realized he had no choice but to command the lead raft. Despite his power and his ferocity in using it, the morale of his army had deteriorated so much that his troops were still balking at making the passage across the strait to the island.

Not openly, no; to all outward appearance, his orders were being obeyed. But resistance can take many forms. Knots poorly tied, logs poorly chosen, vessel designs mismanaged—always with the claim they'd been "misunderstood"—it went on and on. He'd soon realized that the creeping pace at which his troops were preparing the fleet of rafts was itself undermining their morale.

Decisive action had to be taken, and it was. He announced to the whole army that he would be in personal command of the first raft to be launched into the sea and he expected all of his subordinate officers and warriors on the other rafts to launch with him.

Failure to do so would be severely punished.

That was enough. The pace of the work picked up; more importantly, so did the quality of the work itself.

But the time they'd wasted! He had expected to start the crossing in three days. It was now the fifth day after his army had reached the shore—late afternoon of the fifth day. They'd have to wait until the next morning to make the crossing. He begrudged that reality, but there was no getting around it. The moon was waxing and was now better than half full, but he still couldn't take the risk of trying to cross the sea except in full daylight. Leaving aside the risks of the passage itself, forcing his army to make a night crossing would shatter the morale he'd just succeeded in patching back together.

Tomorrow morning, then. Standing on the same small rock spur that Meshwe and Sebetwe had used as an observation perch days earlier, Zilikazi glared at the island in the distance. He'd made another decision over the past few days and announced it to the army also. The only captives they would take would be younglings. Anyone old enough to have been infected in any way by the beliefs of the Kororo Krek were to be slaughtered out of hand.

If there was any doubt, force the younglings to speak. Use torture, use any means of duress to put them to the test. Any youngling who could speak a complete phrase—even a short one—was to be killed.

He made an exception for the Mrem who had taken refuge with the Krek. He didn't understand how they had done it, but it was now clear to him that the Mrem dancers had greatly enhanced the so-called "tekku" of the Kororo shamans.

All Mrem were to be butchered. Each and every one down to the least kit.

By tomorrow night—well, perhaps not quite that soon; the island looked to be big and some would try to flee into its interior—this would finally be over.

Achia Pazik

"I should go with you," insisted Nurat Merav.

"Don't be silly," Achia Pazik chided her. "You've done all you can. Designed the new Dance, and modified it as our rehearsals suggested. It may not be good enough, but there's nothing you will be able to do tomorrow that will change anything. We can't risk losing our best choreographer."

Her mouth twisted into a semblance of a smile. "Also our only choreographer."

Nurat Merav had recovered enough from her injuries to be sitting up straight with no assistance. She was even able to throw up her hands in a gesture of frustration.

"And so what? All of our Dancers—each and every one—will be on that raft tomorrow. If we lose, there will be nothing for me to choreograph."

Standing next to them, young Lavi Tur grunted with amusement.

"And no time either, even if any Dancers were left," he said, using his chin to point to the mainland. "If that huge army gets across, they'll just overrun us. Cut all of our throats for sure and probably hack off our limbs for good measure. They've got to be in a rage already—and if they aren't, they certainly will be after the crossing."

Again, he grunted amusement. He did that a lot. It was annoying. But Achia Pazik saw no point in chiding him about it now.

Maybe later. If there was a later. She was sure he was right in his assessment. Zilikazi and his warriors would be furious with the Kororo Krek and any who were associated with it. If they got across, they probably would kill everyone.

She almost grunted with amusement herself, then. Zilikazi's army would be even more furious after crossing, when they discovered most of the Kororo had fled into the interior. If they thought they'd have nothing to do but quick and easy butcher's work, they'd soon discover otherwise.

There was no point in most of the Kororo waiting on the beach. What could be done tomorrow would be done by the tekkutu and the Dancers on the one raft that would be going out to meet the invaders. The rest of the Krek except a few staying behind to help launch the raft had already started moving inland.

Not quickly. The island's terrain was mountainous, for the most part, especially further into the interior.

They still didn't know for sure, in fact, whether it was an island at all. The scouts had not yet reached the crest of the mountains to see all that might lie beyond. What they had been able to see suggested they were on an island, yes. But there was still perhaps a tenth of the coastline that remained unknown.

And even if it was an island—now, she did grunt with amusement, although not as loudly as the brash youngster—the aggravation of Zilikazi's warriors would still not be at an end. There were caves in those interior mountains, as it turned out. Some of them seemed to be quite large and deep as well as convoluted.

Enough of the tekkutu would remain on the island to keep the gantrak under control. (That had been an adventure! Keeping those temperamental and belligerent beasts from tearing apart the raft that had brought them over to the island had been a close thing. If anyone but Sebetwe had tried to control them, they'd mostly likely have failed.) They could hide at least some people deep in those caves for days, possibly many days.

Possibly even until Zilikazi's army gave up the search altogether. Who could say?

But there was no point in dwelling on that. Achia Pazik was quite confident the new Dance would do what it was designed to do. She'd played no small part in designing it herself, from the experience she'd gained in their rehearsals.

Four days of rehearsals, starting before dawn and not ending until sunset—and the only reason she'd ended then was because the Dancers were exhausted and needed their rest. Never in her life had she been so well rehearsed with a new Dance.

Her muscles still ached a bit, from the strenuous effort. But she knew that by the morning she'd be full of energy and excitement.

All of them would be, Dancers and tekkutu both. A partnership had been forged here that was like nothing any of them had ever seen before. Meshwe had told her that he was just beginning to comprehend the great changes that would take place in tekku as a result. The future looked to be magnificent, he said.

If they got there at all. The only way anyone had ever found to reach the future was through the present, and tomorrow that meant sailing one raft against a great fleet.

True, that one raft would have help. Of a sort. You could hardly call them allies, though.

Njekwa

For the first time in her life, the chief priestess of the Old Faith was considering a possibility she'd never once imagined. What would happen if the rule of the nobles were broken?

More specifically, the rule of their noble, Zilikazi.

The thought had first come to her on the day the army had started down the slope to the sea and word had begun to spread that the fleeing Kororo had successfully made the crossing over to the island. That was something that no one had really expected. For Liskash—for Mrem too, she thought—the sea was a place full of monsters so immense that no one ever seriously thought of venturing far out onto the waters. Most Liskash were even reluctant to approach the shores and those who engaged in fishing, other than in fresh water streams, were considered not much different from lunatics. Either that, or outright idiots.

But apparently the Kororo had managed it. Rumors were also spreading that they'd done so by using their peculiar and little-understood "tekku" powers.

For days, now, the priestess had been pondering those powers. She'd always dismissed them in the past as not much more than superstition. But after watching the Krek's success in eluding Zilikazi for so long, she was beginning to wonder.

What if they *did* have psychic powers that were unknown to the nobility? Might those powers be enough to thwart Zilikazi?

Or might they even be enough to destroy him?

It was possible. For the first time ever, she thought it might be possible. The Kororo couldn't have managed the crossing of the strait unless they could somehow control the sea monsters, could they?

She went so far as to privately broach the question to Litunga.

But the shaman was skeptical. "Control them? I don't think so. If they could control animals the way the nobles can control people, they'd have already been sending monsters to attack us. There are plenty of monsters on land, after all. None of them as big as the sea monsters are said to be, but they're plenty big enough. Have you ever seen a gantrak up close?"

Njekwa shook her head.

"Neither have I," said Litunga, "and I plan to see that remains true. I once saw what was left of a trapper who'd been killed by a gantrak." She used her hands to indicate something about the size of a newborn youngling. "The biggest piece of him they found was about this size. One of his shoulders with bits and pieces still attached to it. Most of him was just . . . gone. Eaten, I suppose."

Njekwa thought about it for a while. "You might be right," she said finally. "Probably are, in fact. But just in case . . ."

She thought for a while longer. "Spread the word quietly to all the priestesses and shamans. Every adherent to the Old Faith should be ready if the time comes."

"Be ready to do what?"

"I don't know yet." Her voice hardened. "Whatever I command."

Sebetwe

He'd come here alone on a little coracle every evening, since the first day they arrived on the island, rowing his way with a crude paddle. It took quite some time, with such a clumsy vessel and means of propelling it, before he got far enough out at sea for the depth to be acceptable to the one who came to meet him each evening.

He—she?—there was no way to know—was the greatest of the Sure Ones. A creature so immense that if you didn't spot the slowly moving nest of tentacles and if the ammonite had its eyes submerged, you might think you were approaching a small island. Birds and flying reptiles *did* perch on the Sure Ones' shells, especially in the evening.

The enormous creature took no notice of them, any more that it took notice of the small fish and big shrimp that were constantly swimming around it and even settling on its body. Sebetwe had wondered, at first, how the fish and shrimp avoided being eaten like all the other sea life that came within reach of the tentacle mass. Eventually, he decided they were feasting on the Sure One's parasites, and somehow the ever-moving tentacles knew they were not to be engulfed.

Such an arrangement suited the Sure Ones. It was the way they dealt with their environs. They were neither predator nor prey. Generally, they ate flesh, but now that he'd gotten more familiar with them Sebetwe knew the Sure Ones ate quite a bit of plant matter as well.

They could swim through the water. Quite rapidly, in fact, although only for short distances. But for the most part they seemed content to drift with the tides and the currents.

Unless something caught their attention. The one thing that was familiar about the minds of the Sure Ones—perhaps the only thing—was their curiosity. You couldn't exactly call it an intense curiosity, because nothing about the great ammonites was intense. But it could be quite unwavering. The Sure Ones were patient in a manner that eclipsed any Liskash or Mrem understanding of the term.

They were one with their world. They ate from it, they let it eat from them. Such matters were not worthy of their notice. Mostly, they observed.

He spent some time, as he did every evening, just floating in the coracle and staring at the Sure One. And it stared back at him. His eyes blinked, now and then. The Sure One's, never.

On the third evening, he'd given this Sure One a name. Bekezel, he'd decided to call it, after the shaman of legend who waited faithfully for her husband to return from a voyage until she died of old age.

The name would mean nothing to the Sure One. The need for a name had been Sebetwe's, not the giant so named.

Just as the words Sebetwe spoke to Bekezel on each one of those evenings meant nothing to the Sure One either. But they mattered to Sebetwe.

The sun was almost touching the horizon. It was time to return to the shore.

"Tomorrow, Bekezel," he said. "Tomorrow, I will come in the morning. And I will need you then. Please do not disappoint me."

Did the tentacles seem to coil with an unusual flourish?

A silly notion.

Probably.

Then again, who knew?

CHAPTER 16

Zilikazi

He'd been puzzled when he saw that the Kororo were only sending one raft into the strait to challenge him. Why had they even bothered? That single raft was smaller than any of the ones in his flotilla—and he had seventeen of them. Even that great number held not more than a third of his army.

But as his armada neared the oncoming raft, he eventually spotted the huge shells that surrounded it. One, two, three...he counted seven of them! For the first time since he'd emerged into his adulthood, he felt a surge of fear.

Angrily, he thrust it down. There was still only one raft and he was now close enough to see that it held not more than thirty opponents. Most of them he assumed to be Kororo, but there were at least half a dozen Mrem there also.

Few of them would be warriors, then. That raft would be carrying mostly tekku shamans and the Mrem dancers they seemed to use as auxiliaries. Did they plan to send the tentacled shells to attack his fleet?

Possibly. It seemed a poor tactic, though. From what little he'd seen of the creatures—ammonites, one of his subordinates called them—they were sluggish and slow-moving. The seagoing equivalent of gigantic snails. He thought it would be easy enough to simply avoid that raft and its escort altogether.

Yes. He'd let them fester in the middle of the

strait with their ammonites while he passed around them and landed almost two thousand warriors on the island. His own rafts moved sluggishly themselves, but he had dozens of warriors available to staff each of the great oars that drove them through the sea. He was almost certain he could outmaneuver his enemy.

He turned and gave the order, which his subordinates began passing through the ranks.

That took no time at all, on his own raft. But he realized quickly that the orders shouted across the water to nearby rafts would soon become so degraded as to be worthless. There wasn't much of a wind, but it was enough to make voices blurred and indistinct when they tried to shout against it.

He'd blundered, he realized. He'd been so impatient to finally settle accounts with the Kororo that he hadn't thought to develop a system—flags, perhaps—whereby he could transmit orders to his entire fleet once they were at sea.

No matter. He could guide his own raft where he would. The rest would follow. They would not dare do otherwise, even though he could sense the great fear that was coiled under the surface within all the warriors on those rafts. They were on the very edge of terror. By now, many of them had also seen the ammonites accompanying the Kororo vessel.

No matter. They were in greater fear of him—and his fury could far exceed that of any pitiful snail, no matter how large.

Sebetwe

"Begin the dance," he commanded.

Achia Pazik

It was a strange Dance. A wedding Dance, in its origins—and it still retained that basic structure. But Nurat Merav had modified it beyond recognition.

To start with, she'd stripped away any trace of its celebratory and ceremonial spirit. That had all been replaced by a great expansion—to the point of gross distortion—of the sexual aspects of the Dance. In essence, a wedding Dance had been transmuted into a mating Dance. And a crude and coarse one, at that.

On the first day of rehearsal, Achia Pazik and her Dancers had struggled to overcome their own embarrassment. Mrem were by no means prudish, but this Dance...!

Then, Nurat Merav had blended into it elements from various feasting Dances—and always the most coarse elements of each of them. The end result had been a Dance so grotesque that no Mrem would have dreamed of performing it in front of any audience.

Except one. An audience of enormous sea lizards. Creatures whose lives were dominated by two simple, crude emotions: hunger and lust.

Meshwe

The oldest and still greatest of the Kororo tekkutu would lead now. Meshwe would be the first to agree that in many ways he had been surpassed by his once-pupil Sebetwe. But none of them had Sebetwe's sense for the Sure Ones, and if he couldn't keep the ammonites steady, they would be doomed even faster than Zilikazi's fleet.

So, Meshwe ignored the Sure Ones. He would let Sebetwe deal with them. He found his tekku, found the minds of his companions in the great art who had joined him on the raft, blended their art with that of the Mrem dancers as they had all now learned to do, and sent that collective mind in search of what were probably the world's purest and certainly greatest carnivores.

The lizards ate *anything* as long as it was meat—and they were instantly willing to tear something apart to find out if it contained meat. Their great jaws could shred sharks and crush sea turtles. No one had yet observed them mating, but it wasn't likely such beasts would be any more delicate and fastidious in that endeavor.

How many of them dwelt in the strait? No one knew. But they were about to find out.

Sebetwe

His initial fear began to fade. He'd worried—they'd all worried—that the Sure Ones would get swept into the tekku maelstrom along with the lizards. But it seemed he'd been correct in his estimate. The huge ammonites simply didn't have enough of the emotions being whipped into a frenzy to react to the great surge of tekku that Meshwe was casting into the sea.

The Sure Ones possessed the urge to eat and the urge to reproduce. But they carried out those activities the same way they did everything: constantly, slowly; most of all, surely. The two emotions that seemed completely foreign to them were impatience and anxiety—without which, frenzied activity was simply not possible.

The most Sebetwe could detect was what seemed to be a heightened...interest, for lack of a better term. But most of that interest remained focused where it had been since the Kororo first came to the sea—on the Kororo themselves.

By now, Sebetwe thought he understood why the Sure Ones behaved the way they did. So little ever changed in their world that they were fascinated by anything new. And since they felt little (if anything) in the way of fear, they did not hesitate to indulge their curiosity.

For days and days on end. A curiosity which, with experience, Sebetwe had learned how to meld with and nurture. In their own placid and cold-blooded way, the ammonites were entranced by him. That was especially true of the one he called Bekezel, the most enormous of them all.

So, the Sure Ones might have felt a mild urge to increase their feeding; or mate; or simply drift away in search of food or mates. But those urges were overwhelmed by the much greater urge to continue observing these enchanting newcomers.

Meshwe

Not so, with the lizards. They had about as much in the way of calm observational instincts as a waterfall.

On the other hand, they *were* curious. But their curiosity had a very tight and narrow focus. Basically, their lives rotated around finding the answer to three questions:

Is this food?

Is this a mate?

Is this an enemy?

For days, more and more lizards had come swimming into the strait between the mainland and the island. They were drawn there, as much as anything, by the simple fact that so many of their kind were gathering there. As a rule, the only thing that drew large numbers of the lizards into one place was an abundance of food.

Or possible food.

But they'd been frustrated for all those days, as well. Yes, there was *something* new in the water. Which might be food and might be mates. Which were almost certainly enemies also; but for the lizards, almost everything animate was a potential enemy.

But they'd been kept at bay by the Sure Ones. Not even angry and frustrated sea lizards were foolish enough to threaten the giant ammonites. Those tentacles might normally be slow-moving, but they were immensely strong—and somewhere at their center was a beak that could cut through or crush anything a lizard could.

Meshwe began stirring them up—not that they needed much stirring to begin with. Within a short time, the frenzy began to build. And this time, there was a clear and unimpeded target for that frenzy.

So much food! So many possible mates, too. Although that was a secondary issue for the lizards. *Everything* was a secondary issue for the lizards, compared to eating.

Almost certainly enemies, as well. But although the lizards were wary of the Sure Ones, they weren't given to worrying much about enemies, other than their own kind. Why should they? A large fully-grown sea lizard was fifty to sixty feet long and weighed somewhere between twenty and thirty tons. Their mouths held four rows of sharp conical teeth which could be half a foot long and could exert a bite force as great as that of a giant shark.

Enemies, pfah.

They were circling, now. Dozens of them, ranging in size from ten to sixty feet long. The smallest ones, of course, stayed at the fringe. They had to avoid crowding the larger ones, lest a big lizard decide a smaller one was an easier meal than anything else.

Nearest to the rafts were seven or eight of the very largest lizards. One of them was sixty-two feet long, measuring from the tips of her snout to her tail, and weighed thirty-four tons.

In whatever manner thoughts moved through such a brain, the lizard decided it was time to take an exploratory bite. What *was* this great, bloated body floating on the surface?

She drove in. Her target was the obvious one. The one in front and more separated from its mates than the rest.

Njekwa

No one could have missed or misunderstood the spike of terror that Zilikazi sent screaming through the minds of his subjects. Certainly not a priestess as old and experienced as Njekwa.

"Start gathering the faithful," she commanded Litunga and the other shamans and priestesses gathered around her. There were nine of them, all told. "Quickly!"

All raced off except Litunga.

"Gather them where?" she asked.

Njekwa looked around. Zilikazi had taken fewer than two thousand warriors with him, the most that could be crammed onto the rafts. The rest, somewhere between four and five thousand, were ranged along the beach.

No, not "ranged," exactly. They were clustered; and, as she watched, the clusters began tightening.

She knew what was happening. Zilikazi had long since crushed anyone in his army who might challenge his mindpower. But that still left at least a dozen subordinates who had noble ancestry and might have the potential to develop a noble's mental control.

All of them had kept whatever such talents they might have carefully concealed, but it was impossible to conceal them entirely. Zilikazi had been satisfied if they were discreet and made no overt show of their power. He couldn't kill everyone who shared noble lineage. Some day, the nobles might evolve into a completely different species, but that was not true today. The nobles still could and did breed with normal Liskash. The only way Zilikazi could have prevented the emergence of any possible rivals would have been to kill all of his own offspring and disband his harem.

He'd considered the first course of action, several times, and might someday do it. But there was no chance he'd dismiss his harem. He was still young and vigorous.

The Liskash officers in the army with noble lineage who possessed at least some of a noble's power would have naturally drawn subordinates around them over time. Now, they reacted the same way to Zilikazi's mental shriek of fear.

The same way sea lizards reacted to the smell of blood in the water.

Njekwa pointed to a low rise in the shoreline perhaps two hundred yards to the south. "Tell them to gather there. Away from the army, and close to the beach."

CHAPTER 17

Zilikazi

Like snakes, the sea lizards devoured their prey whole. Their jaws were double-hinged and their skulls were flexible, allowing them to swallow very large animals. If the prey was too large, though, they were faced with something of a problem. Unlike sharks, their teeth were not well-suited to biting off pieces of flesh. The teeth of the lizards were conical, not serrated. The points were sharp, certainly, but they had no cutting edges.

So, when attacking prey too large to swallow whole, they use a crude and simple method. They bit down—*hard*—and then lashed their long and sinuous bodies, using their immensely powerful tail muscles.

Just to see what might happen, as it were.

What usually happened was that the prey started coming apart.

In this case, Zilikazi's raft didn't—quite—start disintegrating. The logs used to make up his raft had been among the biggest; the ropes used to tie them together had been among the best; and the knots had been well designed and well made throughout.

So, the raft held together when the huge sea lizard clamped down and lashed its body. But the raft was crammed with warriors and it was jolted so hard that fourteen of them were flung completely into the sea and another six barely managed to hang on to the sides of the raft when they went into the water.

The huge lizard relinquished her mouth's grip and circled for another bite, still intent on the raft itself.

Others, however, went after what looked like easier targets. Whatever these things were wriggling and thrashing on the surface.

Within ten seconds, five lizards had come to the same conclusion.

This is food!

It didn't take even that many seconds for the smell of blood—lots of blood—to transmit that information to twice as many lizards, and within a few more minutes any lizard in the strait knew that a feeding frenzy was underway.

✧   ✧   ✧

All but one of the warriors who'd managed to hold on to the raft got back aboard before lizards could take them down. But, of the fourteen who went into the sea, only five managed to swim back and climb aboard to safety.

Such as it was—briefly.

The second bite-and-lash of the biggest of the lizards began disintegrating the raft. Almost at the same time as she relinquished that bite, two more lizards had taken bites on the opposite side of the raft.

That side began disintegrating. Twenty-two more warriors had gone into the sea.

A few seconds later, the big female who'd begun the attack got her first meal of the day. She'd left off going at the raft in favor of something wriggling closer and much easier to swallow.

Her first meal—but by no means her last. Like most large carnivores, the sea lizards were firmly devoted to gorging.

Zilikazi had managed to keep from being thrown off the raft by holding desperately onto the pole he'd had fixed near the front of the raft to hold up his banner. So, he had time—he certainly had the rage and fear—to bring down a wave of sheer mental force and fury onto the creature he knew was responsible. That hateful tekkutu—oh, yes, he recognized his psychic stench! he was the one who'd inflicted so much grief on the army in the mountains—who was the cause of this horror.

Zilikazi could slay anyone outright when he applied

that much power, so long as he could find and latch onto his mind. Which, he finally could. He could now *see* his tormentor, for the first time. The tekkutu standing at the very edge of his own raft.

The wave came down, like a mallet striking an insect.

Sebetwe

Sebetwe felt the blow, certainly. But only in the way someone feels a blow when he's wearing thick, padded armor—and the blow itself is delivered using a padded club. Great pressure, but almost no pain. A powerful jolt, but not a sharp one. It felt more like being suddenly pushed by someone than being hit with a weapon.

A very big someone, true. But not big enough—not when Sebetwe had such sure and certain footing.

He was farther into Bekezel's mind than he'd ever been before; almost communing with the Sure One, insofar as "communing" was a term that could be applied to a consciousness that had neither language nor abstract ideas. It was a mind that had no filters between itself and its environment, because it needed none. It was simply too huge, too powerful, too well-protected to need screens between itself and what it saw, and felt, and tasted, and smelled, and heard. Why bother interpreting reality when it was so engrossing in itself.

Deep inside *that* mind, with *that* mind as his shield and armor, Sebetwe was simply impervious to anything Zilikazi or his ilk could ever do. And his shield and armor were more than great enough to shelter everyone near him as well.

Zilikazi

If Zilikazi had been in full possession of his wits, if he'd had the time to ponder and contemplate the problem, he might have eventually come up with a way to insinuate his mental strength past Sebetwe's protection, in the way a skilled warrior might slip a blade between joints in a suit of armor.

But he had no time to ponder anything and he was not in possession of his wits. He was in a panic, his mind a chaotic swirl. Having no experience with such a state of abject terror, he was hysterical. The blows he lashed out were furious but completely wild.

Within half a minute of the first lizard attack, those wild mental blows had killed six of his own warriors. That wasn't his intent, of course. But just as a fighter who's lost his bearing in a battle strikes out at anything that moves—not knowing who he struck, and not caring, either—so did Zilikazi.

The blows against the tekkutu on the raft in the distance were somehow simply being shed by the hideous creature. So, his terrified rage thwarted in that direction, Zilikazi struck at targets he thought he could reach.

He struck at the lizards first—or tried to. But he had neither knowledge nor understanding of tekku. He tried to strike down giant animal predators in the same way he struck down intelligent beings.

All he accomplished was to drive the monsters into an even more furious frenzy. Three more bit the raft and lashed it; a third of it fell away, the logs separating into small clumps. Dozens of warriors were now in the water, being devoured by lizards.

One lizard—a very large one, if not quite as large as the one who'd begun the attack—came up under the raft, smashing its snout right through the deck before it fell back.

The lizards had begun attacking other rafts as well. The entire armada except the lead raft bearing Zilikazi was now desperately trying to return to the beach from which they'd launched.

They were aided by the waves, but impeded by the current, which in this part of the strait seem to run parallel to the shore. They were also impeded, needless to say, by the lizards attacking them.

Perhaps their greatest impediment, though, was their ruling lord. Seeing them abandoning him, Zilikazi's fury lost whatever coherence it might have still retained.

The traitors! They dared to defy him? He was their master!

All the tremendous force of his mind came down on the traitors. They *would* obey him and return.

He might even have succeeded, so great was his power. But he had no time left.

Another lizard smashed into the raft from below and the vessel finally disintegrated completely. Still clutching the flagpole with its bright banner, Zilikazi went into the sea.

Fury finally vanished. All that was left was terror.

Njekwa

"Hurry! Hurry!" The priestess was almost running herself. At least a thousand people were gathering on the rise. Many of them she recognized as adherents, but many others were not.

Who were they? Most looked to be females and younglings, but there were at least half a hundred warriors in their midst. Looking back as she hurried, Njekwa could see that many more warriors were beginning to drift away from the clusters on the beach.

None of the noble-lineage officers who were starting to gather little armies around themselves were very powerful. For sure and certain, not one of them would be powerful enough to impose his will on all those who contended against him.

So, confusion swirled; doubt and uncertainty coursed alongside. Many of the warriors, with no real attachment to any commander, would be looking toward the largest gathering they could see—the one being formed by Njekwa and Litunga. Few if any of them adhered to the Old Faith themselves, but they knew of it. Some of them had mothers who belonged. Or sisters, or cousins, or even daughters.

It was not only the largest gathering, it was the most visible because it was centered on the one rise in the shoreline in the area.

The pull was powerful. More and more warriors began drifting that way. After a few steps, the drift became a current.

Then all of them felt a new spike driving through their minds, whose meaning was unmistakable.

The current became a tide.

Achia Pazik

Part of her hated the Dance, but it was exhilarating in its own way.

Its own cruel, bloody, ravenous way. Their raft was close enough to Zilikazi's armada for Achia Pazik to understanding what was happening over there.

Death, dismemberment, destruction. *Feeding.*

She fed herself, drawing from it the strength to continue the Dance. The most savage, hideous, intoxicating Dance ever designed.

Nurat Merav should be ashamed of herself.

Nurat Merav

She couldn't see what was happening, but Zuluku and Raish and Selani rushed back and forth from the rock spur to bring her constant reports.

After a while, she thought she should probably be ashamed of herself.

Meshwe

The oldest and most powerful of the Krek's tekkutu, on this day, also possessed in full measure another characteristic of great age and power.

Ruthlessness. There would be no mercy for Zilikazi.

He drove the lizards. Again, and again, and again, and again.

Zilikazi

The flagpole and its large bright banner kept Zilikazi alive for a while. Three times a lizard tried to devour him; each time, the pole and banner thwarted the attack.

The first two lizards were distracted by the banner. The first took away half of it. The second took away the rest.

The third lizard tried to engulf the entire pole and its jaws got stuck open.

Not for long, of course. Not those jaws. But by the time the jaws shattered the slender pole, Zilikazi had swum off.

He was a good swimmer, as Liskash measured these things. And he was full of fear to drive him forward.

He was also lucky. All three attacks had pulled or driven him far outside the frenzy. He was now in the open, more than halfway to the raft that held his enemies.

Perhaps they would accept his surrender.

He wasn't sure he knew how to surrender.

It was a moot point. The lizards who arrived a few seconds later wouldn't have accepted his surrender anyway.

The first one to strike was a small lizard, as such creatures went; not more than fifteen feet long and weighing less than three tons. It tried to swallow him whole but missed and only got his left leg in its maw. An instant later, a second and larger lizard bit his torso and crushed his chest.

A brief tussle followed. The first lizard swam off with the leg. The second started to engulf the rest of the body but a third lizard arrived and ripped off the other leg, the hips, and part of the abdomen.

By then Zilikazi was dead, of course. A few pieces of him were missed by the lizards. The largest was his right arm severed just below the shoulder. Those bits and pieces drifted with the current until they came within reach of Bekezel's tentacle mass. The Sure One scooped them up efficiently, neatly, almost daintily. Seconds later, they vanished into the huge beak.

Most of the rafts, and most of the warriors, made it to shore safely. Still, it had been the biggest feast in any of those lizards' lifetimes. If they'd had bards, they would have been singing lays about it for centuries.

CHAPTER 18

Meshwe

"We have to have the river also," Njekwa insisted. "We have many more people to feed than you do. We will need to fish."

By now, after days of negotiating, Meshwe was more than a little tired of the old priestess. She was stubborn almost beyond belief. The fact that her position was the weakest of the three negotiating parties—the biggest party, but still the weakest—just seemed to make her more recalcitrant.

Fortunately, as had happened several times since

the parlay began, the representative of the smallest of the three parties intervened with a compromise. Perhaps that was because she was also—by far—the youngest of the three chief negotiators.

"You should pay a toll for it, then," Achia Pazik proposed. When Njekwa glared at her, the Mrem Dancer shook her head.

"Be reasonable, Njekwa. The river has its own monsters. If the tekkutu don't control the turtlesnakes for you, none of your fisher folk will last very long if they go out onto the river. Even the marshes are dangerous. Do you expect the tekkutu do that work for nothing?"

Njekwa was still glaring, but the young Mrem simply met the glare with a gaze so calm it was almost serene. She had the priestess boxed in—again—and they both knew it.

After a moment, Njekwa looked away. "I suppose that would work," she said. The glare came back to the surface. "So long as the toll is reasonable!"

Meshwe raised his hand in a gesture of conciliation. "Quite reasonable, I assure you."

It would be, too. Not much more than a token charge, in fact. Meshwe did not really care about the disposition of the river itself. It had already been agreed that the Krek would have possession of most of the island—all of it except the crest and the valley leading from it to the west that the Mrem had been given. There was more than enough arable land on the island to feed three times their number. When the time came that the Kororo numbers had swelled greater than the island could sustain, it had already been agreed that the Krek possessed everything on the mainland coast south of the great river. No one still knew yet what sort of lands lay there, but some of it was bound to be fertile.

Besides, if the Krek decided to start fishing—which they very well might—why would they bother piddling around in the river? They had the sea at their disposal.

Sebetwe

That very moment, Sebetwe was contemplating the same issue. He'd noticed that the Sure Ones enjoyed shade, on those occasions when passing clouds provided it for them. It had then occurred to him that if they built a large enough vessel with a platform supported on double hulls, they could sail anywhere with an escort that no creature in the sea would think of challenging.

They'd have to sail slowly, of course, so the Sure Ones could stay in the shade between the double hulls. Perhaps they could design the hulls with oars and banks for the rowers.

But so what? Fishing was best done slowly.

So he'd been told, anyway. Being a sane and sensible Liskash, Sebetwe had never fished before.

Achia Pazik

By the end of the day's negotiating, Njekwa looked more sour than ever, even though she'd gotten most of what she wanted.

Achia Pazik thought she knew the reason. After

Zilikazi's death, the nation he had welded together by sheer force of mind immediately began to disintegrate. Within two days, eight separate contending little armies had emerged, each with its own fledgling lord.

But the largest of those armies, commanded by one of Zilikazi's former subordinates named Mehuli, had fewer than five hundred warriors and the most outstanding characteristic of their new noble lord—semi-noble lord, rather, and that was being generous—was his fledgling status. His mental powers were still feeble, and might very well remain so.

It was true that for the moment Mehuli's powers exceeded those of any of his seven rivals, all of whom were also fledglings. But he no more considered challenging the Kororo than he would have considered challenging the tides or the sunrise. Whatever might be the nature of their mysterious tekku, the Krek had destroyed the most powerful lord Mehuli had ever known. The world's most fearsome monsters were at their command.

The only thing Mehuli wanted from the Kororo was a great distance. The day after he consolidated his hold over his little army, he ordered them to march back to the lands they'd come from.

Within another two days, his seven rival armies had done the same. All of them were trying to find separate routes through the mountains because none of them was yet ready to match their strength against another. The likelihood was that few of them would manage to do so, however. Most of them would have no choice but to fight over the one route they did know.

That was their problem, however, not the Krek's and certainly not Achia Pazik's.

Unlike Njekwa, she was in a very good mood. The survival of the Kororo depended on their control over the passage between the island and the mainland. So long as they—and they alone—could maintain the peculiar relationship with the Sure Ones that allowed them to keep the sea lizards at bay, they would always have an impregnable sanctuary on the island.

But doing so also depended on maintaining their not-quite-as-peculiar relationship with the Mrem. Without the Dancers, no tekkutu could hope to control even a gantrak, much less the behemoths of the sea.

So, Meshwe had been very generous and compliant when it came to Achia Pazik's demands. And, for her part, she'd been careful to present those demands as pleasantly phrased modest requests. The Mrem were just as dependent on the Kororo as the Kororo were on them.

More dependent, in some ways. Scouting parties would continue to be sent into the mountains, searching for any more small splinters from Achia Pazik's shattered tribe. Each of those parties would have a Mrem accompanying it—but only one. There simply weren't enough Mrem to do the work on their own.

Their numbers had reached eighty-three now, of whom eleven were Dancers. (Twelve, if you counted Nurat Merav.) The valley they'd been given was more than sufficient for them. It would probably be sufficient for ten times their current number, and if they came to exceed that—which she now had every confidence they would, someday—then there were still all those mysterious lands south of the river. She and Meshwe had also already agreed that if the time came, the Mrem and the Kororo would share those lands in an equitable manner.

And equitable it would be. They were too reliant on each other for it to be anything else. Their survival and prosperity depended on maintaining the sanctuary of the island. So long as they retained that, no lord of the lowlands—not even one more powerful than Zilikazi—could possibly threaten them.

The position of the Old Faith, however, was quite different. On the one hand, theirs was by far the largest of the three groups. In the end, more than eight thousand of the people Zilikazi brought over the mountains had chosen to remain on the coast.

For lack of any clear alternative, they had all accepted Njekwa as their leader. But while many of them were adherents to the Old Faith, most were not. So what would happen to them, in the end? No one knew, but Achia Pazik suspected that more and more of them would adopt the Kororo creed, as time went on. And she was quite sure that Njekwa shared the same suspicion.

Well, that was her problem, not Achia Pazik's.

Later that day, she wasn't quite as sure.

"*What?*" She was almost goggling at Chefer Kolkin. "He's insane! Mrem can't do that!"

The veteran warrior shrugged. "That's what I told the youngster. But you know Lavi Tur. He's headstrong. And always wants to try his hand at everything."

Lavi Tur

The next morning, though, the brash almost-a-warrior was feeling a rare moment of anxiety and uncertainty. Squatting on his haunches with his hands splayed on the sand, the youngster stared apprehensively at the tritti sprawled a short distance away in the little arena. For its part, the horned lizard stared off to the side. To all outward appearances it seemed oblivious to the Mrem's presence.

Lavi Tur looked up at Meshwe, who was observing the proceedings with cheerfully-gaping jaws.

As well he might. The old tekkutu was standing *outside* the enclosure.

"Couldn't I try first with a huddu?" asked Lavi Tur plaintively. "Or maybe a mavalore?"

Song of Petru
XIX

Tooth

The Way was Lost
Evil stood across
His Sacred Path
Swords were blunted
Many despaired
To Save us all
He called to Death
Join in my Feast

Feeding a Fever

JODY LYNN NYE

"COME, DEAREST, JUST A LITTLE BITE," PETRU pleaded, holding the piece of browned meat temptingly under Cassa Fisook's nose. The lead Dancer of the Lailah Clan lay in a nest of cushions on a pallet in her hastily-erected pavilion near an oasis at the edge of an expanse of strange desert. The clan had been forced to halt there the previous noon. Few of them could have made it much farther. Only the blessed presence of fresh, potable water had given the sick and ailing the strength to press on to this point. The encampment had become one large infirmary. Cassa's long, slender, black-furred limbs trembled with weakness and the fever.

Petru turned the morsel so that the sun peeking through the draped sides of the tent gleamed off it like the burnished surface of an amber pearl. "You wouldn't want to hurt my feelings, would you? This is the most tender portion of that little desert bird, freshly killed and cooked just to savoriness. I would eat it myself, it is so good. Try just a taste."

The elder female's upper lip curled a little. The scent of the meat had tickled her sensory glands with delight, but she shook her head weakly. Petru moved his hand toward her lips. From her narrow belly arose an audible gurgle. By her expression, Petru knew the sound had hurt, but he offered the food again. Cassa held up a slender forefinger in protest.

"Thank you, cherished Petru, but I can't. If I swallow anything, it will go straight through me."

"Then I despair! I thought you truly loved me," the valet said, wrinkling his nose and allowing his magnificent sable whiskers to droop toward his shoulders. Though he was of a much lower rank than the Dancers, the shining, long black fur that covered his body made him seem to be of noble heritage. His expanse of whiskers was unequaled in the clan, and he used them expressively.

In spite of her discomfort, Cassa chuckled.

"Oh, I do, you big clown," she said. "It is just that my poor body does not love me. I am aged, and I cannot throw off a fever the way that I could in my youth. I fear that Assirra calls me to her side. I will not live to see us arrive in our haven."

"Nonsense," Petru said with a dismissive wave. It was a casual gesture, but in his heart he feared she might be correct. "You just want us to go on carrying you on a litter instead of walking on your own lovely feet."

"If my feet could carry me, I would scamper away from this place! The air is so dry my nose is cracking."

Petru rummaged in his personal basket of cosmetics and unguents. At the bottom—why did things always fall to the bottom when he wanted them?—was a small, heavy alabaster jar sealed with a soft cork.

Avoiding Cassa's hands, he dabbed the herb-scented cream on the leather of her nose. Immediately, the senior Dancer stopped protesting and relaxed.

"Ah, that is better. Assirra must show you special favor. Your lotions are always better than anything the merchants bring me."

"Of course! That is because I make them with love," Petru said. He couldn't keep the note of smugness out of his tone. He was proud of his skill at formulation. "If you will not eat this now, I will soak it in diluted wine and wrap it in a leaf to keep it for later. Shall I open the tent flaps a trifle to let more sunlight fall upon you? Would you like another cushion or two? I have your favorite wool-stuffed pillow right here."

"Yes, thank you, my dear Petru. You always know what I need. Then, let me rest."

The big valet arranged the well-loved and battered suede pillow so that Cassa could sniff the heavy oils of the padding, then pulled the nearest drape around the tent pole to let the afternoon sun touch his lady's feet. With a sigh, she curled into a ball, wrapping her long, slim tail around her body. Petru worried that she would waste away, but rest was the third best restorative, after a cure and food.

He heard a groan and a challenging hiss from the second pallet at the other side of the tent. Cleotra Mreem was having another nightmare. Petru pulled away cushion after cushion until he could uncover the Dancer's face. Its fur was crusted with dried mucus all around the nose and mouth. With the greatest tenderness, he started to brush it away.

Cleotra's eyes flew open. Her glowing pupils bloomed widely in the narrow band of green, and she bared her claws. A dry tongue flicked in and out of her mouth. Petru knew she wasn't really awake. She had a worse form of the disease than Cassa had. She was younger and stronger and could manage food, but suffered fever and hallucinations as well as the choking matter running from her eyes and nose.

"Mistress," he said. "You have defeated the Liskash! It is dead! Victory!"

"No," she muttered. "There are too many of them! The clan will die! They will eat our children! We must save the kits!"

Petru reached for the jug of water beside the bed and poured some onto the soft cloth near the washing bowl. He dabbed at her face with long, gentle strokes as if he was her mother.

"No, mistress," he said, in a low, calm voice that belied his own worry. "The Liskash lies at your feet. It is dead. What could withstand the power of your Dance? Assirra and Aedonniss put their strength into your leaps. It fell, shedding its blood on the ground."

Cleotra's eyes widened. She writhed, clawing at the air with her talons. "Yes! I tore its guts out! I dined on its liver!"

"Yes, yes," Petru said. He jumped back to avoid a swipe. A patch of mucus was dried in the fur just above her left cheekbone. He flicked the flakes and pellets to the floor, and kicked dry sand over them. Cleotra caught him with a wild swing of her leg.

Petru tumbled backwards and sat down hard. Dust rose around him. He cringed at the state of his fur. It would take forever to get all that sand out of his tail.

"How dare you get in my way!" Cleotra screamed, baring her claws. "I am the Dancer of Dancers! My every movement is worship of the gods!"

"Forgive me, dearest lady," Petru said. He knew the diatribe was not aimed at him. It was the illness talking. Cleotra had an evil temper, feared throughout the clan, but she rarely exercised it on him. He took great care not to arouse it. "Oh, no, no, no, mistress, don't, please!"

Cleotra rose to all fours and arched her back high, flinging her tail out of the way. Petru leaped forward with the cloth held out.

It wasn't an adequate barrier. Liquid bowel movements sprayed out of her anus. He caught a small quantity, but the rest fell onto her bedding. She immediately began to scratch at the mess as if to bury it, then realized she had excrement all over her hands. She dropped onto her side and began to cry.

"Oh, mistress, calm yourself," Petru said. He dropped the cloth and scrubbed his pads against the sandy floor. When they were as clean as he could get them, he gathered the Dancer in his arms. She was as a light bundle of sticks covered with dry fur.

Her fever was getting worse. Young as she was, he feared that she might die before Cassa.

Once he had cleaned Cleotra and placed her on a nest of fresh bedding, she was so exhausted by her nightmares that she fell into a deep sleep. Grateful for the respite, Petru went out to clean the stink from his own fur.

The only water to be had needed to be hauled up a pail at a time from the depths of a single well at the heart of the oasis. It tasted sweet, but the Mrem feared that the encroaching sea, not far to the north, would invade the water table from below and pollute this well and others ahead of them with salt. Once that happened, the Lailah Clan would be forced farther into enemy lands. Reluctant to leave his charges, Petru kept looking over his shoulder at the tent where they rested. He disliked change. Change was the enemy, even more than the hated Liskash.

At least the Lailah had had a few months of peace, more so than many of their distant kinsfolk. They had departed the Liskash satrapy of Ckotliss where they had wintered more than a month before. Each clan had had its own place to live among the stone buildings within the high, strong walls. As much as was possible, the Mrem sought to live as though the Great Salt had not invaded their lives and destroyed their lands. Marriages had taken place in the citadel. A few newborns had been welcomed, and several more begotten. Many councils and much healing had taken place, but not enough to undo the evil of having had to depart their homeland with so little preparation. An ongoing interchange of ideas in council was begun among the fragments of the clans now joined together under the banner of the Lailah, but mainly the Mrem were grateful for a place to live safely.

Since the Liskash lord Tae Shanissi was dead and all his court with him, the remaining Liskash fled from the citadel or existed in a forced truce with the Mrem. The good things were a chance to rest and raise healthy cattle, the crops to feed them and the clan on the road, and time to send out scouts to determine the best way around the new ocean that parted them from the rest of the Mrem and safety. The bad thing was they must eventually set out and continue to the west in hopes of meeting up with the rest of the Clan of the Claw. The Lailah could not hope to hold off incursions on Ckotliss by other Liskash wizards who would surely investigate why their brother was no longer communicating with them. It was not altruism on the part of the lizards, but pure self-interest. An empty castle would be a new outpost for the one who could conquer it. The cold ones were friends to no one, not even one another.

The land became more difficult immediately west of the citadel, a natural defense against invasion. The Mrem had a choice between harsh desert and sheer cliffs that overlooked it, a landscape constructed by a vengeful whim of the gods. But the choice resolved itself farther on—the escarpments, receded farther from the salty shore, leaving an expanse of sand and further in, scanty brush in which birds and tiny lizards flitted. There was little cover, but at least it was an easy road, if a perilous one. The Lailah were grateful that none of the herdbeasts or the krelprep would have precious weight run off them on the long journey ahead. Still, they could not linger. The sea encroached daily upon the narrow neck of land. Beyond lay the great desert and who knew what dangers?

The Dancers mourned those of the Mrem whose lands had been drowned. Many lovely valleys were now beneath the waves, and who knew where the inhabitants had gone? The Dancers had performed many rites to lay to rest the spirits of those who had died. Very few survivors were found who claimed to come from those northern valleys.

The Mrem slaves who had been freed within the compound did not trust their freedom at first. Because of the Liskash noble's mind powers, they had given up hope of being considered anything but menial servants and the occasional meat beast by the Liskash. Once the spell had been broken long enough, they began to realize that it was true. When they were convinced by the talonmaster Bau Dibsea and Cassa that they deserved better, they could not show enough how grateful they were. Gradually, they regained pride in themselves, caring for their coats and claws once more. In a grand ceremony with their own ill-trained Dancers performing the rite of thanks before Aedonniss and Assirra, they swore their allegiance to the Lailah clan. Those Liskash who left the Mrem alone or who had treated captives well were left in peace. But the former servants took dire revenge on any of the Liskash who had tormented them. New heads were found dangling from cords along the city gates every morning for a month. The bodies were never found.

Petru did not care where they had been bestowed, as long as he did not have to cope with rotting and

dismembered corpses. He had enough to do looking after his Dancers. His ladies immediately took
the young ones under their tutelage. Already, the
newcomers were thrilling and amazing the Lailah
with the harrowing stories that they acted out. Even
Ysella, most junior of the Dancers, had acquired a
fist of students of her own. They had heard of the
young female's heroic exploits, and begged to serve her
and learn from her. To Ysella's credit, the praise and
adulation had not changed her behavior toward her
betters, among whom Petru counted himself for the
moment. Once she had truly achieved the mastery of
Dance and become a full priestess, he would naturally
cede authority to her, but until then, he tolerated her
antics with the patience of a loving uncle.

The former servants threw their full energies to the
benefit of their new clansfolk. They knew where everything was hidden in the stone chambers, cellars and
corridors. The councilor Sherril Rangawo oversaw the
growing inventory with an authority that irked Petru,
but he could not help but admit that the results gave
heart to the entire Mrem clan. Working throughout
the winter months, the Mrem stripped the palace of
anything useful, especially weapons, along with tools
to make and repair them, carts, lamps and fuel for
same, dried herbs and tinctures for medicine and
lightweight treasures they could use as trade goods
upon the road. Petru himself had gone through Tae
Shanissi's personal chambers in search of adornments.
His stores of sparkle powders, scents and other cosmetics were running low, and the Dancers appreciated

the small touches he added to their beauty before they performed. Once they knew what was lacking in the citadel's own stores, Sherril assembled a list of the supplies that the clan would need upon setting out. Every male and warrior female went on the hunt outside the citadel's walls, and every female, child and elder set their hands to salting meats and drying eggs, herbs and fruit. Wholesome grains and good-keeping tubers were packed into pottery jugs and sealed with wax against insects. Honey, oil, vinegar, and wine were bottled into clay amphorae and set in endless rows in between jugs meant for water that they would fill from the city wells just before setting out. Salt they already had in plenty.

The Mrem had no intention of impoverishing their hosts, for that way lay resentment and possible vengeance. The Liskash themselves must soon move from the citadel, and would require supplies of their own. The Great Salt continued to rise, as much as an outstretched hand a day. The Liskash's jetties that jutted out into the sea were now entirely surrounded, their pilings nearly drowned already. Sometime in the not-too-distant future the encroaching sea would swamp and envelop Ckotliss. The land occupied by the citadel and its rich fields had little time before it was as much a memory as the Lailah's ancient home.

Bau Dibsea announced at a council to which he invited all the townsfolk remaining within the walls that anyone who shared their grain or animals would be compensated from Tae Shanissi's confiscated treasures. Cassa and Bau insisted that the Mrem leave the citadel in as good condition as when they had entered it. As the city would be under water in a matter of moons, it was an empty gesture, but one that they were sure would be approved by Aedonniss and Assirra. They never truly trusted a single Liskash, but they were good temporary masters, and the Liskash responded to that benign treatment. They hated the Mrem, yet they were not soldiers. If they were not misused, they would not try to follow the Mrem westward when they departed to take revenge in the open. Bau was seldom wrong when it came to summing up an enemy. He assumed that the remaining lizards would gather together their goods and animals and flee eastward once the Mrem were gone.

When spring came at last, there was no excuse for remaining. Scouts returned weekly with reports of the terrain to the west. No parties of intelligent Liskash had been spotted; no signs of their passage had been found. The news was not all good, of course. Because the sea had already filled the low-lying farmlands of the north, they would be forced to travel in the open desert.

Petru sighed for the good meals they had eaten over the winter. The months of privation before that had been hard on his lush figure, and those of his ladies, of course. Bau took council from those of the Mrem slaves who had lived to the west and could advise him on the shape of the terrain and the dangers of what lizard-kin roamed there, or had when they were last free. The Lailah were as well prepared as it was possible to be, not knowing how long their journey would last, nor into what dangers it would take them. With great reluctance, they set out.

But the desert *was* vast. While like any of the Mrem Petru reveled the heat, he disliked immensely the endless dust that their passage kicked up. His thick fur needed to be brushed every time they stopped, or he felt he would look unfit to care for his Dancers. Almost daily, the hunters brought in fresh meat from Liskash-kin and birds. Petru treated the journey as though it was a picnic. When the caravan halted for meals, he prepared dainties for his charges and presented them with as much of a flourish as he could muster. Cassa was amused by his antics. For a while, it was easy enough.

The Mrem tired quickly during the first few days, but soon fell into the habit of the march. Fistmaster Emoro Awr, one of the oldest and most seasoned of the warriors, stayed at the rear with a fist of his best fighters, to protect the Dancers, but also to keep an eye on Petru, his dearest love. The riders flanked the Dancers as they walked beside the cart containing their tent and other personal goods. Except for the warriors protecting the train, no one rode but the kits and elders. The scouts led the way, riding back and forth between the talonmaster and his officers to give the news on what lay ahead.

At first the desert looked featureless, all grayish-yellow under a broad blue sky, but Petru soon learned to distinguish differences in the terrain. It was not all sand, but it was hot. Undulating waves of bedrock would suddenly appear in between dunes, leading down into crevasses that were far cooler to traverse than the open surface. Bau Dibsea took counsel from the others, and decided it was wiser to travel at night, when they would not fall prey to the hot sun. Thereafter, the Mrem slept in the crevasses. Some were populated with sting-tails and other perils, but most were safe. Like the scouts, Petru scanned for those darker points of land. When no crack in the earth was available, they trudged over the dunes under the stars, taking their time for the sake of the laboring, panting beasts of burden. The whipping sand covered footprints so swiftly that the best scouts had to wait for the dry storms to abate before leading the train forward. They navigated by the stars and the rising moon. It was in its first quarter, a slender hook the Dancers called Aedonniss's Claw.

Their supplies of water ran out very quickly. The Mrem found the shadowy trails of the animals that occupied the desert in between gusts of wind. Following them carefully and patiently so as not to scare the desert creatures into fleeing randomly, they waited, eyes aglow in the darkness, to see where the small beasts went for water and food.

Some of the scouts that went off on these foraging expeditions never returned, but Drillmaster Scaro Ullenh, a brave Mrem who had proved his worth in Ckotliss as in many other situations before, rode proudly into the temporary shelter, his head held high, with a tale of sweet water, ripe figs, frogs and even fish not half a day's march ahead.

"Broad pools, like blue jewels in the pale gold desert," he said, preening his silver whiskers with pride.

That was their first oasis. The beasts had to be coaxed up and out of the sheltered passageway, but once they got the scent of water, they could not be held back. The lush, green spot was so small, they could have missed it entirely. Scaro preened at having been the one to find it. A couple of the younger nubile females showed him their gratitude, to Petru's amusement. But it was the beginning of the pattern into which their journey fell.

The desert did not give up its gifts freely. The secret of each oasis had to be teased from the terrain and the sands. At their waking at sunset every day the Dancers performed rites to ensure that Assirra pleaded with her husband to show them favor. They never knew how many days would pass in between finding water. The Mrem covered many weary, hot miles, fearing that the wells they sought were only illusions in the minds of the desperate scouts.

Everyone's fears came to pass one moon into their trek. After several successes, the forward observers failed at last to find a well. Day after day, the leaders released smaller and smaller rations of water to the clan to make it last. Petru gave up as much of his portion as he could bear to make sure the Dancers had enough to sustain them. The long, dry trek went on so long that the clan was ready to give up hope.

At last, when they feared they might lose several of their elders and kits to dehydration, the scouts trudged back with good news and half-full amphorae. They had found an oasis, a hollow with several small, deep pools that bubbled up from the depths. It was so remote that the clan passed skeleton after skeleton of lizard kin who had died before they reached it.

Desperate for water, the Mrem had pressed on to the southwest. A scout waited on the rim of the hidden valley and guided them down the slope into a pocket of greenery. The Dancers and warriors tried to prevent the clan from drinking the water before it was boiled, but some, in the choice between life and death, drank of the pool. What, after all, was the worst that could happen? They drank their fill, then loaded up every vessel with the water, and set out again as soon as everyone had regained their strength.

The worst occurred. Within a day or two past the green valley, most of those who drank of unfiltered water became ill. Then, horribly, the illness spread, until very few of the clan was untouched by fever, chills and unsettled bowels. The sickest patients grew disoriented, seeing creatures and threats that were not there. Of these many died. Grief-stricken, their loved ones buried them in the desert.

The talonmaster called a conference of the elders of the clan. With the endless heat like an oppressive hand pressing down upon them, the Dancers and the senior warriors gathered under the waning moon. In the distance, Petru could hear the slither of night creatures. He prayed fervently that Aedonniss would spare the Mrem from the insidiousness of poisonous serpents and stinging insects.

Sherril Rangawo, as usual, the lazy hairball, spoke for those who wanted to stop. The big gray Mrem argued that they needed to halt for a time to heal themselves. Emoro argued against it, pointing out that the scouts had also noticed the footprints of Liskash of all kinds investigating their trail and spoor. They could not hide, nor could they stand against the main forces of Liskash armies. A good deal of grumbling ensued, but the clan trudged on, stopping frequently throughout the nights to care for those whom the disease felled. Cassa promised that they could stop when they found a place reasonably defensible.

Instead, one by one, the Mrem sickened. The disease made their bowels loose, filled up their noses and throats with phlegm, but worst of all, the sufferers began to see hallucinations. Big, strong warriors fell into believing they were kits again. They saw monsters and magic-wielding Liskash everywhere. So did their pack and food animals, who startled at shadows or swirls of dust. The patients began to attack even those who nursed them. The Dancers held together the clan through the firmest discipline, but even they began to lose that grip as fewer of them were able to Dance their supplication to the gods. Bau Dibsea, seeing the numbers of sick increase, had no choice but to order the caravan to stop at the next oasis.

And there they had stayed, for a quarter of a moon, already. The water in the bubbling pool was indeed fresh and sweet. Petru looked down in annoyance at his coat as he went to clean himself. While he was still healthy, and he meant to remain so for the sake of his ladies, he wanted to look his best.

❖　　　❖　　　❖

A few of the youngsters still healthy enough to assist were gathered around the well. In the heat of noon, most lolled flat, their black fur making them look like shadows, on the terrace of stones surrounding the pool or the benches at the perimeter. For a moment, Petru marveled at the presence of such constructions. This oasis, like the last one, was so remote that they had found dead animals in the sands all around it who had lost their bid to reach water in time. Such a contrast to the garden existed within the boundaries of the well's environs that it could be the difference between paradise and purgatory.

Some ancient ruler had commanded that stonemasons and artisans furnish this place as if it was a pleasure spot. Tall carvings and trees stood sentry. Three shallow, rectangular enclosures like low tubs a hand's length in depth stood at the morning, midday and twilight spots around the circles. They were designed for travelers to clean themselves. The drains pointed out of the center, so as not to defile the pure water at the heart of the oasis. One tub was filled with water, and occupied.

Sherril Rangawo, a diplomat of the Lailah clan, glanced up lazily from the water as Petru stalked toward him. He waved a hand over his head toward the nearest bench.

"Valet! My wine cup is over there. Bring it to me."

Petru felt the fur over his spine stand straight up. Sherril well knew that he served only the Dancers, not minor functionaries such as him. But thanks to Cleotra, he was furnished with the wherewithal to make certain Sherril regretted his boldness.

"As you wish," Petru said. He reached over the diplomat's head. As he did, he dislodged a stinking mass or two from his fur. They dropped onto Sherril's face, narrowly missing his eyes. Sherril sat up, sputtering and batting at himself with wet hands. It took only a sniff for Sherril to discover what the unexpected missiles were made of. He let out an annoyed wail. Petru also ensured that a small lump or two of dried mucus fell into the wine cup. He handed it to Sherril. The diplomat downed a draught without looking. The taste, if not the texture, hit his tongue. He sat up, spat out the mouthful in a fury, and glared at Petru.

"Ptah! How *dare* you? You could have made me ill!"

"How dare *you?*" Petru rejoined, propping his hands on his hips in impatience. Despite the state of his coat, he managed an air of magnificent affront. "I have told you before, you do not command me. And every pair of hands is needed to serve those who are ill. Why are you here, and not assisting the healers?"

Angrily, Sherril cleared his tongue and tossed the wine from his cup into the dust.

"I organized these young ones to prepare food for the warriors," he said. He gestured at his wet and now disarranged fur. "Look at me! I had just reached a stage of peaceful serenity!"

The youngsters had roused from their torpor, and were watching the two senior Mrem with eyes so wide that they could have popped out of their heads.

Petru pitched his voice so it could be heard a mile away in the desert, let alone to the edges of the oasis.

"There is no time for peace or serenity! We are

in terrible straits. We have been since the new sea rushed in! We will never be calm or safe until we are with the rest of the Mrem clans on the north side of the great valley!"

Such a speech was not unlike one that Sherril would have made, to rally underlings to do work that he did not want to do himself. The glare with which he favored Petru reflected irritation with a grudging hint of admiration.

"What would you have me do, in this dry-as-a-bone desert?" he hissed. "I cannot cure the sick, and I certainly don't want to catch the illness myself."

"I fear for the lives of our Dancers," Petru said. "You saw, as all of the Lailah did, what became of the tribe who lost theirs. It would tear out the heart of our clan. I have been thinking. I think I know what may aid them."

Sherril was unimpressed.

"And what is that? You are no healer!"

Petru regarded him with haughty displeasure.

"You have no idea as to my training. To become the primary servant of the Dancers requires instruction in many disciplines, including the preparation of simple medicines. But nothing I make for them will mean anything if they can't keep food inside them. They require nourishment."

"We have food," Sherril said grouchily. "We spent an entire season in that stinking Liskash compound to ensure supplies for the year."

"Dried foods, yes. Grains for the animals, yes. But those are not easily digested. I want to find eggs and bivalves and other soft foods high in protein and tempting to a patient's palate. The maps that we took from Ckotliss show that we are not many days' march from a valley with a lush swampland. The Mrem from those lands say the same."

"I know that! For the moment, it is time for me to be clean."

"Good. I shall be clean, also."

Petru climbed down into the bathing pool and nudged the less-substantial diplomat over until the level of the water displaced by both their bodies splashed over the edge. The filth on his coat dissolved out and began to float toward the pool's other inhabitant. Sputtering, Sherril sprang out in one magnificent leap, landing a yard away. He shook his body, spraying droplets everywhere. The youngsters huffed with laughter. Sherril snarled at them. They cringed. The diplomat stalked away, shaking his fur. The drops of water hitting the hot stones hissed as Sherril undoubtedly wished he could do, but such would not be dignified. Petru lounged back into the water, enjoying not only the sensation, but the air of satisfaction at seeing the other Mrem discomfited. Sherril was always seeking privileges above his station. Petru would never do that himself.

But the matter of the Dancers' lack of appetite was something that Petru did take seriously. As night fell, he planned to approach Bau Dibsea with his proposal.

The talonmaster waved him into the tent where he sat with maps outspread over his large folding table.

Bau Dibsea was a large and powerful Mrem whose white chest only threw his black coat into greater relief. The fur around his neck was matted down from wearing a bronze gorget to protect his throat in battle, and he had scars that rippled through the thick hair on his arms and legs. He wore none of his protective armor in the heat, but it lay close by on his sleeping furs in case the alarm was sounded. His staff of authority rested against the arm of his camp chair. Fistmaster Emoro Awr and Drillmaster Scaro Ullenh crouched on their long feet on the rugs that covered the sand, peering at the intricately inked hides.

Emoro gave him a sidelong look as he entered. Petru had taken the trouble to attire himself in his finest necklaces and wristlets, as well as dusting his newly cleaned fur with sparkling bronze powder and enameling his claws with gold, Cleotra's favorite color. He knew he looked handsome, and was rewarded by the expression in his mate's eyes. They did not advertise their relationship widely among the rest of the clan, but they knew Bau Dibsea was aware of it.

At the talonmaster's signal, Petru cast himself at Bau Dibsea's feet and writhed to show his throat in a gesture of obeisance. Impatiently, Bau signaled to him to rise. Petru sat up.

"Talonmaster, I come to you on behalf the Dancers of the Lailah clan, whose well-being is the greatest care in my life, whose beauty delights my eyes upon rising and upon my settling down at night. Nothing matters to me so much as their health and happiness, even my own life...!"

Bau cut him off with a slash of his own, unadorned claw.

"Speak plainly, valet! The day is not long enough to hear your tale. You serve the Dancers well. This I know. What do you want? You have three breaths to make your point."

Cassa might also have demanded the same. Petru was equally prepared to be terse. He dispensed with the rest of his elaborate plea, and laid out his plan in a way that set the talonmaster's head to nod with approval at its brevity and clarity. With a golden claw, he traced out the path on the map on Bau's desk that would take him to his goal in the shortest amount of time.

"... So your wish is to go on ahead of us to seek out these medicinal plants?" Bau asked, when Petru had finished speaking. He looked weary, though at least he seemed healthy. His thick, black coat was dusty. So was Emoro's. Petru longed to offer to brush them, but the talonmaster was not one to accept familiarity from lesser males, and this was not the time nor the place to groom Emoro. Later, in private, when he could take his time, would be better.

"Yes, Talonmaster," Petru said. "The book of ancient lore that I inherited from my granddam describes a fever so like this one that I am certain that the cure must be the same. If our new clan members are correct about what lies before us, the brackish waters ahead of us should contain the appropriate water reeds and thread vines that will stem the symptoms and permit our Dancers to recover. I would also like to gather birds' eggs and amphibians. Both tender meats might tempt the ladies to swallow a morsel or so. If I travel this way," his gleaming talon traced a line from the camp and down nearly to the narrowing coastline and the depiction of marsh plants just inland from it, "it will take two days less than if I go this way." The finger retraced the line. "The dinos are closer to the first way, but I am worried about my ladies surviving until I return."

Bau waved a hand. "You shall go, but I can't send fighters to accompany you. The rest who are still able-bodied must remain to protect those who cannot flee danger."

Emoro looked uncomfortable. He was sworn to obey Bau, but he did not like to see Petru exposed to peril. He would make the argument if he could, but Petru didn't need his help to convince the talonmaster. He opened huge, beseeching gold eyes at Bau, and tilted his head so his throat was revealed again.

"Please forgive me for mentioning it, great leader, but I am no warrior. Can you not allow me even a single fighter to protect us on this task? It is for the sake of the Dancers, beloved of Assirra. I serve Her as I serve them. Not even one?"

The talonmaster's mouth pursed, half in amusement. "Very well. Emoro, who can we spare?"

The grizzled veteran knew better than to suggest himself. He dropped his jaw to think, revealing the chipped lower fang on the left side of his jaw.

"Few are they who haven't had a case of the poops these last few days, Talonmaster, not even the animals," he said with a rueful grin. "The rope enclosure where the herd beasts are penned up is like a cesspit. Even I've been loose around the bowels a little myself. The waking dreams are the worst part of it. I've got an eight or so who can't remember their right names. If Petru can find us a cure, then I'm for it. He knows his craft." He eyed Scaro. "What about you, Drillmaster? You've stayed healthy enough. Petru is right. Even a chance at a cure is better than trying to press on into the teeth of the Liskash in our current state."

The lanky Mrem bowed his head.

"As you wish, Fistmaster. It would be my honor to serve. I will bring the others back safely."

And the story of his exploits upon his return would be certain to earn the admiration and attention of several of the females among them, Petru noted, with an inward smirk. He did not mind what the excuse, if it obtained for him a strong escort.

"It is settled, then," Bau said, nodding sharply. "You may choose a fist of warriors to accompany you. Valet, you have my authority to choose three of our number who are not yet afflicted with the fever to gather these herbs and whatever else you may find in the marshlands. Anyone who is not caring for the sick or protecting the perimeter can accompany you to locate these herbs. Come back as quickly as possible."

Petru righted himself and brushed off the few grains of sand that had accumulated in his coat.

"I shall do so, Talonmaster. I have my workforce in mind already."

❖　　　❖　　　❖

"How dare you tell the talonmaster I would come with you?" Sherril Rangawo complained, not for the first or even fifth time since they had set out from the oasis. He trudged along unwillingly, a pack containing several hide sacks on his back, though he was careful to stay half a step before Petru. "I have many important duties to serve!"

"Nothing is more important than this," Petru said, fixing a fierce eye on the diplomat's spine. He could see it was rigid with indignation even under the scanty moonlight of the new claw. "Lady Cleotra has refused to eat anything for more than a day. More than half of the kits are afflicted. They need soft, fresh foods to tempt their appetites, or I fear they may die."

Sherril ignored him. His long tail switched back and forth to show his annoyance.

"I have a basket for gathering eggs," Nolda said, shrugging a crate woven from straw and stuffed with rags over her narrow shoulders. She had a veil around her face to keep the sand out of her eyes. Her young kit, now several months old, was back at the camp in the care of a nursemaid who was still in good health. He had not shown signs of fever, but she was worried about his dwindling appetite. "We can surely bring enough back for all the sick. I will ensure they return intact."

Petru was flattered that she had volunteered to accompany him. As a Dancer she was sacred to the gods, but he knew her to be resourceful and energetic. He regarded her with affection, his pupils enormous in the dim starlight.

"Dear lady," he said, with a deep bow. "Your grace will aid us in this enterprise. But just let me straighten that cloth for you." Nolda had not yet mastered the skill at tying a sand-shield. She had it wrapped as though she was going to play the part of Mystery in the sacred Dance about the origin of Night. With careful hands, Petru pulled the veil off, shook it out, and wound it over the female's soft black ears and under her chin, leaving the fabric to bell out before her face without touching it. "That's better."

"You take such good care of us, Petru," Nolda said, with a smile.

"You honor me."

Sherril snorted. The Dancer turned huge golden eyes upon him in surprise.

"I beg your pardon, Dancer," he said unctuously. "Sand in my nose."

Behind the female's shoulder, Petru smirked.

Scaro regarded the valet's fussing with little patience. He turned to the final member of the foraging party, a former slave named Bireena. Slender but no longer emaciated, she had short, bronze-colored fur with a dark streak on her forehead, a lighter throat and chin, and enormous, sensitive ears that he found intriguing.

"How far are the swamps from here?" he asked her.

The Mrem shook herself as though she was surprised to be addressed without violence.

"A half day of fast walk," she replied shyly. She carried at least two eights of sacks, more than she ought to have borne, but she had insisted, saying that she was used to burdens. She had a sweet, sad face, with a pointed chin that drew attention to her broad cheekbones and forehead. Scaro wished he could find the Liskash who were responsible for her ill-treatment and tear their guts out, but the chances were great that some of the freed slaves had already taken their revenge on those particular dinos. Bireena was a pretty female. If she had had any spirit in her, she might be a fine companion when they stopped to rest, but he had no wish to take advantage of a Mrem who did not feel she could refuse.

Scaro looked up. The sky was clear, and the wind had died down to a breeze. He smelled the salt breeze to their right. It seemed closer all the time. So did the faint stink of Liskash. He couldn't tell whether the smell came from intelligent lizards or their huge and stupid dino kin. Either way they were bad news. He wished he had more warriors at his side than a single fist. Instead, he took the long, bronze-barbed spear from the pack on his back and gripped it in his fist. He nodded to Imrun and Golcha to fan out to the left and right. Taadar and Nil already were in position to scout ahead and trail behind to ensure they were not being followed.

The smell of Liskash became stronger the farther they walked. He hoped that the lizard-kin would follow their normal pattern of being torpid in the cool night. That way, if he stumbled upon them in their somnolent state, they stood a chance of killing a number of them while those he was protecting could escape.

Close to dawn, the sweet decay of the marshland was almost overwhelmingly strong as the sun warmed

it. The air was moist if not fresh. The ground under-
foot changed from wind-polished sandstone to thin
grass to almost lush plant life. Ahead in the nascent
sunlight they saw the tips of reeds and the sausage
shapes of cattails waving in the breeze. To everyone's
relief, the temperature was markedly cooler than it
had been in the oasis. Fresh water flowed downhill
from the headlands at their left to join the Great Salt
not many hundreds of Mrem-lengths to the right. As
they stepped over one of those rain-swelled rivulets,
the shapes of the plants were thrown into relief.

"That way," Petru said, pleased. He recognized
those shapes. The reeds were of the type that his
grandmother's book described. This land burgeoned
with healing plants. There was more than enough for
him to distil tinctures to treat the whole clan and their
beasts, and to dry herbs against later need. Scaro took
the lead. He let out a whistle that sounded like the
hoot of a night bird. It was answered by a similar
call from Taadar, far ahead.

Bireena became almost animated as they walked
on in the purple light.

"We are near my old home," she said, looking
around, her pupils enormous. "It was such a beautiful
place. We lived at peace for many generations until
the Liskash decided they required slaves. I do not
know if anyone remains in this area."

"I don't smell any trace of Mrem," Scaro said.
"Only Liskash." He had donned his protective necklet
and bronze overclaws, a fearsome weapon that could
gut a giant lizard in two swipes. He bore his spear

in his left hand and his toothed sword in the other. "Stay close to me."

"Bah," Sherril said, looking around him in disgust. "There is nothing out here for the lizards to eat. Why would they be here and not in the citadel?"

Scaro had no time to answer. He used the spear to part the increasingly tall greenery, seeking for stable footing. Shadowy trees stunted by the brackish water that fed them had become covered with twisting lianas. Huge, multilobed leaves tipped water on them as they passed. One gigantic, cup-shaped frond unleashed a torrent that splashed all of them. Sherril looked disgusted. Bireena seemed delighted. It must remind her of home.

"I seek triangle-reeds," Petru said. "Where will we find the greatest number?"

Bireena jerked her head in a rapid nod toward a wall of greenery to the south. "They grow in large clumps along the inner shore of the marsh, just under the drip line of the trees. We will find a broad line of them just on the edge of the water." She beckoned to the others to follow her.

Scaro hurried to catch up as she all but disappeared into the thick marsh. Vines trailing down from the treetops brushed his shoulders. He jumped at each fresh touch.

But Bireena, far from being nervous at the plant life, seemed to have been set free from her reticence. She beckoned to Petru to show him this or that flower, that or this reed. Petru nodded, as though taking an inventory. The footing became more and more spongy.

Scaro disliked the feeling of water seeping between his toes. He clenched them to test the solidity of the ground below. His warriors followed, picking their way uncomfortably. He sniffed. The heavy smells of rotting plants and mud masked the Liskash stink, but it was still there.

Petru, as usual, managed to find the driest possible jumps. With grace surprising in one so large, he leaped from hummock to tussock to clump, all without soaking the fur on his legs. Sherril Rangawo, just behind him, was not so lucky. He had already fallen in once, and his fluffy tail, the gray male's pride and joy, was a stringy mess. Scaro grinned. It was because the councilor didn't trust the valet's instincts. And he ought to. That one had a knack for self-preservation.

The land upon which they had been walking was once headlands, according to Bireena, parted by a delta of a slow-moving, shallow river that poured its brown waters into the once-distant Great Salt. They made their way downslope to the marshland beside the river. Birds hooted their protests as the Mrem walked among their nests and the roots of the trees whose heavy crowns nodded over the flowing river. Bireena and Nolda lifted the leaves covering the nests and peered at each one in turn, marking them for the return journey. No sense in taking eggs yet. The fragile burdens weren't going anywhere. If they happened to hatch, well, tender chicks were good eating for the sick.

"Do you smell that?" Nolda asked suddenly.

"What, mistress?" Petru inquired, hurrying to her

side. The Dancer lifted large, worried golden eyes to him.

"Evil magic is near, Petru. I am uncomfortable. The gods have forsaken this land. Even the birdsong sounds wrong."

Petru raised his nose to sniff. The Dancers had said that Liskash magic had a terrible smell like rotting flesh, detectable at hundreds of Mrem-lengths' distance. Alas, he had not the enhanced senses blessed by the gods. All that he detected was the smell of ordinary Liskash, quickly being overwhelmed by the odors of brackish water and oil-rich plants. Petru's heart sank. This expedition was so important, he felt that others might die if he did not succeed. If they failed, it would be no worse than if they did not try, but he would feel that he let his precious Dancers down.

"Should we turn back, mistress?" he asked.

For answer, Nolda held out her arms and bent her back in a graceful arc. Petru signed to the others to stop. Scaro held up his fist. The warriors halted immediately. The Dancer was about to commune with the gods and her sisters of the foot, to ask divine intention and to beg for protection from what may lie ahead.

The Dancer began to move from foot to foot. Because of the long march, she had foregone all her jewelry, leaving behind bracelets, anklets and tail rings, but her movements were so graceful that it seemed as though she was arrayed in all of those plus translucent veils of every color. Nolda's arms waved like leaves on a playful breeze. She swayed her head from side to side, almost touching her ears to her shoulders. A tiny smile lifted the corners of her mouth as though she felt the goddess rub against her in affection. Petru loved her wholeheartedly at that moment. She was the one of the clan's sacred connections to the gods and all of nature. He was proud of what little he could do to see to her comfort and aid her so she was free to commune with that he could not see and did not pretend to understand. Unlike Sherril, who nodded approvingly at the Dancer's every move.

In the deep green light that preceded the coming dawn, Nolda's graceful leaps and turns seemed to draw upon the marshy land beneath a pattern. It was open on one side in the direction of the way forward, as though asking a question about what lay there. Petru watched her in wonder, hoping that gentle Assirra was paying attention.

Though he was impatient to begin their gathering and get back to the rest of the clan, it was a special treat to see a Dancer undertaking a sacred rite. Not all of the Dances were performed in the open for all the Lailah to see, let alone outsiders. Bireena was rapt at the grace and power. Nolda seemed to be several beings at once: child beseeching mother, mother giving gentle caress, father administering a kind but stern admonition to the eager kitten, then prey fleeing from predator. Nolda's movements became clumsy during that passage. Petru guessed that she was performing as though she was a Liskash, who moved much more slowly and awkwardly than the Mrem. Next, she would surely be the Mrem who successfully hunted and slew her quarry.

Suddenly, Nolda dropped to the ground, shielding her head with both of her hands. She held that pose for so long that the spell of the Dance was broken. Petru rushed to her side.

"Lady, may I help you?" he asked.

"You interrupt the Dance!" Sherril said, horrified.

"No, Sherril Rangawo," Nolda said, with a kind look at the valet. Petru noticed that the nictitating membrane half-covered her eyes. Her limbs were shaking. "The good goddess gives me a warning. It is one we must heed."

Sherril looked around him in alarm as though the gods themselves were nearby.

"What is it, good lady?" he asked. "Are we in danger?"

"We are always in danger on this path," Nolda said, with a sigh. Petru pulled the large pack around from his shoulders to one arm so he could rummage through its contents. He came out with a stoppered ceramic bottle containing the herb-scented restorative liquid he gave the Dancers after major festivals and rituals. He peeled back the wax covering the mouth and offered a drink to Nolda. She sipped.

"Is the peril close by?" Scaro asked. He offered her an arm to help her up.

"Not so close, but we cannot avoid it, Drillmaster. We must be vigilant and clever. Assirra gives us her word that her husband will lend us the will to escape the trap set for us, but not the strength."

"A riddle, Dancer. What is the answer?"

Nolda shook her head. "We must be as swift as

possible. There is a chance to avoid the trap, but it is a small one. Most likely we have a fight ahead of us."

Scaro tilted his head toward the awestruck warriors at his back. "We'll take that fight, lady." He turned to Petru. "You heard the Dancer's words, valet. Let's move faster."

Petru inclined his head.

"I am only too happy to follow the will of the gods," he said.

Now with every sense honed as finely as the tip of a claw, they marched on over the steadily softening earth. The day creatures were rousing. Birds chattered their alarm that the Mrem were among them. Petru stepped carefully to avoid roots that arced up out of the mire with an obvious intent to trip them. Lianas draped over outflung tree limbs brushed their heads and ears. Huge pink and white blossoms that only opened to daylight began to spread their petals, exuding their heady, sweet fragrance upon the already scent-laden air.

Petru stopped just short of the broad cluster of trees on the near side of the sluggish river. With a gleaming, polished claw, colored green for the occasion, he pointed at the bright, yellow-green shoots poking up among the darker, more mature reeds.

"Those are what we need," he said. "Be careful also to take the thin vines clinging to them. The reeds will dry up the bowels. From the creepers, I can distil a powerful medicine against the underlying ailment."

"How do you know it will work?" Sherril asked, his face a skeptical mask.

"My granddam seldom lost a patient," Petru said firmly. "I have used dried plants myself of the same kind. Now, hurry before the sun rises too high! I want the roots as moist as possible. You, cut some of those big, ribbed leaves to wrap them in. Make haste! If we gather enough, we can turn back today, before the threat that the fates send!"

Scaro signed to his ·soldiers. They crouched among the reeds, plucking the shoots as Petru directed. Bireena showed them how to pull the plants up whole, using a twist of her wrist to avoid tearing off the little white tendrils at their base.

"You are very deft," Scaro said. "Not a wasted motion. I admire that." She lowered her head at the compliment, her ears swiveling shyly. Behind them, Sherril made a harsh noise in his throat. Bireena jumped away from the drillmaster. Scaro shot Sherril an angry look. Just when he had been making progress, too!

"Hasten!" Petru said, clapping his hands. "When you have all of these, I see another patch growing just over there."

Fat, green, goggle-eyed amphibians sitting on broad, floating lily leaves jumped away as the Mrem splashed toward them. Taadar, a young Mrem whose accuracy with a lance made even Scaro envious, speared a plump one in midair.

"Breakfast," he said, with satisfaction, packing the twitching body away in his pack.

Rustling in the trees alerted Scaro. He glanced up, but saw nothing unusual. Still, the smell of Liskash was stronger than before.

"Was there a lizard village upriver?" he asked Bireena.

"Yes, there was, but far," the golden Mrem said, her large eyes wide. "They came downriver once in a moon or so to try to trap some of us." She stopped suddenly and looked away from Scaro. That was what had happened to her, he was certain. Her people had been herded together and driven to Ckotliss to be slaves. "But we are not far any longer, are we? The sea has come closer, driving us south."

"That is so," Scaro said encouragingly. "But we have seen none of them yet, so it is well."

"How many remain?" asked Taadar.

Scaro shot him a deadly look.

"How could she know that?" he said. "Take Imrun and go spy out that position. Golcha and I will remain with the gatherers. I hate surprises."

The two young Mrem gathered up their packs and moved silently through the marsh toward the gap.

Petru watched them go with dismay. Two sets of hands that were not gathering plants and food meant more delay before he could return to his Dancers. As much as young Ysella promised that she would see to Cleotra's well-being, he was certain she would neglect small details he would never miss.

Peevishly, he returned to the workers he still had. Sherril was picking through the golden reeds as slowly as a kit trying to keep from eating a distasteful dish. Petru surveyed the pile of shoots on the big leaf beside him.

"Hurry up there," Petru snapped. "Bireena has gathered three times the plants you have."

"I am not a field worker," Sherril replied in annoyance. He raised dripping hands from the muck and flicked a clump of earth at Petru. The valet sidestepped to avoid being splattered. "And as you keep saying to me, I don't work for you."

Petru smirked. "In this case, you do. Move faster. I want to harvest that second clump of plants before the sun is fully up. More! No, not that purple-tipped one! That is gripeweed. It will twist your belly in knots."

Sherril grunted, but moved his hands to a patch of the correct herbs. Not satisfied but resigned, Petru went on to supervise the others. Bireena was the best worker. She showed Nolda and Scaro which plants to choose, picking the most mature of the reeds that would contain the greatest concentration of the healing sap. The threadvines she stored in a separate leaf. Petru praised her lavishly, which made her lower her head in modest protest and Scaro growl under his breath.

Petru shook his head. Silly fighter! Scaro should know by now that he had no interest in the drillmaster's conquests. He was contented with his own love.

The wind began to rush onshore from the sea, bringing with it scents of fish, salt, and an indefinable bitterness that made Petru lift his upper lip to taste it. Definitely Liskash. Scaro rose to his feet. He dropped handfuls of weed and reached over his shoulder for his spear.

"Do you smell that?" Petru asked.

"Been smelling it all night," the drillmaster said, rolling his own upper lip to smell more accurately. "It's getting strong. We ought to get to cover."

"I want to finish gathering these herbs," Petru protested. "The lives of the others may depend upon them!"

"Valet, that's your job," the lean Mrem said, frowning at Petru. "Mine is to make sure you get home to deliver them. Come on. You others, too! Leave the plants. We'll come back when we're safe."

Sherril looked pleased to leave the marshy clumps. He cast away the leaves he was holding and stood up.

"I agree," the gray councilor said. He brushed himself off. It was a futile gesture, since the mud clung to his fur. "Hurry. I don't wish to be left out in the open when the Liskash arrive. Such a prize as I would make would cause a breakdown in morale in the camp."

Petru shook his head.

"I very much doubt that," he said. He turned to Nolda and Bireena. "Come on, then, my ladies! Let's move to safety."

"We've got to cover our tracks first," Scaro said. "Drown everything you're not carrying with you. Try to leave it as natural-looking as you can. Good thing we didn't light a fire."

The first faint hues of orange peeped over the jungle to the south. Petru fretted as he oversaw the burial of one parcel of leaves after another, but he was wary of attack. The drillmaster kept looking at the sky, then scanning the jungle. Now that Petru thought of it, it had been a long while since the two fighters had gone to scout out the riverbank. Why had they not returned?

He took Nolda's burdens and escorted the Dancer carefully over the steadiest footing. Bireena crept along close behind, picking her way with the ease of a native. Sherril, resentfully, brought up the rear with Scaro, who kept the spear at his shoulder in case he needed it.

Mrem could move silently when they needed to. Petru prided himself that not a single blade of grass whispered at his passage. He could do nothing about the frogs that leaped across his path, nor the birds that dived at them, calling out. The increasingly unpleasant smell of Liskash seemed to come from all directions at once.

They made back toward the eastern desert. With sunrise, dew that had settled overnight began to rise in a shimmering haze that obscured the ground. Petru squinted at the rippled landscape.

"Head for the ravine where we slept yesterday," Scaro ordered, pointing to the dark slit between the dunes far ahead. "We'll find a defensible hole inland."

Petru picked up the pace, keeping his arm around the slim Dancer. Nolda protested that she was steady, but he could feel the weakness in her. It was still a good, long walk to the walls of stone. They had worked hard after a long night's march. He could do with a good rest once he had the Dancer bedded down safely.

He was weary, but was his eyesight playing tricks on him? The shadows near the entrance to the craggy pass seemed to move by themselves. Were they animals?

The stink rolled toward them like an oncoming storm. Petru jerked to a stop.

"Liskash! Back! Back!" Scaro shouted.

The shadows jerked into motion. Dozens of bodies rose up out of the sands. Liskash, ranging in size from the behemoth beasts of burden to the small and very dangerous magician race, let out a roar and rushed toward the Mrem.

Where had they come from? Petru threw himself between Nolda and the oncoming horde. He pushed her and Bireena before him and headed back the way they had come. Sherril let out a squawk. He shot past them, regardless of the sodden footing and sloshed his way downstream. Urged on by Scaro and Golcha, Petru followed. They were not far from the advancing Great Salt. He did not wish to have himself or his Dancer trapped between the wide sea and an army of dinos. He looked for a bolthole they could hide in, but the sloping land offered no openings.

"Keep going!" Scaro shouted. "We'll hold them off!"

He unsheathed his sword from the back scabbard and brandished it. He and Golcha ran backwards, trying to keep close to the sound of the threshing as the Mrem fled through the heavy undergrowth. He scanned the rising bodies. Thank Aedonniss that the lizards moved more slowly than Mrem, especially in the cool of dawn. Come the day's rising warmth their natural torpor would wear off, but Scaro hoped they would be safely out of reach by then. There had to be fifty or sixty of them!

The swift-moving ones recovered from the cool of the night before the others. They began to outdistance their fellows. Golcha loosened the throwing knives that he wore in a bandolier across his chest.

As the ravine narrowed, the water increased in velocity. Scaro feared being thrown off the slender path into the rushing stream. None of them knew how to swim. If they were washed out to sea, they were lost, as would be the cure for those back at the camp. All he could do was try to hold off the pursuers until Petru led the Dancer and the others to a place where they could hide. He believed in the valet's knack for self-preservation.

The first dinos, fine scales of a light gray-pink under their short fabric tunics and loose trews, loped toward them on long, thin legs with huge feet. Their skinny snouts opened to show rows of thin, sharp teeth. They hissed greedily, their long pink tongues darting in and out of their mouths.

"They're going to eat us, Drillmaster," Golcha shouted. "Hope I make them choke!"

"They'll choke on their own blood," Scaro vowed. He glanced back over his shoulder at the increasing slope. The vines crowding the sheer stone faces were so thick he couldn't see the others. The water roared as it poured over a cataract. Stones larger than a house stuck up between the rapids. Scaro scanned them with an eye to try to guess if he could jump to the nearest one and make his way across.

No. They didn't have a chance of escape that way. Better to die fighting.

The lightly boned Liskash were almost upon them. Golcha let loose with one of his deadly missiles. It hit the first loper in the eye. It let out a high-pitched squeal and fell backwards, writhing. The four behind it leaped effortlessly over the body. Two of them bounced off the slope and landed just Mrem-lengths away from Scaro, brandishing spears tipped with gleaming bronze. The drillmaster gathered himself and bounded at them.

In spite of their nimbleness, they were as slow to react as the rest of their kind. They missed Scaro with their initial blows. Instead, the drillmaster managed to plunge his spear down into the chest of the nearest one, then turned to rake his rear claws down the throat of the next one. The one with the blade in its eye tried to grab for him with long, skinny paws. Scaro freed his spear with a jerk, then jabbed it downward through the blinded Liskash's other eye. The Liskash fell limp.

Golcha whirled past him, cutting and jabbing at the two lopers that challenged him.

"Taking left," Scaro said. Golcha nodded sharply and concentrated on holding off the right-hand beast. The left-hand loper narrowed its black, beady eyes at him and lumbered backward, trying to figure out an advantageous attack. It jumped at him. Scaro sidestepped it easily and whacked it in the back of the head with the butt of his spear. It righted itself, shaking its narrow head. It turned and jabbed for Scaro's throat with its own spear.

The creatures couldn't be too smart. Even taking into account the slowness of their attack, they missed obvious chances to strike. No, Scaro decided. Their job was to hold the prey in place until the rest of the hunting party could catch up.

Which they did. Liskash riding spindly-legged dinos with long muzzles spurred toward them. Scaro counted four fists' worth. He and the others couldn't stand against a force that large.

"Retreat," he ordered Golcha. The fighter nodded curtly as he grappled with the remaining loper. The hissing dino knew it could not beat him on speed, so it relied upon strength. It wrapped its forelegs around the gray-striped Mrem and held onto him, kicking him with one sharp-toed foot. Golcha bellowed. Blood welled in gouges on his thigh. He fought to free his arm. The dino bent to bite his neck. Golcha brought his head up into its lower mandible. It bellowed. He raked his bronze claw-glove down the dino's upper arm. The bellow turned to a scream. It clamped its limbs about Golcha and crushed him to its skinny chest. The Mrem grunted in pain.

The lizard that found itself facing Scaro made to grasp him in the same fashion. Scaro didn't want to leave his warrior's side, but he had no choice. The creature lunged at him again and again. Scaro dodged and leaped. He had to stay out of its grasp. With his superior speed, he jabbed it again and again with his spear. It was well-armored, and its hide was tougher than he thought. He thrust at its eyes through the slits in its ugly helmet. It retreated, roaring in fury.

Out of the corner of his eye, he could see the others advancing. They were far too outnumbered to do anything. He had sworn to return the Dancer safely to the clan. He must not fail in his duty. Emoro counted upon him! He spun in and kicked the dino in the throat. It fell backward, but caught itself against the vine-covered stones. The blow had been blunted by the dino's gorget. Curse all lizard-kin!

"Aaaagh!" Golcha bellowed. The cry was cut off. Scaro could not spare a glance backward. More of the long-legged dinos had sprung up from the riverbank. He drew a deep breath and stalked toward them, swinging spear and sword. Every step felt heavier than the last one. He forced himself to listen for every sound, pay attention to every move, but his limbs betrayed him. They felt numb, as though they didn't belong to him. He watched the sword rise. Its blade chopped into Liskash armor, bounded off. The spear point thrust toward flat black eyes, was turned aside. The heavy, wet air choked him. He fell back, and the thick greenery swallowed him. Hands, thousands of them, closed on every one of his limbs and tail. He was too weak to throw them off. He tried to catch his breath, but felt as though he was drowning in the very mud around their feet. He gasped, spat, and gasped again.

Curse and curse again! He had caught the fever. Scaro watched as though from a great distance as he and Golcha were wrapped up in hunting nets, stripped of all armor and weaponry, and bundled onto the flanks of enormous dino beasts of burden.

"I'm sorry I failed you, my drillmaster," Golcha said, his voice shaky from the bumps on the path.

"At least they won't have us long," Scaro said. He sneezed, expelling a gout of mucus onto the dino's back. The explosion just barely cleared part of his stuffy head. "We'll die on them and rob them of their victory."

One could tell at once that the scrawny, purple-skinned lizard was the most important Liskash present. His clothes were more disgusting than anyone else's. The Liskash's overly ornate armor and sumptuous fabrics had been painted or dyed in a riot of clashing oranges and greens woven in patterns combined to present a horror of design that offended Petru's artistic sensibilities. He could hardly bear to look at the creature.

A scabrous, whiskery, itchy rope around his ankle tethering him to a post in a clearing hastily hacked from the surrounding forest with scythes and machetes, Petru still maintained his dignity. He would not show fear in the face of the pathetic excuse for a leader of the force that had kidnapped him.

"Release us at once!" he demanded. The smell of which Nolda had complained was stronger than ever before, and he realized the other effect that he had noticed when they had entered Ckotliss, the Liskash stronghold, months before. His own voice sounded alien to him. It sounded weak and mewling, like a kitten's, in his ears. He cleared his throat. "We do you no harm. We are merely passing through this place on our way to rejoin our kin in the far north on the other side of the Great Salt."

"Kin? How many of you are there?" the Liskash demanded. "Answer!"

"I do not owe you an answer," Petru said, raising

his nose in the air. "You assail us from several directions, without explanation and without reason. Why should I trust you with information?"

"I am General Unwal Nopli. My brother the Lord Oscwal Nopli holds these lands as his satrapy. I have every right to hold you and question you. You are trespassing. Your lives are forfeit for coming here."

Petru looked around. To him it looked as though a hasty camp had been set up on the grassy fields of what remained of rolling countryside. The Great Salt encroached upon all but the highest lands. According to the Mrem who had once lived in this region, the streambed down which he and the others had just run opened out into a fertile delta, the end of which must have been drowned in the rising waters. Evidently, the flood came so swiftly it caught the dinos by surprise.

He surveyed the Liskash who occupied the camp. There were females and young huddled near the trees under makeshift shelters of hides and woven cloths. Their clothing, although just as horrible in terms of color and design as the soldiers' uniforms, suggested that they were among the wellborn. Yet, even though the garments were expensive, they had seen a lot of hard wear and little cleaning. He guessed that Oscwal and Unwal were as homeless as the Lailah. Their lack made them more dangerous than Liskash ensconced in a comfortable home.

"What is this?" one of the guards asked. He had upended Petru's personal pack. In his scaly fist, he held out two horn vials of the sparkle powder that Petru wore daily on his fur and with which he adorned the Dancers when they performed rituals. "Some kind of magic?"

Petru made a grab for them, but the lizards at his side held him back.

"They are my property. Give them here!"

Unwal signed to the soldier, who put the stoppered tubes into his palm. Unwal opened first one, then the other, spilling ruby and sapphire powder onto the ground in glittering heaps. Petru struggled against his captors.

"No! You fool!"

"You dare to call me a fool, when I hold your lives in my hand?" Unwal asked. He closed his fist and squeezed. The fragile bottles shattered. He dropped the shards and ground them into the dirt with his heel. Petru swallowed. Now was not the time to voice his outrage, but he vowed the lizard would pay for his loss.

"We do not wish to cause any trouble, Great General," Petru said, switching to his most unctuous and wheedling tones. "Please release us, and we will be on our way."

"No. I require answers. What are you doing here? How many of you are there?"

Petru thought quickly. He would never reveal the true reason for their presence. In spite of Bau's insistence that those who remained behind could defend the camp, the number of Mrem remaining healthy was small and diminished every day. But the Liskash need know nothing of them, not when he had a Dancer at his side. To his surprise, Nolda and Bireena had not been tied up as the males had been. Surely the

Liskash knew that the Dancer was far more dangerous than any of them.

"Our home was drowned by the coming of the great flood," Petru said. He spread out his hands to indicate the few of them there. "We few were cut off from our kinfolk in the north. All we wish to do is rejoin them. We are all that is left of a great city. All we wish to do is make our way to the north. We will be out of your realm by evening."

"Why were you in the Broadleaf Marsh?"

"Foraging. This great lady," he added, indicating Nolda, his voice falling into a persuasive purr, "has found the journey difficult. She is not feeling her best. Our journey rations have not been kind to her digestion. I thought to supplement her diet with soft foods from the marshlands. You would not begrudge her a frog or two? Perhaps some eggs?"

"Bah," General Unwal said, with a dismissive wave. "A female? She should be grateful for whatever scraps you throw her way. She is of no importance except to give pleasure to her owners and bear sons."

Petru felt outrage rise in his ample belly. He lifted a talon and aimed it at the Liskash's nose.

"You! You do not understand!"

Sherril Rangawo cleared his throat meaningfully and lowered his ears in Petru's direction. As little as he liked the diplomat, Petru had to admit that he probably knew more of Liskash customs than he did. His primary concern was the well-being of the Dancers, not petty bureaucracy, but the Liskash ought to know how wrong he was. He opened his mouth to say so.

"Our customs are not the same as yours, General," Sherril said, cutting off Petru's retort. "We Mrem live more simply than you do. We hold our females to be our equal *because* they are able to give birth. But let us not argue over cultural differences. We have no intention to offend. All we wish is your forbearance. If you would allow us to pass unmolested through your land, we would do you a service in return."

General Unwal glared at Petru.

"You let your servants speak before you? I would beat him if he was mine!"

Sherril's mouth dropped open in shock. Petru felt unholy glee swell in his heart. He would take advantage of that misapprehension. *But not now, dear Assirra, while the Dancer is in mortal peril.*

"Why do you think he outranks me?" Sherril snapped.

"I do not converse with those of lowly bearing," Unwal said, not even bothering to address the diplomat. He frowned at Petru. "I never let my servants speak. Why do you tolerate such nerve?"

"He has his uses," Petru said, with a dismissive wave of his hand. In spite of the dire circumstances, he enjoyed the moment. "As you see by his filthy fur, he was searching out birds' nests to provide food for us. But might I ask, Great General, if you recognize me as a person of quality, why you continue to hold us prisoner? We are few." He pointed to Scaro and Golcha. "I have only these bodyguards to protect my elegant person from harm. We could not possibly do you harm."

To prove that Aedonniss had a sense of irony that would have pleased any Dancer performing a tale, at that moment, two of the enormous beasts of burden lumbered into the clearing. The Liskash riding just behind the broad, horned skulls jerked up on the loose end of ropes. Freed by the motion, two huge hunting nets tumbled to the ground. Cries erupted from the tangled mass of twine. Petru was both dismayed and relieved to see the other warriors, Taadar and Imrun. They were alive, but the timing of their reappearance could not have been more unfortunate. Petru had hoped they had managed to remain at large in the jungle to effect their rescue. That faint hope had been extinguished.

"And what are these, then?" demanded General Unwal. "What is the true number of your party? Answer!"

Petru held his chin up.

"These *are* all. I had assumed that these two whom you have just restored to me had fled into the wilderness. Our supplies are nearly gone, as you must know from your brutal search of our baggage. They were hungry, as were the rest of us."

"You don't look as though you have gone without for very long," the Liskash said, lowering his scaly eyelids halfway over his flat black eyes. If he had been a Mrem, Petru would have thought he indulged in irony.

"Naturally," Petru said, refusing to take the bait. "Among our kind, my shape is considered to be desirable."

"All it means to me is that you have plenty of meat on your bones," General Unwal said. "We, too, seek comestibles. I think we need look no further for a time. It is well. We will take one of the less valuable of your number first. That female has well-molded muscles." He pointed at Nolda. "They will be well-flavored, if tough."

Petru was so horrified at the notion that he sputtered.

"Eat Nolda? She is a priestess of my people! I would sooner offer myself to your knives!"

"That would be acceptable. We hunger. Which of you sates it, slave or master, makes no difference."

"No!" Scaro exclaimed, springing to the end of his bonds. "They are all under my protection."

The guards surrounding General Unwal lumbered forward, wielding the butts of their spears as bludgeons. They weren't as quick as the drillmaster, but they had him outnumbered. Scaro fought to avoid them. The heavy wooden staves rose and fell again and again, impacting him upon every part of his body. Petru cringed. The drillmaster fought bravely until a glancing blow took him in the side of his head. He dropped to the ground, moaning. Golcha pulled his senior officer back toward the stake to which they were tethered and tended to Scaro's bruises. Unwal watched the interplay with as little emotion on his face as if he was watching clouds pass.

"You have no power here," Unwal said. "My will is law. Take the female."

"Never!" Petru said, interposing himself between the guards and Nolda. He could sense her muscles tensing to defend them both. It would be a brief victory because the Mrem were such a small group

in the midst of the enemy. "Do not touch her! I...
I...I command it!"

"I do not listen to the commands of chattel," Unwal
said. At last he evinced an emotion. It was boredom.
His indifference inflamed Petru. He felt his chest
swelling with indignation.

"Calm, calm," Sherril said in an even voice, though
Petru sensed he was as frightened as the rest of the
Mrem. "None of us want to be eaten, Great General.
You speak from desperation, unbecoming to one of
your rank. Let us help you. The Dancer would be
too tough for your palate, and my lord Petru here
would give you indigestion. You are hungry, as we
are. Let us seek out better food for you, much more
to your taste."

"Your servant speaks before you again, fat one,"
Unwal said.

"But in this case he makes good sense," Petru
replied. "Forgive the outbursts of my retinue. We
would be glad to forage on your behalf, in exchange
for our lives. Why kill a hunter instead of making
use of her skills?"

"That does make sense," Unwal said, after a moment's
thought. Assirra's paws, but Liskash were slow! "Go,
then."

The two younger warriors, Imrun and Taadar, kept
their heads down in shame as the Mrem were marched
north again to the green bog, burdened with nets and
baskets. Scaro's voice was hoarse as he chided them
for their carelessness in being captured.

"Making mistakes a half-grown kitten would laugh at!" he snarled, then sneezed vigorously. His bruises didn't seem to slow him down. He strode ahead with as much vigor as a considerably younger Mrem. The others hurried their pace to keep up. "You let them sneak up on you! Lizards, who stomp like trees falling! I could have heard them coming fifty Mrem-lengths off. But not you! Oh, no! They come right up on you, close enough to throw a net over your stupid furry heads. Serve you right for being so unaware of your surroundings if they did eat you!"

"Sorry, Drillmaster," one murmured.

"Won't happen again, Drillmaster," said the other.

"You are thunderstorming right it isn't going to happen again!" Scaro said. He sneezed again, spraying green mucus on the ground. Petru regarded the mess with distaste as he stepped over it. "You're on guard rotation from now until next winter, do you understand?"

"Yes, Drillmaster," they said dolefully.

"I can't hear you!"

"Yes! Drillmaster!"

"Huh," Scaro said, and sneezed so hard he barked his chin on his neck guard.

"Quiet!" ordered Captain Horisi, the most senior of the Liskash guard accompanying them. He commanded two fists of four lizards each, who prodded the Mrem on the northbound trail with the stone points of their spears. Their uniforms were as putrid in color and design as the general's had been, tabards of a bruiselike plum overlaying scale mail in a burnt ash gray that did nothing to flatter their ridiculous rainbow-hued complexions. No two of the dinos were the same color. On their backs they carried packs made of the skin of some scaly creature and jugs containing small beer that smelled as though it was already going off. "No talking in ranks!"

"I will, I will," Scaro assured him. *"Once I finish giving these two adolescents a piece of my mind! If this is how they defend themselves, I fear for the lives of anyone else in their care! You wouldn't let a recruit behave so badly! No more would I!"*

Petru, listened with half an ear, but he fretted at every step. Could they find enough food to satisfy the Liskash so they would not attempt to prey upon the Mrem? The Dancer must return safely to the tribe! Oh, how he wished he had never permitted her to join them!

Nolda must have sensed the worry in his soul. She came to walk beside him and laid a gentle hand on his arm.

"We will be all right," she said. "There is no death in the air. Gentle Assirra pleads for our lives every moment from her husband. We will succeed by wit and determination."

"I add my humble prayers to yours, dear Nolda," Petru said. "I wish that you were back..." He glanced over his shoulder warily at the armored lizards following them only a pace or two off their twitching tails and listening as closely as their limited hearing allowed. He raised his voice dramatically. "...Back in our homeland, on the highest ground possible."

Ahead of them, heavy-bodied marsh birds flew back and forth among the hanging vines and thick-leaved branches of the trees. He watched where they stooped for food, and where they deposited the fruits of the hunt. Bright-blue, thin-skinned amphibians seemed to be plentiful as well as frogs in every shade of green. When they reached the boggy shore, the guards put short-handled, almost dull harvesting knives in their hands and pushed them forward.

"Work!" the captain said.

"There is plenty here," Petru said. "Why aren't your foragers at work? I could feed our entire clan—that is, when we were at home—on what I can see within three Mrem-lengths of where I am standing!"

"We don't wallow in mud like you Mrem," Captain Horisi said with a sneer. "Hurry up! You have until the sun's at its peak. Then we go back. If you don't have enough for the general's nooning, the meal will be you."

Petru shot him a peeved look.

"Let us do our job. There is no need for threats."

For answer, the senior pulled a dagger from his belt and ran a thumb up and down the short, curved blade. Petru shivered when he realized that the hilt had been cut from a Mrem's thighbone. If Aedonniss was kind, he would have revenge for that lost kinsman.

Petru turned to the others.

"There are birds' nests in the roots of the biggest trees," he said, pointing. "There, there and there. I've watched the males feeding the brooding females."

Bireena nodded, her large eyes watchful. "I will gather eggs," she said.

"Help her," Scaro ordered Taadar and Golcha. "Take frogs and birds, too. Fish if you can get them." They saluted and trudged into the shallows after the female. Imrun stayed by Nolda's side, helping her to pull roots and plants from the sucking wet soil.

"No, Councilor, that way." Scaro grabbed Sherril by the arm and pulled him toward the patches where they had been picking vegetables before.

"Hands off me, Drillmaster," Sherril said, straightening his back and brushing his fur smooth again. It wasn't easy, considering how much mud was trapped in his coat. "Remember your place! My rank is loftier than any you will achieve in your life."

"With respect, Councilor, time is fleeting," Scaro said, keeping his voice as level as he could. They were badly outnumbered. Aedonniss only knew what would happen if he was the only one to return to the camp without the Dancer. Sherril Rangawo's ego was the least of his problems. He sniffed mightily, trying to clear his nose, and glanced over his shoulder at the Liskash guards following them. "Well, Captain, what do you want us to look for? What tastes good to you?"

The guard, by no means a captain, looked startled to be addressed directly by a Mrem.

"Don't grows about here," he said curtly.

Sherril picked up immediately on Scaro's approach. The drillmaster was a clever one, appealing to the vanity of the guards, who occupied the lowest stratum in Liskash society.

"Well, what did you call them, Captain? Though

my pronunciation may sound incorrect to one such as you, I spent some time in the citadel of Ckotliss, and I know the tastes of the satrap there."

The scaly blue brow ridge rose toward the pink crest.

"You knows Tae Shanissi?" the Liskash asked. Sherril didn't doubt he was impressed.

"Oh, yes," Sherril said. "You may say I was very close to him for a time." He glanced at Scaro, admonishing him with a look not to tell the truth about that encounter.

"Well, we calls them marsh plums, but they isn't fruits. Exactly. But juicy eatings."

This was a slow thinker, Sherril realized.

"I know marsh plums. We call them 'racano.' They're vegetables, but very juicy. You know, Tae Shanissi never got fresh marsh plums, as you call them. They only came to him dried. So you were getting better food than Lord Tae himself."

The guard looked pleased.

"Well, hurry up and finds them! Hasn't ate in days. Don't want stringy meat." He plucked at Sherril's arm. Sherril withdrew it hastily.

"Yes, Captain. As you say, Captain." He glanced around for Petru. The valet stood with his hands on his broad hips, barking orders. The big oaf had managed to conscript the three Liskash who were supposed to be guarding him into picking caltha, a flowerlike pod that contained succulent seeds like those in a pomegranate. He did not so much as deign to hold a bag open for them to throw the fruits into. "Oh, my lord Petru!"

Petru glanced back, startled at the title, then undulated toward Sherril, enjoying the moment. Oh, that big fool was going to pay once they returned to the camp!

"And what do you want, Sherril?" he asked, without a courtesy title of any kind.

Sherril held his tongue. He assumed a humble expression such as he would wear when addressing Bau Dibsea.

"The good captain here would like to eat racano. This ignorant servant of yours knows not where to seek them. From your vast knowledge, tell me where they are to be found?"

"They shelter, as my ignorant servant ought to know," Petru said, "under the leaves of their parent plant, which looks like the folded wings of two doves placed side by side, just above the water of this lifegiving region." He pointed to a flattened, bushy shrub the size of a mature Mrem. Its broad leaves had two rounded edges on either side of the stem, and terminated in a sharp single point. "There is one, and several more beyond. You can just see the rounded shapes of the fruits beneath. If the skin gives slightly under pressure, they are ready to eat. Unripe ones are too sharp of flavor."

"Yes, Lord Petru," Sherril said. He beckoned to the guards to follow him. They did, but when he handed a green-faced subordinate a net to receive the racano, it dropped the seine to the ground.

"Pick!" the green guard ordered. He grabbed Scaro by the scruff of his neck and shoved him down next to Sherril. "Both!"

Scaro bounded to his feet at once, glaring at their

captor, but he was met by a circle of sharp flint spear points.

"Come help me, Drillmaster," Sherril said. He handed the discarded bag to the soldier. "At least we don't have to dirty our paws to take these. They are above the water."

Scaro nodded and began to gather fruit as Petru had instructed them. He cleared the first plant of all the ripe ones and moved onto another bush nearby. Sherril felt gingerly at the first one he encountered, wondering if there was enough give in the flesh to ensure it was ripe. He had no wish to endure the kind of mistreatment that he had heard of from the captive Mrem they had freed from the citadel of Ckotliss. The Liskash were horrifically creative in their torture of those who displeased them. At least underlings such as the guards were not capable of the kind of magic of their superiors. Perhaps even General Unwal lacked that mental control. He glanced back at the green-faced guard.

"How did all of you end up here in the midst of this forest, Captain?" he asked, in polite tones. "It is not usual for your kind to live in wild settings. I thought you preferred stone houses. You must have a very fine home somewhere, Captain." It was purest flattery, as the wrist flashings on the gaudy uniform indicated this Liskash was barely above recruit rank.

"Gnopsmal was walled on a cliff," the guard said, with an expression that might almost have been nostalgic. He took the jug from his shoulder strap and poured some of the yellow liquid into his mouth. "Not as big as some, like Ckotliss big. Saws the floods. Lord says no fear, stays, we ups high. The waters ates the cliff and all falls down half a moon ago on top of port. Ships sinks. Three in four dies. All Mrems still alive ran away. Lord Oscwal takes half army and workers see to rebuild it in the south, high dry. If you lives, you wills become part of the labors on the new walls."

"We would be honored," Sherril said. This was not the time to argue. "I am sure it will be a great city once again. And all of your cropland?"

"Gone first in waters rush," the soldier said curtly. He waved a scaly hand. "Hurry. I hungers!" He withdrew to stand with his captain on a hump of land that rose a mere Mrem's height above the marsh. It was not tall, but it provided a vantage point from which they could see all the Mrem. They didn't need to be swift on their feet; their bows would take down fleeing prisoners. Sherril reached for a racano, judged it to be too hard, and threw it over his shoulder. It landed with a plop on the water and sank. Scaro sneezed, spraying pale green slime over the plant before him. Sherril jumped back, brushing at himself.

"Ugh, Drillmaster, that's disgusting!"

Petru suddenly loomed over them.

"And why are you not working?" he asked.

"You need to gather plants and food, too," Sherril said sourly. Petru shook his head.

"I must maintain my subterfuge of being your liege lord," Petru said. "General Unwal finds me impressive. To surrender that position now would only confuse matters."

"He only seeks to eat you," Sherril said.

Scaro sneezed again.

"Gah!" he said. "My guts are rumbling, even though there's nothing in them."

Petru regarded him with worried eyes. The slender Mrem's eyes had filmed over with their nictitating membrane, but also by a thin layer of mucus. If their strongest arm was falling ill, they were doomed.

"Stay away from his breath," Petru warned Sherril. "I will put together a measure of the potion to aid you, Drillmaster." He glanced back toward their captors. "If I can do it without drawing their attention to what I am doing."

Reluctantly, Petru moved away from them and went to oversee Bireena. The former slave looked up at him with a triumphant gleam in her big gold eyes. Beside her, three sacks had been padded thickly with marsh grasses. The white curve of an egg the size of Petru's fist peeked out from among the greenery.

"What an excellent addition to the larder," Petru said. "You must have been a marvelous gatherer as a child."

"I worked hard," she said, lowering her eyes. "I have always worked hard."

"I know, dear lady." He patted her on the shoulder. More than any of the others, she was unbothered by the presence of armed Liskash. Petru shivered. How horrible to live that way, never being certain of your safety or your future.

"Could you gather a handful of triangle reeds, some swamp garlic and goldthread? Not very much, just a little," he said in a light tone, keeping his voice very low. "Don't put them with the other food. Set them aside on a branch in that tree." He pointed toward a thorny, overgrown black trunk whose roots humped over the watery expanse. Bireena glanced up at him in surprise. The two guards nearest him trudged closer. "You're doing very well. Keep going!"

"Yes, Petru," she said. With a puzzled shake of her head, she moved away into the undergrowth.

As the morning progressed, Scaro became weaker and weaker. He sat breathing hard in between tasks. The guards that oversaw him and Sherril kept pulling him to his feet and throwing him down beside other plants to pick racano or other vegetation, making the birds the others were hunting rise up in alarmed flocks. Taadar and the other warriors helped him, but it was clear the drillmaster's fever was progressing rapidly. The congestion from his nose had moved into his chest. Besides the explosive sneezes, he had acquired a raspy cough. He needed rest, food and a cure.

The means for the last named was at hand. Petru saw that Bireena had followed his instructions. The green parcel he had requested gleamed wetly on the ancient mremgrove. How he could get to it and process it into a potion without being noticed was a puzzle he had not yet solved. Still, he had the benefit of unrestrained mobility. The guards had accepted his peripatetic behavior as normal.

"Will he live?" Sherril asked, when Petru came by to inspect his progress. In spite of the councilor's dilatory methods, he had accumulated four bags of fruit.

"I don't know," Petru said, glancing at the ailing Scaro. The drillmaster held himself against a tree trunk while he stripped clusters of sweet white drupes from its branches. "If we were back home, I would put him to bed for a quarter moon at least."

"He can't let himself be seen as too weak to work," Sherril said. "They'll just kill him. They are so hungry they will certainly eat his body. Do your best to avoid direct contact, valet, and keep the Dancer away from him. We must not fall ill!"

"I know!" Petru hissed. "I am the one who told you that!"

Squawking arose beyond a clump of trees, followed by a triumphant howl. Imrun appeared from the undergrowth. He was covered with mud and broken twigs, but he held a pair of flapping geese by their feet.

"Look at these, Drillmaster!" he cried, holding them for Scaro to inspect. The birds fought hysterically to free themselves. One of them tried to peck at Imrun's eyes. He swung the bird out at arm's length. "I trapped them in a snare made of lianas. You ought to eat their livers. Give you strength."

"Good work, Imrun," Scaro said. "Those'll be good eating for all of us."

To their surprise, the guards came running toward them. They pushed Scaro aside, seized one of the geese from Imrun and tore the screaming bird to pieces. Without waiting for the body to stop twitching, they stuffed gobbets of meat into their mouths. Blood ran down their unlovely faces onto their even uglier tunics. The rest of the guards ran to seize their share. Petru brushed feathers from his coat and watched them in astonishment.

"The Liskash are starving, in the midst of plenty," he said. "Why do they not see all the food to be had?"

Sherril smiled slyly. "These are town-dwellers, valet, the most protected occupants of what must have been a large city. I suspect that their farmers and flocks, and even fishing vessels were swept away in the sudden floods. Even their army is accustomed to having food brought to them instead of foraging. In spite of General Unwal's brave words, I think we see them at the edge of despair. We have not been on the roads for long, but we have always been hunters."

Captain Horisi waded toward them, drawing his knife from his sheath. He stabbed the second bird in Imrun's paw and wrenched its suddenly limp body away from the surprised Mrem. He rushed away, the guards who had failed to take a piece of the first bird striding after him and yelling for a share like hungry kittens.

"All doubt is gone," Sherril said. "Now, how can we turn this to our advantage?"

The greenfaced Liskash came toward them. His gray tongue darted out of his mouth and licked all the blood off his face up past his flattened snout. Petru grimaced.

"You don't normally eat raw meat, do you, Captain?" he asked.

"Hungry," the guard said curtly. "Long time without meat. Herds gone. Officers takes our catch. Like you saws."

Sherril, just behind the green Liskash's shoulder, nodded, his eyes watchful.

"The drillmaster can teach you to hunt birds like the ones Imrun caught," he said. "Scaro has been vital to the survival of our small band. You want to learn from him."

The guard snorted. "No. You catches. I eats."

"As you say, Captain," Petru said, resigned.

As high noon approached, the Mrem collected all the bounty that they had gathered and loaded it onto the back of one of the beasts of burden. Encouraged by Petru to make themselves more useful as tame predators than prey, the soldiers had outdone themselves. Twenty huge marsh birds were strung over a pair of sagging poles carried between Taadar and Golcha. Nolda and Bireena bore baskets of fragile raw eggs layered among spongy leaves, not letting any of the males touch them. Petru flatly refused to carry any of the several bags of racano and other fruit, leaving Sherril, Scaro and Imrun to shoulder the rest. None of the Liskash noticed that Imrun took the bulk of Scaro's burden. The drillmaster staggered to carry a nearly weightless sack stuffed with leaves. Once the beast was fully laden, the soldiers tied the Mrems' hands behind their backs and strung them together with another of the crude, scratchy ropes.

It was a long hike over damp, marshy ground uphill toward the makeshift camp. Like his fellow Mrem, Petru had sampled a number of the fresh fruits and drupes during the harvesting, so his belly wasn't twisting with hunger. He grew very thirsty, though. He wished he could drink some of the dinos' beer instead of the swamp water, but none of them responded to his hints to share.

Poor Scaro had had to break out of the line more than once to go behind a tree. By the smell, he was purging hard. He must have felt like an empty shell. It could be only his strength of will that kept him upright and on the march, though he drooped farther and farther as they went. Bireena and Taadar walked almost pressed up against Scaro's sides to keep him from stumbling. Petru kept the packet of healing herbs hidden in his thick fur. When chance permitted it, he would dispense the first dose to the drillmaster. Scaro was in terrible condition. He wouldn't live more than a day or two without it.

Only fierce orders and blows from spear hafts kept the rest of the Liskash from leaping upon the finds when they arrived back at the makeshift camp. The beast of burden, usually a placid creature, danced and trumpeted to avoid the onrush.

"Well?" General Unwal demanded, from his chair in the middle of the clearing. "What have you found?"

Petru picked the most tender bird and the ripest of the racano. He put them into Sherril's arms and shoved the councilor toward the general. Sherril aimed a sullen look at him, but went to lay the bounty at the general's feet. Unwal's flat eyes gleamed.

"Cause these to be prepared!" he shouted. "Make the rest a feast for all! Well? What is the delay?"

The female dinos near the tents murmured to one another. Captain Horisi cleared his throat nervously and signed to some of the lower-ranking soldiers. One shuffled forward, tilting its head in an abject manner.

"We aren't sure of prepares feast worthy of you, General," he said. "Best cooks goes with Lord Oscwal."

"*Only* cooks," said a blue-faced soldier. "And all our Mrem are gone."

"Oh, nonsense," Petru said. He strode forward and picked likely candidates from the straggled line. "You, you, and you, come with me. The two of you make a fire at least a Mrem-length across. You! Get me some green stakes to use as skewers. Taadar and Imrun, come here now! Show these scaly fools how to gut birds."

With Scaro's warriors as assistants, Petru mustered the servants remaining in the Liskash's aegis to clean and prepare their bounty. They had few cooking pots or utensils. Platters and cups had been hastily cut from raw wood. At least they knew how to make fire. Within a circle of stones the size of his head, they set a blaze that would cook down into useful coals by the time the sun had moved a quarter of the way toward the horizon. Beside it, he spread huge marsh leaves out to act as a makeshift table and instructed his conscript workforce on how to pluck and gut the birds.

"You never saw service outside the walls of the city, did you?" he asked one red-scaled dino who had become a mass of feathers in his amateurish attempts to clean a carcass.

"Only once," the creature admitted.

"Pathetic excuse for an army," Petru said over his shoulder to Taadar. The soldier grinned, showing his sharp teeth.

The bustle of activity had the entire population of Liskash rapt. Noble-born and low-class alike, they pressed closer and closer to the food preparation. One child darted forward and stole a slice of racano from the top of the battered bowl. A gray-faced soldier immediately strode up and swatted the youngster half a Mrem-length with a sweep of its hand. Petru protested, but the guard turned and glared at him, daring him to say anything about the blow or the fact that he tossed the vegetable into his own ugly mouth. He looked speculatively toward the birds beginning to turn on the spits, but Petru introduced his own bulk between him and the hearth. The dino backed away, its eyes always on the roasting geese. It went to pour beer into its personal jug from the big containers at the side of the clearing.

"We need something to fill their bellies until the food is ready," Petru said to Imrun. "Find a bowl or use an oiled hide. Tear up those fresh leaves and squeeze citrus over them. Mix them with the berries and sliced racano and let them eat their fill. Is there oil? No? Bireena, roast the eggs in the embers. They won't take long." He glanced toward General Unwal. "Don't break any or I will have to beat you!"

"Yes, Lord Petru," Bireena said. The threat didn't bother her. Petru felt terrible for making it.

After a portion was served to the general in a cuplike leaf, the males surged forward to gorge themselves.

Petru purposely kept back a third of the food for the lower-caste females and offspring. They were the enemy, but he couldn't stand seeing helpless beings go hungry. Once the women had fed their children handfuls of salad and snatched a roasted egg or two for themselves, they retreated to the huddle of tents. They no longer looked as desperate.

"What a horror it must be to have been born a dino," Petru said to Sherril. "They have no respect for females or care for their offspring."

"Hey, Mrem!" Horisi called. "That one is not working!" He pointed at Scaro. "Is there something wrong with him?"

The drillmaster sat slumped over a stone he used as a butcher block to gut frogs. Golcha and the others had kept him shielded as best they could from the Liskash's attentions.

"He isn't working?" Petru asked, pretending astonishment. "I will discipline him, Captain. Shame, lazybones! Work harder!" He strode over and shook an admonishing finger at the drillmaster. Scaro looked up at him with glassy eyes. Petru worried that he might collapse, but the soldier lowered his ears. He picked up his knife and went back to work. He expelled rubbery discharge from his nostrils among the offal, and wiped his nose with the back of his hand.

"There, Captain," Petru said, dusting his hands together. "I will keep a sharp eye on him. He is just lazy. Nothing more."

"He shouldn't be near the food," Sherril murmured to Petru.

"What harm could it do?" Petru said in an undertone. "They won't be affected. Just don't eat anything he touches. I will make sure there is some that is safe for us."

As the savory aromas rose from the firepit, the Liskash moved in closer and closer, as though they couldn't control themselves.

"They will push us into the flames!" Sherril said in alarm.

Petru moved up close to the nearest dinosaurs and clicked his claws in their faces. The dinos withdrew reluctantly, but within a few heartbeats, they began to move forward again.

"General Unwal, how can I cook you a feast with all this interference?" Petru appealed to the chief Liskash.

"Back!" Unwal commanded, waving an imperious hand. "Assemble by me! Do you want *punishment*?"

For the first time the soldiers looked fearful. They pushed the crowd back until it was behind Unwal's chair. They crouched on the ground to wait. Still uncomfortably close to the fire, Sherril and Petru exchanged worried glances.

"He *can* do magic," Sherril said woefully. "He has not unleashed it on us yet. We must keep him sweet and avoid his wrath."

"I could dance for him," Nolda said, crouched by the hearth cooking fish on hot stones. "I would also welcome the chance to pray to Assirra for further guidance." She smiled thinly. "I'd find it satisfying to offer to the goddess right in front of our enemies. Bireena has some skill on the drum. She could accompany me."

"I offer myself to help," the former slave said, without looking up from the vegetables that she was roasting.

"No!" Petru protested. "Don't reveal yourself, Your Sinuousness! That snake will see you as an asset. We wish to be as uninteresting as possible."

"*You* are not making yourself uninteresting," Sherril said, opening his eyes wide in an accusatory manner. "They can't help but notice you."

Petru looked down his long nose at the councilor.

"Then you are taken in by my subterfuge as well? That if they notice me they will pay less attention to our ailing drillmaster? We don't want to give them a single excuse to harm him."

He could tell by the bemused look on Sherril's face that the councilor had not even considered such a thing.

"Well, hurry up and finish making the meal," Sherril said. "We want to be away from here as soon as possible. We need to retrieve those parcels of herbs before they rot."

"They won't let us go," Bireena said. "We have always been chattel to them. They have lost their servants. They will see us as replacements."

"Well, I am not chattel," Nolda said. "Assirra told me to be watchful and clever, and we will win out against our foes."

"I wish to believe in your dream, Dancer," the tawny Mrem said. At last, she raised her beautiful amber eyes to the others. They were filled with sorrow. "But I have lived in mine too long."

The Dancer patted her gently on the shoulder.

"That nightmare is broken. This, too, shall be in the past. The gods will not forsake us."

Bireena looked as though she wanted to believe the Dancer's reassurance. Petru's heart went out to her. He wanted to believe it, too.

At last the skin of the birds was crisp and the meat dripped with savory juices. Petru cut a piece from the thigh of a plump bird and tasted it.

"As well as can be without spices," he said, nodding to Golcha and Imrun. "Take them off the fire."

Unwal must be served first. Petru laid out his feast with the same flourishes he used when serving his precious Dancers. Savory slices of breast and thigh meat he placed in the center of broad, fresh leaves and adorned them with flowers. He laid these offerings before the general.

"About time," Unwal declared. He grabbed meat with both hands and crammed pieces one after another into his maw. He washed it down with gulps from a beaker filled with the stinking brew the Liskash favored. Petru turned away in disgust.

"Serve the others," he said to the Mrem. "Make sure everyone gets a portion."

Once they had handed out the food, the Mrem retreated to the far side of the firepit. Two of the guards kept with them every step of the way, spears in one hand, drumstick of goose in the other.

Except for regrettable slurping and chomping, the Liskash ate in silence. Petru made certain that the

Mrem had kept back the most healthful portions of meat, though he had hacked it into shards to make it look unappetizing. He placed some of it on a leaf and offered it to Nolda first.

"No, dear Petru," she said with a smile. "Scaro needs this more than I do."

"No, Your Sinuousness," Scaro whispered. "Don't waste it on me. It'll go right through me!"

"I have something better for you, Drillmaster." Petru passed him the heart of one of the birds, done to a savory turn. "The herbs inside this will combat your symptoms. Once we are on our way again, I can brew you the potion that will cure you."

Scaro devoured the morsel, making a face at the bitterness of the green leaves stuffed inside. After a few moments, he swallowed and waited, with a thoughtful frown. The others watched him anxiously. He nodded.

"It's staying put, at least for now."

"Then it's time to appeal for our freedom," Sherril said, casting aside the leaf he had used as a plate. He smoothed his whiskers and brushed his ruff clean. "A good meal will have put them into an amenable mood."

Unfortunately, two good meals also seemed to have recovered the rest of Unwal's arrogance and authority.

"Foolish Mrem!" Unwal scoffed when Sherril made fulsome farewells, almost bowing himself into the dirt with his deep bows. "Of course you can't leave!"

"We must go, Great General" Sherril said. "We have a long journey ahead of us."

"That is of no importance to me."

"We've shown your soldiers where to gather wholesome food," Sherril said, keeping his tone polite but firm. "We have demonstrated how to prepare and cook everything we gathered. They now have the skills they need to make your lives more comfortable until your new home is ready. You don't need us any longer."

Unwal narrowed his beady eyes.

"I need my soldiers to defend me and my people," he said. "You are Mrem, and therefore of a lower order than Liskash. You will gather more food for us tomorrow, and the day after, and the day after that! I order you to build up our stores in preparation for my brother's return. He will be very pleased with me that I have obtained for him such a gift."

"General, we must go. Thank you for your . . . hospitality. Farewell."

"No!" Unwal glared at him. He clenched his fist and turned it fingers-upward. Sherril felt as though that fist had taken hold of his throat. He clutched at his neck. The invisible fingers squeezed tighter.

"No more argument. Now, we sleep. Guards!"

"But, General!" Sherril gasped out.

Unwal gestured outward with his fist. Sherril fell backward into the arms of the soldiers. They dragged him to his feet and herded him back at spear point to where the others were waiting. More guards, still well-decorated with scraps from their feasting, converged upon them and tied tough, braided quirts around their ankles, hobbling them so they couldn't walk normally. The Mrem fought against the binding, but the Liskash had them well outnumbered. As many as eight of them sat on Petru at once to keep him still until he was bound.

Once the Mrem had been secured, a fist of the lizards pulled back to a safe distance where they could keep an eye on them. The Mrem glared at their captors.

"So, the dagger emerges from the scabbard," Taadar whispered.

"This is how it begins," Bireena said, her voice dead and hopeless. "They will keep us until we are useless. Then they will kill us or send us to another Liskash stronghold."

"We won't be captive for long," Petru said. A flame of indignation burned deep in his belly. It was bad enough the general had destroyed his precious glitters, but to presume to keep them captive was outrageous. "You have my word on that!"

"This is your fault," Sherril chided Petru. "If you had not made palatable food, we could have been on your way by now."

"I would not shame myself by cooking *swill*."

"At least we are alive," Scaro said. "If he means to keep us as a workforce, we will find another means of escape. They are slow of wit as well as of foot. They can't keep us long."

"Assirra is with us," Nolda assured them. "Keep your wits about you."

Bireena shot a look of sympathy at Scaro, whose respiration was by then so labored that every breath was audible. Petru knew what she was thinking. The drillmaster was ill. Who knew which others among them would fall prey to the disease?

Toward night, they were given river water and what scraps remained of the feast that Petru had prepared. They were not allowed privacy for personal hygiene. Instead, they took turns going behind the tree to which their ankles were bound and burying their excrement in piles of leaves. Scaro went last. They could smell what he had squatted out for a long time afterward.

When darkness arose, Petru waited. The Liskash could not see in the dark as well as they could. From the thick fur around his neck, he removed the small package of herbs. With flat stones he had taken from the hearth, he ground the leaves together. There was no time for niceties such as precise measurements. His granddam's combination would have to do as it was. He soaked the green mash in a cup of murky water and waited for it to steep. Scaro slept noisily on the ground beside him. Petru sniffed the mixture from time to time. At last it was ready to drink.

He nudged Scaro gently awake.

The drillmaster was instantly on guard. His muscles tautened. Petru held him down to the ground with one meaty arm. Scaro sniffed through his stuffy nose, then relaxed when he recognized the scent of the valet's perfumed fur.

"What is wrong?" he asked in a scratchy whisper. If Petru hadn't had a Mrem's hearing, far more keen than the Liskash with holes in the sides of their heads instead of proper ears, they might have heard him.

"Drink this," Petru murmured, pushing the clay cup into Scaro's hand and closing his fingers around it.

Scaro nodded. He curled himself around the cup

to conceal his action from the pair of Liskash that walked around and around them in opposite directions.

Petru waited until the second dino's legs flashed past him in the moonlight.

"Pah!" An explosion of breath came from the drill-master. "It tastes terrible!"

"It's powerful medicine," Petru whispered. "It will make you better, but you need this twice or more a day over the next four days at least."

Scaro moaned softly, his arms wrapped around his gut.

"If I live."

"You must," a small voice said to them in the darkness. "You must live to lead us home. The goddess sent me a dream. You were at the head of a march of triumph."

Both of them looked toward Nolda, curled up in exhaustion with her back against a tree trunk. Her eyes were open and gleaming in the moonlight. Scaro swallowed audibly.

"I will, Your Sinuousness. I promise. But if I start to show the madness, kill me quickly. I do not wish to put you in peril."

"You have my word," Nolda said seriously. "The gods will welcome you into their arms. But I hope we are free before anything so terrible must happen."

"This is absurd," Petru said. General Unwal stared at him from his backless camp seat which he treated like a throne. They had been rousted at dawn the next morning and dragged before the Liskash commander.

"We are only eight. How can we possibly gather enough food to satisfy your entire group day after day? Let some of your women and children assist us. We will teach them how to find ripe fruit and catch birds."

Unwal lifted a finger. Petru braced himself for the strangulation. Instead, a heavy blow struck Petru from behind. He staggered, but managed to catch himself. The second, however, knocked him to his knees.

"What are ... ?" he began.

The blows rained down endlessly upon his back and legs. He threw his arms over his head to protect it. From the crook of his elbow, he saw Captain Horisi wielding a knobby branch. Petru rolled to avoid the next strike. He sprang to his feet and darted behind the general's chair.

The pair of bodyguards grabbed for him. They were so slow he could have run rings around them, but he feared for the safety of his fellows.

"What are you doing?" he demanded, dodging to and fro. "You may not mistreat me. I am Lord Petru!"

"Slaves that question orders are beaten," the general said, in his flat voice. "Your so-called lordship means nothing here."

"I claim my right from the gods themselves!" Petru said, hoping that Aedonniss wouldn't strike him dead for his presumption. "They will smite you for daring to harm me."

The guards made for him. He dodged them a pass or two longer, but one hooked his hobble-strap with a spear. Petru fell flat on the ground. The dinos surrounded him, beating him with the ends of their polearms. Petru bore the blows with gritted teeth. Ignoring the pain of his bruises, he picked himself up and glared into their faces.

"I will remember every blow," he hissed. "And I will have my revenge."

"Your threats are empty," Unwal said, not bothering to turn around. "Take them!"

"Your revenge," Sherril spat, as they were herded downstream toward the marshes and thrust into the shallows where the racano plants lay. "We're trapped! All we can do is protect the Dancer and hope for rescue."

"I prefer to believe in Nolda's dream," Petru said, with a slight bow to the Dancer herself. "I am keeping my eyes open for our chance."

Sherril threw up his hands in disgust. Two guards, the grayface from the previous day and a yellow-faced dino in a patched uniform, nudged him from behind with their spears. He made his way gingerly into the shallows and began to feel underneath the leaves for the round green fruit. Bireena waded in without being urged. She wouldn't risk getting a beating. With immense dignity, Nolda followed her and began to pick fruit.

Petru's attention was not on his angry companion or the females, but on the guards behind them. They had rheumy eyes. A green discharge dripped from their ugly nostrils. Their voices, when they shouted orders, were muted, and they coughed incessantly. One kept retreating behind a tree to squat.

When they were herded together to return to the camp, Petru whispered his news to the others.

"They have caught the fever!" he exclaimed. Sherril hushed him.

"Nonsense!" Sherril said. "How could they catch our disease? We are not the same species. The raw bird they ate yesterday must have disagreed with them. Or your terrible cooking has twisted their guts. The sickness is just catching up with them now."

"It is the fever, I say," Petru insisted. "My grand-dam would tell you. The symptoms are in her diary! There are illnesses she wrote about that affect all creatures that come into contact with them, although they are affected in different ways. It looks as though this spreads to Liskash and Mrem alike. But it seems to come on with them much faster than it does in us. Hmm." He couldn't keep himself from smiling.

"How can that possibly help us?" Taadar asked. He, too, had begun sniffling.

"It will help us to stay alive," Petru said. "Perhaps long enough."

"Long enough for what?" Bireena asked, her expression one of bemusement.

"Long enough to outlive them," Petru said.

But waiting was not easy or safe. Petru fought as he was dragged forward and thrown to the ground before General Unwal. He pulled himself upright and brushed at his beautiful coat with irritated strokes. The scrawny dino pointed at the sagging nets on the back of the carrier beast.

"Eight birds? That is not enough food for all my people! You have failed to follow my orders!"

"We gathered all we could in the time we were given," Petru said. "My Mrem held nothing back. Do you accuse us of theft?"

As if a wall fell upon him, a mighty force struck him to his knees. Petru struggled to get free from those holding him down. He realized in horror that no living creature was touching him. The general stood above him. He held nothing in his hands but power. Madness caused his flat eyes to gleam.

"Tomorrow, if you fail to bring us enough to eat, you will be the roast on the spit."

"It's been four days, Talonmaster," Fistmaster Emoro Awr said. "The foraging party ought to have come back yesterday."

The grizzled fistmaster crouched before the senior officer in his tent. Bau Dibsea looked poorly, in Emoro's eyes. He must have been sickening up, too.

"One day's delay is not enough to worry me," Bau said. "Why are you concerned?"

"You know Petru. He fears for the Dancers' lives. He knew what he needed to make them better. He would hurry back as quickly as he could move and prepare his medicine. I am sure that something has happened to him. Them."

"There's nothing we can do about it, Fistmaster," Bau said peevishly. "We can't send out searchers. There are barely enough of us still standing to protect us against a Liskash incursion."

Emoro lowered his gaze slightly.

"It isn't just me. Young Ysella came to me. She is still well and fit. She's put together a group of her apprentice Dancers. They are supple and strong, and it wouldn't hurt to have those favored by the gods with me. They are prepared to go in search of Petru. He has always been kind to them."

"Spoiled them within a pad's width of her life, you mean," Bau said, but his tone was indulgent. "I can't risk the lives of our only healthy Dancers."

"Young Gilas wants to come as well. He would do anything for Ysella. I know it's not much, Talonmaster, but I have a feeling something went wrong. We must bring them back. Lady Cleotra is fading away, Talonmaster. We need Petru's cure."

Bau sighed. His breathing sounded labored. He needed the cure himself. Emoro had found his own throat was getting a little scratchy over the last few days. How long until he was raving and lying in his own muck? He feared that finding Petru was the clan's only hope of surviving. At last, Bau nodded.

"Very well, Emoro. Go, but return safely, and soon!"

Petru woke on the fourth morning, annoyed. He had had a terrifying dream in which he ran from the sickbed of one Dancer to another, watching each of them die of the fever. The labored breathing and coughing was getting no better. He rolled over and poked Scaro in the side. The drillmaster flipped over suddenly, glaring at Petru.

"Isn't the potion helping?" Petru asked in a low voice.

"A little, valet," the drillmaster whispered. "I can breathe a bit. And I'm not so weak as I've been."

"Then why are you still coughing and sneezing?"

"It's not me," Scaro said in surprise.

A fit of sneezing erupted. Both of them turned their heads toward the noise. One of the guards sat on a stump a few Mrem-lengths away. His flat black eyes were filmy. He brushed slime from his nostrils with the sleeve of his coat.

"Well, that's a pleasant sight," Petru whispered. "A pity we can't do anything to make it worse."

"Yes, we can," Sherril said with a feral grin. "We will take vengeance for our own entrapment and the many Mrem they enslaved over the centuries."

Bireena's eyes gleamed at that last.

"How, Councilor?"

"With the tool we have at hand," Sherril said. He turned to Scaro. "Drillmaster, I have a special assignment for you today."

While they hunted in the marshland, Scaro pushed his meager strength to the uttermost. He made certain to touch or breathe on every Liskash in the company at least once during the day. When he felt a sneeze coming on, he ensured that one or more of the soldiers was in range of his explosion of mucus. If he wasn't coughing or sneezing, he made certain to touch or fall on them, making them touch him. Petru watched Scaro's antics with growing pleasure. Within hours, nearly every Liskash displayed one or more symptoms of the fever. It seemed that every one of the dinos, including the beasts of burden were coughing or sneezing. The ones watching the Mrem hunt were almost tottering with weakness. Where the Mrem had a certain immunity garnered over the years, the Liskash had none. And the fever took hold with tight talons. By midmorning, several of them were wheezing. Captain Horisi was dehydrated and shitting himself behind every tree. The Mrem pretended to see nothing as they worked.

"Hold there!" cried the grayface guard, pointing a trembling finger at Taadar. "That one is armed. Take him! Tie him up!"

The young warrior struggled in the grasp of three sniffling soldiers.

"I have nothing but kivor leaves," Taadar insisted, holding them out. "Take them. I mean no harm."

"A knife! He intends to slit our bellies!" the grayface shrieked. Petru came over to investigate the fuss. He took the leaves from Taadar and sprinkled them on the ground.

"Look here, Captain. Nothing. Calm yourself."

The guard bounded away from Petru and disappeared among the trees.

"They will kill us!"

On the way back to the camp, they saw the body of the grayface. He had collapsed in a heap on the path and died, a look of terror on his face. Petru kicked the body as they passed it.

General Unwal marched over to Petru and struck him across the muzzle with the back of his hand.

"What happened to my soldier?" he demanded. "Have you bewitched us all? How did you kill my man? Was it some kind of Mrem magic?"

"I have no power," Petru said. He ignored the blow, holding himself tall and looking the officer straight in his eyes. "Perhaps the privations of the last weeks left him vulnerable to illness."

"That skinny one has been sick since we took you all," Unwal said, pointing at Scaro. "He must have infected my soldiers!"

"How could it be the same illness?" Petru asked. "We are Mrem and you are Liskash. Scaro has not gone mad, and he still lives. Your soldier must have been suffering *before* our arrival."

"My men are coughing and sneezing as he was. Only my power keeps me from having the same symptoms!"

"And have you no doctors? Hmph!" He shook his head in scorn. "I should have known Liskash were too far removed from nature to know anything of value! I am a herbalist of some repute among my people. Let me go out later to gather plants to make medicine."

"See that you do!" Unwal thundered. His skinny purple body juddered as a sneeze took him. He clutched his sides with his thin hands. "I will be watching you! Now, bring me food!" Petru turned to hide his smile. The general's symptoms were coming on rapidly. He pointed at his volunteer workforce.

"You, you and you! Begin to gut those frogs and thread them on the spit!"

Nolda sidled up to Petru as he went to oversee the females plucking the handful of geese that Taadar and Imrun had captured. The rest of the Liskash were so lethargic that they weren't crowding up to steal fruit or meat.

"You won't give them the cure, will you?" the Dancer asked. Petru was devastated to see that her eyes were becoming filmy. Because of the beatings and hard work, they were all susceptible to the fever.

"Never, Priestess," Petru vowed. "Not if they kill me. But I must cook and not be cooked. A pity that a nourishing meal might help them to stave off the fever."

"Burn it, Valet," Sherril said. "Ruin the food. Let them go hungry as we are. Once they are too weak, we can slit these hobbles and run away. Soon they will be in no condition to chase us."

"I can't," Petru said, with a glance over his shoulder at Unwal. "He's no fool. He will know if the geese are too long on the spit. Later today I will make them take me to hunt for herbs. I will promise a cure, but I will formulate false medicines. Once they are helpless, we can escape. I need to get back to Lady Cleotra."

"Why wait until the fever takes them?" Taadar asked. "Bireena and I have been working hard all morning." He beckoned to Bireena. The former slave hobbled toward them.

"Lord Petru, I wish to help you," Bireena said, her expression carefully blank. She even kept her tail still. "I have herbs to season the meat."

"What, did you manage to find spices?" Petru asked. "He opened the huge leaf she handed him. It was full of gripeweed. The grin spread across his black-furred face so widely that it could have touched his ears. "Oh, this will be a most flavorful meal!"

"Be prepared to flee when the moment is right," Sherril told the others. "I will give you the signal."

"We'll be ready," Scaro said. He still looked as though a strong breeze would blow him over, but his determination held him upright.

When the geese were done, Petru arranged a platter with the most tender and perfectly roasted pieces of meat, alongside a salad of green leaves mixed with white and purple berries, and flavored with wild scallions. It looked as delicious as anything he might serve his precious Dancers. With as much grace as the hobbles between his ankles would allow, he presented the platter with a flourish to General Unwal.

"This is the finest of our produce of the day," Petru said. "I hope you will enjoy it."

"I shall," Unwal said. He stared at Petru, never looking at the food. "Eat it."

Petru blinked.

"What?"

"If it is so fine, you won't mind tasting it for me. All of you," he said, gesturing the other Mrem forward. Guards surrounded them and forced them forward with the points of their spears. "Come here."

"But why, General?" Petru asked. He wondered if the purple Liskash could see into his mind and see him chopping up gripeweed to mix into the salad and the sauce on the meat. The smirk on the dino's face suggested that he could. Petru felt his insides twist.

"You are so solicitous of our health and well-being," General Unwal said, pointing a skinny finger at him. "I do not believe slaves care so much for their masters. My men were not ill before you came. You must be poisoning them. This could be an attempt to poison me. Therefore, you will eat what you have prepared for me."

"Oh, no," Petru said, holding up his hands. "I couldn't. This is a feast for you, good General."

"I don't believe you," Unwal said, his eyes fixed on Petru's. He tightened his fingers. The valet felt the invisible hand tighten on his windpipe. He released the hold and signaled one of his men to bring him beer. A green-faced dino hurried to do his general's bidding. Unwal took a long drink from his enameled beaker and smacked his thin lips. "Eat, or you all die. I am patient. I can wait."

Petru gazed at him, focusing all the hate in his body on the creature before him. His vengeance was coming.

"So can I." He reached for the platter.

"I don't sense Liskash nearby," Ysella said. The young Dancer stalked along the crumbling path toward the rushing waters of the new sea. Every so often, she glanced at the broad expanse of water, expecting it to reach up and sweep her off the rise. If it was true that the Great Salt grew every day, then they were in danger.

"Can't you smell them?" Emoro asked, wrinkling his scarred nose.

"I can, but there's something wrong with the smell."

The five tawny-coated females following in Ysella's train, her apprentices, nodded their agreement.

Emoro had to concur with the females' opinion, but what else could he do? He had to find Petru and the priestess Nolda and bring them back safely. The trail led in this direction, at least for a while.

He had set them a rapid march from the camp over the last day and a half. When they reached the marshlands that had been Petru's stated destination, he had found signs of considerable activity. Threshed paths went off in all directions from that point. Broken branches leading downhill alongside the river to the north made him think that Petru had run into some trouble. Emoro followed traces, spotting a footprint here, a chopped branch there. He listened, but he couldn't hear any voices, only birds and other creatures calling. Where was Petru?

The Liskash stink was everywhere. He couldn't rely upon his nose, but he trusted his eyes, and the Dancers had a way of sensing the presence of the cursed dinos. They chopped and pushed through the thick overgrowth, hoping to discover the route taken by their lost loved ones.

Downhill to the north, he had come across a discarded bronze claw hand. He recognized it as one of Imrun's prized possessions. More crushed and torn foliage, being swiftly overgrown by the hungry jungle, told him that there had been a struggle there. Scattered handfuls of fur also decorated the bushes, including thick, plushy black tufts he knew had come from Petru. They had come this way. Were they prisoners? Had they been killed? Emoro felt his soul sink, but he had to press on to discover the truth.

The young females had the kind of energy that Emoro had once possessed. He was reluctant to risk sending them out as scouts, but they were eager to help. Two of the tawny lasses raced down the path and disappeared over a slight rise.

They returned almost immediately, looks of horror on their faces.

"They're all dead!" one of the girls wailed. "Bodies everywhere, Mrem and Liskash!"

Ysella let out a little chirp. All the courage she had shown had fled.

"It must not be true!"

Emoro pushed them aside and ran down the forest path. His heart pounded. Petru dead? The Dancer lost to them? He could not imagine either of those horrors. The young females and Gilas ran beside him, then outdistanced him. Ysella emitted her peeps of terror, showing again how young she was. Emoro wished he could console her, but he feared what he would see.

Gasping, he burst through the last hanging branches. With a backwards bound, he caught himself just Mrem-lengths from the edge of a precipice. The path was sheared off as though by an axe.

"Where are they?" he demanded. One of the girls pointed downward.

Emoro prided himself on being battle-hardened over his decades of life, but he was shocked by what he saw at the foot of the cliff. The massive tumble of stones and masonry in the lapping water spoke of a horrifying cataclysm. An entire city looked to have perished. Ysella burst into tears.

As the girls had said, Liskash and Mrem corpses littered the rockfall. Birds and other scavengers worried at the bodies, shrieking their delight at such a bounty. A black shadow stretched over a piece of shattered wall caught his eye. The body was broad enough to be Petru. He couldn't see the Dancer, but surely she must lie near the valet. He would have protected her to the end. His heart clenched in his chest. He must not weep. He had to rescue the bodies and give them decent burial.

"We must get down to them," he said. Desperately, he sought about for a path down to the water's edge. The broken land started to crumble at his feet. Perhaps he could hug the cliff face and climb. "Stay here," he cautioned Gilas. "Protect the Dancer."

"No, Fistmaster," Ysella said, catching his arm as he dropped to his belly. Her voice was suddenly steady. "Don't go down."

"That is Petru there. He is dead!"

She pulled him back from the precipice.

"Breathe, Emoro. Smell. There is no life here, but these died too long ago to be our kinsfolk. I swear it. Smell."

Emoro fought back his grief. He was annoyed that his nose was becoming clogged with the oncoming fever, but he blew it clear and inhaled deeply.

The stink of rotting corpses almost knocked him over. He looked down. With new eyes, he surveyed the scene. That poor Mrem on the rocks was not Petru. Its fur was far too short. The skin that showed in rents torn in its coat by the scavengers had turned a dark purple green. He nodded.

"Thank you, Dancer. You're right. These poor souls are half a moon dead. When our clan passes this way, we'll give them decent burial. But now we have to go back again to find...to find the priestess. But, where?"

For answer, Ysella closed her eyes. She began to move backward and forward as the goddess began to speak through her. When she opened her eyes, it was as though another Mrem occupied her body. She turned and began to walk sure-footedly along the cliff to another path, a wide, well-traveled road. It, too, stank of Liskash, many centuries' worth.

The females cleared the way for Ysella. She walked, seemingly heedless of the vines that trailed down onto the road. A wide bridge of boards and ropes took them over the roaring falls to the far side of the river. They passed small outbuildings and empty paddocks, a brewhouse and a flour mill, showing that the Liskash had abandoned the area completely when their city collapsed.

The sun climbed up from their right shoulders, over their heads and descended halfway along their left by the time they heard sounds other than their own breathing. Ysella seemed to be in a trance almost the entire time, not stopping for food or water. Emoro wished he had some of that gods-given strength. His worry was causing him to flag. He needed to rest, but he had to go on. If there was a chance to find the others alive, he had to be alert for it.

The sounds of voices shouting mixed with screams brought Emoro out of his torpor. He judged them to be about fifty Mrem-lengths ahead. He signed to the youngsters to halt.

They stepped off the main path and crouched down

to arm themselves from their packs. Gilas had full armor, as had Emoro. Each of the young females had a gorget to protect their vulnerable necks and clawed gauntlets on their hands. Each of them had daggers and knew how to use them. Emoro and Gilas took their spears from their packs and held them to stab, not throw. At Emoro's nod, they crept forward toward the sound of voices. He couldn't distinguish who was speaking, only they sounded like they were in terrible pain. He was all too aware of what the Liskash did to prisoners. He hoped that he would be in time to save his kinsfolk.

The smell of death also impinged on his senses. They came upon piles of carcasses, but these were fresh. No Mrem were among these dead. The picked bones were those of frogs, geese and fish, no more than a couple of days old. He also smelled worse odors: blood, vomit and feces. On top of all that was a sweet, familiar aroma. He lifted his upper lip to smell it more thoroughly. His eyes narrowed.

"What is that?" one of the girls asked, keeping her voice low. "It smells like . . . perfume. Flowers and spice."

In spite of his worry, Emoro couldn't help but smile. "It's Petru," he whispered. "I don't know if he lives or not, but that's his scent. Come on. He needs us. We need to spy out what is ahead."

They crept forward, stopping to listen every other Mrem-length.

Not far ahead, Emoro heard a terrible moan.

"That's Scaro," he said. "I'll bet my left foot on it. Come on!"

As silently as shadows, the Mrem wove in and out of trees and skirted bushes.

Just short of a huge tree, Emoro stopped. His eyes watered at the sharp, noxious odor. He'd found the dinos' latrine. Someone else was there. He went on high alert. But the shadow was not a Liskash. Huge gold eyes stared at him out of the shadow.

"Who is it?" a female voice whispered.

"Fistmaster Emoro Awr," he whispered back.

"Blessed be Aedonniss!"

He crept closer and recognized Bireena. She was kneeling, not the usual pose to evacuate one's bowels. He realized she was sitting next to a body. Emoro looked at it in horror.

Scaro lay sprawled on the ground, his eyes open and staring. They had discarded his corpse on the midden heap! Emoro swore he would have vengeance for that insult!

Then the "corpse" moaned.

Emoro ran to kneel beside his drillmaster.

"What did they do to you?" he whispered, helping him to sit up.

"They?" Scaro replied. *"He!"*

"He? A Liskash?"

"No! That Petru. His potions are *noxious*. I've grunted my guts out almost hard enough to turn me inside out! The rest of us are no better. Bireena's been watching over me like gentle Assirra herself." His eyes were glassy, but they fixed on Emoro's. "But it worked, Fistmaster. By the gods, it worked. That valet is the smartest Mrem who ever lived."

Emoro almost sat down on the pile of leaves and dung.

"He's alive?"

Scaro laughed, then winced as his belly spasmed. Bireena gathered his head into her lap and stroked his face.

"Maybe you'd better go and see for yourself, Fistmaster. But leave me alone for a while. I'm in no shape to move."

The drillmaster curled up around his abused belly and went back to moaning. Emoro chuckled to himself. It wasn't the way the randy drillmaster would have liked to be alone with a nubile female, but for the moment, he wasn't complaining. Emoro pushed through the trees and into the clearing.

Petru sat in the general's chair with his feet propped on Unwal's corpse. The clearing stank of excrement, but the only dead were the Liskash general and a couple of the guards. All of the Liskash had leaped upon the food and devoured it, but they had all been exposed to Scaro. In their weakened condition, the Liskash succumbed to the fever in a matter of hours. They had become disoriented and thirsty. Naturally, they had begged for drink. Petru was happy to provide it to them. Nolda, Bireena and Sherril had poured the small beer liberally to one and all.

The general had been wrong. The gripeweed had not been in the food, but in the beer. Overcome with the illness and the twisting in his guts, Unwal had fallen over dead in between the main course and dessert. Petru kicked the body again. It was beginning to stiffen. It would do as a footrest until it started to stink. The others, all the females and children, and half the soldiers, had become meek and docile, begging him to help cure them of their loose bowels. Only time would do that, he noted with satisfaction. He lifted his lip to take in the stink, even to revel in it. Sometimes triumph smelled bad. He might never drink beer again.

"Petru!"

He looked up. Delight shot through him faster than the spasms of pain in his belly. He saw the face of the Mrem he loved above all, and beckoned to him.

"Emoro! Come and see our triumph!"

Once back in Mrem camp, Petru prepared his new collection of threadvine and water reeds into a strong infusion that he gave to all the sufferers in the camp. The herbs arrested the symptoms and began to reverse them rapidly. Cleotra regained her wits and her appetite after one day, and was beginning to put on a little bit of weight. Cassa, too, was able to retain food. Petru fed her tiny bites and sips of mild foods until she felt well enough to sit up and drink soup on her own.

"I chopped some lily herbs fine. It gives the broth flavor, but it is also good for your blood," he said. "Is there anything else I can do for you?"

"Oh, I missed you, Petru," Cassa said with a smile. She was still weaker than he would have liked, but so much better than she had been even the morning they had returned. "I prayed to Assirra to favor you. I am so grateful that she intervened for you with Lord Aedonniss." She rubbed her ear against his cheek affectionately as Petru arranged cushions behind her back. Thankfully, he could now keep all his beloved patients clean. His own coat had had to be washed many times to get the stink of the Liskash camp out of it. He wore his favorite perfume and a puff or two of silver sparkle powder. How he had missed his adornments while in captivity! "So you defeated an entire village of Liskash with a handful of leaves and a sick warrior?"

Petru smiled.

"Lady Nolda told us she had a vision that this battle would be won with intelligence and patience, not strength," he said. He couldn't help being pleased with himself, but he had to bestow credit where it was due.

"Yes, she told me," Cassa said. They looked toward the sunny edge of the hide tent, where the slender sable female and Cleotra lay side by side on broad cushions stuffed with sweet grass. Cleotra's famous temper had been calmed now that she was cured of her fever. Nolda's kits tumbled and wrestled in the sunshine a Mrem-length away. Cassa beamed on them all with maternal pride. "They will recover very soon, will they not?"

"Yes, dear lady."

"I can hardly believe that Sherril Rangawo was actually of some use to you!"

Petru could have embellished the truth, but there was no need.

"He was a true Mrem, although he moaned all the way on the walk back here, a night and a day and another night. If he'd had his way, I would have had to carry him on my back, but there was no chance of that. My duty and my strength were in the service of the Dancers. Young Ysella was a credit to us and your training. Emoro and I want you to know how brave she was. But, Bireena! She showed so much ingenuity and fortitude that she could have been born Lailah."

"I will take her into my care," Cassa promised. "And Scaro Ullenh? He sounded as if he was the sickest of all."

"They are already mending," Petru promised her. "All of them. We will all live to continue our journey."

"Under your protection?" Cleotra asked teasingly. "You have the wit and determination to be a great leader. I hope you always shall use your gifts to aid us as Aedonniss and gentle Assirra do."

"Oh, I would not put myself on an equal footing with the gods," Petru said. He looked at her playfully from under half-lowered lids. "They put the ingredients in my grasp. I only prepared the feast."